SON OF NO MAN SERIES

ESPARAN

BOOK 4

SON OF NO MAN SERIES

ESPARAN

BOOK 4

D. LAMBERT

Esparan
Son of No Man Series Book 4
Copyright © 2021-2024 D. Lambert. All rights reserved.

4 Horsemen
Publications, Inc.

Published By: 4 Horsemen Publications, Inc.

4 Horsemen Publications, Inc.
PO Box 417
Sylva, NC 28779
4horsemenpublications.com
info@4horsemenpublications.com

Cover and Typesetting by Valerie Willis
Editor Laura Mita

Library of Congress Control Number: 2022938095

Paperback ISBN: 978-1-64450-618-9
Hardcover ISBN: 978-1-64450-696-7
Audio ISBN: 978-1-64450-616-5
E-Book ISBN: 978-1-64450-617-2

TO MY KIDS.
MAY THEY LOVE THE WORLD AS MUCH AS I DO.

Table of Contents

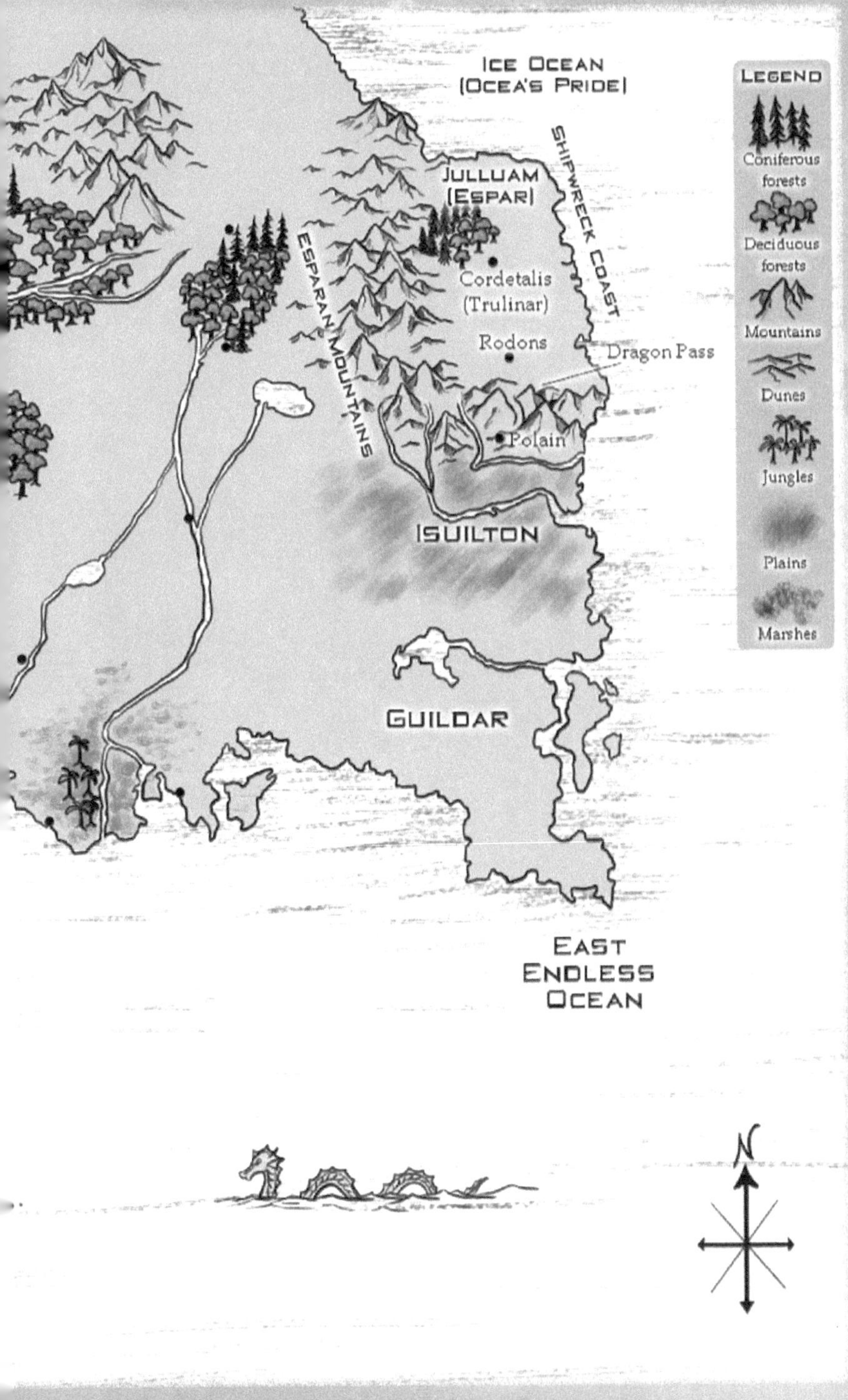

ICE OCEAN
(OCEA'S PRIDE)

JULLUAM
(ESPAR)

SHIPWRECK COAST

Cordetalis
(Trulinar)

Rodons

Dragon Pass

ESPARAN MOUNTAINS

Polain

ISUILTON

GUILDAR

EAST
ENDLESS
OCEAN

LEGEND

Coniferous
forests

Deciduous
forests

Mountains

Dunes

Jungles

Plains

Marshes

N

"Revenge binds and blinds."

-Prince Marfaie Vornan,
Prince of Tanble

Chapter 1

A season's worth of marching, a dozen engagements, a kidnapping, a betrayal, and a dead dragon had brought Tohmas Galanth to the budding village of HillTop far from home, welcoming his enemy as a friend.

For these forces, the battle was over. They had passed the night celebrating or resting. Traders moved among them. Injuries were tended to. The dead, surprisingly few, were burned. A single large pyre burned overnight in the Northlander camp, where the wind could carry the stench into the woods.

Tohmas, in his role as Prince of Galanth, had spent the night planning. Three nations camped beside the lake, and all answered to Tohmas now. The Esparans, following him as a Prince of Espar, took up the hill overlooking the lake. The hardy Northlanders, allied through their Darknim DoomDragon, had expanded from their defenses at the base. The Rydans, the wild plains people, were encamped on the frozen lake, loyal to Tohmas because of his link to their chief.

Between the Northlander and Esparan camps, the dead black dragon lay sprawled in the new dawn. Rydans had picked at the meat, but most of the beast remained, the impenetrable scales preventing harvest.

"You look proud of yourself," DoomDragon muttered in his soft, unaccented Esparan as he joined Tohmas and his prime protector, the Rydan Carsh, overlooking the battlefield.

"We had a busy day yesterday," Tohmas replied. He had come to know Darknim DoomDragon by fighting him, yet he felt closer to him than to any of his Esparan allies. With DoomDragon, Tohmas did not have to pretend to be a proper prince. "The alliance worked out, didn't it?" He glanced at the dead dragon. "Maybe not as smoothly as we'd planned, but still!"

Darknim laughed and cast a long stare down to the waking armies. The old Northlander, who indeed had seen six decades of winters, stood as tall as Tohmas and just as wide. Only a small part of his bulk was his dragon scale armor; most of it was his muscles. His ax hung over his back, the arc of the blade making dragon wings over the Northlander's shoulders. He seemed undisturbed by the array of burns, blisters, and scratches he had earned during his battle with the black dragon. Someone had salved them, but they were open. He had found new boots to replace the burned ones.

Below them, the stirring warriors gave the still-steaming corpse of the dragon plenty of space. Most were still in their beds after a late night of celebrations.

"No, not exactly as we planned," Darknim agreed.

"Naw bad," Carsh replied from his customary place behind Tohmas. Tohmas glanced back, reminded that his closest friend had been wounded. As a Rydan, Carsh matched Tohmas' daunting height but was lean with muscle. He still had mud crusting in his beard and in the cracks of his skin after falling from the dragon's mouth. Cutter Darak had stitched Carsh's back, and in true Rydan fashion, Carsh hid any indication of the pain he was in.

The Rydan wiped his muddy hand on his chest over the mountain cat's ear of his tattoo. He then paused, tilting his head like a listening deer. Tohmas tensed when the Rydan pulled a second knife, indicating readiness for battle. He had to remind himself not to overreact; unless he was surrounded by trusted friends, Carsh would always have two blades out. He had carried one temporarily because only DoomDragon and Tohmas had been present. A second warned someone else was approaching.

Sure enough, Prince Barnon arrived at a run. Wheezing, his breath puffed as a cloud as he halted at Tohmas' side. The wind picked up. Without the warmth of the sun yet upon them, the air was chill.

"Prince Tohmas! Riders approach from the south!"

Tohmas fought a grimace. Something about how Barnon said the title "prince"—which by itself was tedious—sounded threatening. With Barnon's presence, the performance had to begin. Tohmas was, once more, a Prince of Espar.

"Blue and gold standard. Prince Dragal has arrived," Barnon added, following on Tohmas' left while Darknim came up on his right and Carsh followed, protecting his back. Tohmas had no doubt his Rydan bodyguard was keeping a close eye on Barnon.

Tohmas cocked his head. "I did not realize he was on his way."

"I did," Darknim replied brightly. "Prince Marfaie insisted I wait until he was here before killing you all."

Barnon glanced at Darknim, suspicion on his face one blink then forcibly erased the next.

"You knew as well, did you Barnon?" Tohmas asked, trying to distract his "uncle" from his unease. "Dragal and I agreed to come north when DoomDragon captured Sol," Barnon replied, focusing on Tohmas. "Dragal couldn't get out right away what with his—" Barnon cut himself off, stumbling on the poorly-guarded secret surrounding the prince's health. He had told Tohmas about the coughing death, but it was not meant for other ears. Tohmas had not yet decided how best to use the information, but it would not matter if Barnon himself could not keep the secret.

Swallowing quickly, Barnon added, "Said he should arrive before the New Year. According to the scout, he ought to be here by nightfall."

Tohmas clasped Barnon's shoulder. "Good! Then we have time for some drinks." He guided him into the command tent.

Even the doubtful Prince of Rabarch was able to sit back in his chair in the presence of the Northlander without complaining. The conversation quickly went to Barnon's real reason for traveling north: Prince Sol's imprisonment by Prince Marfaie of Tanble. They passed wine and Rydan wildwater around the table freely. It was pleasant to hear the formalities dropped.

"My casters can find Prince Sol," Darknim said, "but Marfaie will not make it easy to get to him. He knows you will come after him."

"If you think the Circle of the Raven can best Master Terant, then we have hope. Marfaie can't be looking for revenge, or Sol would be dead," Tohmas said.

"Sol is bait. He knows they will seek their brother," Darknim confirmed. He wisely made no assumptions about Tohmas' interest in his wayward relative.

"Find him, and I will personally retrieve him!" Barnon declared, taking another drink. For a moment, Tohmas forgot Barnon was his elder. It had been years since Barnon had been forced to engage in battle, except for joining Tohmas late in the campaign against DoomDragon. Prior to that, Barnon had fought only as a boy under the care of his brothers. Tohmas thought it ironic that he had at least twice as much battle experience as his "uncle."

But Barnon had swiftly swallowed two helpings of Rydan wildwater. The potent drink probably had something to do with his sudden enthusiasm.

Darknim and Tohmas exchanged glances. Tohmas knew they were of the same mind; keeping Barnon and Dragal out of the way would be vital to their success.

Barnon prattled on, detailing the conversations he and Dragal had shared through Dragal's BookKeeper Olmer, who had the best memory in the world according to Barnon and could recite entire conversations flawlessly mooncycles after he had heard them. A marvelous man, if quiet and humble and...

A caster, Tohmas realized. *Master Kitable will not be happy.*

The Prince of Rabarch was able to carry the conversation with himself long enough for the sound of hooves to be heard in the trampled slush outside the tent. The protectors answered, which spurred Tohmas to investigate. The others followed him out.

A crowd of Clandac protectors, recognized by the green ropes on their shoulders over their coats of blue and gold, surrounded Prince Dragal. The Protectors of Galanth formed a barrier between the new arrivals and Tohmas' tent, defending Tohmas from even a known ally until told otherwise.

Carsh behaved like the prime protector he was meant to be and called them off. A gap formed in the line of protectors.

As soon as Prince Dragal dismounted, Prince Barnon staggered forward. "Just in time!" he cried, rushing up and clasping his brother's forearm. He then flopped into a hug.

Dragal was smaller than the last time Tohmas had seen him. The mild gut he had been developing at his age was gone, and his face was longer. Although the man walked with confidence, Tohmas sensed something unsteady in his steps. There was weariness in the prince's eyes that had nothing to do with long days of riding. His height was still imposing, but his limbs were a less formidable size. Even his prominent beard looked thinner.

"What mess have you gotten into this time?" came the gravel response from the eldest of the Galanth princes as he eased his brother back to his feet.

Prince Barnon was all smiles. "No, no! Victory, Brother! We have won! You are in time for the festivi-vities!"

Disbelief crossed Prince Dragal's face. He searched the area as if to confirm his location, then furrowed his brow and answered, "There were plenty of Northlanders left from what I saw." His eyes found DoomDragon, and he snarled. "In fact, there's one now."

Tohmas had not thought much about the people who had accompanied him from the tent until Dragal fixed a disapproving glare on him. Carsh, a Rydan on one side. Darknim, a Northlander on other. *What a group we are.*

"The enemy does not have to be dead for there to be victory," Tohmas replied.

DoomDragon seized the opportunity to introduce himself with a grin and a formal Esparan bow.

"DoomDragon?" Dragal snapped. "You are the bastard who captured my brother," he accused with another disapproving look, this time for Barnon.

Like a scolded son, Barnon hung his head.

"Actually, Prince Marfaie is responsible for that," Tohmas interjected.

"Marfaie?" Prince Dragal said the name like a curse.

"Apparently, he has a grudge against your family, and Sol's capture is being used to that end." Tohmas regretted the slip, but no one else seemed to notice the use of the word "your" instead of "our."

Barnon had been embarrassed when explaining the feud between Marfaie and the sons of Zayban, but Dragal showed no regret. Instead, mention of the insult fanned his outrage. "That son of a demon should have been gutted years ago. I will not have—"

"We will be organizing a rescue for Sol," Tohmas interrupted. "If you are staying, your swords are welcome."

Dragal's stony stare, once a wall of solid rock, had lost much of its strength. When turned on Tohmas, it felt made of gravel instead of granite.

"With this Northlander?" Dragal demanded, gesturing at DoomDragon as if shooing a miscreant hound.

It was hard to believe the two men were the same sixty years. Darknim DoomDragon had been named the DoomDragon of his people for a good reason; the aging Northlander was in perfect physical form. Darknim's eyes matched Dragal's for color, but the chill in Darknim's confident stare made the ice wall infinitely stronger than the crumbling stone wall.

"We share an enemy in Marfaie," Tohmas replied. "DoomDragon can find where Sol is. I appreciate any advantage—"

"Champion!"

It was not often that Tohmas, as the Prince of Galanth, was interrupted. He was caught off guard when a woman's voice suddenly broke into the conversation.

Carsh grinned. "Let 'er thru!" he called.

"Loni," Tohmas recognized.

Sure enough, the shapely Celebrant of Inac passed between the protectors and knelt in the mud at Tohmas' feet. Her arms, wrist to shoulder, were bandaged, and one hand—the one without her brand to the Goddess of Fire, Inac—carried a complex wrapping of white as well. She knelt with both arms under her as if to hide the bandages, but the white stood out. Under the muck, she wore a scanty red dress with a low corset like a whore. A wet cloak hung over her bare shoulders, the hood pulled off to show her tangled head of auburn hair.

"Champion?" Mooncycles before, Tohmas would have winced to hear the word hissed from Dragal, but he had won too many victories to be bothered by the condemnation of his eldest so-called "uncle."

Celebrant Loni leaped to her feet, her face flushing in fury. "Champion of Inac and bringer of victory! All hail to the Prince of Galanth and Champion of Fire! Who are you to doubt him? Who are—?" Undeterred by rank or wealth, she wagged a finger at Prince Dragal.

In some ways, it was a shame to see her tirade end, but since Dragal's face was flushing to match the Celebrant's crimson robes, Tohmas intervened.

"Celebrant Loni, we are blessed that you have returned safely!" Loni had left HillTop somehow in the early winter without giving a reason. He did not know where she had gone, or why she was back now, but that would have to wait.

"I am undeserving of blessing, Champion," she whispered like an apologetic child. "I went to do the Goddess' will and sought a blade worthy of you. I found the sword, but it was taken from me. I lost it, Champion. I failed you."

Baffled, Tohmas could only stare at her.

"We found her frozen in the snow on the banks of IcePeak River," Dragal said curtly. "I take it you know her," he finished, disapproval seeping from every word.

Carsh grinned wider and chuckled. He certainly knew her and knew her well. Inac was also the goddess of lust, after all.

Refusing to allow the prince's glower to discourage him, Tohmas answered, "Yes, I know her." He may not have taken her to bed, but he knew Loni well enough. She had been absent from among the whores of their tag-along supply and service unit Fixer City, and Tohmas had missed her fanaticism. He knew Kitable would not share his opinion; Loni was an untouchable, immune to magic. Although she seemed unaware of her abilities and could not manifest the power like other untouchables, Kitable still spooked at the mention of her name every time.

"A sword?" Tohmas asked her. Under his unsteady hand, the hilt of SoulBurner warmed under his touch.

Understanding, he drew the sword, a blazing aura lighting around him. He was grateful for Kitable's absence. No one jumped at the untouchable powers that came with the light.

He had, however, forgotten about another possible caster in their midst. One among the Clandac protectors did not wear a green rank

rope, and it became clear that the tall man was a caster when he physically winced. Unlike other wizards, BookKeeper Olmer did not try to escape the magic-nullifying light. Instead, he jotted something down into a well-worn book, a deep frown creasing his face from forehead to chin.

Celebrant Loni lifted her head, her wide eyes gleaming in the red light. Recognizing now what she was seeking, Tohmas presented the blade to her.

"The sword!" she shouted as she jumped to her feet. "You have it!"

"The Goddess herself walked from a fire to deliver it," Tohmas confirmed. The words came out with certainty, no matter how strange they sounded. "You did not lose it."

At first, Tohmas thought the woman might try to kiss him in her excitement, but she remembered her place at the last moment and instead knelt in the mud again. It did not seem to bother her that her dress was now streaked with filth to her ankles.

She whispered the prayer of Inac at a blinding speed. As soon as she finished, Loni was on her feet, and her wide green eyes sparkled at him.

"Champion of Fire, you never disappoint! The purpose of the Goddess has been completed! I have much to do!" she declared. With a smile that Tohmas never expected to fade, Loni pivoted to face west and sauntered away without waiting to be dismissed. "My Lady's duties await!"

He assumed she would find her way back to Fixer City. The camp had changed in the cycles since her departure, but woe be to any who got in her way. She would find a way.

When Tohmas looked back at Dragal, the older man was eyeing SoulBurner, so Tohmas released his grip and offered it to Dragal.

"Champion?" Dragal repeated as he tested the blade. Predictably, there was no light when the Prince of Clandac held the sword, but the writing on the edge was still visible. "A blade for the war that brings peace to Espar?" Dragal read. "Strange thing for a Goddess of War to be looking for peace." He returned the sword to its rightful owner.

DoomDragon replied, "She is also Lady of Victory. How can she have victory if she only ever has war?"

Reminding Dragal of DoomDragon's presence, Tohmas realized, had been a mistake. Dragal's face darkened with a scowl. "Says the man who fights another man's war," he said.

"To the man who refuses to fight his own," Darknim replied swiftly.

Tohmas stifled a laugh, hoping Dragal had not spotted it.

"Shall we move out of the wind?" Tohmas said to prevent them from coming to blows. "Prince Dragal, after you," he finished with a gesture to the tent.

Dragal would have to enter or refuse the hospitality, and even the eldest prince did not seem willing to be that rude. Still, he could not help adding the final word as he passed into the shelter. "I do not trust Northlanders." He erupted into a fit of coughing as the warmer air hit him.

Barnon shrugged apologetically, then followed Dragal in.

Darknim watched the men go with calm displeasure in his stare. "A man who does not trust Northlanders gives himself a good reason not to trust Northlanders."

"We will only have to tolerate him for a short while," Tohmas promised. "Will you still ride with me?"

The heavy shoulders of the Northlander rose and fell with a sigh, but in the end, he nodded. "My ax is with you against Marfaie. The Northlanders will follow me as long as I carry the title of the DoomDragon." With a shake of his head, Darknim DoomDragon frowned. "Arrogant, intolerant, impatient, and rough: Prince Dragal is the man Marfaie described."

"Meaning he is the man you agreed to help destroy." The Northlander nodded. "I will keep that in mind," Tohmas said.

He followed the others into the tent, readying himself for an entirely new type of battle.

With every breath, Rakhund felt the absence of the dragon's soul like a gaping wound in his chest. He knew the sensation would eventually fade to a dull knot, to join the one that still lingered from his first fallen dragon, but for now, the lack of the soul gnawed at him like a disease.

After nearly two centuries, the great black dragon Rakhund had enslaved was dead.

The first warning had been the loss of the bindings between the dragon's handler and the dragon. At first, he had thought the handler had come in direct contact with wizard powers, but Rakhund's permanent control spells had been untouched, which just meant the handler was dead. That had suited Rakhund well enough. The boy could be replaced. He had assumed the dragon would try to flee during the brief reprieve without a master, but it still had to sleep. When it did, Rakhund's hold would be renewed. He had only to wait.

But then the permanent spells broke, the dragon killed. The memory of the sensation still made Rakhund's heart tense. Without his dragon, he was weak, incomplete. He needed his prestige back immediately.

By the time Rakhund's patron heard about the loss, Rakhund intended to have remedied the problem. He would not be seen without a bound dragon soul, even if the humans did not recognize such a thing.

Rakhund left behind the quiet majesty of his dead volcano's caldera and traveled out alone into the wilderness of the north. Unconcerned by the last of winter's winds and snow, he hunted with his eyes on the skies. His black robes hid his features but did little against the chill. For that, Rakhund had his spells and his natural scales. He crossed great distances, requiring little by way of rest and nothing by way of sleep as he traversed the open, rocky terrain.

At length, he felt the presence of dragons and followed them back to their lair.

For days, he watched the pair of red dragons. His dragons had been Blacks before, the strongest of the Magma dragons. The skill to dominate Blacks had put Rakhund into positions of authority among of his kind once. But now, there were no others of his kind to impress, and the black beasts were too rare. The demons who had crafted the mightiest of the dragons had left enchantments that killed the beasts once their masters were gone. Too few escaped dragons had bred before the spells sapped them of life.

Finding a Black once had been fortunate. Now, it seemed likely to be impossible.

Taking two dragons instead of one would grant him similar strength. The spells would be harder to cast and hold, but the resistance of each

dragon would be easier to manage. Reds were less vicious and less clever than their volatile, larger cousins. Rakhund's last Black had been a veteran of the demon wars, sturdy and experienced in resisting a demon's hold. Two younger, naïve Reds would easy.

Sitting in the moss of the stony fields, Rakhund cast for days, pulling in the powers of his core to build the spell. He used the magic to craft a composite stone, built pebble by pebble from the hills of the dragons' home, their sacred place. Once he had two such creations, each the size of his fist, he imbued them with more magic, fashioning a spiral of confusion. Confused, they would never be able to defy him.

At midday, when the beasts were sleeping, Rakhund took both stones and crept into the caverned home of the red dragons. Hidden by magic, he placed the first stone onto the steaming wrist of the bull dragon and let it fuse to the scales. The spells flickered to life.

As he placed the second stone onto the female, the bull awoke, his nostrils flaring. His roar was instant and fierce, and Rakhund thought he understood it.

"Demon, I smell you."

But it was too late. The stones worked their powers over the mind of the beast, and the dragon's search was distracted and uncoordinated. While Rakhund sat hidden in illusions, both dragons searched for him. Too confounded to hone in on the source of the smell, they had not found him by the time his following spells, which had to be set by touch, were ready.

When Rakhund bound himself to their souls, both dragons went still. He felt their fury, for they recognized what had happened and despised him for it, and he was comforted. He had lived his life with that hatred seething within him. He had felt incomplete without it.

Rakhund forced the larger bull dragon to carry him as a rider back to the hills outside of Arcott. The innate heat of the dragon, hot enough to scald exposed flesh, was nothing against his magic.

With the souls of the dragons now held, Rakhund reported to his patron. Dragons were again ready to be commanded.

An army marched against Prince Marfaie now and needed to be destroyed. That was fortunate, for Rakhund wanted to kill something.

Chapter 2

Kitable, Master Wizard of the Princedom of Galanth, awoke after his restless sleep, no closer to deciding on a course of action than when he had lain down.

He had questions. The Lie Light had shown falsehoods in Tohmas' promises to his people. He was lying about everything from his origins to the current war. All Kitable thought he had known was falling apart.

He had considered Tohmas a friend as well as his patron, but it had been Tohmas' father, Prince Habal, who had protected Kitable from a death sentence. If Tohmas had been complicit in Habal's murder...

The green and silver robe didn't sit right on him as he donned it. How he could be loyal to Galanth's colors if Tohmas Galanth was guilty of murdering his own father?

Thinking to confront Tohmas at once regarding his discovery, he pushed open his door.

He halted on the top step of his vardo. Seven Northlanders sat around his campfire. Colt, Kitable's driver, stirred a large pot over the fire and served them tea from the steaming pot. As no one dared set their waggons close to Kitable's vardo, there was sufficient space to accommodate the entire Circle of the Raven in their garbs of furs and feathers.

Kitable had dueled a master wizard the day before and was still expecting that enemy to re-appear. He also knew Terant's ex-apprentice, Seria, was somewhere in the camp, having promised to help DoomDragon. But of all of these threats, none compared to the Circle

of the Raven, DoomDragon's team of intuitive casters. Together, they had created illusions better than anything Kitable could counter. He did not fully understand their formidable abilities, yet was supposed to be allied with them.

I'm too tired for this. Tohmas had asked him to "play nice," yet Kitable passionately hated dealing with other casters, particularly ones that had tried to kill him. But appearing weak in front of enemies was dangerous.

Taking a deep breath, he ran his eyes over the seven stout elders. Seven pairs of eyes looked back up at him. Colt, engulfed in a large quilted coat, carried on as if nothing was amiss, filling the cup of a man in a white bear skin.

Each Circle member wore the pelt of a given animal; the man standing to greet Kitable had a white wolf skin over his shoulders. Despite being the youngest of the elders, he looked close to DoomDragon's age, making him twice as old as Kitable. Behind him, a thin crone-like woman in a full coat of snowy owl feathers unsteadily came to her feet to shadow her younger counterpart.

Recognizing the leading pair, Kitable's gut clenched. He had nearly been killed by these two in their last altercation.

He felt no need to introduce himself; by their lit faces, they knew who he was. They had come to meet with him.

Play nice, he reminded himself.

"The wolf pelt," Kitable said to the youngest elder, trying to make his voice gentle.

The man chuckled and bowed his head in acknowledgement. "I am Tril. I am flattered you have recollection of me. And yes, you took my pelt," the Northlander said in surprisingly good Esparan.

"You can have it back, if you like," Kitable offered.

Elder Tril shook his head. "That Aspect was lost to me. I have a new one. You may keep the pelt as a gift. I hope it keeps you warm."

In the soft voice of the Northlander, it sounded like a blessing.

The crone spoke next, her voice a croak as she unsteadily stepped up beside Elder Tril. Kitable did not understand any of her words.

Elder Tril tilted his head up to Kitable. "Master Kitable, this is Elder Ela, the Voice of the Circle of the Raven. Because she has little skill with your tongue, I will repeat her words for you."

Kitable shrugged in acceptance; he could not think of any valid reasons to refuse. The prince wanted them to get along. For now, he would try. His conversation with Tohmas would have to wait.

He came down the steps. Last night, there had been two stones at the fire, but now there were nine. Since that left him a choice, he picked the stone closest to the vardo and sat, allowing the Northlanders to take their seats again. The heat of the magic stones could not reach Kitable, but Colt brought him a fresh cup of tea. They were all enjoying tea, Kitable noticed. *I don't own that many cups. Did they bring their own?*

As they sat, Elder Ela spoke again, rasps and half words that sounded Rydan.

Elder Tril smiled and said, "We offer you praise for your skill in breaking our Circle." Kitable frowned, and the man explained, "When you stole my pelt, I could no longer complete the Circle."

"Which is why it took you so long to attack again," Kitable reasoned. He looked around at the mix of men and women facing him. "Seven of you? I was dealing with seven?"

Elder Tril's smile showed sharp fangs. "We are the Circle," he said, as if that was the only possible answer. "We further offer you praise for your skill in escaping our Vision in your search of the Northlands," he translated for Elder Ela.

When it came to Kitable's eventual success in seeing through their illusions, Kitable felt more ashamed by his earlier failures than pleased by his single, limited success. He had, once only, seen enough to reveal the alliance between the Northlanders and some Esparans. It had been a pittance but it had prompted Tohmas to question the war and discover the alliance between Prince Marfaie and DoomDragon.

Despite his efforts, Kitable had never been able to repeat the feat.

"Where is woman?" Elder Ela said in carefully whispered Esparan, surprising Kitable.

Elder Tril translated the inquiry as, "Where is the woman who helped you in your visions?"

"Visions?" Kitable echoed. "You mean Scrys. But ... helped me? No woman helped me. Seria was my enemy. She did not help me." Something stirred in Kitable's mind.

"You did not know," the woman elder mumbled. "You did not ask for her help."

Scowling, Kitable resisting the urge to cast. He tried to keep his voice level but heard it rise. "It is rude to read someone's thoughts. I happen to be one of the few people who could block you, but I will first request that you stop your thought magic. You cannot control—"

"We do not seek control. We are the Circle: we seek only knowledge," Elder Tril interrupted diplomatically as the woman in owl feathers gave a hoot of laughter.

"For DoomDragon, I will hinder the *visaln*," the woman agreed. Kitable guessed the word meant their magic.

Elder Tril spoke into the silence: "But the woman who aided you, even if you were not aware, must be known to you."

Realization struck Kitable. He frowned further.

He scanned the nearby camp, undiscouraged when he did not find her; she would be watching. Now that the only other caster in the camp had been killed, Kitable suspected Shimmer Weaver and her father Dust had taken to following him instead.

"Weaver!" he shouted. "Get out here, now!"

Sure enough, Shimmer Weaver stepped out from behind a nearby waggon. She brought with her a cloud of magic, although it was invisible to anyone not sensitive to it.

He regretted calling her; her exposed belly and high-slit dancing skirt were not seemly. Shameless, she joined them around the fire, her crimson hair flowing down her back. Her lack of physical cover was at odds with the density of magic layers wrapping her.

He would have to chastise her later for getting involved in his spells. *And point out that wearing a coat would help protect whatever shred of modesty she still possesses!*

"The red-haired girl..." Elder Tril whispered.

Magic flared, and Kitable scrambled back, coming to his feet beside Shimmer Weaver. He activated an additional shield from his hovering spells, having no idea what spell had been cast by the elder.

The untargeted power flared then faded in a single blink. After the flash, it reduced to a powerful thrum on the wolf elder. To those not able to sense magic, he would have seemed to be dodging nothing at all.

"That was ... weird," Shimmer commented, her voice tense.

Kitable was impressed. He had not known she possessed the ability to sense magic innately. Few did.

Despite his effort, Kitable identified no spells around Elder Tril. *How did he cast without speaking at least an activation word?*

Letting them know he was puzzled might allow them to believe they held an advantage. He instead watched, trying to solve the mystery without revealing how little he understood about their strange powers.

In the ongoing buzz of magic, the wolf eyes tracked something Kitable could not see. A dozen heartbeats later, Elder Tril lifted his head and stared at Shimmer with an intensity Kitable did not like.

"The man you live with," the elder prompted.

"My father?" Shimmer offered.

"With red hair like you. He works with plants."

"He is an apothecary."

The elder cocked his head. "I do not know that word."

Elder Ela caught up to the conversation, for she took advantage of the brief silence to snort and chastise, "Tril!"

The Northlander turned on his seat by the fire, his face stern. "He can help you!"

Every mother the world over apparently made the same noise. Like a scolding parent, Elder Ela tsked at the younger man.

Elder Tril did not let it stop him. He faced Shimmer again. "She is sick, but your father can help."

Shimmer blinked several times, finally easing the tension from her shoulders. Kitable recognized she too had been ready to cast.

"You...you want to hire us? For a remedy?"

The Northlander nodded. "Medicine. You have medicine we do not. You can help her."

"I will bring my father around as soon as I can," Shimmer agreed tentatively. She glanced at Kitable, but Kitable gave her no sign. It was odd to recognize she was looking for his advice. Or was it protection she wanted?

With that settled, Elder Tril let his intense stare drop. The magic faded away, the *visaln* finished. The Voice of the Raven was still shaking her head, but she did not speak.

The wolf eyes came back to Kitable. Kitable realized how much he had appreciated the brief distraction.

"You have questions."

CHAPTER 2

Clearing his throat, Kitable lowered himself back onto the stone by the fire. Shimmer Weaver took the stone beside him, completing the circle of nine stones. Colt, chuckling, brought Shimmer a cup of tea.

Knowing he had to seize the opportunity, Kitable decided to focus on business. It was easier to push aside doubts for now.

"I need to know about the wizard you worked for: Master Terant."

Elder Tril glanced at Elder Ela and received a nod of agreement. "Ask your questions," he said.

Answering the summons of his patron, Master Terant Palnon stood outside the doors to the Grand Hall of the Manor of Arcott and straightened his robes one final time. It had been three days since his duel with Kitable, and he was still limping from his fall. His left shoulder throbbed, and his right knee tweaked when he walked stairs, but it was improving. His injuries gave him another reason to hate the Galanth wizard.

Terant pushed wide the doors and strolled into the grand hall. A fire burned at the far end, the enormous fireplace the only ornamentation in the largely empty hall. The windows spaced between the pillars sent low sunbeams through the dust as Terant headed for the seats by the fire. The constant hum of hovering spells surrounded him like a circle of bodyguards, impenetrable. He could not be seen as weak, even when meeting with allies.

As Terant approached, he spotted Grigson by a window, his back to Terant. The old cheat had worked hard to make himself presentable. With enchanted sight, Terant saw the many hovering spells and guessed them to be twice as numerous. On a mundane level, Grigson also wore his finest tunic. A dozen or more gold and silver trinkets decorated Grigson's gaudy black and silver outfit, each glowing as magical to Terant. The man's prematurely white hair was neatly gathered in a short braid.

Four chairs made an arch in the warmth of the fire. In the far north, burning wood was uncommon, but a Prince of Espar would not sit by a dung fire. Making use of the cleaner fire, two servants prepared a meal behind the prince. Prince Marfaie sat with his feet up, his thick boots steaming the melted snow off.

One other seat was occupied; Rakhund was already in attendance, cloaked in black and slouched in the fine armchair.

Once Terant reached the level of the window, Grigson left his vigil and together they presented themselves to their patron. The air tightened as they approached, the wizard powers agitated by Rakhund's presence. Terant understood well why Grigson had kept his distance until absolutely necessary. Terant compared it to being around a man who smelled like pig slop; it made it a little harder to breathe, and he always wanted to toss the offending individual into a river.

The fifth chair that usually stood across from the prince was absent.

The prince himself did not rise to meet them, but he nodded to each of them as they took their seats. Despite having recently passed his forty-fifth birthday, Prince Marfaie had the look of a draft horse: tall, long-faced, and stiff when bored. He wore his black and silver colors in everything from dyed seal-pelt boots to the silver-thread collar of his tunic. Daggers made of fine carbiron, stronger than bog iron and rare outside of Lour, lined his belt. His short staff leaned against his chair, forever within reach. Under Terant's enchanted vision, the prince looked much less intimidating than Grigson, but still, Terant took heed. Grigson used trinkets to make up for what he lacked. Prince Marfaie of Tanble needed none. The tattoos across his face marked him as a warrior, but the hovering spells made it obvious that fighting was only one of his skills.

Princes were not known for their abilities with magic. This was a secret Prince Marfaie revealed only to his closest allies.

"It is certain. They bring war to us," Prince Marfaie said once Grigson and Terant were seated.

"Why continue the march?" Terant asked. Prince Tohmas and his allies had been in Solta to defend Prince Sol's claim to the land. Now that the Northlander invasion had been stemmed, their duty ended. Armies were expensive and war was dangerous.

"Darknim can do nothing else," the prince replied.

Terant nodded. It was not Prince Tohmas' slight he had to gauge; it was Darknim's. Darknim DoomDragon had sat among them, yet he now backed Tohmas. The lands that made up the Princedom of Tanble had once belonged to the Northlanders; no doubt Darknim wanted

them back. And would Darknim not seek Marfaie's head now? He had been betrayed.

It seemed Prince Tohmas of Galanth had promised him aid in this revenge. All the forces at his command were heading north.

"So it was not a ploy?" Grigson asked. He picked at the cooks' pork pie, left on a side table to cool, as he spoke. Nearly every finger of the man's hand had a ring on it. "I thought perhaps you had Darknim swap to mislead the southerners."

Marfaie scowled, the tattoos on his face stretching down. Like his finest warriors, the black claw marks stretched across the prince's face to remind them of his authority over the armies. It made his frowns look deeper and his scowls darker. "He has broken his oath."

With a shrug and a sigh, Grigson dismissed the problem, and the too-hot pie. Although they had worked together, none of the foundlings were friends.

"What of Seria?" Grigson asked, casting an eye at Terant.

"My apprentice is still loyal," Terant reported. "Darknim thinks he has an ally in her, but she answers to me. I have left her with them for now."

"Grigson, I want you in there," the prince commanded. "These alliances are new and fragile. Break them."

Grigson sat upright, quickly bowing his head in acceptance, his smile broadening. Certain chores were surprisingly pleasant to the conman. Sneaking into an enemy camp seemed to be one of them.

Terant sat a little straighter as well, an idea forming. He had been setting a trap for Master Kitable before being summoned. The issue troubling him had been how to get the enchanted item into Kitable's sphere of influence without moving it in magically, which the wizard would detect. If Grigson was—

"Master Terant, I understand Kitable is still a problem. As is the Northlander Circle now," Prince Marfaie interrupted.

The reminder of his failure to kill the Galanth wizard made Terant grimace. "They have an untouchable in the camp, a Celebrant of Totho by the name of Calanor. Kitable used him to dispel me. Thankfully, he is no warrior. We should see little of him."

"You have a plan?" the prince asked.

"I need to get Kitable away from the Circle and out of his vardo's defenses. If Grigson will be nearby, I have a suggestion."

"And the Circle?" the prince answered.

Terant took a long, slow breath. The gathering of seven casters into a Circle was formidable, but the Northlanders had no finesse in their magic. He had seen two of the Circle do battle once, but their specialization in the milder elements and domains made them impotent. With the appropriate defenses, he would be immune to their influence.

"I want the Circle broken," Terant agreed, "but until Kitable is neutralized, that must wait. Having him help them would be ... tricky. Eight casters are a bit much, even for me."

"So modest," Grigson said with a laugh as he rose. "If I am to get there before they get wise to us, I must start out."

Nearby, an unbalanced tray poured grease onto the fire and smoke billowed out. The cooks cursed. Grigson, closest to the fire, waved his hand to clear the smoke from his face as he stepped away. Terant detected a wave of magic hidden in the gesture, but it only cleared the region near the trickster.

Terant set a Wind Barrier between his patron and the fire, pushing the smoke back. Coughing was heard from behind the barrier as the cooks struggled to get clear. The prince, protected by the spell, did not move.

Grigson shrugged at the disruption and left, nigh on skipping in his excitement. Terant had no doubt Grigson would thoroughly enjoy pulling the forces of Galanth apart.

As he looked back at the prince, Terant realized the meat pie was gone from its resting place. He smirked. Grigson's fine tunic had not been nearly as well fitted as the man left. He assumed he had missed the spell Grigson used to tip the grease into the fire and distract the cooks from his theft of the pie.

Before heading back to his study, Terant paused to look down at Rakhund who had, as usual, said nothing. In ten years of working with the man, Terant had never seen his face. He had heard his voice only when he commanded his dragon.

"And what of you, Rakhund?" Terant asked. "With your dragon dead—"

"He has replaced the Black," Marfaie interrupted. "Two Reds fly at his command. I cannot risk sending another foundling but I do not

want magic getting involved against Rakhund. I need Kitable out of the way before the dragons burn the rabble to ashes, Master Terant."

His assignment clear, Terant bowed.

"I will visit Sol," Marfaie added, for a moment his eyes on the copious amount of smoke behind the Wind Barrier to his left. "I am confident his brothers are going to mount a rescue, and I cannot allow that. I will assign one of the foundlings to monitor him. If a rescue is attempted, Sol will either be moved or killed. But until then, perhaps he can provide insights that may help us."

"I have a trinket that can help. Shall I bring it by this evening?" Terant offered.

"I would appreciate that, Master Terant."

Dismissed, Terant hobbled out. He left his Wind Barrier up, sparing the prince from the smoke until the grease had burned off and only the crackling of firewood heated the room.

Chapter 3

Prince Sol Galanth of Solta paced.

The room was half the size of his tent in Solta. It took him four strides to cross from the fireplace to the bed. Two cycles into his imprisonment, he made the trek from one wall to the other without conscious thought.

That was the point. When he paced, he could think about everything else.

Sol had been misled for ten years, then betrayed and captured. Master Clarin, Sol's prime protector, had been serving Sol's enemies since he had positioned himself to take the position a decade earlier. With everything, he had been working for Prince Marfaie of Tanble to bring down Sol and his brothers.

Days after learning of that betrayal, Sol had met Prince Marfaie himself. He'd revealed that DoomDragon was his puppet. Marfaie—a man Sol thought had been dead for a decade—harbored his own plans for Sol and his brothers. Sol was helpless to stop him.

Sol had started pacing to give his feet something to do while he cursed and plotted then cursed some more.

Servants came and went, delivering clothing, food, and water to his room, but spoke not a word. Twice in the two cycles, they arranged a bath, although the water was frigid, and he was left drying himself on his own dirty clothing. Every few days, they took him to a small courtyard.

In the snow, given a merger coat, he was allowed to see the sky for a few candles before being returned to his room.

Days had turned into quartercycles, then a halfcycle, and he had no indication that he would be released. He did not even know if Marfaie had demanded ransom. Or maybe he had and been refused.

He paced more vigorously, cursing his brothers, then his nephew. He was certain, for a time, that they were to blame.

Somewhere near a cycle of his imprisonment, he decided to escape from the courtyard. It failed, and he was beaten for it. He did not see the courtyard for another five days.

Sol started hearing voices in his empty room, answering him when he muttered and paced. Knowing the isolation was beckoning insanity, he found parchment, ink, and quill in the desk and turned to the written word. Daily, he recorded his thoughts, forever ending with a curse for Marfaie. The acidic ink stained his fingertips yellow and made them raw.

He remembered little of the second mooncycle in the room. After the third attempt at escape during an outing, Sol endured a worse beating, and the insanity he had kept at bay broke through.

The journal he had been keeping had no entries. He vaguely remembered dreams of plugging the chimney, setting the room on fire, and even drowning himself, but he had lacked the conviction to follow through. Days blurred together. A haze remained.

One day, he decided to run around the courtyard. It was surrounded by walls; running was not an escape. But in running, he discovered how profoundly weak he had become.

Determination had set in. He ran in the courtyard, pushing himself to near exhaustion, and then paced in the room. His movement woke his mind from its slumber. His body repaired and built back up.

Running gave him time to think. He ran past where he had punched the wall in a rage, nearly breaking his hand. He ran past the corner where he had climbed, only to be tackled by guards. He ran through the pond where he had considered drowning himself. He tried to make more rounds before he was taken back to his room.

He thought about his life, his wife, and his sons. He thought about life before, when he had followed his father on the rides to set a neighboring warlord down or displace a rebellious soldier claiming independence. He reviewed those long rides, seeing fear in the faces around him.

He had not understood then. He had considered his father a protector of the people. Now, he saw it for what it was: conquest. Zayban had claimed land, gifting them to his sons upon his passing.

The princes kept peace in Espar, their only opposition each other. Sol had never been a warrior. Before DoomDragon and his Northlanders, he had never fought a war.

He thought about the campaign in Solta, repelling Northlanders. It made less sense the more he reviewed it. DoomDragon had destroyed at least four villages farther north in one season, then stalled at Darbin for years. If DoomDragon had struggled to breach those walls, why had he not gone around? Sol's soldiers would have been unable to harry them. The lands surrounding Darbin did not allow for choke points. Sol had been pinned. DoomDragon could have taken Darbin, had he wanted it.

He did not want it, Sol decided in his pacing and running. *Just as he did not want BellRoost.* Once Tohmas had come to BellRoost, DoomDragon had changed strategies and taken it in a single day.

Sol's efforts to keep the Northlanders at bay had been futile for years. Now, he could see it.

Tohmas saw it, Sol recognized. He had tried to warn Sol in BellRoost. He had seen that the position had been precarious. Prince Marfaie, the man back from the dead, had bled Sol and, through him, his brothers.

Sol planned vengeance as he paced and ran. His favorite was tying Marfaie to a starvation post as a traitor. He held that image in his mind before he slept every night, vowing to make it come true.

At noon on a warm winter's day, Sol's door rattled. He stepped back, expecting an early meal, but was surprised by visitors. He had not had a visitor since Marfaie had come to him nearly two mooncycles before, but these men were not the arrogant prince who had taunted Sol.

A servant in a tunic of black and grey and a sour, stern expression was the first through. His sunken eyes were wide and glassy like a bookkeeper's. The man was as short as a teenager but had a beard that boasted full maturity as he stood in the shadow of two larger warriors.

The two warriors ducked to get through the door behind the servant. Their faces were marked by the traditional tattoos of rank, something Sol understood had originated in tribe life but had somehow come to be a part of Tanble's military ranks. Both men had four tattoos,

marking them as part of Marfaie's high-ranking Bears. He thought that apt considering their fuzz, size, and surly manner.

"Come along, Prince Sol," the servant said, beckoning like calling a dog to heel.

"Who, by the hells, are you?" Sol asked, his voice croaking. The fine cut of the man's tunic and the many layers of carved bone adornments implied wealth, but Sol could not identify a rank on the man.

"I am Melnor," the man replied, tipping into a small bow. "I am a servant of Prince Marfaie. I have come to bring you to him. Come," he said again, gesturing. The smile under the beard was broken by worn teeth.

Feeling less at ease with Melnor than with the warriors and their swords, Sol stepped away. He struggled to control his ill-used voice. "What if I refuse?"

Melnor's wide eyes blinked as if the thought had never occurred to him. "I suppose I would force you," the man said with a shrug. "These two can do it or..." Melnor put a hand into his pocket and pulled out a cumbersome key-like object as long as a hand. Where Sol expected the blade of the key, a row of tiny spikes protruded. "...or I can force you to."

The menace in the voice was sincere enough to convince Sol that arguing was not worth his while yet. The object, whatever it was, looked unpleasant.

Escorted by the brutes, Sol was taken down new winding stairs. Passing the groomed halls and their shuttered windows, he arrived in a basement lined with natural stone. A single room, lit with torches, had been carved out of the rock. Smoke curled up the stairwell above them.

Melnor faced him again. "Strip, dear prince. The chains await."

"Now just—" Before he could properly begin his protests, iron grips fell onto Sol's shoulders. The Bears leaned over him.

Melnor pulled out the object in threat.

Sol eyed the strange key, wondering if it was meant to be a torturer's tool. With the lines of spikes on it, he did not want to figure out how it worked, but neither was he willing to bow to every whim of Marfaie's servant. Sol was a Prince of Espar. He would not be treated like a slave.

Sol drew himself up further, denying the rise of memories. He had survived beatings three times already, and he would again. He had not spent two mooncycles in isolation to cower before a scrawny servant.

"Don't threaten me, boy." Sol pulled away from the Bears. With his restored strength, it took both soldiers to hold him back.

Sol stared down at Melnor, meeting the man's eyes instead of staring at the strange tool he did not understand.

Melnor laughed, and it was a speckled sound. "Prince Sol, my threats are not empty. This device is tied to a powerful spell. Although I doubt you'd appreciate its complexity, it is a Five-way Domination spell that can force you to obey. If you do not do as you are told, you will be forced to. It is that simple."

Sol regarded the object again and realized he did not recognize the metal. Its dull brown-black was unlike any iron or copper he had seen, but it looked strong. At the least, the spikes remained sharp despite the age of the implement.

Regardless of how much the sight of the instrument made his stomach twist, he was still a prince.

"Then make me, you whining demon," Sol said, finally feeling full strength return to his voice, "because I'll not do it myself."

Melnor gave a tiny shrug, as if a child had declared war on him for the day, and muttered something quietly to the key.

Cold cascaded into Sol like ice water, sweeping along each limb and then across his body. It ended by stabbing, like a hundred tiny spikes, into his mind.

Strip, a voice commanded, *then present your wrists.*

His tingling arms and legs answered despite his opposition. He released the lacings of his boots and kicked them off. His hands undid his belt, dumped it on the floor, then pulled off his tunic. Off came the trousers and hose, and all were heaped together, freeing him to extend his hands to Melnor.

"You demonic—"

Silence, the voice commanded, and Sol's words stopped. He tried to shout, filling his mind with curses, but nothing came out. He could not move, not even to scream in frustration, as shackles were set on his wrists and attached to iron rings imbedded in the wall behind him. Tied by his wrists, Melnor and his two Bears left him.

Slowly, the cold lessened, leaving only the natural chill of the deep cell. As the time flickered by, Sol took to pacing again, limited to only

two steps thanks to the chains. He was reminded of the cold bath, but moving allowed him to warm somewhat.

Marfaie was punishing him. Marfaie was angry. That meant something had gone wrong for the Prince of Tanble.

Sol felt the first bud of hope.

When Marfaie joined Sol in the cell, Sol was rubbing his hands together to keep feeling in them. Thankfully, there was no sign of Melnor and his key trinket. Still, Sol acutely noted that Prince Marfaie carried a cat o' nine tails.

Marfaie had changed out of his usual grey and black tunic with carved ivory and bone and wore a simple brown tunic and leggings. For the first time, the Prince of Tanble's arms were bare, giving Sol a clear view of the many tattoos decorating his forearms in addition to the five crisscrossed claw marks on his face. The markings of his arms were fine and detailed; Sol had never seen anyone so intricately tattooed. It was writing, albeit in a language other than Esparan, and that unsettled him profoundly.

A warrior arrived, pulling Sol's chain to pin him to the wall, his hands bound before him and unable to protect his modesty. The warrior then retreated, leaving Sol face to face with Prince Marfaie.

Without a word, Marfaie lashed the whip at Sol. The tip cut thin lines over his left shoulder. Sol started back, crying out in surprise.

But through the burn of the whip, he still held onto hope.

Sol's voice croaked when he laughed dryly. "Something wrong, Marfaie? You don't look happy."

The Prince of Tanble leaned in, his face a finger's breadth from Sol's. "Oh, I'm ecstatic, Sol. Dragal has come north." The thick skin of the weathered man crinkled in scowl.

Worse than the pain of the lash, Sol's heart ached. He had known that he was bait for his two living brothers. He had been praying they would somehow know, but now that hope was dashed.

Sol flexed his arms against the chains, but he could not strike out. Instead, he could only stare at the man in brown across from him.

Marfaie's scowl hardened. "Now, with Barnon already committed, I have all the sons of Zayban in one place, far from their manors and allies. I am amazed they value you so highly." Dismissively, Marfaie turned away.

Despite the dread he felt creeping into his stomach, Sol stood tall. "What about Tohmas? You didn't mention my dear nephew."

Marfaie spun and the whip lashed out. This time, it slashed against his legs, but Sol held his feet. This pain did not matter. His running had burned his legs worse.

Sol smiled victoriously. He had seen Marfaie's wounded pride.

"Habal's dead," Marfaie said, his voice forcibly tight as he pulled the whip into a position of readiness. "I don't care about his son."

Sol shook his head, knowing his smile would goad Marfaie but, for a moment, not caring. He had only words with which to wound his torturer.

"Oh, you seem to care. Your magic tricks got me, but they missed Tohmas. And so long as Tohmas remains, Clarin's usefulness is limited; Master Kitable will keep him in check. Your Northlander army cannot—"

The lash took him across the chest, and Sol lost control of his voice and his legs, falling to his knees. Every breath shook as the lines of fire bled down his front. Another lash came across his shoulders, keeping Sol from gathering himself or his thoughts. He lost count after that, his mind too shaken by pain.

But through the pain, he kept thinking of his stubborn nephew. There had to be a reason for Marfaie's rage. The sons of Zayban were not defeated, not yet. Tohmas had seen through DoomDragon's tactics in BellRoost. He had outmaneuvered DoomDragon more than once. Sol had to assume he had done so again.

At length, the lashes stopped. Sol took long, deep sighs, with each breath repeating the same conviction: the sons of Zayban were surviving. There was hope.

"Tohmas and his Rydan rabble will never reach Arcott," Marfaie said. "We will break them in the march."

In the pause, Sol lifted his head from where he had shielded it under his bound hands. Forgetting himself entirely, a smile crept onto his face.

"Rydans?" Sol said. A chuckle escaped him. "How many Rydans? A lot, I hope! I knew Tohmas had allies in the south, but I never imagined he would have enough clout to bring them up!"

To Sol's delight, Marfaie's face fell.

Sol guarded with his forearms, but the whip strike was sloppy and only grazed his skin. The budding hope swelled. "And coming north,

coming to Arcott, are they? That means my brothers and nephew defeated DoomDragon!"

This time, the whip struck deeper. Involuntarily, Sol's arms withdrew, and he took two lashes across his shoulders and back instead. He felt blood run from the cuts, hot against his cold skin, yet it still did not bother him.

"I have no need of them!" Marfaie declared as he swung.

Seeing Marfaie's face contort in fury emboldened him. Despite the agony of his body, Sol smiled.

He's scared.

"Did you lose control of your puppet Northlander?" Sol whispered.

Marfaie lifted the whip and Sol drew back instinctually, unable to do more than hunch in anticipation. There, he paused. His hand lowered, his jaw tense enough to choke the words as he spoke.

"Do you think your title will save you? Princes do not kill princes. We all promised." With his free hand, Marfaie grabbed at Sol's throat, yanking him forward. The Prince of Tanble tightened his grip and Sol choked, but his legs did not have enough energy left to even kick at his attacker. Light flashed behind his eyes. The room darkened.

"You will not be given that respect, not when you have the blood of my brother, of a prince, on your hands." He leaned away and took a long breath. "But let's talk a bit longer." He released the hold on Sol's throat. "Let's talk about those forces. Let's talk about your dear brothers, and what you know about your nephew's allies."

Sol took a long breath. His vision hazily returned, the dark shape of his enemy forming in the limited torchlight. "Piss off," he said, deliberate force in each word.

"Then Melnor will join us. I've had my fun. It's time to get answers."

The tiny man with the key entered the room. Sol's chest tightened in raw fear.

He kicked out wildly, desperate to do something—anything—to keep the magic at bay.

Prince Marfaie stepped out of range but struck back. The whip slashed its nine claws over Sol's chest once more.

The pain overwhelmed his senses one last time. Consciousness left him. It was a form of victory.

Nowhere had the celebration of New Year been louder or more raucous than in Fixer City. The mobile camp of tradesmen, whores, and merchants attracted men and women from all factions—Rydan, Esparan, and Northlander—and taught them what a real festival should be. The party lasted the entire night, calming as dawn peeked over the grey hills. The new year had arrived. With it came spring, filled with promise, particularly for the forces that were freed from the commitments of war.

Dust Weaver rearranged the shelves of his vardo shop Match and Mixer as the sun rose on New Year's day. He replaced the more entertaining herb and drug mixtures, which had been popular overnight, with hangover cures and pain relievers. With the brewer's vardo not far, Dust expected to have plenty of customers in the later candles of the morning.

Once done, Dust joined his daughter Shimmer by the campfire for breakfast. Although she had been up all night with him selling concoctions under a magic lamp, Shimmer looked as if the celebration was about to begin. With her long red hair tucked under a gold wrap, she needed only to remove her overcoat to be in dancing costume. But she, like him, was ready to pack up. A prince had come from the south because the war was not yet over. A new enemy had been identified holding DoomDragon's chain. The march would head north.

Dust had conceded that he and Shimmer would likely go north with them. There was nowhere else Shimmer wanted to be.

Having been kept up by the business, Dust was still yawning as he picked at a chunk of bread and drank the tea Shimmer had prepared, the pot filled with water by her summoning spell. As he sat, Dust reviewed the herbs he would need to support an old Northlander woman's failing heart.

"Some things never change, eh Dust?" a voice said.

Leaping to his feet, Dust knocked his tea and plate over the fire and onto Shimmer. Shimmer sprang to her feet across from him with a curse, scowling at her stained skirt.

The speaker had aged so little in the last decade, he still looked to be in his prime. Grigson's hair had gone white sometime near the age of twenty, giving him a ghostly complexion. Although it was hard for

Dust to know, he suspected there were spells present on the unobtrusive jerkin and tights the man wore to blend in with the merchants of Fixer City.

To Dust's dread, Grigson narrowed his smoky blue eyes over Dust's shoulder.

"Then again, perhaps some things *have* changed. You have improved your taste in partners!"

Dust squared his shoulders, stoutly blocking the path to Shimmer. "Hello, Grigson. It's been a long time." He clenched and unclenched his left hand, telling Shimmer to stay clear of the confrontation.

Grigson's eyes flicked down to the gesture. The man cracked a wide grin. "You still using code like that? I did teach you Sendings, didn't I?" Although Dust knew Grigson was from Lour, he had none of his usual emphasis on the consonants when he spoke. He sounded almost Galanth in his choice of accents.

The reminder that Dust's magic would be outdone by Grigson chilled him. Dust did not stop Grigson from crossing through the campfire circle to address Shimmer. Despite his desire to blast the man to pieces, that was fated to fail. Grigson would not have come unprepared. And if Dust defended Shimmer, Grigson might think she needed protecting. The old thief would try to get her alone.

Grigson's stare swept up and down Shimmer's decorated clothes, as bright as Dust's but closer cut. Using the stain from the tea on her right thigh as an excuse, he stared at her legs the longest.

Shimmer could present herself as any number of characters, and Dust knew each by her posture and expression. This time, she chose her true self.

She straightened. Although she had to raise her chin to meet his eye, her expression made it clear she was still looking down on him.

Dust winced. Defiance here was an invitation to Grigson. He would see it as a challenge.

The conman held his place, testing the limits of Shimmer's magic defenses and her convictions.

"What do you want, Grigson?" Dust asked.

"I need information, old friend. I was hoping you and your partner could help me."

Grigson raised a long-fingered hand and, like a lover's caress, moved to brush aside a lock of red hair from Shimmer's face.

Magic sparked against the conman's white skin. Reflexively, Grigson withdrew his hand, but neither of them moved more than that. Shimmer's stare narrowed vindictively. It was a simple enough spell, visible and obvious in its purpose. Shimmer had been studying magic books since being able to read, and she never left Match and Mixer without defenses.

Grigson's smile grew. "I taught your father that spell. You think I can't counter it?"

Shimmer sank into one hip, a hand on her waist, and flipped the lock of hair out of her face. "Shall we dance?" she invited.

Again, Grigson ran his eyes up and down Shimmer's form, but this time Dust saw the flicker of magic over his eyes. Shimmer let him assess her, not caring. With a hushed whisper, she matched his spell, activating Spell Sight. She mimicked his scrutiny of her, even duplicating his intrigued but cautious expression.

Dust held his breath, wondering if Grigson might have met a match in Shimmer. He suspected they had equal hovering spells, although Grigson certainly had more experience.

"Tempting," Grigson admitted, but he stepped back. "I see the family resemblance now, Dust. Looks like her mother." He paused to lift his eyebrows at Shimmer in taunt. "I wonder what Loria would think if she knew where you were."

Shimmer snorted dismissively. "Wow. Threatening to tell on me to my mother. She knows."

Grigson's confident smirk did not waver. "Does her husband know?"

Hesitation flashed across Shimmer's face, and her eyes flicked to Dust. Ready to play the part of the father, Dust shrugged widely and joined his daughter in front of Grigson. "Darmac knows damn well she's alive," Dust said. "And Shimmer already knows her history, Grigson. I have no secrets there for you to exploit. Now go away. I left that life."

Bowing his head in mock defeat, Grigson retreated a step. "Just a chat then, old friend? For old time's sake?" he requested, his voice conversational.

Dust's heart sank. He knew that shrewd smile. Although he dreaded to think it, Dust had a terrible feeling he needed to hear what Grigson had to say.

"It's alright, Shim," Dust said. "Go get cleaned up."

She paused, no doubt hearing the tension in his voice, but Dust gave her no other signal and she had to let it go. Shimmer still gave Grigson a long, suspicious look but obediently left the fire for the waggon.

"Sweet little girl," Grigson said, staring after Shimmer for far too long. He chuckled at seeing Dust's scowl. "Oh, Dust, don't worry. I wouldn't dream of touching her. I remember what happened to the last people who did."

Grigson slowly turned back to Dust, his crooked smile knowing.

The warmth drained from Dust's face. His hands went to fists at his sides.

Grigson's voice lowered. "She doesn't know, does she? Your sweet little girl wouldn't be so proud of her father if she did. No, she'd fear you." He stepped up to Dust, passing through Dust's external magic shields and positioning himself to loom over the apothecary. Feeling trapped by the man's words more than his physical position, Dust did not move.

"Four men," Grigson whispered. "Four young, strong men. I even know where you hid the pieces, Dust Weaver."

Dust felt no guilt, but the thought that Shimmer might find out made his confidence fail. She would not understand. She didn't even realize he knew what had happened on the road outside of the village of Vait five years before.

"What do you want, Grigson?" Dust asked once more, but this time hushed in surrender.

"Rydans, old friend. I want to know about Rydans. I want to know their habits, their language, their customs. I want to know everything about them. Then, and only then, will I leave you and your little girl alone." He glanced at the waggon meaningfully. "Her respect is worth it, don't you think?"

Dust nodded. It was.

Tohmas visited Prince Rairn in the dusk, enduring the cold reception of the Barlabian without complaint. In the morning, he returned, answering the concerned reports from the healing mother. While his twisted foot only needed rest, Prince Rairn became acutely ill after sunset. Overnight, he deteriorated. His sudden fever left him shivering on the warm blankets of the Healing waggon, unable to eat and unwilling to try. The healing mother gave cautious reports, fearing disease would take Rairn soon.

Out of sight, Tohmas stood beside the entrance and watched.

Rairn had survived a decade of war against DoomDragon. He had allied himself with Tohmas, then betrayed him to fight against him. In the end, he had been defeated. Esparan traditions protected the turncoat prince, but Tohmas saw no reason to observe them. Although he would never reveal it, the fever had started, and would end, by Tohmas' hand.

Rairn had betrayed him. He would not be allowed to do so again.

DoomDragon found Tohmas still positioned by the door at dawn. HillTop had been without a Celebrant to Pari over the winter, but with Dragal's arrival bringing new celebrants, a dawn service to Pari drew out the gathering of Pari. As a result, the Healing waggon was empty. To Tohmas' amusement, the fragment left in charge of this Healing waggon while the rest attended the service was Tohmas' cutter Darak and his dog Stitches. The hound with the mottled coat lay beside whatever patient Darak was tending.

For a long moment, DoomDragon stood beside Tohmas and stared at the unconscious, sweating Prince of Barlaby within the waggon. Then, with a frown Tohmas was learning to heed well, the man sighed.

"The gods do not favor him these days."

"Perhaps this is Inac's answer to his fluid loyalties," Tohmas replied.

The Goddess embodied justice, but she was also the Goddess of Vengeance. He was certain she approved of his actions here.

Cutter Darak shot him a dark look, which made Tohmas smile and turn away. His silent presence had not bothered anyone, but the conversation threatened to wake the patients, and it was still early dawn.

Darknim's expression changed from gravity to bemusement. The Northlander chuckled through his beard as they left, a Prince of Espar chased out by a lowly cutter.

Four protectors set themselves ahead and behind Tohmas with practiced precision, clearing a way through the sparse crowds. Smelling of bodil tea, Carsh came to Tohmas' side looking fresh and ready. But his eager prancing was slower; he was hungover despite the tea. The New Year's celebration had raucous among the Rydans, as usual, it seemed.

For the first time in his memory, Tohmas had avoided the revelry. Too much was at stake for him to be among the partygoers.

They walked through the camp in silence, stepping over the debris from the merriment of New Year and victory. Apparently, Esparans traditionally exchanged footwear as part of the celebration, meant to herald in new paths and adventures. The dozen shoes strewn around made Tohmas wonder how many people had cold feet come morning.

Carsh's Esparan Follower, the boy Sabian, was the only one permitted to enter the command tent once they arrived, but Carsh assigned him to guard the door and did not let him join them in conference. *There's another who did not participate in the revelry.* Sabian, although he was barely eighteen, was too serious about his studies with Carsh to partake in any such nonsense.

Once in the tent, where only Carsh would overhear, Darknim raised a bushy eyebrow and said, "You are two men, Tohmas of Galanth."

"Oh, I am only one man. I just act like a different one when the need arises. Sit for a drink, Darknim?" Tohmas pivoted a chair on its back legs to offer it.

The Northlander leader smiled broadly. "So long as I get to make the drink. Rydan wildwater is not easy on old stomachs this early in the morning."

Given leave, the old man set up a brazier and placed a pot to boil. Darknim sat on the ground beside the pot, crossed his legs, and stared up at Tohmas. Taking the hint, Tohmas left the chairs and sat in the dirt beside the newest addition to his forces and handed over three mugs. Carsh joined by crouching, a Rydan position of planning.

While they talked, Darknim sorted leaves from a satchel and selected a handful, which he threw in the pot. Carsh made a face in jest.

Soon the smell of bark and grass wafted through the tent.

"Elder Tril tells me our enemy now controls two red dragons," Darknim said.

The calm of the Northlander's voice made Tohmas laugh aloud. *This is the leadership I sought, calculated in all things.* Growing up, Tohmas had been told that fear was unacceptable. Opposition was a chance to excel, to be challenged and so rise stronger. Lately, he had spent too much time comforting his Esparan commanders when odds shifted against them. It was refreshing to have someone who needed no comforting.

"Two? One fire-breathing monster is not enough?" Tohmas asked.

Darknim shrugged. "Wouldn't you if you could?"

Tohmas considered the problem. At length, he decided, "We'll need some advice on this one. Who better than my *wisavi*?"

The Rydan word had been bestowed upon Kitable by Carsh to protect the wizard from the anger of the other Rydans. Rydans had no tolerance for casters of any kind, believing any magic user was a villainous "flyer" bent on dominating people, butchering prized horses, and stealing daughters. Although the Rydans would still tear out Kitable's throat if he was ever caught casting, they could accept him as powerful in matters of the mind so long as he was a *wisavi*, Tohmas' advisor.

The wizard was still getting used to the title.

Carsh popped to his feet and trotted to the entrance. From his place on the ground, Tohmas accepted tea from Darknim and watched Carsh scrutinize the tent flap. Sabian's pale eyes watched carefully, the Follower trying to see unspoken commands.

Kitable had set spells over the tent at one point, and Tohmas thought he understood what Carsh was planning. Sabian did not seem to.

When Darknim cocked his eyebrow, Tohmas laughed. "Just getting his attention."

Taking a thin knife, Carsh scratched the flap of the tent. Tohmas felt nothing, but Carsh smirked widely, skipped back, and stood ready. Sabian cocked his head, feeling, but he shook his head. Unlike Carsh, Sabian had not yet developed the ability to sense magic.

Sure enough, Wisavi Kitable appeared in the middle of the tent. He was poised as if expecting an attack, his hands up and a trinket of black wood in hand.

Seeing only the grinning prime protector, he cursed and stood straight.

"You could just call me! A candle's worth of casting, and you just scratched it into oblivion! I've got Scrys on the place! Just call my name! I will hear you!"

"Need some help with this one, Kit," Tohmas replied, waving the wizard over.

"Of course, no problem," Kitable replied. "I wasn't doing anything important. I never do between your summons. I just sit there, twiddling my thumbs until some barbarian fiddles with my spells and scares me into popping in!"

Tohmas waited.

Kitable, spotting the Northlander sitting on the floor beside the table, winced. The wizard blinked several times, likely reviewing what he had said so far. He begrudgingly shook his head.

"My apologies, my prince. I did not realize you had company." Kitable's voice was a resentful grate.

Darknim barked thick laughter. "I love it! He apologizes not because of his behavior, but because he was caught!"

Extending a steaming cup to the wizard, Tohmas invited Kitable forward. Carsh would not miss his tea.

"My outburst was entirely justified," Kitable said. With a final sigh, he took a slow seat beside Tohmas, accepting the tea with uncommon hesitation.

It struck Tohmas as unusual. Did he not like the smell of the woody Northlander tea? He had not thought Kitable picky about tea.

"So, what are we talking about?" Kitable prompted as Carsh crouched back down with them.

"Dragons," Tohmas replied. "Two, apparently. Red ones."

"Prince Marfaie has them under his control," Darknim added, smiling over his steaming cup like a man discussing his grandchildren.

Tohmas expected another tirade from the wizard, but DoomDragon's calm seemed to be contagious; Kitable sipped his tea mildly.

"Dragons don't get enchanted easily, if at all. They're resistant. No wizard can properly control dragons." He paused, his brow furrowed. "But Prince Marfaie can?"

Darknim sipped his tea. "The one controlling them is called Rakhund, and he is not a wizard. I have seen him only a few times, but he hates wizard magic abjectly."

"Anything to do with your ax?"

Darknim cocked his head. "Not that I know of. Why?"

Tohmas felt the Northlander's tension; he seemed to be fighting an urge to reach for the weapon in comfort.

Kitable shrugged. "Just curious. Your ax is strange magic."

"Untouchable?" Tohmas questioned, thinking of SoulBurner and its ability to destroy wizard magic.

"SoulBurner makes me nervous," Kitable admitted, his grey eyes flickering down to the blade on Tohmas' belt as if to be sure it wasn't being drawn. "But this is different." He looked back at Darknim's blade. "That ax is an insult, like the powers within are a terrible mistake. Seeing as it's so old and can slay dragons, I thought perhaps it was related to this Rakhund."

DoomDragon shrugged. "The ax came from the Circle of the Raven and is from time before time. That is all we know."

Kitable nodded pensively as he went back to his tea. He kept a wary eye on them all, although Tohmas wondered what he was looking for.

When nothing else was forthcoming, Tohmas asked, "So who is Rakhund?"

"He is the first of the foundlings of Tanble," Darknim said.

"Foundlings?"

DoomDragon nodded. "Including me, there were four elder foundlings, but Marfaie has brought in other, younger ones in recent years. When they are young, he teaches them absolute fealty to him and him alone. You killed one; the boy controlling the black dragon we defeated."

"So that was not Rakhund?"

"No. Rakhund seldom leaves his home. He assigns younger foundlings to the task of controlling the dragon. Or dragons now."

Kitable shook his head, the tea lowered in his lap. "But it's impossible to control a dragon for any length of time. Maybe give it a command or two, but not long term. They cannot be enchanted."

"Rakhund has done it for as long as I have known of him," Darknim replied. He shrugged apologetically to the wizard. "I do not know how."

Leaving Kitable to consider the problem, Tohmas asked, "What of the other foundlings? Will they be a problem?"

DoomDragon seemed to be reading the steam of his tea as he replied, "The younger ones are not a real threat; they will simply be another sword opposing you, no better or worse for their upbringing. The elders..." Darknim grimaced. "Well, we are the survivors of the hundred that were chosen. We have been... distilled you may say. You have already met one of the other elders, Master Terant."

Kitable jumped, spilling tea onto his hands. He swapped his grip to shake off the hot water as he admitted, "If he's an indication of the skills of these older foundlings, then Rakhund will certainly be formidable. Terant has been a challenge. If we move into his territory, I expect to be pressed. He's creative and, though I hate to admit it, incredibly powerful."

Carsh snarled, and Tohmas had to smile. In this opposition, Carsh saw opportunity. He, in true Rydan fashion, believed the challenge had to be met with enthusiasm.

Tohmas chose consciously to follow his example.

"What about the fourth? You, Master Terant, and Rakhund make three."

Darknim shrugged. "Grigson is the last. A skilled spy. He uses magic, but mostly trinkets instead of his own powers. Although he is most proficient at gathering information, he is not above assassination. He claims he can look like anyone. Deception is his best ally."

There, at last, Tohmas had something he could do. "Runnah!" he called.

The protector who answered the call for a messenger presented himself smartly, only to pause in confusion when faced with an empty table. He located the prince and his allies on the ground just in time to catch the token Tohmas threw to him.

Before he could say anything, Tohmas noticed Protector Sanba had a black eye. He cocked his head. "Protector? Trouble last night?"

Sanba straightened his shirt and glanced at Sabian. Carsh's follower was leaning back, watching carefully but fiddling with a knife.

Sabian's knuckles were skinned.

"Some fools started a fight," Sanba replied. "Just a scuffle. Nothing serious."

"Sabian was involved?" Tohmas asked, narrowing his eyes on the young man. He spotted a handful of other scratches and bruises.

The protector said nothing, openly looking at Carsh's follower.

"They were cheating some Rydans," Sabian replied curtly once it became obvious no one else would answer the question. "We thought it would be better if we argued with them about it, else the Rydans would've done the arguing."

Sanba shrugged, one part agreement and one part confession. "Wasn't too bad. Only four of us were involved, and the other guys were far drunker. We won."

Tohmas tried not to smile but failed. "How many of the 'other guys'?"

Sabian shrugged, the answer irrelevant.

Sanba was pensive for a moment, then said, "Ten down by the end. Maybe fifteen altogether. At least four ran off..." He put on an innocent expression. "Was there something you wanted, my prince?"

Chuckling, Tohmas accepted the incident. It had been wise for the protectors and Sabian to intervene. Rydans cared too little about Esparans to pull their punches. At least with these two, he could assume the ones "down" were beaten, not killed outright.

Turning his attention back to the affairs on hand, he said, "Fixer City is officially closed."

Protector Sanba, his newly grown beard thickest under his ears, frowned deeply. "Sorry, my Prince. What?"

"I want you to assign the Fyrd of Border to the task of closing Fixer City. We did a census before; expand on it with the bookkeepers. Get a full tally of everyone. No one new joins. They are now a full part of this army, and I want them to act like it. From here on, they obey me. If they don't like it, they leave before we march."

Sanba bowed his head in acceptance and left briskly. He was already calling for additional protectors. They would make it happen.

Four, including Sabian. "They got off light. Only fifteen!" Tohmas said.

Carsh laughed aloud, but Sabian looked embarrassed and did not meet Tohmas' eye.

Kitable rubbed his temples. "I guess I will tighten up the defenses here."

Something in Kitable's voice sounded unusually worn. "There a problem, Master Kitable?" Tohmas asked.

Tohmas had his suspicion confirmed when Kitable winced. But the wizard glanced at DoomDragon, then shook his head. "Not the time," he muttered. He gave Tohmas a long look. "I will see what I can do to prepare for Rakhund while watching for Master Terant and Grigson too I guess."

Kitable already sounded tired. He sat as if on pins, nervously glancing about.

Tohmas held up a hand to stop the wizard. "I have some ideas. For now, focus on getting something that might free or kill those dragons. As much as Terant worries me, two red dragons will end this march instantly. Thank you, Kit."

The wizard left his tea as he rose. "I hate war," he said as he turned to leave. "Pity I'm the only one in the group who seems to."

Sure enough, Carsh was grinning hugely, every sharpened tooth bared. He crouched on his toes as if waiting for something exciting to be said so that he could jump up.

Challenges had to be met.

The three remaining people sat and enjoyed the tea. Tohmas thought it probably one of the last moments of serenity he would find for some time.

"The Circle also found Prince Sol," Darknim volunteered after a pause.

"So the reports I have of him being located in Chock Keep, conveniently just a day or two outside of our march to Arcott, are not true?" Tohmas asked. Darknim pursed his lips in a frown. "Don't worry; I was certain that report was a lie."

"He is located in the Merile Manor, at the far end of the Tracker Mountains."

Tohmas did not need the map; he had been staring at it for days. "So in the opposite direction."

"He is not worth retrieving," Darknim said, his voice still calm, as it had been all along.

Tohmas was not as certain. Prince Sol did not matter to Tohmas, but he mattered to Barnon and Dragal. They expected Tohmas to act like family. They needed to rescue Sol.

"I agree, Darknim, but the sons of Zayban will not. Our main forces are going north. I will take this to Marfaie himself, and I will burn down Arcott. As for Sol..." He glanced at Sabian standing guard, his stance wide and balanced in Rydan style. The boy was learning well. "...I will have the Rydans help."

Perhaps Darknim was right after all; by balancing Rydan customs with Esparan politics, Tohmas felt divided. It was becoming increasingly hard to keep the two roles separate.

Maybe he was two men. But even if that was true, it was not something he could keep up.

Kitable ducked out of the command tent, his mind tangled by the problems.

Grigson: a spy, assassin, and magic-user.

Master Terant: a master wizard rewriting magic as he went.

Rakhund: a wizard but not a wizard who commanded two red dragons.

Somehow, he was meant to manage them all, while still monitoring the forces for internal magic concerns like the Weavers.

And for what? For a march commanded under false pretenses. For a lie and for a man complicit in the murder of the man Kitable had sworn his life to. It left a stone in his gut.

Kitable turned away from the path to his vardo, too agitated to return home. He was risking his life yet did not believe Tohmas anymore. If he did not trust the man, and certainly he did not, why should he obey? Why stay at all?

He could forsake the patronage of the Prince of Galanth. Who would stop him? Although he had once feared Carsh, he knew his methods now. He could leave and no one would be able to catch him.

But do what? His life had been in service to Galanth. He did not know where he belonged if it was not in Galanth. Habal had offered him shelter when he had been hunted. Kitable had intended to take

his service to Tohmas, but now he felt uneasy just being near the current Prince of Galanth.

He walked through the mud and slush, feeling the uncommon desire to hit something. This could have been simple. He wished he had never seen the vision of Habal's death. He wished he could have remained ignorant, believing that Tohmas was a generous soul helping his uncle with invaders.

But Tohmas Galanth was so much more than that.

Kitable marched on, threading between tents and stepping over strewn footwear. He had no idea where he was going until he reached the end of the canvas tents. Across a gap, the sounds of cooking fires and conversation reach him. The pelt and bone tents did not sag under the wet as the canvas ones did. Smoke curled above the tents with the scent of rabbit and pheasant.

A man sat on a stump to Kitable's left, taking in the same view of the Northlander camp. Unlike Kitable, the man was Northlander, his layered pelts and furs making him as dark as the stump he used as a seat.

Before Kitable could give him more than a cursory glance, magic flared, and Kitable leaped back. He snapped a word to activate a defensive spell, but the magic did not reach for him. Instead, it settled around the figure on the stump, then vanished.

Elder Tril's bags circled his eyes like a mask. His stare darted around at first, then swept through the area as if he had landed from a Relocation spell and was getting his bearings. When he found Kitable, his stare fixed upon him, and the man grinned through his thick blond beard in a manner that reminded Kitable of Prince Habal and a prison cell from two decades before.

"Master Kitable, it is good to see you again. Did you enjoy the New Year's celebration?" the Northlander asked

Kitable frowned. "I don't partake in such nonsense. Today is no more special than yesterday," he groused, straightening his robes and standing tall.

Elder Tril cocked his head, suddenly looking more like a wolf with his crooked smile. "Every day is special," he replied as if teasing. Despite his accent, it sounded like something Habal would have said.

Elder Tril was missing his footwear, Kitable realized, yet his feet were pink. In the shadows, frost claimed the peaks of the frozen ground, but the paths were sucking mud that climbed up Kitable's legs to his knees.

The elder must have been among the Esparans overnight to lose his shoes. Tril's face was unknown to the Esparan; they would not have recognized him. He could have walked among them observing and none would question it.

"You're supposed to exchange shoes, not discard yours," Kitable pointed out.

Tril looked down at his feet and wiggled his toes, smearing the mud between his bare toes. "I traded with a sprite of a girl. Could hardly squeeze them on! Once my toes went numb, I hung the shoes by her door. She'll need them in the winter when her baby is born."

Kitable coughed uncomfortably. For a baby to be born in the winter, the woman might not even know she was pregnant yet. More divinations, causally mentioned like a comment on the weather. The elder's powers were formidable, albeit focused.

"Prophecies?" he tentatively asked. He wasn't sure he wanted the answer, but these new casters were a threat, another part of Tohmas' plans that Kitable did not understand.

But perhaps it's not my problem, he mused.

"The second aspect. I carry more now. I see more." Tril drew his feral gaze up to meet Kitable's. He touched his hand to the pelt on his shoulders, stroking the white fur affectionately.

In a blink, magic flared again, and Kitable forced himself to keep his place. He could not be seen jumping at nothing. He knew this magic. This was a divination, nothing more. It was harmless. It could not touch him anyway.

The elder's eyes did not entirely focus as the magic faded away.

"I see doubt," Elder Tril said sadly. He blinked, a sort of whiteness leaving his eyes, and came to his feet. Even standing, he was a head shorter than Kitable and had to crane his neck up to meet Kitable's eyes.

"I doubt many things," Kitable replied diplomatically. "It's my duty."

The Northlander bobbed his head, wiggling his feet into the mud. How they were not blue, Kitable did not know. "I know. I've seen that."

Kitable snorted. The Elder couldn't "see" Kitable. The defenses Kitable erected every morning hid him from divination magic. His shields made him invisible to all kinds of Scrys or attempts to locate him. An amateur, even an instinctual one, could not hope to breach those spells.

"But you do not doubt in their prowess, do you?" Elder Tril asked, cocking his head the other way. His white wolf pelt mirrored him from the other shoulder, making Kitable's skin crawl. He felt like the eyes of the dead animal were watching him.

"Whose?"

"Tohmas and Darknim," Tril replied as if the answer had been obvious all along. "You cannot doubt that they can do it? Save Espar? Bring peace?"

Forgetting the wolf, Kitable looked down at the shorter elder, confused. For the first time, he noticed the lines around the elder's smile—he smiled often. His skin was thick as hide, burned by wind and sun both until permanently dark. But his eyes were as bright as a child's in their excitement.

"Peace?" Kitable echoed. "This is your DoomDragon's purpose?"

"*Our* purpose," the elder corrected with a wider grin that showed his canines.

"Yours?"

"No, *ours*. Yours and mine. Ours. Peace from the Ice Fields to the DragonTail Mountains, all of Espar as one. That is the purpose."

A chill swept through Kitable. He checked the surroundings but found them empty. It was too early for the revelers to be out on this side of the celebration. The dawn was hard on hungover heads. They were alone. Why did he feel as though he was being watched?

Perhaps he sees through me?

Despite himself, Kitable stepped forward and lowered his voice. "All of Espar?"

Tril's words were eager. "Whether or not he knows it, DoomDragon walks on this path now. Neither really knows what they are doing, but they will come to see it soon." The elder squinted in thought, his eyebrows dropping low. "You did not know?" His eyes were distant once more, and magic flowed in from below as if his words were the question for a Reflection spell.

Kitable activated Spell Sight, stepping back to watch the colors wrap the elder from the ground up like a bonfire reaching for the sky. As bright as a noonday sun, the auras made Kitable shield his eyes reflexively. He had to turn his head—his hand did nothing to block the sight.

In a blink, the magic went out like a snuffed candle.

Tril swayed on his feet, stumbling when his foot stuck in the mud. He caught a nearby tent post, his eyes slow in focusing. Part of Kitable wanted to assist, but he did not dare touch the man who channeled such volatile magic.

Tril's voice was soft. "You did not know, not yet. Many things you do not know yet. You are choosing. But now you know. Now, perhaps you can decide."

Kitable tensed, lowering his hand slowly as the Northlander straightened himself. He shook his head as if trying to clear it.

"You can't know anything about me. I am defended against divinations. You can't see me in magic," Kitable said, but his voice fell, his words a hope, not a fact.

"What I do is not the same as you. I cannot explain it well, but I could show you. I can get you answers, answers for the things you saw but could not understand."

Peace had not been Tohmas' goal, not according to the Lie Light during his speech. But what if that was the result, despite his intentions? Curiosity piqued, Kitable felt his head nodding despite his trepidation.

"I can help you better control your magic," Kitable offered. "Help me learn more about this alliance."

The grin widened. The elder reached out slowly, his hand bunched in a fist.

Kitable stared at the fist for a long moment before mirroring the man and knocking his fist against the Northlanders. "Another tradition you've picked up from Esparans?"

Elder Tril shrugged. "Your traditions will be my traditions. We are one people." He squinted again. "Or we will be. Maybe." He shook his head. "I will call upon you when I can. We will see our people through this time of upheaval. We might even survive."

CHAPTER 3

The elder twirled and stomped off into the Northlander camp, leaving Kitable staring at his knuckles, where a hole had appeared in his Molded Shield.

Chapter 4

Tohmas changed his stride when they reached the edge of the Rydan camp. Among Esparans, he was a prince confident in his protectors. Among Rydans, he was a leader ready to defend his title. Here, he had to be ready to draw a blade and defend himself. He had to be a warrior.

Carsh moved away subtly, no longer defending Tohmas.

A hoot went up, and the followers gathered around them. But Tohmas passed between them and sought Burlotak at the *shella*. His Followers on his right, Carsh and his Followers on his left, he stopped before the *shella* and saluted, fist to his shoulder, to acknowledge Tamv's authority despite the man's absence.

Burlotak mimicked the gesture, crossing his muscled arm across to his broad shoulder and partially covering the grinning fanged jaw of a wolf tattoo on his chest. His grass bracelets loudly clattered, being mostly beads and little grass. Tohmas knew the significance of the bracelets; only the Chief had more Followers, and Burlotak's bracelets were only one step away from being stained in chief's red.

But so long as Tamv lived, Burlotak remained the chief's loyal Follower.

"I must send some Followers to guard Esparans on a foolish quest. Will this still allow you to fulfill the will of Tamv?" Tohmas asked loudly.

He knew seeing him garbed in Esparan armor and hearing him talk Esparan had unsettled some of the Rydans. Loyalty to the clan was all, yet he was now among others, seemingly forgoing all Rydan authority.

Tohmas could not let them doubt that he was still the son of Tamv, even if not by blood. The chief's will was paramount.

"Easily," Burlotak replied. His grin matched the one on his chest, complete with sharpened teeth. "Are they so in need of babysitting?"

Tohmas smiled derisively. "They are princes. They are useless."

Not like me, Tohmas finished for them. *I am more than them.*

They nodded around him as if hearing the unspoken words.

Tohmas turned to his Followers and selected three. Each left with a whoop, eager to prove themselves by readying their horses the fastest. They would not leave for days, but that did not matter. The display was essential to defending the prestige they had earned.

Tohmas was unsure the quest was all that important in the end. Prince Dragal seemed to have come north looking for a way to deny his illness the privilege of killing him, and he had insisted on going himself to rescue Sol. Barnon had followed for reasons Tohmas did not understand. They had limited their protectors to a dozen each so that BookKeeper Olmer could conceal them. With Tohmas' forces moving north, the hope was that Marfaie's wizard would not notice the smaller group traveling in the shadow of the mountains.

Tohmas had deliberately chosen Rydans who had no aptitude for detecting magic, and he had warned Olmer to be subtle. Magic would not be tolerated by any of them.

And while the two princes made their way into the cover of the mountains to rescue their brother, Tohmas would lead the army north. Eventually, he planned to set a siege outside of Chock Manor as if he believed Sol was within. It would be a pleasant reprieve to be without other Esparan princes.

At some point, he would draw out the dragons, he knew. Two red dragons could destroy everything if they arrived before Tohmas was ready. Even Kitable had not come up with a permanent solution yet, and Tohmas did not want to pit his wizard against the beasts without a plan. Killing the single black dragon had been fortunate, but it had nearly halved his forces. DoomDragon's ax had been the key. The enchanted weapon could not kill two dragons at the same time.

Remembering his purpose, Tohmas faced Burlotak once more. The chief's Follower had not moved from his place, arms crossed, on the threshold of the *shella*.

"We head north to take the capital of this prince," Tohmas said, framing it to appeal to the Rydans. "But we might meet dragons. The Esparans are cowardly. The courage of Rydans does not panic under the shadow of dragons. Will the Rydans lead the way?"

Burlotak nodded stiffly in approval. "May we meet dragons to slay."

The Followers cheered wildly, boasting calls and war cries sounding in agreement.

"And may they be crushed under the hooves of our steeds," Tohmas replied.

But as he headed back to HillTop, Tohmas shook his head. It was foolishness to go seek enemies such as those. The Rydans would have it no other way, yet Tohmas doubted.

It was a doubt he could not admit to even Carsh. Having been raised by Tamv since he was child, Tohmas was the infallible eldest son to the Rydans. No hesitation could be allowed. It was loyalty or death.

When Tohmas picked Followers, Krahr was the first to be chosen. He was the best of the trackers, and one of the first to have pledged himself to Tohmas a decade prior. Eager, he arranged his supplies swiftly, then met with the other chosen to discuss their plans for the Esparans.

In the early dawn a few days later, Krahr presented himself to the Hand of the Outlands. The forces had arrived at a branch in the mountains, where rocky terrain and steep peaks lined their east flank and extended southeast. Their goal was still north, Krahr understood, but the three chosen Rydans were not heading that way.

Krahr hoped the quest would bring them battle.

Before the Esparans arrived, Tohmas crouched with the Rydans and drew them a planning circle. Krahr now knew they were heading for a *shella*, although the Hand called it a "manor." The prisoner within needed to be freed. Any pillage was his to take.

Pleased to be able to demonstrate his skill in battle, Krahr accepted eagerly. He started to reconsider as he met the men that he and the other Followers were to protect.

Old, Esparan idiots. Krahr knew they were important among their people—they called them princes—but he could not understand why.

Perhaps they had once been skilled. Maybe the Esparan had not thought to criticize them, like a pup deferring to their elder once grown.

As the Esparans made to leave the Rydans, with a glance at each other, they decided their positions. Dakn took point, being the youngest and the best with throwing spears. Atop his bay mare, he led the way into the eastern mountains. Vengr, positioned to second point, joined the Esparans.

Krahr waited for the Esparans to leave, having taken the rear guard.

Since the Rydans had met up with the Esparan army, Krahr had been trying to learn Esparan and felt he knew just enough to understand these princes. He suspected that was one reason the Hand selected him, but he hoped that his skills with the curved blades of the *hooknyes* were another.

Krahr understood when the Esparan in blue and gold asked Tohmas, "Are you sure about this?"

Each of the princes had their own warriors with them, easily recognized by the colors of their shirts. Those warriors were better suited for questioning Tohmas, if anyone was. Krahr looked forward to seeing Tohmas put them in their place. There was no stronger Leader than the Hand except the chief himself, and Krahr was always pleased to see such a fact proved.

But Tohmas did not beat the man for asking the question. *Perhaps the Esparan is not worth that effort*, Krahr thought.

"You'll find no better than Rydans, Prince Dragal. They are invaluable in battle. If we assign any more, we will surely attract attention. Move quickly and return soon."

Strangely, the words did not sound like orders. Still, the older man nodded and turned his horse to follow. The entire group left at a canter.

Krahr waited a moment longer, knowing his horse could easily catch up. He checked with his Leader one final time.

"Obey them when you can. I want them all back." His voice was soft in the Rydan.

Krahr saluted, then urged his horse Vatnorish into a run. His Leader had said "want," not "need." Krahr would put his own life and those of the other Followers first. But since Tohmas wanted these Esparans alive, Krahr would do his utmost to make it happen.

Krahr wondered if it might be most efficient to leave the Esparans behind in the mountains and just rescue the prisoner themselves. At least then, the Esparan princes would come to no harm.

He decided to discuss the idea with Dakn and Vengr when the Esparan required rest.

Despite being open for use, the Temple waggon of Clandac, built shortly after Prince Dragal's arrival to the army, was still being finished as the army marched. The red paint, contrasting the white, green, and blue of the other Temple waggons, seemed to absorb into the wood, leaving it a ruddy brown instead of fire red. Celebrant Sedgan overheard someone arguing with the painter hanging from the side of the waggon as he tethered his horse to the waggon's hitch and hopped through the partially finished door. The waggon rolled on, rocking little to his weight.

Like the exterior, the inside was unfinished. The altar was central and immaculate though, the sacred fire of Inac set squarely atop it. Sedgan recognized the style; unlike his traditional lamp, this altar had a reservoir of oil within it. The wick for the blessed flame was so thin that it was all but invisible. The setting of glass and rubies around the light lent itself well to the mystical aura of the miraculous fire.

Prince Dragal had traveled with haste. The four celebrants were the only four non-military men forced into coming, except for BookKeeper Olmer. From what Sedgan had seen so far, all four religious leaders resented their separation from their usual homes and acolytes and wore perpetual grimaces.

Celebrant Utheran of Clandac, who emerged from the back room as Sedgan entered, was taller than Sedgan remembered. His frown had become permanent in the many wrinkles on his face, particularly around his narrowed, suspicious eyes. His clothing was more ornate than most celebrants' and heavily emphasized Clandac's white and blue with silver and sapphires, despite Inac's traditional colors being red and gold. Only the presence of the symbol of the Goddess hanging around his neck identified Utheran as loyal to Fire.

Hidden under his red and orange robe, the same symbol was burned into Sedgan's chest. No human hand had been involved; Sedgan had

woken to the feeling of his skin being scalded when alone in his waggon after a night with Loni. The next day, he had learned that Loni spent the entire quartercycle in the care of the facets of healing, too weak to stand. Sedgan had no doubts who had been in his waggon that night.

He felt the scar itch as if to remind him of its presence.

Although Celebrant Utheran smiled at Sedgan, the scowl remained in his eyes. "Ah, you must be Celebrant Sedgan of Galanth."

With effort, Sedgan smiled politely. "I am so pleased to see you again, Celebrant Utheran. It has been many, many years."

The celebrant shrugged, dismissing their previous interactions. Feeling Utheran was trying to provoke him, Sedgan smiled with greater sincerity. He had not come to make friends with Celebrant Utheran. It seemed he would not be disappointing anyone.

"What do you want, Celebrant? Come to defend that ridiculous title you gave your prince?" Utheran asked.

"You wasted very little time in condemning it," Sedgan said, wandering toward the altar. The waggon skipped on a stone, jostling the occupants and making the light flicker.

"There is no such thing as a 'Champion of Inac,'" Utheran said, pursing his lips as if lecturing a child as he regained his footing.

Sedgan ran a finger down the smooth altar. "I suppose that if I arrived at a camp, and someone told me the man leading it had walked up to a dragon and talked it into leaving the path, I would tell them it had been a stunt to gain fame."

"Indeed," Utheran agreed. He watched Sedgan's hand as if expecting him to snatch one of the altar's rubies.

"And if, in that camp, someone said his prince could play with fire between his fingers, I would suggest he check his eyesight," Sedgan continued.

"Exactly."

"And if they then said that the Goddess Inac herself had stepped out from a burning waggon to deliver into that leader's hand an enchanted sword that no wizard yet has been able to explain, I probably would tell them to stop spreading foolish rumors."

Dropping his hand before him, Sedgan waited. Utheran seemed to have run out of words but narrowed his squint further, waiting for Sedgan to make his point.

"Of course, the trouble here is that I have seen all these things and more. I doubted, oh how I denied it, but I can tell you now that these things are true. If ever the world has had a Champion of Inac, it is Prince Tohmas. You would do well to heed that."

Utheran snorted, not pausing to even consider Sedgan's statement. "Nonsense. That you profess to believe this heresy is an insult to proper followers of Inac! That is not how it is done, Celebrant Sedgan."

Sedgan thought it odd that the next words he spoke had once come from Loni. When first they had met, Sedgan had also accused her of heresy. "We cannot afford to be so caught up in etiquette that we forget our purpose. We are here to serve Inac, and Inac has made her will known."

Utheran waved his hand dismissively. "You cannot believe that."

Sedgan laughed, deliberately mocking. "If you don't believe it, you will be made to."

Utheran pulled himself to his full height, his chest puffing out in defiance. "Are you threatening a fellow celebrant?"

Matching him, Sedgan pushed out his chest, and his robes parted. The scar of Inac's symbol attracted Utheran's gaze, and he stared at it as Sedgan replied, "Not a threat, a warning. She will come next, and you will understand why standing against us is madness."

He turned on his heels and left. Sedgan had already told Loni where to find the Temple waggons of Clandac. It would not be long. Utheran would never step a foot outside once she was done with him.

Either way, Sedgan's duty was fulfilled.

Grigson waited until Celebrant Sedgan had left before returning to the Temple waggon's backroom. The real Celebrant Utheran lay dead on the bed, blood from a deep wound on his ankle forming a puddle as red as the walls of the waggon. The supposed cause of the wound—a stray iron nail as big as Grigson's finger—stuck out from an unfinished board on the doorframe at the perfect height to catch the unwary.

Had he known Celebrant Sedgan of Galanth would be stopping in, Grigson would have arranged to the death to cast the blame onto Sedgan. But it was too late for that. Grigson dared not attract too much

attention yet, so the death would appear an accident—something sure to start rumors of bad luck among the religious. He still thought it fitting that the last man who would see "Celebrant Utheran" alive would be someone Prince Dragal could easily be convinced to mistrust.

Before he could remove the celebrant's robes, Grigson heard the door of the waggon swing open, and light steps entered. Checking quickly to make sure he had no blood on him, Grigson returned to the altar room, bracing himself against the frame to resist the rocking of the waggon. He was extra careful to step over the nail.

He recognized the woman who had entered from rumors, although her appearance had changed once more. Previously, Loni had been wrapped in thick bandages and bundled against the cold because of her injuries. Now, Loni FireDancer walked with a dancer's grace, each step arching, balanced, and poised. Her gown was fiery red from breast to ankle, but the orange blouse beneath it had been torn at the collar. A sparkling array of gold and rubies overlaid her neck as if to hide the inappropriate exposure of skin. A dozen more pieces of jewelry decorated her from armband to anklet. The most prominent of them was her headdress; a golden flying dragon was set in the tangled mess of her ruby-red hair.

A most unusual feature drew his eyes; Loni carried an ornate dagger on her hip over the dress. While Grigson had seen a similar blade both on Utheran and Sedgan, the sight of it against a woman's curves surprised him.

Arrogance had been an obvious choice for Sedgan—the man had been looking for a fight and had so found one—but the way this woman walked left Grigson unsure if she was trying to seduce him or kill him. He wondered which persona would be most appropriate.

Before he could decide, Loni looked him straight in the eye and said, "Recognize the Champion or get out."

That makes it easy. What else could any celebrant say in reply?

"Don't be absurd!" he replied, sauntering up to stand over her. He was surprised she did not shrink back; Utheran was easily twice her size and a substantial part of it was muscle. She was too small to offer...

She stepped forward, and a feeling of illness flooded through Grigson. Every hovering spell he had attached to himself suddenly quailed and tried to cower. The sensation was so unsettling that he failed

to recognize she was about to strike him. She slapped him across his face with the back of her hand.

Normal reflexes did not answer through his shock. A cold feeling, contrasted only by the burning on his cheek, swamped him. In a moment, he was completely disarmed.

His magic was gone.

Grigson staggered away. He came to his senses leaning against the door to the back room, held up only by the handle behind him. He had never expected to find a caster among the celebrants, let alone one capable of landing an Eight-layered Dispel through every one of his defenses in a single blow.

Feeling he was already too far at the disadvantage, Grigson activated a spell hidden in one of his rings. The ring responded; Grigson sensed the magic strike the woman squarely between her breasts.

Grigson paused for a moment, waiting to see her expression change, but nothing happened.

The Blind Love spell was one of Grigson's most powerful tools. She should have been suddenly his ally, fooled by magic that bypassed almost all defenses to think him a lost lover or similar friend.

Yet the woman in front of him continued to stare him down, her expression of ire stone.

The spell failed, he realized. The spell had failed, and she had, with a touch, dispelled him.

Untouchable.

Grigson had avoided the Temple waggon of Wind because of Terant's warning, but it seemed Inac had her own untouchable!

"Demon-kissing luck!" he cursed.

Hooking up the handle and swinging the door wide, Grigson bolted through the curtain hung on the doorway and into the back room. Skipping over the dead man, he activated another item, one that opened a brief doorway in the wall, and dropped out of the moving waggon. The magic dissipated as soon as he was through, closing the escape. He had enough forethought to pick the side opposite the painter, lest he surprise the hapless man off the waggon's side.

Once outside, Grigson stripped off the celebrant's robes. Since his spells had been broken, the likeness to Utheran was gone and no one seemed to look at him twice as he briskly trotted away.

Damned untouchable, he cursed as he walked. In confrontations between untouchables and wizards, untouchables won. Thankfully, there were few such individuals around, and they tended to be oblivious to their talents.

Let the crazy woman deal with the body, he thought. Perhaps she would think the man on the bed was the same who had fled from her. But she had not seen his illusion at all; she had seen his real face. She would have seen through the magic.

Muttering more curses, Grigson headed back toward where Fixer City trundled after the army. He was not quite ready to infiltrate the Rydan camp, so he would conceal himself in Fixer City. Dust was no friend, but he had at least given Grigson enough information to conceal himself.

He would have to get a message to Prince Marfaie about the second untouchable. Loni was a threat to all magic.

He found himself a place in Fixer City just as a census was being completed.

Clever idea, dear Prince, Grigson thought as he gave a fake name to the bookkeepers. *Clever, but too slow. I'm already here.*

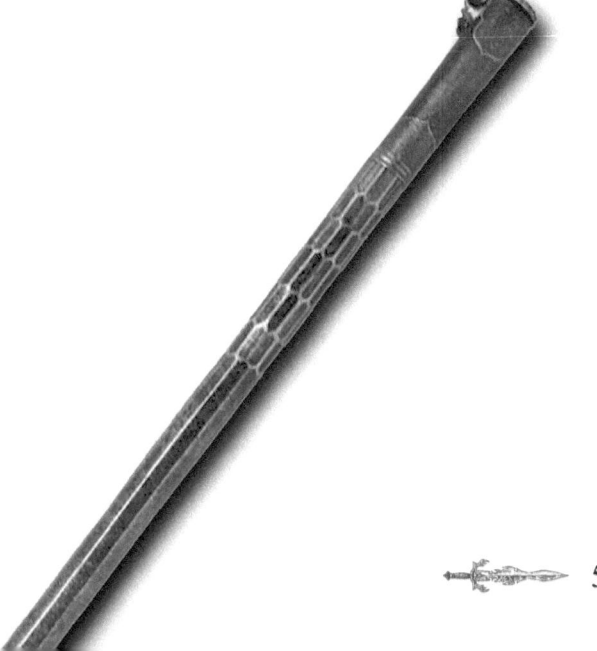

Chapter 5

Kitable let Colt pick the parking place for the vardo. It didn't matter to him whether he was right next to the command tent or a league away; he could Relocate over instantly. And he never had to fight for a good place. Once he was recognized, he had a clearing around him. He appreciated the distance others kept. It meant one less thing to pay attention to.

He kept tabs on where the Weavers set their moving shop, Match and Mixer, but Colt seemed to know to keep a distance from them. Kitable had considered the location of his vardo random until he opened the door one evening for his meal and found Elder Tril at the bottom of his steps.

It made him bristle. Had the elder predicted where they would set the vardo? *Is anyone else able to pre-empt my actions?*

He had already dissected his defenses and could find no path through the shields against divinations, so how was this man able to consistently anticipate him?

The elder smiled up at Kitable, deepening the creases around his eyes and mouth. Kitable thought he would struggle to recognize him if he wasn't smiling.

"We can talk," he said.

"I happen to have time. Join me for dinner?" Kitable agreed tentatively. Had that been a prediction too?

"I brought my own," Elder Tril replied, pulling a wrapped package from under his shirt. He rolled a log over to where Colt had set the warming stones and now heated their meal on a cast-iron rack. *Probably for the best*, Kitable acknowledged. It didn't look like Colt had prepared extras. This was a stew made from leftover goat and vegetables. The vegetables were probably nearly a mooncycle old by now; they looked like the same ones from the roasted platter nine days ago.

Settling comfortably on the log, Tril opened his package and pulled out dried strips of meat, a handful of greenery, and a shriveled fruit Kitable did not recognize.

Unsure where to start, Kitable said, "I appreciate you taking time to visit."

Elder Tril pulled off his thick mitts, selected a piece of meat and popped it into the corner of his mouth. He chewed as he replied, "It was time. You have questions."

"Of course I do. How—"

"Not about us. You have questions about the past, something you have seen." Tril interrupted, his mouth still working the jerky.

Kitable straightened, feeling threatened. "I do not like being Scryed upon. I will not allow..."

Elder Tril gestured soothingly. "No Scry, Kitable. I do not mean to intrude. I see things. They come to me. In fact, I believe I saw what you saw. I saw your discovery. Your patron. Your old one."

The world narrowed around Kitable, a lump forming in his throat. Emotions tangled together, partly annoyance at Tril's ability to see through his defenses but mostly grief for Habal. The Reflection of Habal's murder had stuck with him, intruding into these thoughts when his attention was meant to be elsewhere. He could not shake the memory. Part of him did not want to.

"How?" The word slipped from him.

Elder Tril shrugged, finally swallowing the jerky and smiling again. "I am not like you. I am one part golden light and one part spiral."

Kitable looked at him, blinking in astonishment. Realizing Colt was offering him a bowl and possibly had been for some time, Kitable accepted the bowl and spoon absently. Thankfully, only Colt was close enough to hear and, being deaf, he would overhear nothing unless Kitable connected deliberately to the man's stone.

"You do not like admitting you do not know," the Northlander said softly.

"I survive by knowing more than other people," Kitable confessed.

It had been a long time since he had confided in someone. He had not expected to ever trust another person and certainly not another caster. Yet something about the Northlander put Kitable at ease. The man was gentle despite the power he wielded. And he seemed to, unlike anyone else in the damn war, care.

"You learn, so you can stay ahead," Tril said, nodding sagely. "I like that about you. You want to know more. You will learn. You will never stop learning. That is why I don't want you to leave, why I came to talk and to help you listen. We need you."

Leave? He had indeed been contemplating abandoning his oath. The promise of peace for Espar, although he could not understand how such a thing could happen, had kept him in the army, working for a goal he thought Habal would have wanted. But he did not trust Tohmas. *Does Tril see that?*

"And you have an opinion on my findings?" Kitable asked obliquely, the closest he could bring himself to asking the Northlander for help.

Tril's eyebrows united low over his blue eyes, blending well into the white pelt on his head and shoulders. "You saw what happened. What if you could not just hear the words, but understand them? Understand what the Rydans said?"

He had no doubt seen what Kitable had. *And what did he think of the murder?* he wondered.

His words were choked. "A Translation applied through a Reflection? That has not been done before," he choked out. His mind spun through the possibilities. It had never been described before, but it was feasible. Overlapping the components...

"Let me show you?"

The request was tender, pleading.

We need you, Tril had said. For all of Tohmas' cavalier plans, Elder Tril had a different purpose in mind for the Prince of Galanth and his army. Whether or not the prince agreed seemed irrelevant; it was less about whether he wanted to be a part of this grand plan and more about whether they could achieve it.

Peace for all of Espar. Was that possible?

Kitable put the forgotten bowl on his lap and reached out a hand. Elder Tril's grin stretched wide, and he placed his thick hand in Kitable's.

Magic rose from the earth like a new vine, twisting around them and entwining their clenched hands. Elder Tril closed his eyes, but Kitable kept his open, watching as the smile faded from the elder's face. His brow creased, lips pressed, and tears formed in the corner of his eyes.

Grief, Kitable recognized.

With the next blink, the clearing and meal were replaced by the shared Reflection.

Tril squeezed his hand, making Kitable realize he had tightened his grip in anticipation of the scene.

Tohmas, tanned and freshly tidied up, sat at his father's side in the elaborate sitting room, discussing his experience in the Outlands. Bragn, the Chief's son, sat opposite them with the two Rydan escorts behind him. Without warning, Bragn lunged and drove a knife into Prince Habal's gut. Tohmas' came to his feet, a blade in hand. Confusion on his face, he crouched over Habal, assessing the wound. Tohmas did not put his blade away as he checked on his father, a detail Kitable had missed last time.

"Leave him! He is our enemy!" Bragn called, pulling on Tohmas' shoulder.

"You attack without thought!" Tohmas snapped, this time his Rydan words translated. He threw Bragn back as he yanked his shoulder free of the Rydan's grip. "Think of the consequences! If he dies..."

Bragn's face darkened sharply in anger.

"You cannot be loyal to both." Bragn brought his knife down in readiness.

Tohmas was on his feet instantly, his knife low in a matched position, poised.

"This is not—" But Tohmas' words fell on deaf ears. With a snarl, Bragn launched forward as if expecting to repeat the gut blow he had delivered to Habal.

But Tohmas caught Bragn's wrist, twisted it expertly, and stabbed the knife through the Rydan's back in one smooth action. It was over in a blink.

Tohmas' expression was stone; Kitable recognized the now-prince was blocking his emotions. *Did he regret his action?*

In the next flicker, Tohmas dropped the dead Rydan and went to Habal. He applied pressure to the wound that had left Habal unable to cry out.

When the two older Rydans joined him, they moved cautiously. *Fear,* Kitable recognized this time. They were, for a moment, unsure of Tohmas' reaction to their presence.

"We can help," the taller one said softly in Rydan. He knelt, his touch light on Tohmas' shoulder.

"You cannot save him," Tohmas said with a growl.

"But we can save you," the shorter one replied, taking a place opposite Tohmas, across Habal as he lay gasping. "If the Esparans come now, they will blame you. You are still unknown. Let us clean this up. We will hide the wound. We can call it a sickness, and they will never know."

Tohmas glared up, his jaw clenched. He checked on Habal, but the truth was clear; Habal would die no matter what he did. He released the pressure on Habal's wound and allowed himself to be guided away. As the Rydan washed Tohmas hands, Tohmas asked, "What of Bragn?"

The tall Rydan shrugged. Already, the blood had been hidden by spells. No more stains seeped into the floor. "He is dead. By the agreement, that makes you the first son of Chief Tamv. But that has been your place for years. Now, it is formalized."

Tohmas stared at the dead body on the swept floor, the Rydan's chest tattoo twisted as he lay bent. Kitable was not sure he heard the Rydan's words at all. "He was reckless."

"Our chief knew that," the Rydan said. "You will not be blamed. We will see to it. But, take heed, son of Tamv. The Esparans must not know how their prince died. We have lived among them for many years and tell you truthfully; they will kill you for your part in this. He is already lost. Do not allow this tragedy to take your life as well."

Kitable's heart sank. What *would* have happened if the protectors had come in on this scene? Would they have killed him? It seemed possible. Tohmas had been an unknown to them. The extent of his ties to the Rydans and his ability to speak their language was still largely unknown. But this idea of being a son of Tamv, that was new even to Kitable.

In the vision, Tohmas nodded grimly, his expression again flat. Once the Rydans had cast their spells—it still surprised Kitable to see

them casting—Bragn's body vanished, no evidence of the dead man remaining.

Tohmas turned away to call for help, claiming Prince Habal had collapsed. In the fuss, no one noticed the missing Rydan.

The spell broke, and Kitable was again outside his vardo. The sight of the sweating, shaking, dying Prince Habal on the floor lingered in his mind.

Blinking, Kitable realized Tril had finished and was now staring at him.

He released Tril's hand.

"You have what you need," Elder Tril said. He shook with the effort of standing, collapsing onto the stone.

Kitable reached out, helping the man steady in his seat. Concern blossomed in his chest.

So powerful, yet so vulnerable.

"Was that why you came? You came here to show me that?" Kitable asked.

Tril nodded weakly, his smile sad. "You needed to know. I am sorry. So hard to lose one you care for."

The words acted as a trigger; magic shot back up and over the Northlander. Kitable fought the instinct to withdraw, worrying that the exhausted man would be overwhelmed by the magic. But it was brief flare only. In a blink, the powers faded once more.

Seeing Elder Tril's face, Kitable admitted he had been optimistic. Although the magic had been brief, Tril's expression made it clear it had hit him hard.

Tears swelled in the older man's eyes, his beastly stare distant.

"Bad news?" Kitable guessed.

"The worst," Tril said, blinking back his tears. "I will search for more information. I will..." Magic flared again, making the elder slouch.

"You need rest," Kitable insisted. "I'll get you home."

Dodging the Circle of the Raven was taxing; Terant was unexpectedly disoriented as he arrived back at his scrying circle in the Manor

 **ESPARAN**

of Arcott. The woven pattern on the flagstone, situated in a courtyard where rain never fell, made his eyes cross as he got his bearings.

Attack was the only option, but the Circle of the Raven could confound almost any wizard, Terant included. He was never quite confident enough in his Scrys knowing the Circle was against him.

So be it, Terant thought. He just needed the right moment. If Kitable was not around, he could kill the Circle. Then, once he could trust his Scrys, he could target Kitable directly.

Terant lurched to his feet, his head pounding. He paused in confusion. He had dropped the Scry but taken time to recover. He should not be—

The thought trailed off when he realized he was not alone in his courtyard.

There were three of people dressed in strange robes made, seemingly, of ribbons. They had no distinctive color markings—he could not assign princedoms to them—but they all wore a foreign golden symbol on their chests.

Two were men, but the one directly in front of Terant was a tall, blonde woman with dark streaks in her hair. Jewels were imbedded in her hands at the knuckles, and the twinkle of a gem glittered at the corner of each of her eyes.

Both men were clean-shaven and bald, and each had a gem at the center of their foreheads. The younger of the two, who looked to be about thirty, wore fewer, wider ribbons, and held his right hand clenched across his front as if holding a small object.

Terant's heart kicked up instantly. Who were these three and how had they gotten into his courtyard? What defenses did he have? Had they done something? *And why can't I act?* He wanted his staff, but his hands were empty and his tongue seemed unable to form the word to summon it.

"Terant," the woman said once his eyes focused. "*Neh brasso pitact.*"

An instant later, proving he had been subjected to at least one spell during his distraction, he heard the words in Esparan: "We have a proposition for you."

Like a wink, Terant felt a flip of magic in his mind and he cringed. Magic was anchored to his thoughts. He had been bound.

Subtly, the younger man's hand turned. The man was not holding an object; he was holding a spell. He had anchored Terant's mind while he had been scrying.

He's stomach sank, sweat forming on his palms. How had they attacked his mind without him noticing? With the stranger bound to his mind, Terant was magically naked. With a thought, the stranger could kill him instantly.

Terant quickly brought his fear under control. *I was an easy target during my Scrys. They had an anchor, but they are not using it.*

Gathering his thoughts into controlled bursts as protection against mind-reading, Terant raised his head and inquired, "A proposition?"

"You seek the means to upset the Northlander Circle," the man on Terant's right stated. The words came first in the strange language, repeated in Terant's mind in Esparan a heartbeat later.

"Is the Circle of the Raven a concern of yours?" Terant replied, assuming that his words would equally be translated.

"We are the Watching Circle," the older man said from Terant's left, making Terant turn his head in the opposite direction.

"We want the Northlander Circle broken," finished the woman, bringing Terant's attention to the center once more.

Except for Darknim and his Northlander Circle, Terant had never heard of any other Circles. Now that one Circle had betrayed him, he was not particularly keen to work with another.

But he was curious. Setting one Circle against another might defeat the Northlanders and their new Galanth friends faster. And with one of the casters holding a thread directly into his mind, Terant did not feel it was prudent to argue overtly.

"I am interested," he said, "but why is the Circle of the Raven a concern to you?"

"They are an abomination," the woman said with such vehemence that she nearly snarled.

She was followed by, "They must be disrupted," from both of the men.

Linking? They spoke as if knowing each other's thoughts. The Circle of the Raven linked often enough for Terant to recognize the effect.

"So you would assist me?" he asked. If three more casters wanted to join the game, then Master Kitable seemed suddenly much less of a threat.

The woman pointed to Terant's feet. A piece of strangely thin vellum lay on the ground before him.

"This spell will keep retaliation from reaching you in time."

Terant picked up the sheet and scanned it, but it did not make immediate sense. It was a spell, written in wizard's cant, but he did not recognize many words. He got the impression it was a form of Seal spell, but it seemed to be defining an impossible area.

"It will keep him from getting in your way," came the older man's voice from Terant's left.

"And why should I do this for you?" Terant inquired boldly. Gems and ribbons aside, these were casters. He was at least entitled to some respect among his peers.

The younger man rotated his hand slightly, and Terant felt a pull on his mind. Before he could react to the implied threat, the woman interrupted.

"Because we have just given you your payment." She glared at the younger man in reprimand. "That spell," the woman continued, her expression easing as she looked back at Terant, "contains code you have never seen before. You know you can adapt those components and make your spells stronger."

"But if you do not break the Circle of the Raven..." the older man said.

"...we will take back our gift," finished the man on Terant's right.

It was possible they were referring to elaborate thought magic to remove his memory of the spell, but Terant suspected they were likely threatening to kill him.

They had walked through his defenses and written a level of code he had never even read about. Besides, he had been planning on killing the Northlander casters anyway. It was easy to nod in agreement.

"We share a common goal," he told them as if he had chosen to cooperate amidst other options. "I shall see if this spell can be used."

All three bowed their heads slightly in semi-salute and together said, "Be quick about it."

When they vanished, it was through a Relocation spell cast while linked, and it consisted of seven words less than he would have expected.

The thought that their magic was so condensed left him stunned. He dared not move until he felt the thought spell release from his mind.

I will have to study this spell. He did not need long with the Northlander Circle—they were all old, feeble magic users—but he did not want Kitable interrupting before he could finish off at least a few of the annoying elders. All he needed was one elder. Elder Ela if he could. But any of them would do.

And with the mysterious aid, he was certain he could get at least one.

After many days of riding, the Rydan found the *shella* they had been seeking. Krahr led the Esparan princes and their protectors to a hiding place overlooking the building. There, the Esparan made plans.

"Nothing magical on the walls or gates," a measly man with no hair on his head told the princes. Krahr did not understand the Esparan word "magical," and decided to ignore it. By the nodding heads, he thought it probably meant defenses. "I can get the door to open, if we are swift."

Prince Dragal, garbed in gold and blue as always, seemed winded despite being well rested. "Dusk tomorrow," he said. "We ride up without colors, make them think we're one of theirs. Olmer can open the gate. We break in, and take back Sol. Those walls are sparsely guarded. Marfaie does not think we know where to find our brother."

"Are we certain he is here?" the younger prince, the one in white with red, asked.

It was the bald man, Olmer, who answered for the winded prince. "He isn't in Chock Keep. There is nowhere else in any of the records. He must be here." Olmer looked again at the old prince for approval. Krahr was not sure why, but the prince in gold and blue allowed the bald man to continue the conversation as they set details.

Krahr listened to the princes talk and had to remind himself that Dragal, the older, weaker man, was leading. He had a prime protector, as did Barnon. They were the stronger warriors. They should have been leading.

Dakn and Vengr joined Krahr in listening in. He knew by their restlessness that they saw the same flaw in the plotting as he did.

None of the Esparan seemed to be concerned about the enemy killing the prisoner. The princes had put themselves at high risk, determined to rescue their brother, yet now their tactics put Sol's life in peril. If the enemy thought they were likely to lose their prisoner, the final insult to the princes could be delivered by a knife through Sol's heart.

But Tohmas' orders were to see all the princes through, and that included the captured one. If the Rydans allowed the princes to sally out and threaten the enemy, Krahr was certain Sol would be killed, and Krahr would have failed his Leader.

The three Rydans drew lots once the Esparan had settled to sleep. Of the three stones, Krahr drew the black pebble. He would go ahead of the team. Seeing no need, he did not tell the Esparan, and he did not let the sentries see him as he departed.

It was nearly dawn by the time Krahr had made his silent way to the walls of the building and, concealed against shadows, climbed them. He then made his cautious way into the large stone building.

The building was more extravagant than any Krahr had seen before, making it hard for him to navigate. Krahr was familiar with a *shella*—a single-story thrush and thatch shelter only a chief had the right to use. Here, there were enclosed paths between vast rooms and rooms above as well as below. There were plenty of hiding places, which he was grateful for, but sometimes candles of time passed between safe opportunities to move in the choked space.

Slipping past Esparan soldiers dressed in black and silver at each corner, Krahr drifted through the stone corridors of the strange building. Near evening, he found a guarded room.

Krahr pulled himself out a high window and scaled the outside of the building, dozens of paces off the ground. Through the window matching the locked room, he was pleased to find, beaten and bruised but mobile, an Esparan man. Sadly, neither he nor the prisoner could fit through the window.

It was one thing to know where to find the man, but another to keep him safe from the wrath of their enemies.

Krahr made his way back into the hall. The beams of the ceiling were solid when he tested them, and he was able to climb up. In the dim light of the torches, the ceiling was in deep shadows. Moving at a hunter's stalk—slow enough to draw no attention—he made his way

to the guards. Like naive deer, the enemy did not look up to see him creep in above them.

Krahr dropped down between them. He stabbed his *hooknyes* simultaneously through their throats. As he pulled his hooknyes free, the guards slumped to the floor, blood pooling under them.

Skipping over the pools and knowing he still had time, Krahr crushed each of the hands and so destroy the soul-binding powers of the knuckles within. He then took what weapons were easy to carry.

The door did not open when Krahr tried it. He had to adjust a kind of lock, pulling a heavy latch up. Ultimately, he removed it from the braces entirely. Thinking the rod well worth trading to another Rydan, he slid it into his bag. Now the door opened easily.

The man—the prince they called Sol—had once been fuller, but meat had shrunk off his bones and left his skin sagging. He was still a tall man, and he stood proudly bare-chested despite the many whip marks, both old and new. A bruise darkened one eye, curling the face into a scowl. It seemed to hurt him to stand tall, although he did it anyway.

For a moment, the man stared at Krahr like a child trying to recognize a new clan marking. Krahr's tattoo was prominent on his chest—a swordfish—but he was not renowned enough to expect anyone to recognize it.

"Rydan?" the Esparan stuttered. "By the hells, what are you...?"

Krahr shushed the man. Craning his ears in the silence, Krahr heard a tolling bell, and he thought he could make out the shouts of angry men and the clash of weapons. It was dark already. The other Esparan were making their attack.

To identify his loyalty, Krahr punched his right hand into the left palm in salute to the Hand, but the confusion did not leave the Esparan.

"If you are here to bring my sanity into question, then consider it done and go away. I've got too much of a headache."

Dense Esparan doesn't understand me, Krahr thought. To make it plain, Krahr explained: "Tohmas."

The man started, his good eye narrowing suspiciously. "What about Tohmas?"

Knowing he lacked fancier words, Krahr pointed at the man. "Sol?"

"I'm Prince Sol, yes," the man replied, filling Krahr with confidence. *Right room. Right man. Good.*

He beckoned for the Esparan to follow him out of the room and pointed to the dead men by the door.

Sol stared at the guards for long moments. Finally, puffing out his cheeks, he faced Krahr. "Lead on, Rydan," he said.

Giving the Esparan a nod, Krahr turned to leave. But when brisk footsteps approached, Krahr ducked back into the room and against the wall quickly, leaving the doorway open.

Sol retreated to the middle of the room, disoriented and standing awkwardly unhidden.

The man who rushed into the prisoner's room was thin and poorly grown, but his robes were rich in Esparan fashion. He squinted his fishy eyes at the prisoner and lifted a metal tool that Krahr did not understand but sensed was dangerous.

Despite the two large warriors accompanying the little man, Krahr thought the greatest threat was the strange man and his spiky tool. Lunging out from the wall, he sliced his *hooknye* across the little man's wrist. Before the man could turn or scream, Krahr ducked low across the man's path. With his left hand, he raked the *hooknye* through the man's abdomen. He was rewarded by a shriek that became feral in panic and pain.

Krahr came up between the enemies and the Esparan prince he was meant to protect. The little man's intestines fell to the floor and the stranger followed, crumpling. Krahr smirked when he realized the man had fallen on the strange spiky object.

"Rydan! Get him!" one of the warriors shouted, swords already in hand to attack. Krahr knew better than to pit his iron chipped knives, sharp as they were, against leather and metal armor; his targets were the enemy's exposed arms. Dancing forward, he skipped beyond one sword and ducked a second. He scored a single deep gash to the sword arm of one of the warriors, and the Esparan dropped his sword.

Keeping moving, Krahr slipped between the two men, then around one's back. He ducked low, but the Esparan anticipated the cut for the hamstring and blocked Krahr's *hooknye*. The guard then stabbed at Krahr's face.

Krahr dropped to the floor and the attack missed. He swung himself up quickly, sweeping his foot to his left. The warrior stumbled against Krahr's kick off balance because of his missed strike.

CHAPTER 5

Pivoting without even fully rising, Krahr slashed at the inner leg of the warrior, and the *hooknye* lived up to its name by hooking into the flesh. He cut a long tear through skin and muscle. The blood pulsed out.

Color drained from the warrior's face within a breath. His reactions were sluggish when Krahr aimed a new slash across his throat, killing him.

Krahr held his fighting stance as he faced the first warrior he had disarmed. He was surprised to find the Esparan already dead.

Sol stood over the body, the warrior's sword in his bloodied hand. *Not bad for an Esparan*, Krahr thought. Maybe Sol was not as frail as he looked.

Baring his teeth in an approving grin, Krahr tilted his head to the door. Sol nodded agreement, and with Krahr leading the way, they made their way out.

Barnon felt nothing like a prince as the sun set over the Tracker Mountains, blanketing night over Merile Manor. Torches and lamps flickered to life, and Barnon wondered if one of them would light for Sol. Was his brother be trapped in a dark cell? Or was he in one a well-lit room in the Manor, playing a game of Royal Courts with his captor?

Is he here at all?

Dragal had no words of comfort for Barnon. With two decades between their age, Dragal had been more like a second father than a brother for Barnon. He and other seasoned warriors had guided Barnon after their father's death, preventing the youngest son of Zayban from ever becoming the warrior his brothers were. Although Barnon had been taught swordplay, it had never been utilized.

Fighting alongside Tohmas over the winter had taught Barnon some, but none of his experience seemed relevant as Dragal set out the plans to attack Merile Manor. When last Barnon had gone into battle, leading his fyrds with the Galanth army, the thought of being in command of so many people had terrified him. Now, it was the presence of so few that worried him.

At some point overnight, one of the three Rydans had disappeared, and no one seemed to know why or where the man had gone. When

they asked the other Rydans, they shrugged at the Esparans, either not understanding or not knowing the answer. No one seemed to know what to do with the missing man's horse. Since it bit or kicked at anyone approaching, they had to leave it.

The disappearance, particularly leaving his horse, nagged Barnon, but Dragal declared they would go on. Come dusk, they made their slow approach, counting on anonymity and BookKeeper Olmer's defensive spells. Once at the gate, action exploded. Olmer muttered a word, and the gate flew wide. A horn sounded. Enemy soldiers fired their arrows and attacked with spears and swords.

Barnon's horse seemed to know what to do. The warhorse lurched into the opening, knocking two surprised guards prone with a kick. The horse pivoted, taking Barnon with him, and they were quickly among enemies. Barnon brought his sword to bear, feeling the punch of every arrow that hit his shield like a warning clap. His prime protector stayed diligently on his flank. The other protectors surrounded the princes. Enemies could only approach through the defenders.

As Dragal had predicted, the forces were thin around the gate and quickly overrun. That worried Barnon further.

What contingency does Prince Marfaie have? He worked with the Circle. Does he not know what they are capable of?

With the gate secure, the attacking party regrouped. Dragal assigned the protectors into squads to search the Manor.

If I was Marfaie... Barnon thought. If Marfaie knew the rescue was imminent, would he risk losing his prize? Terant was meant to be busy thanks to Kitable but...

A shrill whistle interrupted Barnon's thoughts. The remaining Rydans sat suddenly straight on their horses. They repositioned themselves, and their huge warhorses to block the movement of the protector teams Dragal had assigned.

"Go back," one of the Rydans insisted, pointing to the gate and into the fields outside the fort. "Done. Go back."

Dragal bristled like a porcupine. No matter how tall he sat on his warhorse, he could not look down on the Rydan because of the almost two-hand difference between their horses, but Dragal had a way of looking up that felt like looking down. Giving orders to Dragal *never* ended well. Barnon winced in anticipation.

"Get out of our way, savage, or I will cut you down! My brother is in there! I will not allow anyone or anything stand in my way! Move aside!" Dragal's voice boomed as if the command came from the God Pari himself.

The two Rydans exchange glances, but it was more amusement than concern. It was as if a child had picked up a stick and was threatening to beat them. They looked keen to find the mother so she could spank her child.

"Dragal?"

The sound of an Esparan voice calling made the raiding party turn in their saddles. Perched atop a quaint riding horse, Barnon was shocked to see Sol coming up beside the party.

His heart leaped in such joy that he forgot his sword, and it clattered to the ground. He almost dismounted to greet Sol to confirm to himself that it was real when he remembered the immediate danger of their surroundings. The defenders of the manor were being held off by the protectors, but the threat was still real.

Sol wore no shirt, his breeches looked like had been unchanged since his capture, and he had clearly been beaten repeatedly. But he was alive, and he was here, making Barnon laugh.

The missing Rydan held the reins of the horse, his broken-toothed grin widening at the shock he had caused among the Esparans. He then whistled again. Barnon checked with the other Rydans, but they did not seem to acknowledge the whistle. Before Barnon could ask, Sol spoke. His voice was more like Tohmas' soft tone than Barnon remembered it being.

"It's alright, Dragal," Sol said. "We can go now."

"Protectors, form up," Dragal shouted, taking charge again. "Escort. Let's…"

The Rydan's horse arrived through the gates at a gallop, narrowly missing a protector. Immediately, the returned man mounted his horse. *Answering the whistle,* Barnon realized.

"Let's go," Dragal finished, although he glared at the errant Rydan as he finished the sentence.

Flawlessly, the protectors took their places in a caging formation around Sol and his rescuer. Barnon joined Dragal and was soon

protected by the same cage as the party rode out. The sparse defenders of the manor offered no further contest.

Once they had returned to the cover of the mountain, the party paused. Olmer reported casting spells to buy them time to organize the flight from the area.

The Rydans clustered together, the returned one telling the two others a grand tale in a babbling, incomprehensible ramble.

Sol dismounted, his legs shaking as his bare feet touched the mountainside.

Barnon jumped down and grabbed his brother in a hug. He regretted it when Sol winced.

Sol was cut up everywhere from his shoulders to his feet. Seeing his body gaunt and haggard, Barnon grabbed some rations from a saddle bag and presented them.

Sol lowered himself to the ground as if his knees had forgotten to bend. He held the hard bread in his hand for a long moment, his gaze vacant.

The moment Dragal's boots hit the stones, he was cursing. "Demon-cursed savages! Disappearing on us like that was damn risky! And for what? Running around without an escort outside the walls! You were liable to get shot! Or seen! Had you alerted them, we all could have been killed! You put the entire mission in danger!"

The Rydan paused his storytelling and cocked his head at Dragal as if trying to understand what the crazy man was raving about. With a shrug, the Rydan gave up and turned back to his friends.

Before Dragal could launch into another tirade, Sol's quiet voice interrupted.

"He saved my life, Dragal."

Dragal whirled to face his brother. "Demon shit! We were on our way!"

Sol shook his head and broke a tiny piece of bread off. He chewed it carefully as if the motion hurt. "Lanor," he said. "Marfaie had a servant by the name of Lanor. He had a magic trinket. If that Rydan had not gotten to me when he did, Lanor would have controlled me. It could have been me you fought."

"Princes don't kill princes," Dragal declared. "We may fight, but in the end, no Prince would ever—"

"Prince Garit Carnilan of Meloch," Sol replied.

Barnon did not understand how the quiet voice could have so much of an impact on Dragal. The oldest of the brothers was suddenly silent.

Prince Garit had been the prince of the third northern princedom, Meloch. DoomDragon—under the command of Prince Marfaie—had killed Prince Garit.

If he thought Sol might escape, it seemed possible Marfaie would have commanded his death.

Facing the Rydans and catching their attention, Barnon nodded his head to them. "Thank you," he offered.

Dragal clapped him on the head. "Don't be stupid. Princes bow to none but a god. Come on. We have a lot of territory to cover before we can regroup. It's not safe here. Olmer! What have you got by way of speeding spells? We need to reach the ClipClaw Mountains."

With Sol hardly watered or fed, the party took the horses to the open flats near the west hills and started their run. Sol had to be tied to the saddle, and Barnon kept a close eye on him as they rode.

The Rydans again split to protect and lead them on. Barnon felt all the safer for it.

Chapter 6

The Esparan army reached Chock Keep early on the 15th day of the 1st cycle and set their simple camp outside of arrow range. They left the majority of the supplies packed in readiness, untacking the horses only partially and leaving their saddle bags nearby. The "tents" were nothing but spare blankets propped on scavenged branches. The camp-fire was real enough, thankfully, and warmed the evening for Lance and his companions as they waited.

Sori joined the gathering by the fire, bringing a pot of tea. Carthy, one of Lance's older friends who was sitting across from him, yawned as he groggily took a cup from the Rydan woman. As small as she was, Sori did not struggle to pour the large cast iron pot, although she had to adjust the angle to avoid catching one of her many knives on it.

"You'd better wake up," Lance warned. "Can't have you drifting off when the call comes."

Carthy smiled kindly at Sori like she was a favorite daughter, not a grown woman carrying a half-dozen weapons. Despite being of mar-rying age, Sori still had not shown interest in any Esparan man, and Lance doubted she ever would. She had supposedly had three husbands in her short life, the last of which had died just before she and her com-patriot had tried to kill Lance and somehow ended up seeking refuge with him instead.

In the cycles since her arrival, Lance's guardsmen had learned not to bother Sori. With her assistance as a cook, mender, and cleaner, she

had become as much a part of Lance's corner of the army as any of the wives. But never into the bedrolls of anyone except Lance.

Sori had declared it was her duty to warm the bed for him. When her companion Tanuka had left to rejoin the Rydans, Lance had accepted sharing his tent and bed with her as the only way to keep the small Rydan outcast alive in the cold. Sleeping beside her without sleeping *with* her was a distinction that was difficult to maintain. His heart still belonged to another, yet he suspected Sori snuggled against him for more than just warmth. He dared not broach the topic with her. Her Esparan, although well-practiced, was still weak. She may understand too little, or maybe too much.

"Will it keep me awake?" Carthy asked the Rydan woman.

"Drago Pestin," Sori replied, naming the herb. Recognizing Carthy's confusion, Sori smiled sweetly and added, "Yah, good tea." She filled Lance's cup without spilling a drop of the dark-brown tea.

Carthy happily closed his bleary eyes to savor the flavor as he sipped it.

"You shouldn't have been visiting Fixer City so late last night," Lance said with a smile. He blew on the tea, cupping his hands around the cup. The fire made him want to remove his coat, but he knew he would need it soon enough.

"Had I known we would be up all night, I wouldn't have," Carthy replied.

The other guardsmen, sitting at another campfire with their horses tethered behind them, laughed raucously.

"Yes, you would have," Kevan called over. He lifted his cup in salute to Sori, who had already made the rounds. "What's her name, Carthy? That husky dame you found in your prayers to Inac? Callalilly?"

"Cali," Carthy said, his smile wistful through the steam of his drink. He peered at Lance, his grin suggestive. "Got handholds on her but not someone to cross. Could probably knock any one of us off our feet with a sucker punch. Especially Kevan."

"I think we all know who the sucker is here, Carthy," Kevan shouted back. "She's cute, but I like them to be shorter than me..."

Lance stopped listening when he felt a creeping chill sweep over him. It was so distant, it was little more than a breeze across the camp.

None of the others seemed to notice, but it made Lance instantly shiver despite the heat.

Lance tightened his fists in reflex. He knew that feeling: magic. His bracelet of river pearls, shared between him and the woman he loved in Gaidol, pressed firmly against his wrist. The unnatural cold passed.

It was probably friendly, Lance reminded himself. He knew Kitable and the Northlander Circle would be in action tonight. It was no wonder the magic was potent enough for him to sense.

A horn sounded over the army, and the ribbing between the guardsmen instantly stopped. Lance knew he had been right about the magic; if the horn was sounding, it was time to move and that meant Master—*Wisavi*, Lance corrected—Kitable and his allies had covered them with an illusion. The Circle of the Raven had predicted the attack.

The dragons of Tanble were flying against them this night.

The horn call was to move out immediately. Like Lance, every one of the guardsmen were immediately mounted, their mugs and plates stored in saddle bags or tossed to Sori to gather. The Rydan woman slung her sack over the packhorse Lance had bought her and stood at the ready, the lead in hand, just as quickly. The fake tent was abandoned, the tea dumped, and all the cups stowed in a blink.

Lance, as a member of Prince Tohmas' command, knew the rest of the plan: follow the other Fords north-west as fast as possible.

His soldiers knew only that they had to follow him.

"That's all the time you've got! Anything not packed is to be left. Move out! Now!" Lance called, as he mounted his black stallion, Bolt. The Fyrd of Arrow was the furthest into the field and would be the last to leave. They had to march the quickest to have any hope.

He saw some of the soldiers pausing, looking confused as they struggled to cram the rest of their provisions into a sack. When they watched him march past them, they scrambled into ranks and followed. With Lance leading, the Fyrd of Arrow made their way through abandoned campfires and debris. Those on foot broke into a short jog, spurred by the sounding of "haste" from the horns. Lance looked toward the call but saw nothing, not even stars. The magic that had swept over the area now shielded them.

"Lance?" Carthy asked from atop the horse beside Lance. His voice was softer than Lance had ever heard before in their ten years of shared combat. "What's that sound?"

Barely audible over the clatter of the marching soldiers, like the thump of a wave in the distance, Lance made out the beat of huge wings.

Having no intention of revealing the danger to the general forces, Lance replied equally softly. "That sound's something nasty, something we're leaving behind. Got it, Guardsman?"

Upon leaving his homeland, Lance had been surprised and flattered by the several dozen Gaidolon guardsmen who had followed him. These veterans had abandoned their lives and families to honor the lifetime of battles they had shared. He enjoyed the camaraderie but sometimes forgot that he outranked them.

But they never forgot. When he addressed them by title, every one of the guardsmen straightened on their horses and replied, "Yes, Sir."

Glancing around, Lance saw it in their faces; they knew. They recognized the deadly sounds moving in over them by primal intuition. But they would say nothing, recognizing Lance's tacit command to remain silent.

"Can we go harass the rest of the column?" Kevan asked after a pause.

"Yeah, get these idiots really moving?" Carthy added.

Their voices were soft but urgent. Unlike the tried and tested guardsmen, fyrds were made of common men enlisted to defend their homeland. Except for the training and experience they had received as part of Prince Tohmas' forces, the men and woman marching were not warriors.

Over Lance's shoulder, the march was becoming ragged. Some individuals moved into a sprint, not seeing the threat but feeling the danger. Many others were turning around, looking for pursuit and losing the pace. A handful were halting in concern.

The Rydans had already cleared the field, carried out of harm's way by their swift steeds. The men and women of Lance's fyrd had no means to escape apart from their feet. They would be the last to leave and the first to be eaten.

"Carthy, lead on," Lance called as he pulled Bolt to a stop. "The rest of you, spread out. Corral anyone back to the main forces. Set the pace for them. I'll take rear." He watched the unit of riders flawlessly break,

the guardsmen taking their horses at a canter to cover the width of the marching men.

Carthy remained for a moment. "I can never tell if you do these things out of bravery or stupidity, Lance."

Lance shrugged as he turned Bolt back toward the ranks and the dragons. "Same difference!" he called.

As he made his way to the far end of the ranks, Carthy's voice rang out behind Lance. "Pick up that pace! No, you don't get to stop for your buddy! Tell him to stop dragging his feet and move it!"

As he passed through the ranks, Lance saw many blanched faces.

"You deaf?" Lance snapped, kicking a stunned man to get his attention. "Horns said march, double pace. So march! Move!"

Startled out of his freeze, the man broke into a brisk walk. Although it seemed random, he did travel in the right direction.

Similar voices boomed over the ranks.

"Move your feet! You can do better than that! My grandmother can do better than that! One two, one two..."

"You call that a double pace? Try using your left *and* right leg!"

"You fall out of ranks again, and I'll take your arm off. If I'm going to have to carry you, I'll make you lighter!"

Harassed by the guardsmen, the ranks picked up the pace but kept control.

"Next one who steps out of line loses a foot!" Kevan shouted. "I warn you, my ax is already sharpened!"

Lance was herding another panicking soldier when the fire crashed down.

He wasn't sure if he kicked Bolt into a gallop or if the horse just took off, but Lance was immediately among the ranks, just outside of the rush of dragon fire that scorched through where they had so recently been drinking tea. He turned back around at once but could not see the source of the fire. Soot covered the area, new flames catching in the grass. The heat made Lance's face feel sunburned under his helm.

The fyrd's panic intensified, and it took all the guardsmen to keep the group moving in the right direction. Carthy adjusted from the front, heeding the instructions from the horns when a call corrected their direction. It was no longer a march but a harried flight. The only thing

saving from them trampling each other was that most ran at a similar speed. Lance could not tell if that was luck or training.

From the back of the fyrd, Lance could do nothing but individually kick those who froze.

"Can't get them all," a voice shouted, and Kevan came into view, chasing the corner of the fyrd back toward the main forces. He angled them to the trail and away from the fire.

"I can damn well try," Lance retorted. To prove his point, he scanned the burning field once more.

He saw silhouettes in the smoke and fire, distant enough that they must have been trying to catch up when the blaze started.

A rumbled followed, and through the light of the fire, the great shape of a red dragon landed among the stragglers.

Lance leaned way back, trying to see the head of the beast. Two enormous horns curled from its foreheads like those of a mountain ram. The wings were stretched leather between thin, fan-shaped bones that pumped with power enough to toss boulders. The maw of the beast looked like a spike pit trap big enough to hold four men before being sated.

Two of the dawdlers were crushed outright by the enormous feet. Two others screeched as they were burned by being too close to the beast. Then the dragon reared its head.

He'd seen that before. They reared their heads before blowing fire.

"Run!" Kevan called.

Bolt needed little prompting; the warhorse pivoted and took off down the slope, first toward the dragon, then perpendicular to it. Sure enough, flames chased him, flowing away from the main forces. Bolt's hooves pounded through rock and dirt, outdistancing the blaze initially by only a hand's breadth. Lance held onto reins and mane both, unable to guide Bolt through the smoke and trusting his horse to find a way.

When Bolt slowed at the top of a rocky ridge, there was no longer fire nearby. Releasing his hands finger by finger, Lance sat up.

Bolt was now off to the side of the retreating forces. The fires had licked across the last of the ranks, killing many but allowing others to limp on. Beyond, within the camp they had set, more screams of pain and terror rang out. The dragons, for Lance could now see the second,

stomped gleefully through the empty tents and campfires, blasting fire across the field at random.

No one left behind would survive. And if the fires spread, it may burn toward Chock Keep as well. Had Prince Marfaie damned his own soldiers as well?

Feeling Bolt calm now that the dragons were not on their heels, Lance guided the horse to the ranks. The panicked run of the soldiers had slowed to a brisk jog, one they would be able to hold for candles more. They had a long way to go in the night.

We need to do a roll call, Lance realized. He could already tell dozens were missing, whether left behind or caught in the blast of dragon fire.

And the night wasn't over yet.

Tohmas stood, for the first time in his life, atop a platform to observe a battlefield. Despite a year of arguing against the tactic of his grandfather, tonight Tohmas needed to be away from the front lines. Thus, the engineers had built a platform in the hills behind Chock Keep, allowing him to look down across the silent keep and the army camped beyond. Although he stood two strides above the ground, he felt confident he could leave quickly if the illusions failed and he found himself the target of dragon fire. He had SoulBurner ready.

Kitable stood beside him. The wizard had cast a spell, lighting the area as if by moonlight. No torches had been lit. As far as Tohmas knew, the Northlander Circle of the Raven did not require light.

Carsh paced below, irritably flicking his knives in the amplified moonlight. Although Tohmas felt nothing of the powers working both below him among the Northlanders and beside him in Kitable, Carsh's prancing made it clear the Rydan sensed it. Thankfully, the talent to detect magic was rare, and Tohmas thought it likely Carsh was the only one bothered by the magic. Sabian, the boy shadowing Carsh as surely as Carsh shadowed Tohmas, stood nearby watching. He was attentive but did not appear to detect anything.

"Just don't draw SoulBurner," Kitable warned Tohmas quietly, for the second time. "That damn thing will dispel all my hard work and get us eaten."

"I know," Tohmas replied. He wanted the comfort of a weapon in hand, but he understood the need for magic here. Even the enchanted sword could not kill two dragons. He needed to reach Arcott alive to unseat Marfaie. Their best hope was for Marfaie to think them dead. Kitable claimed the Northlander Circle was capable of creating an illusion showing the army's destruction. Tohmas was counting on it.

Kitable touched Tohmas' shoulder, and Tohmas felt a jolt of cold through his leather and chain armor.

When he next blinked, his vision had changed completely. The flickering campfires of his army were now hidden in hundreds of red silhouettes of people below. The horses equally glowed red and orange like contained fires on their tethers. Similar silhouettes hovered farther across the field, seemingly suspended in the air. *Defenders of Chock Keep, standing on the walls,* he realized. The stones of the castle were not visible to him, too dark in the night.

"Demons, Kit, that is just weird." Tohmas muttered.

The wizard harrumphed. "It's called Dragon Sight. Useful for seeing in the dark. Live creatures appear as red or orange, while non-living things will be grey, blue, or green."

Tohmas cast his eyes over the camp below, marveling at the different shades of orange for beasts and humans. "This is how dragons see?" he asked.

"I have no idea. Pure speculation on behalf of the inventor of the spell."

A bright red light appears in the sky overhead like premature dawn to Tohmas' enchanted sight. Just a moment behind it, a second appeared. To be visible at what he assumed was the horizon, they had to be massive in size. Tohmas' throat went dry.

Elder Tril had warned them. Two dragons. Two angry red dragons.

Tohmas had killed a black dragon, but that had been a close thing. Darknim and his ax had made the killing blow only a flicker before Tohmas had been immolated. The fear he had felt—his back to a stump, his sword ripped from his hand, and his allies all fallen—flooded over him. Blacks were larger than reds by almost half, but the thought of trying to tackle two reds at the same time felt all the more daunting. Blacks and reds were magma dragons, their scales hot enough to burn. One such beast among his men could end the entire army.

And there were two.

"Can you see that, Kit?" Tohmas asked keeping his voice steady forcibly.

"I bound you to *my* spell, my prince," Kitable replied from beside him. "Yes, I can see them. The elders were right." Kitable's voice was slightly impressed. "I'm ready to throw your horn calls," the wizard added. The idea of redirecting the source of the commands had been Kitable's, since trying to hide the commands from the enemy would invariably have some of the Galanth army miss them too. Better that the commands simply come from a place Tohmas was not.

Tearing his gaze from the red doom flying toward the camp, Tohmas glanced down to check on the Circle. Where there had been only people, now he saw eight people and seven animals. The humans were hunched and frail, but the beasts with them ranged from a tiny flittering songbird to a hulking bear. Instead of red or orange light of the living, each animal's outline sparkled in mist-like golden light. Only one silhouette—Darknim's—stood alone.

Tohmas was at a loss.

"Kit? Why are there gold animals under the platform?"

"I'm going to think about it later," Kitable replied, his voice still mild. "I have no explanation for the appearance of the Circle right now. I can, however, tell you that they have established their link and their illusions are in place."

Tohmas turned his attention back to the camp, pushing the strange golden animals from his mind.

"Far crier," Tohmas called. "Sound the up and out. Flystead is on vanguard now, moving south-east. Rydans need to break off, straight west. Tell them all to move it."

The horns called out the orders, but it was still a long, painful wait before Tohmas saw a response in the silhouettes below. The Rydans were the fastest; almost instantly mounted, they shot out in full charge away from Chock Keep. Following Tohmas' instructions, they then made a slow arch to re-join the group in the south.

The other fyrds were slower, being on foot.

Everything felt like it was moving underwater, slowed by the distance from which Tohmas observed. With the speed of the dragons, it would be a close thing. While most of the forces were out of the region,

the last of the fyrds were still clearing the field when the steady wings of the dragons brought the beasts over the camp. Tiny flickering campfires still burned in the false camp, looking like firebugs next to the bonfire of the dragons themselves when seen with Dragon Sight.

A handful of human and horse shapes had lagged behind, whether from physical ailment or disobedience.

But that's not what the enemy sees, Tohmas reminded himself. If the Northlander Circle was doing their duty, anyone watching the area still saw a busy camp below those dragons. Perhaps the illusionary people would flee now. Perhaps they would freeze in panic. Tohmas could only see the real people, a few dozens of them, rushing about now that the danger was upon them.

There was nothing he could do.

Deceived, the dragons launched their fire into the illusionary camp. The real people were caught almost by accident.

The magic coating Tohmas' vision did not know what to do with interpreting dragon fire. The blast that cascaded down came out as blinding, brilliant white, like burning sand on a sunny day, and flowed down from the sky like an incinerating waterfall.

"Illusion is holding. The Circle is manipulating it to adjust for the presence of the dragon," Kitable reported softly. The wizard surveyed the Northlanders below them. "Not bad. For all that magic, no one's unconscious yet."

The fires below caught in white light but eventually shifted to more typical yellow as they moved through the cleared land outside the keep. Tohmas and his men were heading into the mountains, where the rocky cover would provide protection, but Chock Keep faced the burning fields. At best, their forests were lost. At worse, their lives would be too.

Tohmas turned his attention back to his forces. "Far crier; Flystead leads the way, a quarter turn west," he ordered. The horn sounded, although Tohmas heard it come again from somewhere in the abandoned camp outside Chock Keep. The vanguard obligingly shifted their hurried pace to the west.

"Do you think the dragons know?" Tohmas asked, watching the dragons thrash their tail through rubble, sending sparks and kindling soaring through the night sky. While they caught a few stragglers, most of their efforts were against empty tents and abandoned campfires. "You

once told me they were resistant to magic, particularly when they are pissed off. Can they tell it's an illusion?"

Kitable shrugged, his eyes fixed on the beasts below. "The illusion is very realistic. It shows us all panicking and running around their feet at the moment. Some of the soldiers are even on fire."

"But do the dragons see that?" Tohmas pressed.

"I don't care if they do," Kitable replied with a sigh. "We need the person commanding them to see it. These dragons have to be under tight control. Right now, since their orders must be strict, they can't deviate from the directions, even though they may know what they are doing is meaningless."

Tohmas waited another dozen moments before correcting the fyrds once more again, this time east. They wove between hills.

While the army moved away, the dragons let loose more torrents of white fire, burning spots in Tohmas' vision as he watched them destroy the camp. One of the great beasts landed and threw its entire body through broken, deserted defenses and campfires. A roar sounded out. Several horses in the ranks spooked. The dragons stomp through the rubble. Nothing remained, but they continued to crush the ashes of the fires under foot, leaving the edges of the fire to spread.

"They look angry."

"They are sentient," Kitable replied factually, although he finally looked away. Tohmas could not read the wizard's features with the strange vision to tell if the wizard was sympathetic or not. "Every action in their lives are being controlled. They cannot go where they wish to go or do what they wish to do. They are screaming in fury and frustration, only no one can hear them. It is torture." Kitable went back to watching the field.

"So that's why you said the one type of magic you refuse to use is domination."

"A fate worse than death," Kitable replied.

They observed the remaining destruction in silence. Tohmas finally left the platform just as the dragons left the charred, burning fields and returned north on leathered wings.

The combined forces of Esparan and Northlander marched between foothills above a long, snaking river. The air was warm on the slopes, once the sun had time to heat the stones, but it chilled quickly in the shadows. It rained. When the rain lifted, clothes hung off vardos as they traveled to dry.

Elder Tril wondered if any of the Esparans would have treated him differently had they known he was part of the Circle that was keeping them safe. Working in teams, the Circle continuously hid Tohmas' forces from the Scrys that could guide dragons to them. Would any Esparan have smiled at him? Given him the path? Perhaps thanked him? He had attended their New Year's celebration without being recognized. He walked often in their midst relatively unnoticed.

Tril arrived at Kitable's vardo without any Esparan giving him more than a cursory glance. Keeping pace, the wizard's vardo trundled along with the carts and supplies of the main forces, driven by the deaf coachman.

Tril had not visited Kitable since their last conversation. Although he could not yet call the man a friend—he doubted Kitable had any such relationships—he still felt they had developed an understanding. Tril was now known by Colt. When Tril arrived, Colt indicated his master was in and bid Tril knock on the vardo door.

Tril declined. He knew interrupting magic was hazardous. He would simply wait. He was used to waiting.

Yet waiting was no longer easy. Once, he had been happy to walk and draw in divinations to examine. Kitable had caught him out doing just that New Year's day. With each vision, he sought what had influenced the many possible futures, seeking to predict or alter them. In between those sessions of deliberate contemplation, his vision had seldom bothered him. And once, he could have blocked his mind against the visions if he had wanted peace for a time.

But the powers had grown since his new aspect. With every vision he called in, he was subjected to others unbidden. The visions had proven their worth, but it was a mixed blessing. While he could no longer cut off the *visaln,* he had learned much about the Esparan and their goals through them. He needed to see more, yet feared it as well. There was danger coming. He needed to understand it to prevent it, if only he could find a way through the cacophony of the visions.

Speaking with Master Kitable would soon cause his *visaln* to present him with a multitude of consequences that would make his mind swim. Even the simple act of opening his eyes could trigger a similar cascade. The answer, he was certain, was buried in the barrage. He had to find it. Kitable was the key to unravelling the problem.

Tril walked gingerly beside the waggon, his hand on a staff of twisted willow cut for him at Elder Ela's insistence. Even with concentration, he could not clear his mind of the blurry, half-formed images.

"You look awful," Kitable's voice said, and Tril chanced to look up. Seeing the wizard standing in the door to his vardo made the visions flare, but they were not too piercing. Briefly, Tril saw the wizard kissing a beautiful blonde woman, but the glimpse was short. He could not even tell if it had been past or future.

"How long have you been walking beside my vardo?"

Tril shrugged and forced a weary smile onto his face. The wizard was smiling too. *Kitable is happy to see me,* Tril thought. He hadn't predicted that. Kitable had been tepid in their interactions, but upon reflection, Tril could see the interactions had warmed. The wizard insisted they conversed to serve Galanth, but perhaps there was more than that.

That thought triggered more visions, but Tril forced them out. They were not important, not yet.

"You might as well come in," Kitable invited. "At least we can talk while the horses do the work."

Gratefully, Tril followed the wizard up the stairs and into the warmth of the lit vardo.

Despite previous meetings, Tril had never been inside the waggon, and he rapidly understood why. Bookcases, a single bed, and a series of tools and boxes filled the space until there was only room to walk two strides from end to end and half a stride from back to front.

"You have never invited any caster in here," Tril said, feeling astonished by the trust being extended.

"You are not a wizard, not really," Kitable replied. "Besides, even if you could control the spells you cast, you only channel divination. You're more of a threat to yourself than to me."

His disappointment must have shown on his face for Kitable frowned in apology. "I meant no offence," he said, awkwardly trying to make amends. "You have proven yourself uncannily accurate in

divination. As much as it is a weak domain, your control of it is impressive. I am pleased to be continuing our conversations, Elder Tril." He cocked his head. "That said, I suspect this visit is more personal than informative. You did not knock."

Tril knew Esparans preferred chairs, but since Master Kitable did not have any, Tril lowered himself onto the floor. Kitable joined him there. In the small space, their knees nearly touched.

"I have a problem," Tril said.

The Esparan wizard snorted. "You most certainly do. You are using magic constantly. You said that meant visions, but how do you control that many divinations at a time? Doesn't it cloud your mind? Burn?"

"You can tell?" Tril asked, propping his staff against the corner. It fell as the waggon jostled, but Tril did not bother replacing it.

"I'm probably the only person in the army that could, although Miss Weaver might not be far off," Kitable said. "I can sense the presence of magic, Elder. So long as I'm nearby, I can feel every vision that pops into your head. It's erratic, and it's powerful. It might not be dangerous to me, but I cannot imagine it is good for your sanity."

"I am keeping it quiet," Tril said, taking a steadying breath. Visions pushed into his mind, but he shoved them aside again. He needed Kitable's help, but not with his *visaln*.

"No, you are quieting it down after it has already nearly split your skull. That's like saying your child is quiet because after it screams, it whispers."

"The *visaln* is not meant to be suppressed."

"Yet, the human mind cannot handle power such as this," Kitable objected. "You look worse than I did after my worst enervation! I refuse to believe that those random bursts of visions are at all..."

Kitable's words triggered another flare of divinations and Tril flinched. With piercing clarity, he saw the Esparan wizard chastising Prince Tohmas for something and the image, even through the pain in his head, made Tril smile. The prince was also smirking.

Once the wizard recognized that a vision had interrupted Tril's attention, he stopped the tirade, both in vision and in truth.

Silence followed.

"The *visaln* strengthens with use. Mine is using itself rather a lot," Tril confessed.

"And the more it comes to you, the stronger it gets. A nice spiral, Elder Tril. What happens now? Are you going to be knocking yourself out every time you blink? Is it burning you yet? Demons, do Northlanders even get spell burn?"

"It is a gift," Tril pressed.

"I can stop it."

The words made Tril shiver in his seat. He had not come to the wizard for this, and he had certainly not expected that there would be anything Kitable could do. Would he have seen it? Could he see what the man meant even now?

A flurry of answers floods his mind. Once, only the most likely futures, the strongest, would have presented. But now it seemed as if every possible scenario swam through his head at the slightest invitation.

"Your casting is different from mine," the master wizard was saying as Tril's consciousness returned to the vardo, "but the concept is the same. You draw in the magic, form it, then release it just like I do. But what I do with spells, you do intuitively. Regardless, if I block the drawing of the powers, the visions will stop. Will you let me do this?"

"It is my gift," Tril said again. There was a shuffle across from him, but Tril had closed his eyes again and did not see the wizard move. By his voice, it sounded like he had sat back.

"Fine. Let the damn thing kill you. I don't know why you came here if you do not want my help."

The answer to that question was obvious, and the *visaln* showed it to him in great detail.

Screams and burning… damaged furs and broken bones… shattered ice. There was fire from the sky and collapsing walls. Tril saw terror in his friends' eyes and faces of deathly grey as falling blood stole life from his comrades. Although the methods varied, the results were always the same: the Circle was going to die.

One after the other, the visions of Master Terant's attack on the Circle of the Raven replayed in Tril's mind. Sometimes the man walked in, other times he simply appeared. In some, he was not seen at all, but the fire that fell from the ceiling of the Earth Lodge still told Tril that the Tanble wizard was responsible. Fires burned in most visions, but sometimes the ground swallowed them up, and other times light

engulfed them all. One of the worst ones showed the Circle lying dead in their seats, unwounded, just snuffed out.

The visions came too fast. Careful consideration should have been able to find what had led to each, but now the visions pushed each other out of the way. He did not know where to start. No vision seemed any more or less likely than any other.

But he had to know. If he could not determine the cause, he would be powerless to stop it. As the visions had shown him a hundred times over, the Circle would be broken.

Forgetting Kitable, Tril drew his consciousness in. He tried to slow the visions, to take each into his mind and study it. With each analysis, he felt himself pulled deeper into his *visaln*. Every thought triggered another vision, and each new one knocked him farther from the conscious part of his mind.

Master Terant was coming. More visions showed him in person than Scrying in. He'd use fire if he could, but if blocked, he could blast them with force or attack with rip the Earth Lodge apart with an earthquake. If he could, Terant wanted Ela dead first. Without a voice, the Circle would not act. But if she survived, they could fight.

Kitable could help, but only if he put himself in harm's way. In many visions, Tril failed to convince the reclusive Esparan wizard to assist.

How to bring him onside?

Even with Kitable's involvement, the results remained catastrophic. The Circle was broken in every scenario. He tried to follow the visions back to find a choice that could lead to a new conclusion, but he lost track of which vision belonged to which ending.

He could not save them.

His heart rebelled. Even if he had to search another thousand visions, he would not let the Circle of the Raven break. He had to find a way.

But when he pulled anew at the visions, blackness snuck in, the flow of magic sweeping him away. All the visions broke through, bombarding him.

DoomDragon leaving.

Prince Rairn dead, poisoned by a righteous hand.

Prince Dragal's death by the same hand. His illness would never have the chance to end his life.

Dragons in the skies as a funeral pyre burned.

An arrow in the back.

A dark figure with scales.

Fire that burned through mountains.

In the raging currents of the visions, Tril's consciousness went under. The visions lost form and took on the colors of magic elements. Every color and shape tangled around him, dragging him through a blackness so deep, the light of the auras cast no shadows. He was helpless as the magic carried him deeper into darkness.

Ahead, hanging in the void, a spiral of light shone like a galaxy of twisting auras larger than the night sky.

In a final burst of vision, Tril saw himself falling. Between him and the spiral was a great chasm and the pull of visions would pitch him into it.

His heart sank, for he knew he was lost.

A howl sounded behind him, and Tril's movement slowed. The wolf was coming. His aspect was chasing him and gaining quickly. He felt her approach and her devotion.

He was not done yet.

Hope rekindled, Tril turned away from the spiral and fought the pull of magic. His feet slid across the smooth surface of the dark ground, the visions sweeping him toward the light despite his protests.

A golden shape appeared in the distance. In the blackness suffocating him, his white wolf sprinted to him, fast outpacing them visions.

In a blink the wolf was beside him, shouldering the magic out of the way and snapping at the visions that tried to sneak around her. With shaking hands, Tril grabbed onto the fur of the winter wolf as she turned her back to the starry display of magic and ran.

The powers chase him, but the wolf was faster. With teeth barred and hackles raised, she darted among the visions, distancing him from them stride by stride.

The darkness faded. Tril felt a floor beneath him. Blinking away spots of light, he opened his eyes.

Kitable sat across from Tril with his hands folded on his lap. He seemed to be concerned, but insufficient time had passed for him to respond to Tril's lapse.

Tril felt his chest slowly release tension. He was safe. He had not fallen into the chasm.

"Master Terant," Tril said softly, concentrating on each word to keep himself centered, "is going to attack the Circle. I cannot stop him."

If he was surprised by the assertion, Kitable did not show it. When Tril's eyes finally focused on his surroundings, Kitable's expression was pensive.

"That's what you saw? How certain is it?" the wizard asked.

Tril trembled under the surge of visions offering to answer the question. Somewhere in his mind, the wolf growled at the unwanted powers. When she snapped at them menacingly, they drew back, and Tril could think again.

"I have seen hundreds of visions. If there is a future in which he does not attack, it is too faint for me to find. He is going to attack us, and worse, he is going to kill us," he said.

Kitable sat forward with a concerned frown. "Now that you have told me this, can we prevent it?"

Tril smiled wearily. It was good to hear optimism. "Not that I have seen, but that is why I am here. I need your help."

Kitable placed a hand on his beard and was quickly lost in thought. Tril wondered if his own eyes had looked so vacant when he had been pulled from his mind.

"We can either try to stop the event entirely, or we can aim to minimize the damage since we know it's coming," he mused aloud.

"Tell me what you would do," Tril invited. In his mind, the wolf winced, but he knew she was willing to endure this for the sake of the Circle. Between the two of them, they could master the visions long enough to find the solution.

Kitable paused. Tril was reminded that only a quartercycle ago they had been enemies. Although Tril sensed the beginnings of a friendship, it was too young to hold the weight of such decisions.

"For DoomDragon," Tril insisted.

"For Galanth," Kitable answered, a small smile sneaking onto his face. While their reasons differed, it was clear their goals were the same.

Kitable took a deep breath, then suggested, "I could shield the Circle, rotating the spells. By the time Terant works his way through, I'd have a new one in place."

New images overwhelmed the wolf, but she rallied to chase the weaker ones back. Those that made it into Tril's consciousness showed fire and death.

"He will find a way through," Tril warned. He joined his strength with that of the wolf and pushed the visions out before they continued to the ending he had already seen. Reliving the death of his friends, he was certain, was not good for what was left of his sanity.

"Not surprising. I know how powerful that man is. Perhaps we could set an alarm then. If you call me, I could..."

Tril shook his head again. The visions were the same as the previous ones, but this time Kitable died as well. In some, some of the elders lived, sometimes with Kitable and sometimes without, but the Circle was still broken.

"Not enough," Tril said as the visions were chased out once more.

The wizard rubbed his temples, his expression sour. "Then we need additional assistance."

Others could help? Tril's hope renewed.

The visions stirred, and the wolf raised her hackles. There were too many options. Tril was not keen to have them invade his mind.

Oblivious to the storm Tril was facing, Kitable continued, "If I'm going to confront Terant, I need something unexpected. He knows about the untouchables, so I can't use that." There was a chuckle as he came to his conclusion. "Carsh."

Images of the Rydan prime protector darted through Tril's mind. He was juggling blades in one and chasing a blonde-haired woman in the next. His reputation as an adversary to Kitable was well-established among the Esparans.

Kitable continued, "But we will have to find a way to get him where we need him. That means another caster or a trinket. Terant might be able to modify a trinket. Having another caster is necessary." The Esparan puffed out his cheeks in a sigh. "Bookkeeper Olmer is unlikely to be any good at duels. That leaves either the Weavers or Seria."

By sheer numbers, the visions overwhelmed the wolf and drove her to the edge of Tril's mind before she could dig her claws in. With the way open, the visions flooded in.

He saw Kitable a hundred times over. Kitable on a hill with his hands up holding a wall of green force against a fire that threatened to

end the Galanth army. Kitable sitting behind the young Weaver with one hand on the back of her neck and the other hand reaching around her to hold her wrist. Kitable in a tent as rain pounded and the frozen image of Seria was used as a guide for spells Tril did not understand. Shimmer was curled up beside him.

The future snuck in. Kitable casting, Shimmer at his side. Kitable enchanted and near death, Shimmer's spell freeing him. Kitable in a room surrounded by trinkets and tools, Shimmer sitting at a nearby table. Her patience at the end, she gave an exasperated cry and, grinning, threw an ink pot at the master wizard.

More visions followed in a blurry cascade. There were visions of the girl dancing by a fire while Kitable sat back and scowled, and others when she slept on the floor of an inn room, the wizard asleep in the bed above her. Scenes repeated with slight variations: sometimes they would argue, other times ignore each other. Spells were cast from every angle. Dances were completed to different rhythms.

The call of the wolf warned Tril that he had been swept away for a second time, but Tril could not find purchase on the smooth black surface of the strange place near the spiral of light. He fought the visions, but they carried him on. His wolf was with him, wrapped in visions and unable to escape. Her attacks slowed, exhaustion setting in.

He skittered toward the chasm, foreseeing only his demise.

In an instant, every vision disappeared. Tril found himself standing on a black surface, the distant spiral silently drifting overhead. The wolf at his side, there were no powers. With one hand on her shoulder, he walked back into his mind calmly.

He lay in the silence for what felt like forever, but when the eternity ended, he opened his eyes.

The ceiling of a vardo stared back at him.

It was gone. Although his aspect comforted him from the back of his mind with a whine, a different part of his skull was sharply empty.

The *visaln* was gone.

"I blocked it," came Kitable's voice.

Tril slowly returned to a proper sitting position. In his failing consciousness, he had slid down the bookcase. Now sitting up, he found the wizard sitting cross-legged on the bed.

Tril had no idea how long he had been unconscious or when the man had moved. If the number of pages of the book on Kitable's lap was any indication, Tril had been lying prone for the better part of a candle.

"The *visaln* is a gift from the gods, Master Kitable," Tril gingerly protested. A multi-colored, fiery wall surrounded him, hovering on the edge of his vision. He had to turn his head to see it, so faint was it.

"I doubt the gods intended you to pass out on my floor," Kitable replied with a shrug as he closed the book. He lowered himself back to the floor to sit across from the Northlander, a hard look in his eyes. "I do not want you passed out on my floor at the least. If necessary, I will argue with the gods on the matter. Unfortunately, it is only a temporary solution. When the spell ends, you will be right back where you started. I might be able to teach you to cast this shield if you want."

Tril's Northlander heritage objected when he nodded, but he had no choice. The *visaln* was, as Master Kitable had said, spiraling. If Tril did not slow it down it would destroy him. Although the gods might be angry with him for rejecting their gift, he would have to release the *visaln* only in short bursts until he was able to better control it. Eventually, perhaps, he would manage the flow, but until then, the Esparan's spell could save his sanity.

For now, he had gleaned what he needed. "You can trust Shimmer Weaver, Master Kitable. You work well together."

There was either disgust or disbelief in the expression of the wizard, but he did not put words to his discomfort. Instead, Kitable said, "We can use Carsh and the Weaver then. I would ask you how Seria would fare, but I dislike her and you need rest. I will cast the required spells tonight. The moment Terant attacks, we will know, and we will come to your aid. I will kill Terant this time."

Flipping the book open again and carefully folding the pages back, the wizard finished by saying, "In the meantime, I will show you how to stop your mind from breaking into a thousand pieces."

At the urging of the three Esparan princes, who had a schedule to keep, Krahr and the party rode night and day. They stopped only as was required for the horses, the princes traveling in silence despite how

desperate Prince Barnon seemed to be to speak. Krahr took it to be yet another sign of weakness.

Once beyond the mountain range, they crossed farmland and forest under a bright spring sun. Now confident they were safe, the princes filled Prince Sol in on the war since his departure and revealed where they were heading: to catch up with Tohmas' forces, hidden now in another mountain range. The rescued prince listened intently but said little. Krahr thought it very Rydan.

Between them, the Rydans renamed the princes.

Prince Dragal, the eldest and most irritable, became "Porcupine" because of how he constantly bristled. They heard him cough, knew the sound as *rehbrehd* and took to avoiding him.

The middle brother, Sol, was dubbed "Glint": a hint of worth, like the glint of shining metals, but none of them seemed certain if there was value or not. Sol seemed to have great courage but now seemed as dull as ore. That apathy would help him keep his head in battle but unless he found passion, Krahr knew Sol would be dead by summer. A soul without spark had no light to share. He had to regain it or he would fade away.

Barnon earned the name "Gelding." They all thought he could be a strong man, like a strong warhorse, but he seemed to be holding himself back. Sadly, geldings never regrew their balls, and the Rydans had little hope that Barnon would come into his own in the shadows of his brothers.

After four days of riding with Porcupine, Glint, and Gelding, they reached the smoky ruins of a large stone building. They crossed the burnt plains and made their way around scorched stones to the foothills. Vengr returned to them, reporting he had found the messenger Tohmas had left them.

The cool spring sun pressed against their backs as they moved through a corridor of stone. Krahr saw the tracks of the waggons that had gone ahead of them in the dust and turned stones of the path, although they were old. The good weather was an asset for hard riding, but it would grant no concealment to either Tohmas' ranks or Krahr's charges. Thankfully, Dakn had been disguising their passage since they had left the *shella*. It was easy enough to hide the passage of a small group. Tohmas' forces would have no such option.

The messenger was a pair of the Eidenlandsa, or "Northlanders" to the Esparan. The elder man sat stooped on a boulder along a short path into the mountains. His beard was thin for a Northlander, but he carried a spear, which he lifted as he stood. On his hip hung a sling. The younger of the pair was a boy short of maturity. Although the resemblance was strong between them, the child seemed too young to be the son of such an older man. The boy matched the man in every garment, even holding a smaller spear and carrying a sling.

When the princes and their assigned Rydans stopped, the boy stepped forward.

"I am Kohd," he said in halting, weak Esparan. "This Bak, Eldafather. We lead you on."

In a croaking voice, Prince Sol said, "Northlander?" The surprise was heavy in Sol's voice.

"Why should we trust you, Northlander?" Dragal said, grousing like the spiny animal he had been nicknamed for.

The older Northlander, Bak, did not understand at all, and he looked at the child for a translation. Kohd narrowed his eyes, peering up at the prince as if solving a puzzle and, after a long hesitation, answered, "They hidden. We show." The boy lifted his hand and presented a small leather token.

Prince Dragal took the token and examined it closely. After having gone over every detail of the faces and edges, he wrinkled his large nose and declared, "It's Tohmas."

"Tohmas?" Sol asked. He glanced around, as if seeking the prince. When his eyes landed on the Rydans, Dakn, Vengr and Krahr all answered simultaneously; they placed their right hands into their left palms in salute to the Hand. To Krahr's amazement, Kohd also performed the action, and he seemed to do so before he saw the Rydans do it. That made Krahr cock his head and watch the child all the closer. *Did he understand? How?*

"Tohmas," Bak repeated. The two Northlanders slid down the boulder and landed on the smoother path beside the horses. Bak took his first steps farther into the mountain path, then paused and looked back, waiting for them to follow.

Porcupine rattled his spikes once more. "Surely having you ride would be faster."

Kohd puzzled his way through the sentence carefully. He turned to his eldafather and repeated the sentence, but the words came out sounding more Rydan than Esparan, amazing Krahr. Bak shook his head in refusal, replying with swift words.

Of course he would not know how to ride! How many Northlander horses had he seen? None! The animals did not do well in the harsh winter of the north.

Kohd turned back to the prince and delicately said, "Bak run." Pressing his lips in pout, he eyed the horses and added, "I ride?"

Bringing his horse Vatnorish up, Krahr placed himself above the boy. The Northlander father tensed, his spear lifted into position for a throw. When Krahr reached his hand down for the boy to take, the spear lowered.

Rydan horses could most easily take a double load. Vatnorish may not be used to carrying a wife, but he had been trained for it. The boy's weight was hardly anything, and Krahr wanted to speak to the boy without the father on hand. Perhaps they had more in common than Krahr had believed.

Once the boy was settled, Kohd called to his eldafather, "Lee onn!" Krahr laughed at the Rydan words.

Chapter 7

The crowd, frustrated and anxious, gathered along the uneven path in the mountains. After the long night traveling under force and the recent threat of dragon fire, the people were on edge. Grigson only need to say a few choice words to people of influence.

Let's see how Prince Tohmas handles an angry mob.

Grigson helped them divide, giving Tohmas two sets of demands. Once the light of dawn allowed it, half of Fixer City tried to retreat from the mountains, while the other half insisted on halting for rest.

Assisting Grigson unwittingly, Prince Tohmas' representatives responded with force. The guardians of the fyrd on rear guard reminded them people of Fixer City that they were Tohmas' subjects now and corralled them like cattle back to the main forces. Those who wished to halt were harassed into marching again with blows and threats.

Their anger reached a boiling point, something Grigson encouraged. In protest, Fixer City stopped entirely, standing on the roads and refusing to move. To their credit, Prince Tohmas' men did not cut down the dissenters. Instead, Grigson caught word that Prince Tohmas himself had come to address the masses.

Grigson made sure he would have a good view from within the security of the crowd.

Before the prince's arrival, Grigson spread more rumors and outrage to outspoken individuals to make sure they were all suitably annoyed by the time Prince Tohmas, with his shadowing prime protector, arrived.

Grigson was surprised the prince had not brought more of an entourage but considered the oversight fortunate. The lack of military threat would help embolden Grigson's primed dissidents. The prince took a place on the rise ahead of them, where the road narrowed between the hills.

The most opinionated person was Croc Dounnan, a squat, sour man who had set up an intimidation racket within Fixer City. Grigson knew the man had once been a prosperous pimp, but Celebrant Loni had chased the man out. Croc's newest venture was providing thugs for Fixer City's less reputable members, and he had ignored Prince Tohmas' message about Fixer City coming under the army's control. Since the army forbade such practices within their ranks, Croc stood to lose his entire business. He eagerly took Grigson's words and prompts.

Once the prince declared he would keep them moving forward no matter how much they wanted to go back, Croc was atop a waggon's bench, ready.

"You cannot keep us here if we wish to leave! Fixer City is independent!" The crowd shouted agreement with their fists raised high.

"No, you are not," Prince Tohmas answered, his booming voice silencing the crowd. Grigson saw more than one set of eyes in the crowd flick down to the sheathed sword on the prince's belt, the greatest symbol of physical and religious wealth any of them had ever seen. He sensed hesitation in them instantly, but it was not enough to dissuade them entirely.

"I gave you the opportunity to leave," the prince said, pacing the width of the road. "I told you if you stayed you had to be willing to follow my command. You stayed, and I set things in motion believing you were earnest in your decision. You are I are both trapped now."

Those nearest the prince nodded. Grigson suspected that the prince could have declared that the path home was being lined with rose petals, and they would have nodded. No one seemed to want to argue unless there was some distance between them and the prince's sword.

Thankfully, Croc had positioned himself behind a wall of innocents. He retained enough bravado to shout, "No one told us the path lead into the mountains! There is no advantage here! No people! No profit for us!"

Prince Tohmas stopped, but his shadowing prime protector carried on pacing. Grigson admired the strategy; eyes went to the Rydan and his knives and the people at the front shrank back. There was no room to step away, but they managed to give the Rydan slightly more room.

Standing firmly and speaking over the heads of the crowd, Prince Tohmas addressed Croc directly. His voice softened, yet seemed to gain force. "Right now, our enemy thinks us dead. I will not allow even one of you to leave and endanger my soldiers. You are no longer just trailing behind us; you are a part of these forces, whether you like it or not."

A strong argument, he admitted. Most of Fixer City knew a soldier or two, so the prince appealing to the need to keep the army safe was potent. Some of Fixer City were families to those soldiers. Many more were friends.

Croc—*bless him for being so self-centered*—still replied, "We are free men and women here! No oath was taken. You cannot hold us against our wills!"

The calm voice of the prince did not shift. "Are you objecting to my keeping you and your thugs here, or to the idea that I might extend my protection to these people and render you useless?"

Croc went white. Grigson had to congratulate the prince; Tohmas had spies in Fixer City. Grigson wondered if his own name or face was known to those spies and started making a mental list of people to examine more closely.

The crowd turned to regard Croc as the ex-pimp stuttered briefly, unable to reply. Grigson felt the lack of response deflate what tepid support remained for his position.

"Fair ladies and good sirs," the prince said into the pause, "I present to you the new Guardian of Fixer City, Zarac Dounnan."

A strapping man in a new green tabard stepped forward, his shoulder bearing the blue rope of guardian rank. Grigson thought him familiar and wondered if he had seen the younger man around Fixer City.

In the next heartbeat, Grigson recognized the last names matched. The family similarity between Croc and this guardian was obvious.

Well done again, Grigson thought.

"Through your new guardian," Prince Tohmas said, "I am giving you a voice in my ranks. If you have a problem, bring it to your guardian or his wardens. If they cannot solve the issue, Guardian Dounnan will

bring the issue to me, and I will fix it. Once out of the mountains, I will release Fixer City. Until then, get your vardos ready because we are moving out!"

Guardian Dounnan did not move from his resolute position as the prince pivoted and left the crowd at his back, clearly fearing nothing from any of the members of Fixer City. Grigson finally appreciated why the prince had left his protectors behind; showing force to these people would have made them resent him further and could have led to open rebellion. Instead, he had placed them in an equal position to the other fyrds.

Once the prince and his prime protector were gone, the new guardian relaxed and released his wardens from their ranks to mingle. Guardian Dounnan greeted individuals of Fixer City by name, giving Grigson the impression the young man had previously been part of the community.

Grigson was considering starting a fight—no one would ever know who threw the first punch at the hapless warden—when Celebrant Loni in her long, red dress sauntered in from behind him. Despite himself, he scampered away, fearing for his spells, but her goal was elsewhere.

"As foretold!" Celebrant Loni cried to the parting crowd. They cleared a road between her and the guardian. "See how the Champion acts in the name of the Goddess! Behold all, the power and wonder of Inac and those in her service! Zarac, once you were nothing but your brother's slave. Now you have found your true purpose through Inac's graces!"

Thinking the goddess was not known for her graces, Grigson found the sentence ironic.

Guardian Dounnan accepted Loni's statement with reverent poise. Grigson took that opportunity to leave, accepting that the combination of military power and religious support would not be outdone fast enough to make Fixer City useful in destabilizing the forces right now.

He needed to gather information, and that would be best done outside Fixer City. Grigson still had not discovered how the Prince of Galanth had arranged for the army to "disappear" instead being burned by Rakhund's beasts. Most importantly, he had to inform Prince Marfaie of this deception. But with ongoing magic fluttering in the

air above Fixer City, magic communications would be risky. Revealing himself now would be fatal.

It was time to leave Fixer City.

He could not live among the Northlanders; he had been told Northlanders had varying magic "gifts," and he was not yet sure if any of those gifts may reveal him at an inopportune moment. Infiltrating the Rydans had been his initial target, knowing that impersonating them was an easy way to sow resentment between Esparan and Rydan, but their societal norms threatened him. Every Rydan had a place in the clan, and trying to bring himself into someone else's was likely to be detected, even just as a discrepancy and so it was a weakness. Being challenged by a Rydan boded ill; he could not defend himself without magic and that would be disastrous among the magic-hating people.

As he turned from the crowd and left Fixer City for the main camp, Grigson set himself two tasks. The first was to end Celebrant Loni's support to Prince Tohmas. So long as the religious forces also supported the prince, Grigson was limited. Further, the woman's power as an untouchable made her a threat to Grigson, Master Terant and even Prince Marfaie. She had to be contained before the forces of Galanth reached Arcott.

The second goal was to find a position in the army, as close to Prince Tohmas as he could. He had heard of a Rydan woman among the ranks who did not follow Rydan traditions. He even knew the woman had lost her husband some mooncycles back, although she had not witnessed the death. Best of all, she was living in the camp with a Gaidolon high guardsman whose rank matched that of the Galanth guardians. Through her, Grigson could move onto his next sabotage.

In the little Rydan Sori, Grigson had the perfect target for his Blind Love ring.

He still slashed two sets of harnesses on his way out of Fixer City. Every little bit helped.

Chapter 8

"Too complicated!"

Shimmer father's voice cracked in indignation. Shimmer snickered. Dust had spent his life perfecting his acting skills. She had seen him stand in front of princes and tell bald-faced lies without hesitation. He had argued with brutes twice his modest height without flinching. He had once convinced a rich patron that he was Espar's most prominent chef, despite not knowing the difference between a pot and a kettle.

But putting him next to Master Kitable flustered the poise right out of him.

Camp had been set twisted around a river valley in the mountains. At the elevation, the trees were small and provided little cover. The sunset glowed from behind the mountains in the distance, casting long shadows but leaving the sky cerulean blue. While the Circle of the Raven kept illusions hiding the main forces, Master Kitable himself had set the defenses to hide any casting from scrying eyes. The layers kept it from being visible even to Shimmer as she stood below it. To her, the sky above was empty except for the distant misted clouds, even though she knew a dozen spells were directly above her.

The Weavers had selected a boulder on the outskirts of camp as a practice platform. Master—or should it be "wisavi"—Kitable's vardo beside the stone acted as a deterrent. No one else dared set their waggons within a dozen strides. Shimmer sat atop the boulder, her feet dangling.

"It's not *too* complicated; it's just complicated," the master wizard said firmly. He held the image of a tiny dragon in his hand, the sunset flickering off silver scales.

"Needlessly complicated then. For a fraction—"

"You will not know where your audience is," Kitable argued. "You cannot expect to get away with a light illusion. You need wind as well and, most importantly, no illusion aura!"

Dust harrumphed and tossed his cloak wide. The patterned inside was designed to dazzle, but it did not make Kitable even blink. "Precisely! *Too* complicated! It's one thing to conceal it from a standard version of Spell Sight, but these people could use any number of variations. No one..." Dust fumbled on his words for a moment, suddenly recognizing who was talking to. "...no one, that is, except you, I assume, can channel enough power to counter every combination!"

Seeing Wisavi Kitable's scowl, Shimmer laughed aloud.

Kitable glared over at her.

"So why don't we split the responsibility?" Shimmer asked as she slid down to land between the two men. Her father looked relieved, but Master Kitable only wrinkled his nose.

"Because I need you for something else," he replied.

Shimmer felt her heart skip several beats in excitement. She knew he couldn't be talking about working with her personally, but for a moment, she pretended he was.

"Just make the illusion opaque, and it will cast a shadow," Kitable told Dust. "That limits the size. Research something that sounds like a dragon and plan to make it big. Really big. I will provide a code for hiding the illusion auras."

Dust swallowed audibly, his eyes on the tiny dragon in Master Kitable's palm. "It's too big!" he weakly objected.

With a flick of Kitable's wrist, the image winked out.

"Practice it," Kitable said.

"If Shim and I worked together..." Dust prompted gently.

Seeing Kitable's eyes turn to her, Shimmer smiled.

"No, I need her for something else," he repeated.

"You going to tell *her* what it is?" Shimmer asked. She placed her hands on her hips firmly and stepped up to Kitable to bring herself between him and her father. She felt two layers of shields pass over her

as she approached. Only once before had she managed to get closer to him than this. Every other time she had crossed paths with him conscious, he had kept at least this much distance between them. She assumed it was true for everyone he met.

"Well?" she prompted when he failed to reply.

"I need you to attach yourself to Sabian," he replied.

Shimmer snorted, making a face. "Companion Arvanon? Why?"

Kitable shifted his weight back, distancing himself subtly from her. He seemed more comfortable the farther he got from her. He had to plan his words, but when he spoke they tumbled from him.

"I am anticipating a problem. I want Prime Protector Carsh to assist, but I will need my strength, so I do not want to be responsible for moving him. I will provide the spell, as I assume you cannot perform a two-person Relocation. But I need you to anchor it. It needs to be flexible. The target may change."

She felt his stare like a touch, and it made her heart flutter. He rarely met her stare unless it was to scold her.

"I can do that," Shimmer said, hearing her own voice stutter. "I am *very* flexible."

Dust choked loudly.

Disappointedly, Master Kitable did not seem to notice her word choice and inflection as he carried on obliviously. "You will pretend to be taking interest in Sabian—he's not been called companion in some time—and since he and Carsh are never more than a few paces from each other, you should be on hand when Master Terant attacks. You will bring Carsh with you to the Earth Lodge. Stay out of the fight; Master Terant is well beyond your skill."

Shimmer stood dumbfounded, her voice lost. *Is that concern in his voice? Is he worried about me?* She could not read his expression.

Her father cleared his throat behind Shimmer. "You really want to do this, Shim?"

Shimmer didn't need to look back to know her father was frowning at her. He had no tolerance for risk, but Shimmer had no intention of abandoning Kitable now.

Kitable beat her to the response: "I don't see you have a choice," he said, breaking the stare with Shimmer to address Dust. "Prince

Tohmas made it clear that Fixer City now answers to him. You didn't leave, Weavers."

Shimmer smirked. "Sugar sap," she said.

Kitable eyed her. "The writings of Everand. The clamp beetle prefers sugar sap over fruit acid. Trapping the beetle is best done with sugar sap."

Shimmer waited for his conclusion, unsurprised that he had recognized the quote.

"You are suggesting that I would be more popular if I was sweeter," he said. His smile was bitter when he added, "Do you realize that a clamp beetle fed sugar sap does a poorer job cleaning truffles, the very job they are trapped to perform?"

"But if you don't catch them in the first place, you can't put them to work," Shimmer replied. "So stop offering us the fruit acid, would you?"

He shocked her and stepped forward, standing suddenly directly in front of her. Shimmer's heart flipped backward, and her skin tingled in anticipation of contact, despite knowing he would not willingly touch her.

"I take your point, but I do not have the time to negotiate. Can you, or can you not, do as I require?"

Shimmer struggled to find her voice again under his grey-eyed stare. It had been cycles since she had felt the magic around him pulse with each breath he took. The closeness thrilled her.

In that, she had her answer. Watching Kitable work even from a distance delighted her, regardless of his constant criticism.

"I am an actress. I can do it. I'll help Papa when I can too. If Terant doesn't attack when the illusion is needed, I can directly Boost him." Seeing Kitable's disgusted expression, Shimmer chuckled. "Just because you have never found someone you trusted enough to..."

Her sentence fell off at his scowl, and she realized her error. To save both Shimmer's life and that of a friend, he had tied his energy to hers directly once, risking his own sanity and life. For a moment, she had entirely forgotten the chance he had already taken. Somehow, they had not discussed the event since.

"Weaver, plan your spells," he said, his voice tight in annoyance. He turned his back to her and went to his vardo, dispelling and then resetting his defenses as he moved. She watched him go, but she was no closer

to understanding his wards after observing him. The sound of the door closing startled her.

Shimmer found Dust behind her still, patiently waiting. With a nod of his head, he indicated they should go.

"As they left the campfire circle beside Master Kitable's vardo, Dust grumbled, "Well, this should be interesting."

She winced.

"Interesting" was what Dust said when he did not want to offend or discourage her, like when, as a child, she created a clay statue of an owl that looked like a blob, or when a spell had glaring errors that would change its results. "Interesting" was a polite way of saying "not good" in her family.

The spell Master Kitable had given them was complicated beyond anything either of them had attempted before. *Did I get us in over our heads this time?*

But the excuse to be near Kitable was welcome, even if she had to pretend to be on the arm of someone else. She would just pretend Sabian was Kitable.

"It will be worth it," she replied.

Dust had a glimmer in his eye when he tilted his head at her. "We can make it worth it."

Rairn had seemed to recover but relapsed shortly after Tohmas visited him again. The Barlabian protectors predicted his death; a dozen remained loyal to the prince while the others became mercenaries in Fixer City. The soldiers themselves slipped into Tohmas' ranks, swearing new oaths. Their confidence in their prince was ruined, satisfying Tohmas. Darknim had conquered Rairn's princedom, but the final blow against the man was being dealt by Tohmas' hand.

Now certain the turncoat prince would never wake, Tohmas left the Healing waggon behind. Darknim had come with him but said nothing as they parted ways. Tohmas could not be freed from his other shadows as easily; Kitable remained at his side. Since Carsh was also present, so was Sabian. As part of their preparations, Shimmer Weaver hung from

Sabian's arm, apparently making rude comments in his ear. Sabian spent his time trying to smother undignified snickering.

Sabian was playing his part remarkably well. Tohmas hoped the boy remembered he was meant to be looking for threats as well.

Before Tohmas reached his tent, a whooping, celebratory call interrupted. Tohmas recognized Krahr's voice announcing his Rydan Followers' return. Carsh whistled, giving the Followers a target amidst the tents. The army had camped alongside a low hill, forcing the party to weave along sloping paths between ranks and campfires in the sunset. While the Rydan steeds managed it deftly, the Esparan ones lagged behind.

Tohmas paused among the tents of his protectors. Admitted through the protectors on Tohmas' order, the three Rydans presented themselves with the Esparan princes a hundred yards behind them.

Kitable and Carsh both followed Tohmas to meet with the Rydans. Although he had been told the reason behind his wizard's determined proximity, it crowded him.

Sabian instantly stepped away from the girl, leaving Shimmer pouting. Tohmas' Followers did not acknowledge Sabian, but Tohmas was not fooled; they had taken note of everyone in the area who could remotely be a threat, and Sabian ranked high on that list. The boy and his knives had gained a reputation in Carsh's shadow.

In their ignorance, all three Rydans dismissed Kitable's presence.

Once their assessments were completed, the Rydans went down into ready kneeling positions in front of Tohmas. One by one, the three Rydans placed an object in front of them. Vengr placed a porcupine quill in front of him, Dakn placed a shaving from a horse's hoof, and Krahr placed a metal rod that had probably been a latch.

Three items. Three princes.

The porcupine was simple; Dragal had been grouchy, but that was no surprise. The hoof chip implied some degree of importance—what Rydan was not proud of his horse?—but a horse that injured its hoof was not at its full strength. So someone had potential but had to improve. The metal rod was something of value, being stronger than stone or bone; one of the princes had impressed the Rydans with their fortitude. He was not sure which represented Sol and which Barnon, but at least there were three items.

Next, the Rydans presented their spoils, which were sparse. There were a handful of iron weapons, a couple of arrows (Rydans loved taking the feathers from them to use on spears), someone's laces, and a bent copper table coin which would work as decoration more than currency.

Seeing nothing he wanted, Tohmas gave them leave to take their prizes as the Esparan caught up. Krahr seemed exceptionally happy with his metal rod as he left. Their victory calls shot through the valley, and the whistles that answered guided the returned Rydans to the Rydan camp atop a valley's edge.

Tohmas wanted to follow; he was curious to hear their stories.

At length, Dragal, Sol and Barnon joined Tohmas atop the ridge where the command tent stood. They were led by a Northlander who looked a fair bit like Elder Tril. A boy rode on the man's shoulders.

With a nod, the Northlanders left, finished the duty their Circle had assigned them.

"Damned savages!" Dragal declared as he dismounted, not even waiting for the Northlanders to be out of earshot. Barnon moved to help Sol off his horse, but Sol dismounted too quickly to accept the aid.

Tohmas quickly identified Sol as Krahr's metal bar. While he had been beaten badly and carried a host of scars and bruises, the Prince of Solta had become tempered. When Sol looked around, he did so with the iron stare of a Leader. Krahr must have seen the same thing.

"Is there a problem?" Tohmas asked, waving them into the tent as protectors took charge of the tired horses. "I see Sol has been recovered. That seems like a good thing."

Carsh, with a shake of his head, assigned Sabian to watch outside, and Shimmer slunk back onto the boy's arm. Kitable ducked into the tent ahead of Tohmas, permanently at the prince's side while they awaited Master Terant's attack. He found a place in the corner quietly.

Tohmas pulled a chair for Sol, but the man did not collapse into it as he had expected. Instead, when Sol sat, it was controlled and calm.

Rydan influences, Tohmas thought. Was Sol hiding his body's weakness? Smothering it with a strength of will?

In respect for his efforts Tohmas made no mention of his ginger motions and turned immediately to business.

"Runnah!" Tohmas called, and a protector answered by popping into the tent. "Please have DoomDragon and the guardians join us,"

Tohmas said, tossing the man a token to identify the command's origin. The protector nodded sharply and left at a run.

After sourcing cups, Tohmas grabbed the wineskin from the top of a chest and tossed it onto the table. The prime protectors took their places in silent watch over their princes, although the space behind Sol remained conspicuously empty. Carsh had been sitting at the table for most of the winter and took that place instead.

"Those stupid savages damn near got my brother killed!" Dragal declared as he finally settled. "One of them snuck ahead. If he'd been spotted, we'd never have gotten close enough to the gate for Olmer to open it." Dragal paused, but Tohmas suspect it was not voluntary. He was out of a breath and stifled a cough. After a few short breaths, he continued, "And if Marfaie or any of his brutes found out we were there, they'd have taken him away. Sol himself said that one of the lackeys had magic! Could have bewitched all of us! That Rydan should never have gone out without telling us!"

"Unfortunately," Tohmas peaceably said, "they tend not to discuss things, at least not in detail." He took a deep breath to calm his own impatience. "I, for one, am glad to see Sol back. Marfaie's quarrels was with the sons of Zayban. It is right you all be there to settle this."

Dorakon growled, then coughed. "So why are we taking the long way around? The path through the mountains will take much longer."

Tohmas smiled. "I will explain."

With a sympathetic roll of his eyes, Carsh tossed the wineskin from the center of the table to Tohmas. Tohmas nodded to his brother in appreciation and, forgoing a cup, drank. He was going to need something to calm his head. DoomDragon was expected shortly. That was going to be difficult. Dragal was still in too foul of a mood.

He passed the wineskin to Sol on his right.

Before he could begin to explain the illusion and escaping the dragons, Tohmas stopped. Behind the burn of wildwater, there was a strange aftertaste.

"Get to it!" Dragal groused. "We need rest for—"

Realization struck him. "Tarol!" Tohmas snapped, lunging to stop Sol from bringing his filled cup to his lips.

Carsh was faster. A knife sunk itself into the wineskin in Prince Sol's hand. Sol was so startled, both the wineskin and his cup hit the

table. The contents spilled back toward Carsh like tendrils as Dragal, mid-tirade, went silent.

"Tarol root?" Barnon echoed, his voice choked. "Poison! Runnah!" Barnon shouted, making Tohmas smile. The Rydan word was being universally accepted, at least whenever the protectors were around. "Get Cutter—"

"Not necessary," Tohmas interrupted, dismissing the protector messenger with a wave of his hand. "I will be fine."

The youngest son of Zayban stared at him with wide eyes. "If it is concentrated enough to be tasted in wildwater, you must be treated immediately! Tarol root is deadly! You have—"

"It is only poison for those who have never had it before. I was exposed as a child."

They all paused, eyes on the stain darkening the surface of the table. It looked like a twisted tree, like the Galanth crest.

By their panic, none of them knew about the poison's limitations. *That means they are unlikely to be immune...*

Had any of the others besides Carsh drank first, they would have soon broke with fever and tremors. A dose high enough to be tasted over wildwater would kill even a grown man swiftly. The only question was whether the assassin had known that Carsh and Tohmas would be unaffected, having been exposed among the Rydans since an early age. All Rydans knew it was a good dye for clothing and knew that children who did not chew it early got sick from it later.

"Who had access to this tent? Who could have placed the poisoned drink?" Dragal demanded. "And where is that Northlander? Wasn't he meant to be here?"

Tohmas winced. "Tarol root is a plant from the Outlands. DoomDragon probably has never even heard of it."

"But he is not present. Convenient!" Dragal persisted.

"I only just called for him! He did not know he would not be here, would not be the first to drink."

"Unless he too is immune."

"Which is highly unlikely, considering how hard it would be to get tarol at all this far north!" Tohmas shot back. "Dragal, if we lose DoomDragon, we lose the Northlanders. Be more cautious where you throw accusations!"

For a moment, Dragal paused, and Tohmas was unsure if it was the chastisement or a lack of breath.

Sol wiped his hands on his trousers gingerly to be rid of the residue of the drink. "So, a Rydan?" he asked.

Mentally, Tohmas cursed both in Esparan and Rydan to hear the suggestion. He was having a hard enough time keeping them from killing the Northlanders. He did not want them turning their suspicions on the Rydans now.

Just as he opened his mouth to correct the notion, he paused. *This is an opportunity.*

He put on a thoughtful expression and said, "I have to look into it. There are only so many places one can get tarol root. Burlotak is responsible for the Rydans. He will likely have a few things to say about this."

Not wanting to approach himself, Grigson hired Croc and his goons to fetch Celebrant Loni. After setting a drugged wine jug into place, Grigson put goblets on the table inside the small, simple vardo and then followed Croc into Fixer City at a safe distance.

Through his contacts, Grigson had learned the Prince of Galanth was in the Rydan camp tonight. Even if it was not for long, Master Kitable's attention would be on the prince as he dealt with the volatile people. Kitable's paranoia was renowned, as was his suspicion and dislike for the Rydans. Kitable's focus on the other side of camp gave Grigson his first opportunity to cast unobserved.

Grigson was disappointed by how easy it was to lure Celebrant Loni out of Fixer City. While Grigson watched, Croc walked up to Celebrant Loni and ask her to join them. The woman left her entourage, her campfire, and her friends without looking back.

Once he was satisfied Loni was on her way, Grigson returned to his procured vardo and settled outside.

For this night of the mountain trail march, the camp had been set in a broken valley of stone. Unable to rely on grazing, livestock and steeds were rationed onto grains. Here, the mountains made for good cover, and the valley bottom was smooth, not nearly as treacherous as

Grigson had expected. The rocky terrain even gave him a cave to set the vardo next to.

Loni's appearance was filth; her red dress and orange blouse had not been changed, it seemed, since they had last met a quartercycle before. He was not sure if she slept with horses to perfect the amount of dirt, but the smell of her made him suspect it. Still, her blouse was low cut, and she had cut a slit in her dress to show off her long legs. Her combination of beauty and disarray both aroused and repelled him.

"Celebrant Utheran!" Loni called with strangely genuine cheer as she approached him. Croc's bushy eyebrows furled at the title, then at Grigson's attire. Grigson had been forced to discard Utheran's robes previously, but he had found suitable replacements. No magic was required in the disguise. Loni had seen through his illusions and, not knowing what the real Utheran looked like, she still believed he was the celebrant. News of Utheran's death clearly had not reached her ears.

Smiling as sincerely as he could, Grigson rose. "Celebrant Loni, thank you for coming." He gestured to the vardo door behind him. "Would you join me for a drink? We have something to discuss."

The suggestive smile of the whore made Grigson smile wider still. Had it not been for her being untouchable, Grigson would have taken her to bed as she seemed to think he intended to. Her body was worn, but Grigson had always been impressed with the teachings of Inac, Goddess of Lust. As far as he understood it, sleeping with each other was a form of worship.

But he dared not touch her.

The celebrant cooed, "Certainly." Swinging her hips emphatically, she climbed the steps into the lit vardo. Careful not to come in contact with her, Grigson followed her in.

Untouchable or not, she was still mortal.

With the heavy dose of his Sweet Dreams concoction in her wine, Loni was unconscious shortly. Grigson did not even need to make much small talk. The woman seemed to prefer the sound of her own voice.

Once he was certain she was unconscious, Grigson called in Croc and his friends.

"Tie her up, gag her, and put her in the cave. Don't let anyone see you. First chance you get to leave, take her to Arcott. The rest of your pay is there."

The thugs accompanying the pimp rushed in, accepting rope from Grigson. They already knew about the exit through the back of the vardo that lead into the cavern. If Tohmas kept his army in the shelter of the mountains, the Esparan forces were still five or more days away from Arcott. By cutting across the flat plains outside the mountains, Croc could make it in only three days. He had a map to help.

Grigson left the vardo, joining Croc on the steps. He handed the man a wand.

"Here. I will seal you in to hide you from Kitable. Once the army has moved on, point this at the wall and say 'open wall.' You will then be free to take her away." Croc shrugged and shoved the wand into his belt. "I have a final request," Grigson added and the squat pimp raised an eyebrow. "I want to cast a spell on you to help you travel safely. Will you allow it?"

With far too little hesitation, Croc shrugged and said, "Go ahead. You're the one paying." He clapped a hand to his belt pouch, which clattered loudly in demonstration. The first part of their payment had already been delivered. The promise of more was powerful motivation.

But it was not enough for Grigson. He could not have them changing their minds. Loni was too valuable. Marfaie would not be pleased if the delivery was incomplete, even if the prince did not know she was coming.

Swapping to wizard's cant, Grigson cast a Geas spell and laid it, entirely without resistance, onto Croc. He kept the casting as subtle as he could, so as to not alarm his target.

Once done, Grigson pulled out a beaded bracelet that he had taken from Master Terant.

"Keep this with you at all times. By it, my prince will know you and give you your payment."

Croc's glazed expression focused on the beads, and his blunt hands accepted the magic item. He was still slightly dazed as he turned to the vardo to join his goons, the orders now permanently imbedded in his mind and impossible to disobey.

"And never touch her," Grigson added. "Let the others do what they want, so long as she lives, but you may not touch her or allow her to touch you."

Croc nodded, and the gesture gained force as he came to his senses. The Geas had been accepted. So long as he never tried to disobey, Croc would never know he was controlled.

Even if he knew, he can't escape now.

The beads would keep the anchor active and warn Grigson if the Geas slipped. Thought magic was tricky. Overnight, it could be dispelled by sheer bad luck. If that happened, Grigson could replace it from afar through the enchanted item Croc now carried.

It never hurt to be extra prepared.

Once Loni and her delivery team were in place, Grigson dropped a conjured wall of stone over the cavern's entrance. The magic auras faded as he turned his back and left them.

Grigson checked the skies again. The flare of magic had been brief, and the cave should hide Croc and his magic items now. He did not think he had been noticed. Even Master Wizard Kitable could not be everywhere at once.

He shed the robes a final time, tossing them into an empty vardo. He wondered absently what the woman of the home would say to her husband when he found them but decided it did not matter. Grigson clamped one of his engraved hair pins to the cloth of the next tent before moving on.

He already knew where he was going, the Fyrd of Arrow. There, he would find the little Rydan outcast he needed.

Not surprisingly, Burlotak approved of Tohmas' plan. He seemed impressed that his Leader's son had come up with the plan himself, but Tohmas was accustomed to Burlotak's low opinion of others. While the Rydans marched, Tohmas spread his Followers out. It took four days for them to all be in position.

Overnight, given leave, the Followers started the executions. At first light, Tohmas moved in for the final confrontation.

He acted without Esparan involvement. The Esparan princes and their soldiers still saw him as Esparan, one mask he wore among several, and he did not want their delusion disrupted, not yet. As much as he

pretended to be otherwise, Tohmas was still Rydan at heart. And this was a Rydan affair.

If Burlotak could be seen as next in line to take Chiefdom should Tamv falter, Baont was third. The Rydan had once lived near the Second Clan territory with his large family and, early in raids against Second Clan, had made himself useful to Chief Tamv. Unlike Burlotak, who had been a friend and Follower of Tamv for decades, Baont had been an ally only, one that had outlived its usefulness. Tamv's last orders to Tohmas had been to destroy Baont.

Rydan justice was simple; those who had the strength dealt out punishments to those who did not. But Baont was powerful and well-connected. Killing him outright would separate Tamv's supporters from Baont's, dividing the authority of the clan. Thankfully, someone with a poisoned wineskin had given Tohmas the solution.

Tohmas had to act directly against someone as high ranking as Baont, which meant leaving his protectors behind. He hoped no one would try to call on him in the early morning.

With his Rydan Followers grinning behind him and Carsh walking at his side as his brother, they entered the Rydan side of camp and located Baont's fire.

The older man raised his eyes at the approach but did not pause eating until the sons of Tamv were standing at his campfire circle. The man's wife and two daughters, only one of which was of an age to be claimed, moved to one side of the fire, leaving the man and his two present sons across from Tohmas.

"Have you a quarrel with me, son of Tamv?" Baont asked, echoing Tohmas' words from the challenge that had killed Baont's youngest.

Tohmas smiled. How he enjoyed the simple ways of the Outlands compared to Esparan politics.

"You attempted to poison a gathering of Esparans two days ago, Baont, in my tent," Tohmas replied.

"I hear I used tarol root," the man snidely replied, peering up against the sunrise Tohmas had strategically put at his back.

"Which has been found in your belongings." It did not matter if it was true; it would be accepted as truth since Tohmas had spoken it and none alive dared contradict him.

"...and which would have done no harm to you or Carsh," Baont pressed as he rose. His old *stafnye*, a double-bladed staff, was on hand. Two of his sons hesitantly stepped up in support. The sons of Baont were outnumbered and, more importantly, outskilled by the Followers behind Tohmas.

"What is my crime, then?" Baont asked directly.

No one cared if Baont poisoned Esparans. Every Rydan knew tarol would be of no threat to Carsh or Tohmas.

"You transgressed my hospitality. They were under my protection," Tohmas argued.

"Followers of yours?" Baont raised an eyebrow.

Tohmas nearly laughed. *Now that was a trick question!* If he wanted to have Rydans accept the people in the tent, the easiest way was to make them Followers, but they were weak, they were irritating, and they were Esparan. Naming any of the princes as Followers would only diminish his position.

But Kitable had been present too. A wisavi was respected as an advisor, not for skills in combat. They had no way to judge Kitable's skills except by Tohmas' success. Since Tohmas was powerful, Kitable was held in high esteem.

"You attacked my wisavi," Tohmas said.

The sneer fell from Baont's face.

The crime had been named. Now Tohmas was ready to deal out Rydan justice.

"So, you finally have your excuse." Baont sighed as he leaned over and picked up his *stafnye*. Standing tall, he set the lower blade in the ground, holding the shaft below the top blade, ready to spin it into striking position. "You know it will not be enough. My sons will carry my family, even if I die."

At a gesture from Carsh, the Followers tossed in the severed heads of Baont's nine other sons. The two remaining boys bared their teeth, but they knew better than to attack blindly in anger.

Men would freeze, flee, or weep when facing their death. An Esparan might have tried to bargain, but any Rydan begging to spare his life rendered his word and honor worthless, making him deserving of death. That much was simple.

Baont rotated his *stafnye,* ready to fight. His sons lifted their weapons to do the same. They were dead, but they would die fighting, as true Rydans.

Tohmas drew SoulBurner into the dawn. The glowing aura scattered the shadows of the doomed Rydans.

The Rydan weapons provided no resistance to Tohmas' enchanted blade. Inac's fire blazed across Baont's throat after only two strikes. Carsh's knives found places between the ribs of the sons. In in flicker, Baont's family was done.

The threat to Tamv's position as Chief of the Rydans ended. None could contend with Tamv. Tohmas' duty as son of the chief was done.

Baont's wife was free to return to her father or brothers, but the daughters were a different matter. Not old enough to be a wife, the youngest was a good-looking child who promised to be a strong woman one day, so Carsh allowed her to be claimed by one of his Followers. Tohmas gave the eldest girl, who carried a knife to go with the poison of her stare, to one of his Followers. He watched with approval as the girls were carried away.

The mother sat by complacently. Assuming Carsh and Tohmas continued to do well, her daughters would hold a place of authority as wives to their Followers. It was not quite as prestigious as Baont's rank had been, but they were being promised a good life.

Burlotak presented Baont's head to the table of princes the next day, claiming they had found the man responsible for the attempted poisoning.

Meanwhile, Tohmas set his sights on finding the actual guilty party. The saboteur had to be close by. He would discover them and bring them down, quietly, when the time was right.

"Found them!" Terant declared to no one in particular. He fell back from the spell casting, ending up on his back in his courtyard. The space was sealed but open to the sky; his vision returned to show a weak, cloud-covered sun. A chill wind, despite the presence of warming spells on the walls, cut through. He was coated in sweat, like a runner after a

long sprint. He fought sleep, staring at the sky and trying to think clearly through the enervation.

Never before had he channeled so much magic. No one person was meant to control that much! His mind felt thin as he left the spell behind. *Did I push too far?*

Still, he could not deny the success. After a quartercycle, ten long days, Terant had finally broken through the illusions of the Northlander Circle and found the Galanth army.

For the first few days after the dragons had been sent in, Terant had thought victory complete. Grigson had been the missing piece; he had not returned. Prince Marfaie was adamant the spy was not dead, but they heard nothing. Prince Marfaie's mood had gone from elated to tepid rapidly. By the third day, Terant had been instructed to investigate the remains of the army thought to be immolated by fire.

Dragon fire could make bones into ash, but the remains had been too sparse. The ploy was obvious. The army had fled. And because of the fires, no one had been around to verify the deaths they had assumed.

Marfaie's mood had turned furious.

Despite knowing the sons of Zayban were in the mountains, locating them had been impossible. All the power of the Northlander Circle had been set against Terant. He had been unable to overcome them alone.

But with the help of the strangers, he had finally broken through.

Pushing himself up slowly, Terant felt his muscles ache as if he had lain on the stone all night. Thankfully, he was not spell burned at all; he had used up all the power, leaving none to harm him.

The sun slipped behind a darker cloud, and the thin light dimmed. With the cold coming in, he shivered. He did not know why his heating spells, meant to keep the snow and wind out of his courtyard, had failed, but he decided against replacing them now. Enervation could render a wizard unconscious. For the moment, Terant was too tired to cast anything.

Passing through the wards, he shuffled into his hall and chambers. He forfeited rest at first in favor of reporting to Prince Marfaie. With subdued satisfaction, he reported Rakhund's failure and the new location of the Galanth army six days from Arcott.

The prince took it surprisingly well. Understanding that Terant was not in any condition to attack immediately, they set their plans for the morning, and Terant returned to his quarters to sleep.

Rakhund met Terant in the morning. Given a map of the area, Rakhund and his dragons took flight. Terant watched them disappear over the horizon, a feeling of foreboding sinking into him. He had never seen Rakhund leave the region around Arcott. Even without their master, the dragons were formidable. With their master on hand, they would be unstoppable.

There would be no mistakes this time.

Terant went to his courtyard and cast Scry. It was high time he brought his wrath down upon the Northlander Circle for their betrayal. With the help of the strangers, he was more than ready.

Chapter 9

One of the Healing waggons rolling along the mountain road with the Galanth forces carried a prestigious patient. Prince Rairn of Barlaby lay in fitful fever and sickness, his twisted ankle healing slowly. Rumors said that the gods were punishing the man for his disloyalty during the battles. Tohmas knew the real reason.

One day after Baont was brought to false justice, Prince Rairn lost the battle against his fever and died in the night. The healing mother of the waggon reported the news to Tohmas, asking if they should have the celebrants prepare a pyre.

Rairn had been a prince. There were protocols to be observed.

"I will think on it," Tohmas replied. He had no intention of stopping his march to honor the man he had killed, but how would the other princes react? Knowing he had little time before word got around, Tohmas requested the princes converse. He included Rairn's death in the message, seeing no benefit to catching them by surprise. Dragal in particular would be less explosive if he had time to think things through.

Tohmas had intended to attend prayers while waiting for them, but Kitable arrived before he could take a place at the altar. Without preamble, the wizard declared, "Elder Tril says Terant's coming, and soon. The Circle of the Raven strongly recommends not marching out today. Stay here for the funeral."

Tohmas' gut tensed.

"Prince Rairn's death has not been announced yet. I informed only the princes. What else does this Circle know?"

He had left DoomDragon out of the missives to avoid triggering Dragal's rage.

The Master Wizard of Galanth shrugged. "The Circle knows a lot of things they probably should not, and their predictions have been accurate thus far, which is why I am concerned. Elder Tril has also said Master Terant will break the Circle before we reach Arcott."

"*Will* break? You've always said 'will try to break' before. Why the change?"

Kitable let out a long breath. Their private conversation became crowded as the other princes began to arrive ready, Tohmas was certain, to argue the need for a formal pyre for the dead prince. Ignoring the traitorous prince seemed likely to undermine their own sense of importance. Formalities kept the masses in line.

"I have only dealt with Master Terant personally twice," Kitable said, lowering his voice. "Our first meeting left me unconscious, afflicted with spell burn the likes of which I did not know existed. The second meeting, I would have lost if not for Celebrant Calanor's help. Master Terant's spells are not only complicated, my Prince, they are essentially impossible. At some point, that man is going to find a way through my defenses. If he uses any of his engineered spells, the Circle will be dead before I can Relocate to help. We have hidden from him thus far, but Tril is adamant that advantage has been lost. I'm doing my best, but I am not confident I will succeed against this man."

Tohmas had never heard Kitable so hesitant. He'd been flustered before, but this was different. *Is that fear?*

"Yet today, staying here, is somehow better?" Tohmas asked, trying to mitigate the damage.

"Not just better," Kitable replied. "Apparently, today is our *best* hope of minimizing Terant's damage. Tril explained as much as he could, but the variables make it impossible to offer any true certainty, except that Terant is coming, today, if we stay. Knowing that, we can be ready for him."

Seeing the princes taking seats at the enormous, pitted, and stained table, Tohmas nodded and let Kitable take his customary place in the

corner. The smell of the spilled wildwater had lingered, giving the room a sour smell that sharpened as he approached the table.

Dragal took the initiative, laying his hands over the stain and formally stating: "We need to honor proper observances for any prince who passes."

All eyes turned to Tohmas, anticipating resistance.

"I agree," Tohmas said, the words sounding strange to his ears. "We will wait out today, set a pyre, and then move on in the morning."

Dragal sputtered, his arguments thrown by the agreement. Having little else to discuss immediately, they parted soon after.

By midday, Tohmas stood on a vantage point overlooking the final preparations of the pyre. Servants erected a nearby canopy with stones as anchors to protect the princes from possible rain, despite a cloudless day. Anyone who wanted to pay tribute to the dead was welcomed, and that resulted in a gathering of the traveling army's most notable members in the stone valley, although Tohmas could not find Celebrant Loni.

The rest of the princes joined Tohmas at the canopied rise, each wearing attire more formal and clean than Tohmas had seen in cycles. Sol even had a new prime protector. The jumpy man extensively checked the canopied area, including questioning Shimmer and Sabian. Wisely, the man avoided Carsh, whose reputation was too well known for even a newcomer to fail to heed it.

Nerves were expected in light of his new rank.

Below the princes' canopy, Celebrant Sedgan lit the pyre from the Blessed Flame of Inac. The Celebrant of Inac for Clandac had met misfortune days before and died, leaving Celebrant Sedgan once more in charge.

"No band of mourning?" Kitable wryly asked as he drifted into a watching position behind Tohmas. Where the wizard had spent the morning, Tohmas did not know.

"Do you think anyone will notice?" Tohmas answered, taking a seat, expecting to be at the pyre for a long time. He did not point out that Kitable was also missing a strip of white cloth over his arm in honor of the dead prince. No one had expected the wizard to, but all of the other prices wore one.

Kitable snorted but did not otherwise reply.

People would notice the lack of a mourning band. Dragal might dispute it with him. The people who knew Rairn as the coward he was would understand why Tohmas refused to honor the traitorous prince.

As Dragal crossed Tohmas' mind, the eldest son of Zayban arrived and took a seat beside Tohmas. He immediately leaned over and said, "DoomDragon was there when Prince Rairn died."

Tohmas had difficulty keeping the anger out of his voice. He had worked too hard to keep the Northlanders and the Esparan together to have Dragal pull it apart haphazardly. "DoomDragon worked with Rairn for mooncycles. They were allies."

"Only until the Northlanders turned against their Esparan patron," the Prince of Clandac pointed out. "I heard Prince Rairn and DoomDragon had exchanged harsh words after. DoomDragon did not tell Rairn when he made the bargain with you. Rairn even took control from DoomDragon when he thought he could."

"Of course, Darknim didn't tell Rairn about allying with me. His loyalty was too fluid for DoomDragon to trust him."

Dragal sat back in his chair and put a thin hand to his chin. Listening closely, Tohmas heard the man wheeze with each shallow breath. "DoomDragon went to the Healing waggon the day Rairn took to fever, then again the day before he died. Do you expect me to accept this as a strange coincidence?"

Tohmas was tempted, in defense of Darknim, to point out that DoomDragon had only come to the waggon because Tohmas had been there, but he thought better of bringing himself into the light of suspicion. Dragal had enough suspicions already.

"Yes," Tohmas said, soft but with emphasis. "A coincidence, nothing more."

Dragal's retort was cut off by a cough. Tohmas turned his head. If Dragal had been Rydan, the clan would have chased him out by now. He was weak, and this kind of disease was known for spreading. But he was Esparan, so the cutters gave him treatments. They did not seem to working, and Tohmas resented how they put his men at risk.

The sentence was left incomplete; Dragal recovered but seemed to know Tohmas was not going to be swayed. When DoomDragon arrived, Dragal spared a moment to glare at the Northlander.

CHAPTER 9

Darknim took one look at the chair that awaiting him, moved it back two steps, and sat on the ground in the space he had cleared. DoomDragon had no doubt been told about Master Terant's imminent attack, but there was no evidence of tension in DoomDragon's calm posture now. He was a pragmatic man. If there was nothing he could do about the magic threat, he would not waste energy fretting.

The moment DoomDragon had arrived, Seria slunk up from the crowd below. Her steps were cautious, but Tohmas attributed that to the harshness of Kitable's stare. She requested permission to sit with Darknim, and DoomDragon accepted by pointing at the ground beside him. The tiny woman folded her legs and sat next to the giant Northlander, then she stared at the fire to avoid the venomous stare of the Galanth wizard at her back.

Carsh moved up on Tohmas' left protectively, putting himself between Tohmas and the caster.

Wanting something to think about besides politics, Tohmas examined the crowd below him. After the pyre was lit, Celebrant Calanor, the Celebrant of Totho, presided. Calanor's ties to the God of Wind made him the expert in matters of death and transitioning into the afterlife.

Celebrant Calanor stood just outside the heat of the fire with his stormy eyes on the rising smoke. Illness entitled the dead to the stars, unlike others who would be buried, taken by the earth-god Pari to a mystical place underground to be judged before their release to Totho and the heavens.

Looking at Celebrant Calanor now, Tohmas was struck by how plain the man was. Being a Celebrant of Totho, his long white robes with the hood and a scarf over his face were customary. Calanor's maimed hands remained tucked in the enormous sleeves, concealing the torturous injuries he had survived. Those events had brought Calanor close to his god in more ways than one; in nearly killing him, the trauma had opened him to untouchable powers. For the most part, the celebrant restricted the use of his magic to communicating when his mutilated tongue could not, and his usual target was his only acolyte, Timon. In the crowd, Timon stood at his celebrant's side, close enough to meld the acolyte's grey robe with the pristine white robe of the celebrant.

Four gods provided life and all the gifts of the world, but only two were represented in Tohmas' forces. Calanor commanded the respect of

Wind, and Celebrant Sedgan had proven himself sufficiently to speak for Fire. But no Galanth man or woman represented Water or Earth, and that unexpectedly worried Tohmas as he watched the pyre. He had started with a balanced four, but sabotage within their ranks had killed two and no one had dared step into their places. Seeing the reverence given to Sedgan and Calanor, Tohmas realized he needed to bring the balance back.

If he had control of four celebrants, he would further extend his influence.

Out of the corner of his eye, Tohmas saw Shimmer jump. Tohmas checked with Kitable and saw his wisavi looking off into the distance, his eyes vacant. Soon Shimmer bore an expression of intense irritation to match Kitable's. Before Tohmas could open his mouth, Kitable vanished.

"Of all the demon-cursed timing... Carsh!" Shimmer called, stepping up on Tohmas' left.

For a brief moment, the prime protector refused to offer his hand. Knowing the greater threat was Master Terant, Tohmas gave the Rydan a stern look, and Carsh placed his hand gingerly in the hold of the dancer.

"Demon piss," Shimmer muttered as she took Carsh's wrist just above where the knucklebones in his bracelet were rattling. "That's got to be the largest Seal! Fourth marker?" she wondered aloud. "Gods, sixth marker!" she finally cursed. "We're going to have to do some running."

The next word out of her mouth made both the redhead and the prime protector vanish. Carsh winced and closed his eyes before the spell took them away.

Elder Tril had been right. He only hoped this "best chance" would be good enough to save the Northlander Circle.

Before Tohmas could offer an explanation to the princes who were staring at him accusatorially, a voice sounded over the pyre below.

"Tohmas!" shouted Prince Rairn's voice, "Murderer!"

Covered in wispy tendrils of black smoke, a human face appeared above the pyre, snagging Tohmas' attention. The crowd gave a collective gasp, inching back as the form appeared. For a moment, they froze like Tohmas, unable to believe what they saw.

CHAPTER 9

The ghost of Prince Rairn of Barlaby, who Tohmas had poisoned over a halfcycle in revenge for his betrayal, grew above the pyre. It turned its shadowy gaze on him and him alone.

Beside Tohmas, Dragal made a choking noise then, like everyone else, looked at Tohmas for his response.

Tohmas' heart stopped in his chest, and he drew himself slowly straight in his seat.

"*D'aems*, I did not see that one coming."

Terant's Seal was the largest Kitable had ever seen. He had expected the spell from the start—there was no better way of keeping other casters from interfering—but not like this. Instead of just covering the Circle's Earth Lodge, Terant sealed off half of the Northlander camp, blocking all anchors.

But Seals did not stop physical passage. He just had to get to it.

Kitable wasted no time on dispels—Terant would have defended the Seal. Instead, Kitable sorted quickly through the markers he had set through the camp as anchors. One was available on the edge of the Seal spell. He anchored and activated the Relocation spell.

He reappeared in the middle of the Northlander camp, the strong pulse of magic on his left.

The Weaver would be able to do the same, and Kitable did not wait for her. Running through the Seal, he aimed for the Earth Lodge at a sprint. The taller pelt and bone tents forced him to weave, skipping over fires and dodging confused Northlanders until he spotted the shale stones of the Earth Lodge. Somewhere within would be the ice pool Terant was so determined to destroy.

Kitable halted. The Earth Lodge was silent, the Northlanders at their chores banally in the surrounding area. The animal skin roof hung low over the walls, packed with lichen to hold out rain. Not a pebble was out of place on the dugout walls.

Yet magic was layered on the door and auras flashed within, made visible by Kitable's augmented Spell Sight.

Terant was already here.

There was only one entrance into the unfortunate place, but Kitable did not spare the tunnel-like doorway more than a glance. A dozens spells guarded it. None of Terant's creations looked friendly.

Kitable's next spell had been such a success the last time he had cast it, he had decided to keep the recitation permanently.

He defined the area and activated the Backdoor spell. The wall of the hut disappeared, displaying those within.

His heart dropped.

"Ah," came a bemused voice, "Master Kitable. How kind of you to join us."

Except for his magic, there seemed little remarkable about Master Terant. He had a plain face, a shaved chin, and an average build. If he had not been surrounded by magic, Kitable would have expected to find the man selling turnips at a farmer's market. He had come in person, which meant he was trapped by his own Seal spell.

The destruction made the inside of the hut look like it had been ransacked by Rydans. One elder, Kitable could not even tell which, lay groaning beside the opening Kitable had just created, while the rest huddled against the wall to Kitable's right. Tril and Ela stood between the rest of the Circle and Terant as if to defend them. Tril's shield against visions glowed under Kitable's Spell Sight and probably had provided some defense against Terant's assaults. Only Ela and Tril were without wounds or burns. In many cases, the pelts of their aspects had born the greatest damage and were singed or patchy.

Kitable made a point of not wasting words when dealing with wizards, but today was going to be an exception. Carsh and Shimmer were on their way. He wanted their help.

"Master Terant," Kitable calmly said, "you are without your apprentice this time. You must realize you are outnumbered."

Kitable analyzed Terant's auras as he spoke. The assortment had changed since their last duel. Kitable could immediately spot five shields for stopping Eight-layered Dispels, and at least ten that would prevent physical damage. Carsh was going to be hard-pressed.

So am I, Kitable thought. Even with his enhanced Spell Sight, it was possible he could not even see all of the defenses. The auras looked like they were drifting between shades, changing their elements before his eyes, but that had to be a trick of the light.

To Kitable's relief, Terant seemed willing to carry a brief conversation, turning away from the Circle.

"What did you do with her anyway?" Terant asked.

"Seria? She likes Fixer City. Spends her time selling perfumes and cantrips for children. Fits right in." He knew she had been spending time with the Weavers on occasion, but the rest were lies. It did not matter anyway.

From the far side of the hut, one of the elders crouched and reached out a hand to their fallen companion. The movement caught the attention of the northern caster, and he sneered at them. The Circle tensed, clustering closer together.

"I cannot have you all interfering any longer. I will deal with you, Master Kitable, in a moment," Terant said, raising his hand.

Kitable saw Carsh and Shimmer arrive, coming in at an angle to the opened that was not visible to Master Terant within. As they paused by the opening, Shimmer whispered in Carsh's ear. Kitable saw spells bind to the prime protector's weapons, not to the man himself.

Clever girl. She was separating the magic from the man, making targeting that much harder.

The Rydan slunk around the corner and into the hut like a shadow. With his head turned toward the Northlanders, Terant did not see the Rydan's approach.

A spell formed on Terant's hand. For the potency, Kitable feared the Circle would soon be ashes if he allowed the magic to progress. Yet try as he might, he could not identify the spell Terant built.

Doesn't matter, Kitable decided. He activated a small Solid Force Cage and targeted the area around his foe's hand. The wizard couldn't be targeted, but nothing was protecting the air from a force spell. A destructive spell confined to Master Terant's hand would help speed along the duel nicely.

Disappointing Kitable, Terant dropped his spell, recognizing the counter.

"Your aim is impeccable!" Terant commended.

The elders had reached their downed member. Terant let them surround the injured protectively. Kitable did not blame him; his confidence was well-founded. The man was incredibly well defended.

The words had done their duty. It was time for action.

Kitable activated a dispel, taking out a pair of shields and keeping Terant's attention on him for a moment more.

From the other side, leaping from the shadows, Carsh attacked. His blade should have been struck a defense, but Shimmer's enchantment meant the Rydan's knife instead sliced through the shield. The dispel bound to the knife was used up, but there was suddenly one less shield between Kitable and his target.

Carsh's next strike was deflected by a second defense, but the Rydan simply ducked beneath the reciprocating flare of magic. Coiled low, he shoved up and forward as he rose, pushing against the defense.

Terant spun to face the Rydan, shock on his face. But the surprise faded quickly, replaced by irritation.

Kitable took advantage of the distraction to fire another series of dispels, seeking to open a path to the man himself. A few more spells, targeted by Shimmer as she peeked around the corner into the hut, enchanted Carsh's knives breaking shields when the Rydan could not otherwise bypass or break them. Kitable's spells knocked out two more shields just as the Tanble wizard released a fresh assault.

It was a burst spell. Although it was easily deflected by Kitable's defenses, Carsh slammed against the wall of stacked shale. The Rydan landed on his feet, shook himself, and ran back at the caster, lichen clinging to his back.

Kitable expected the Circle to fare less well, but the energies of the blast inexplicitly focused in on Elder Ela alone. As if she had been struck in the forehead, her head snapped back. She fell backward into the arms of her friends.

Despite the noise of Carsh's assaults and Terant's casting, Kitable heard Tril growl.

Kitable physically moved forward through layers of the shields, using the openings Carsh had formed. His Eight-layered Dispel hit another defense and eliminated it. Behind Terant, Carsh was close enough to glance an attack off the man's Molded Shield. The impenetrable defense deflected the blow.

Ignoring the Rydan, Terant's next spell was for Kitable. It looked simple enough to be stopped by the first shield, but the spear-shaped spell punched through and peeled away, revealing another dispel within.

After it cut through the next shield, a third layer appeared, aiming to take out another shield.

Kitable activated a Reverse spell, which spun the attack back at Terant. The man had the sense to drop the open spell before it could do damage.

Should have known he would never cast simple spells.

"Entertaining, but I have a job to do," Terant said. His grimace eased into a smile.

A word more and the prime protector was thrown back for a second time, this time immediately pinned to the ground by alteration and destruction. While the prime protector struggled, Kitable dispelled the last of Terant's defenses against fire.

Ignoring Kitable, Terant faced the Circle.

Kitable stepped into the path of the attack, activating a Flame Dart spell. The dart struck Terant's shoulder too late to disrupt the power that cascaded toward the Circle. Kitable felt the magic like thunder from his feet up.

A single physical shield remained when the magic cleared.

A dispel? Some kind of multi-way destruction? Kitable did not know what had hit him, or even if he had succeeded in protecting the Circle at all. *Had that been for me anyway? Or for us all?* It seemed similar to Kitable's Uncover spell; it had left Kitable largely undefended.

Tension rose in Kitable's chest. He forced his panic down and focused on his task, the next spell.

He activated a contingency and a new defense sprung up. A second word put up decoys for Eight-layered Dispels, which was the most likely next attack. An Eight-layered Dispel would disable remaining enchanted items and, if it landed Kitable, would eliminate his hovering spells. Striped of his spells, death would follow.

Tril had mentioned one such possibility. *Hope we're not in that future.*

Carsh joined Kitable between Terant and the Circle elders. He was wary, but his resolve was clear. Shimmer had no doubt helped him escape the spells, which both impressed and worried him. If she was spotted...

He pushed her out of his mind. Carsh did not seem any worse for wear. *He's not tired; he's angry. Good.*

Before he could choose another spell, a wall of magic appeared in front of him. Kitable took an involuntary step back. He recognized the flashing magic barrier from his duel with Clarin; it was destruction and death in a dozen forms. And it was defended heavily.

Carsh looked to Kitable for a response. They, with the Circle behind them, were trapped against the wall.

Compared to Terant, Clarin had been an amateur, and the solution then had been to oppose the open spell, knowing Clarin could not match Kitable's endurance. Kitable had no hope of doing the same to Terant.

He had two people in mind when he activated his counter spell. The first was Clarin, for providing his introduction to the attack and the second was Tohmas, for having inspired the counter.

"Lady's Skirts." The words activated the hovering spell still tethered to Kitable.

A second wall of magic appeared between them. Like the wall of fire Tohmas had once used to push back the fires sent to burn him, Kitable's identical wall advanced against Terant's.

He did not have to beat Terant. He had to match him.

One by one, Kitable copied Terant's destructive magic, undoing the spell one element at a time by exhausting the powers. Feeling like he had tethered a tornado, it was only Carsh's firm hand on Kitable's own Molded Shield that kept Kitable from being pushed back. The flurry of magic spun the air.

The walls imploded inward, destroyed.

Terant's expression, Kitable was pleased to see, was mild surprise.

Carsh seized the opportunity: two of his knives banged into the Molded Shield of the Tanble caster. Following the knives, the prime protector launched himself at Terant.

Kitable slapped up another defense, then joined Carsh's assault. His attack was grabbed by a Reverse spell and shot back at him. He dove aside instead of countering. Carsh was forced to do the same by a Flame Dart spell.

The ground rumbled and shook, tossing Kitable as he tried to rise.

Through the instability, Kitable made out the smooth black aura around Terant that meant earth alteration. *An open spell? An earthquake?*

But the majority of Terant's defenses were down. Kitable had a path in.

From the ground, Kitable activated an Eight-layered Dispel and fired it at Terant. It hit the man's shoulder, not his core, but the uneven footing didn't throw his aim.

But the spell had no effect, hitting a hidden shield. *Wasted.*

The ground beneath Kitable bucked, then cracked. Carsh was pinned near the Northlanders, a tendril of magic from Shimmer working to free him. The room tilted with waves of energy rolling out from Terant as if with each heartbeat. Kitable skidded, grabbing at the breaking ground to slow his fall. Behind him, a crack opened wide enough to form a pit, part of the ground dropping away. Desperate to shake Terant's concentration, Kitable activated a blinding light, but even before the light dimmed, he knew it had failed. The shaking continued, as wild as a green horse, kicking him from each handhold and making it hard to think.

Focus damn it, he scolded himself. He needed to get through the Molded Shield. The Eight-layered spell had failed. He had to cause serious pain to stop this spell.

Terant's shields kept Kitable's magic at bay, but only the Molded Shield was stopping physical attacks now.

If I can get Carsh through...

Kitable found purchase against the wall and rolled to face Terant. The crack between him and the Northlanders widened, the depth blackness below.

He had no spells that could break a Molded Shield. *Has to be a full cast.*

Not only did the casting take a great deal more time, but it would also occupy all his attention and prevent him from defending himself. If Terant found a way through Kitable's remaining shields, Kitable might not live to complete the full cast at all. And even trying to cast required him to cast through the waves of rocking earth as the surroundings crumbled and cracked around him.

But I need that Molded Shield down.

So through the tremors, Kitable began casting.

Having not had warning from his patron or his allies, Grigson was pleasantly surprised by the activities of the morning. First, Prince Rairn died overnight. Second, magic flared around the pyre fire, demoralizing and accusatory. Third, more spells clashed around the Earth Lodge of the Northlanders.

Typical Marfaie, Grigson mused. The Prince of Tanble preferred the many-armed attack. Against this force, it was necessary.

As he headed for Fixer City, Grigson spotted the shadows of dragons approaching over the mountain tops. Tohmas and his army were to be hit from all sides. *Four attacks,* he realized. Rakhund from above. Terant among the Northlanders. Seria—or was it Marfaie acting himself?— at the pyre. Grigson would be the strike from among the forces, although it would have to be improvised. *Pity, I didn't get more warning!* Kitable's defenses had made communication too inconvenient.

But I can improvise.

Knowing he needed to avoid the dragons, Grigson hastily made his way to the edge of the valley where the camp had been set. He pointed the dragons out to everyone he passed, spreading hysteria until a solid panic gripped the people of Fixer City. Once he found a deep enough cliff, he created a hiding place. He made sure he was not observed during his casting, but he was confident Kitable would be too distracted to notice.

Sitting in the entrance to his cave, Grigson pulled a hairpin from his pocket. Using it to define the other dozen such pins he had left throughout the camp, he lit fires through Fixer City. Content to see the smoke rising from the already-panicking camp, Grigson lit a magic light and closed the cavern behind himself. The ground rumbled as the red dragons landed on a nearby peak.

Fires from within, fires from the pyre, and now fires from above. Galanth's glory ends in a blaze tonight.

Celebrant Sedgan left the funeral pyre shortly after he lit it, leaving the acolytes to maintain it. Loni had not been at the funeral pyre, a fact that unnerved him. Loni normally seized every opportunity to preach Inac's

will to the uninitiated; she would not have missed the crowd. Fearing the worse, he went in search of her.

As Sedgan set foot in Fixer City, the first cries of alarm sounded. Following the cries, Sedgan was shocked to find a tent on fire, the smoke curling above like twisted wool. Without thinking, he activated the enchanted ring he wore, destroying the small fire. Not so much as an ember remained, the blaze snuffed out in a blink.

The people of Fixer City, being dependent on their vardos and waggons, were not usually careless with fire. There were no nearby fire pits, nor could Sedgan see a lamp.

Where had the fire started?

A woman rushed up, a pot of water in hand, but she paused beside the extinguished debris. Confused, she dumped her water on the halfburnt remnants. So cold were the ashes, the water did not even produce steam.

"Is this tent yours?" Sedgan asked.

The woman nodded absently, not looking up. She touched the ashes gingerly. Once she confirmed they were cold, she pulled off the burned cloth and exposed the contents. Much of the inside had survived, implying the fire had started on the canvas itself.

"Careless to leave a fire unattended," Sedgan said.

"I dinn't do any such thing!" she shot back, her voice heavy with a northern drawl. She had the build of a Northlander, although her features were finer and her hair was loose down her back. She wore digger's chaps and tall boots, all of which were filthy. "What d'you take me for? I dinn't do this."

Sedgan snorted, certain the woman was lying. But before he could speak, he heard, "Fire! Fire! Help! Fire!"

Following the voice, Sedgan found, around the corner of a vardo, another fire near the roof of a sales waggon. Again, he saw no nearby campfire. No light source would have been needed here, outside in the middle of the day.

The truth became obvious.

Arson.

While the closest person tried futilely to slap at the fire with a blanket, Sedgan stepped up, pointed at the target, and activated the ring once more.

The licking flames along the eves snapped out of existence, leaving charred wood behind. He had to repeat the spell to eliminate the fire that had jumped to the roof of the vardo.

The people stared at him, their blankets and wash basins drooping in their hands.

He squared himself proudly, keenly aware of his celebrant robes. "Such misuse of fire angers Inac. I will not have—"

Another cry went up, this time incoherent panic. Thinking the arsonist had been moving through the waggons, Sedgan marched toward the cry. He smelled no smoke but thought he could hear someone calling the alarm further ahead. The thickness of the crowd stopped him, and as he tried to push his way through, he suddenly realized these people were looking up.

Up, where the first of two red dragons had perched on a peak overlooking the camp.

His heart fell into his ankles, and he entirely forgot to breathe.

The army was trapped by the mountains on either side, the only way out the path to the north or south. None of them could move fast enough to outrun these beasts. Dragon fire could easily immolate them all.

Drawing a slow breath, Sedgan forced his hands to stop trembling. He could do nothing about that except trust in those who were more powerful than him. Master Kitable would have a contingency for this. Prince Tohmas must have a plan. They had killed a dragon once. For the sake of everyone, they had to do it again, somehow.

The crowd around him had gone silent in shock. Farther out, Sedgan heard people screaming.

A plume of smoke curled skyward ahead, a mundane fire where there should be none, black smoke rising. In the fires, Sedgan found hope.

"Enough staring!" he shouted, finding a nearby waggon and climbing atop its counter. He managed to capture the attention of half of the crowd, praying it would be enough. "Those dragons are not our concern; leave them to greater men, for they will protect us. Our duty is to reach out to Inac. Seek all fires, campfires, candles, lanterns! Extinguish them all, leaving only the Blessed Flame of Inac. Seeing only that light, Inac will heed our call for victory. Tell everyone. Seek the fires! Put them out! All of them, out! Go!"

Little by little, he roused the gawking crowd from their terror and gave them purpose. With his acolytes still tending the pyre, a Blessed Flame, he recruited the people of Fixer City as his followers, insisting they spread the word. When he stumbled upon Loni's followers, he used them to spread the word even further. Methodically, Sedgan's teams swept through the camp and put out fires, including those caused by the arsonist. With all of Fixer City united, the fires would not be allowed to spread.

Sedgan avoided looking up, knowing it was useless. Either the dragons would burn them all, or they would not. If they did not, Sedgan would have Fixer City in order.

He would have to find Loni later.

Chapter 10

Rairn's face was unmistakable in the twisting smoke of the pyre. Tohmas rose to his feet. Facing the specter with a crowd watching was unfortunate, but it seemed unlikely Rairn's returned spirit was going to oblige him by moving to a private setting.

A hundred folktales played over in Tohmas' mind. Ghosts belonged in legends, not in life. Was Totho unable to catch the soul of the dead prince? Had the Wind God sent the soul back to confront his killer?

"Traitor and murderer!" the ghost shouted over the gasping, slowly receding crowd. "I lie dead because of you."

Tohmas shook his hand to clear a tremor. SoulBurner's power pulsed in its sheath, comforting him against the works of Totho. Inac was with him, but he did not know if it would be enough to stop another god. The God of Wind had dominion over death and spirits. The crowd was peeling away, although many people remained frozen. They were pinned between a rockface, the pyre, and the rise with the canopy for the princes. While he recognized a panic would be potentially deadly, he did not yet know how to defuse the threat.

"Silly illusion," Darknim grumbled, rising from his seat on the ground beside Tohmas. "Simple too. People will believe anything."

Tohmas' heart steadied with reluctance. "It's a spell?" he stuttered.

DoomDragon cocked a thick eyebrow at him. "Glows yellow. Wizard!" he called, glancing over his shoulder to where Seria was slowly rising. "Cast your magic sight. I see powers at work here."

"You can see magic?" Tohmas snapped, too shocked to keep his voice soft.

Darknim gave him a bemused look. "The *visaln* of many Northlanders manifest in that sort of vision. She can confirm it. It is magic."

Tohmas could not help himself: he released a sigh of relief. He had enough trouble dealing with celebrants. He had no idea how to handle an emissary of the gods. Magic, on the other hand, he understood.

With a hand ready over SoulBurner's hilt, Tohmas stepped out from under the shelter. "Sabian!" Carsh's follower tilted his head in acknowledgement. "If I can lure the caster out, put a knife in him." The boy slunk away like a serpent into the grass, a blade in each hand. "Rairn!" Tohmas called next, and the crowd stilled, watching him. "You look terrible!"

The specter had grown to twice the size of a person, but Tohmas felt the power of its stare lessen now that he knew the truth of the illusion.

"My death is on your hands, Prince of Galanth. The favor of the gods has left you!"

"Will you not answer me?" Tohmas asked. "I am told this is a spell. Is it pre-written? Unable to—"

"Your mission to the north will meet with despair and destruction. You will fail, and you will fall into Inac's fourth hell, there to burn for eternity!"

"SoulBurner disagrees with that," Tohmas answered, moving toward the pyre. The crowd jostled to let him through, the fringes thinning as people snuck away. A group of protectors followed a dozen paces behind Tohmas, but Sabian, still stalking, made a circuit.

"Killer! Traitor! Murderer! You will meet the justice of the fires!" the specter cried fiercely.

The crowd withdrew further from Tohmas.

Tohmas paused in front of the fire, under the swirling smoke that was making the shape of the Prince of Barlaby. Seeking to steal back the authority of the God of Wind, Tohmas searched and found Celebrant Calanor standing stoically at the head of the pyre.

"Tell me, Celebrant of the Gust, is this specter truly of Totho?"

Calanor's eyes were sparkling in amusement, his smile hidden by the beaded scarf. From beside his celebrant, Acolyte Timon spoke the words Celebrant Calanor had given him.

"This is no specter, only smoke," the boy declared loudly.

Of course, Tohmas mused. Calanor was untouchable; wizard magic could not affect him. He probably could not even hear the words that resounded over the crowd.

"If you are merely an illusion, then you are not going to like this!" Tohmas called up.

He closed his hand over SoulBurner's hilt. The red aura burst out, surrounding Tohmas in light despite the blade remaining sheathed. The power of the sword seemed stronger, perhaps in answer to the magic that needed dispelling, and even Tohmas blinked in surprise. When the dots cleared from his vision, the specter in the smoke was gone.

Letting go of SoulBurner for the moment, for he knew it would make him invisible to the caster if they were watching via magic, Tohmas turned to the crowd.

"You will have to do better than that, wizard! Your ruse has been revealed. Show yourself!"

Under the canopy, the other princes stood now with their prime protectors at hand, making Tohmas sharply miss Carsh. Sabian still stalked in the crowd, but the boy had not developed a knife dancer's sense for magic. Seria, standing among the princes, had cast Spell Sight but offered no insight either.

"Murderer!" bellowed the still-disembodied voice of the Prince of Barlaby. "You will bring only ruin to all who follow you."

The spell for the voice must be beyond the reach of the light. The ghost is oblivious to its own destruction.

But while the specter declared Tohmas' doom to a crowd that was no longer listening, a new spell appeared.

Seria shouted in warning, but Tohmas could not see what her shining vision showed her. The gust of wind that rushed against him forced Tohmas three steps toward the blazing fire of the pyre. Against the gale, Tohmas brought his hand over SoulBurner. The red light destroyed the magic, stopping the wind and saving both Tohmas and his protectors from crashing into the pyre.

Tohmas did not move forward despite the heat from the fire behind him. "Coward! Do your worse, demon! By Inac's power, I stand against you."

Wind blasted away from him, directed at the canopied area instead of Tohmas.

Tohmas could not be targeted so long as he held SoulBurner, and BookKeeper Olmer had already laid spells of protection over both Prince Sol and Prince Dragal. Seria seemed to have defended DoomDragon, for the Northlander withstood the blast easily. This left only Prince Barnon without defense when the magic struck. The choice was wind, perhaps to further the illusion of the ghost and the role of Totho. Along with the Prince of Rabarch, the three prime protectors were tossed back. Thunder sounded in the clear day, and the crowd cowered.

"Bringer of death and despair! Your way is cursed! Your mission is fated to fail!" Rairn's voice shouted. Dark laughter traveled around the pyre like a trail of whispers. Many ducked their heads in fear, but Sabian lunged at the sound.

"False!" The high, unbroken voice of the Acolyte of Totho cut through the noise. "Lying, false ruse! Your sacrilege will not be permitted! Behold the true power of the wind!"

The wind rose again, blustering in from every quarter. Muttering curses, Tohmas climbed back up the hill to the canopied area. Prince Barnon had taken a seat, cradling a clearly broken arm as a cutter saw to him. The other protectors hit by the first wind lay further back, having fallen from the crags. No cutter tended them; it was too late. Tohmas was, for the first time, grateful for Carsh's absence; he had been spared the fate of the other protectors.

Seria scampered clear, but Bookkeeper Olmer was caught by the aura when Tohmas placed himself among the princes and openly drew SoulBurner to defend them. Tohmas got a glare for the error. Ignoring the man, Tohmas faced the rising wind, SoulBurner glowing in his hand.

It took him another moment to recognize that this wind was not magic. The gusts easily passed through the red light of Inac. DoomDragon confirmed it: "No auras this time!"

His white robes flapping, Celebrant Calanor stood at the head of the crowd, the pyre at his back spiraling up into a pillar of fire. Tohmas had seen the winds once before during a battle, but those had been controlled to push back the enemy's attacks. This time, there was no order. A tornado raged across the fire, tossing flames and embers in a whirlwind so high that Tohmas thought it would light the stars ablaze. The crowd's

shouting could barely be heard as the gusts encircled, then swarmed, the people. The canvas canopy over the princes ripped from its poles and flew away. The remaining people ducked low to keep their feet. When Tohmas next met Seria's eyes, they were her natural pale blue, her Spell Sight dispelled by Calanor's untouchable magic.

The power of Totho, God of Wind, was made manifest in all its raw, uncontrolled temper.

With each pass, the wind lost strength, like a passing sigh released. The whirlwind slowed, reducing to a flurry around the celebrant by the pyre. After another few heartbeats, Calanor's robes were the only movement, gently swaying in a breeze that finally allowed the people to draw breath.

A long moment passed before anyone moved. The pyre, to Tohmas' shock, was entirely out. Cloaks, hats, and occasionally shoes were strewn about, and Tohmas could not even see where the canopy had landed. Still, unlike the gusts that had thrown the prime protectors to the ground so violently, no one had been knocked over by Totho's storm.

Celebrant Calanor, not looking the least bit weary, calmly returned to his place by the extinguished pyre, folded his maimed arms together into his sleeves and lowered his head. If needed, Tohmas had no doubt the man could repeat the windstorm.

When there were no more curses and threats of eternal damnation, Tohmas assumed the illusion of Rairn had been dispelled.

Tohmas cleared his throat and slowly sheathed SoulBurner.

Having no chair—they had been swept away—Tohmas took a seat as imperiously as he could on the ground. DoomDragon quickly joined him. The other prince joined one by one.

He then located red robes among the gathering. He could not see Celebrant Sedgan, but the acolytes were present. "Acolytes of Inac, fetch Inac's Blessed Flame. We must relight this pyre," Tohmas declared.

As an acolyte ran for the Temple waggons, the remaining crowd alternated between staring at Tohmas and staring at Calanor. Neither acknowledged them.

Before the new light arrived, a rumble rolled over the area like long thunder.

Tohmas' gut clenched, a feral urge to run flooding over him. The crowd froze like frightened ground squirrels.

CHAPTER 10

They all looked up.

Atop a nearby peak, perched like a gull on a ship's mast, an enormous red dragon had landed. It was distant enough for the roar to echo but close enough to still cast a long, terrifying shadow over the encamped forces.

Tohmas wanted to crawl into a den and hide, lest he be eaten. He was a skilled warrior but standing against a dragon was folly. His first thought was to escape.

He touched his hand to SoulBurner a second time, using the presence of the brief flame to mutter a quick prayer. *We prepared for this.*

He just had to hope that the plans had succeeded. There was nowhere to run.

The screech of the dragon sounded again, and Tohmas thought it was laughing.

In the Circle's hut, the shaking ground prevented Kitable from finishing his spell. He could focus enough to hold the magic but could only build it piece by piece between waves of crashing earth. It was taking too long.

And Terant appeared to recognize what Kitable was doing: casting. A full cast occupied his attention.

Terant dropped the open earth magic, leaving the earthquake to peter out. Replacing the black aura, the gusting aura of destruction surrounded Terant in a blink.

Kitable's stomach dropped. He paused casting, unable to advance the spell he was building but too stubborn to let it drop.

Four elements, destructions. All.... Kitable tasted bile in his throat. *That's a Disintegration spell.*

He had no defenses remaining that would save him. He restarted casting, building the spell as quickly as he could accurately, hoping he would have time to add something once through it, but Terant's casting was fast. In too-few words, the Disintegration spell was completed and shot at Kitable like a spear, aiming to dissolve his very essence into nothing.

An orange-shimmering wolf landed between Kitable and the enemy caster, taking the blow in her broad shoulders. The spell ripped through

her fur, opening her to muscles and spattering blood along the broken ground and the Northlanders' elders.

Showing no sign of pain, the wolf pivoted on the uneven terrain and planted herself between Kitable and Terant, bearing her teeth widely.

Kitable had no idea how the wolf had not been destroyed. A Disintegration spell of that magnitude destroyed all elements of life. It should have rendered the wolf, or any other creature, into nothing.

Able to focus as the quaking stopped entirely, Kitable spotted the outline of a man overlaying that of the wolf. Thanks to Spell Sight, he recognized the thought magic; Elder Tril was manifesting a thought into a physical being. The wolf was not real, and Terant had *not* included the element of thought in his Disintegration spell.

Tril's aspect, the animal spirit, had taken physical form. And he was not the only one.

An orange-shining bear ran into Terant at full speed bowling over the wizard despite his Molded Shield. One of Terant's spells threw the bellowing north bear back, but when Terant next raised a hand to attack, a hawk swooped in. Terant had to duck to protect his eyes. Although his shield kept the bird at bay, the instinct to protect his head saw the master wizard fumble a word and lose his spell.

Kitable hurried to finish his full cast. He held the last word, waiting for an opening.

The other Circle members took their turns harassing the Tanble caster. A fox lunged in from the side, forcing Terant back then falling as a hare got under his foot. When Terant finally regained his footing, he came face to face with the Prime Protector of Galanth.

Freed with Shimmer's assistance, Carsh wasted no time. Knives joined with the claws, talons, and teeth as they sought a way through the impenetrable Molded Shield.

Terant's hovering spells were being destroyed as well. The hare underfoot knocked aside the light of one of his bound magic spheres as it hopped over the rubble behind Terant. The hawk took out another over the man's head as if snaring a sparrow. The bear sliced through a spell meant to stop force magic. Somehow, the aspects picked off the hovering spells, striping Terant steadily of his defenses.

Kitable held his spell, looking for a way through the crowd that clamored over the stones.

A binding spell from Shimmer slipped into the room and touched Carsh's knife. Spell Sight identified the minor destruction spell. *Clever,* Kitable admitted. By binding Carsh's blade instead of attacking Terant directly, she bypassed the deflective spells between her and the enemy. The blade pierced through the Molded Shield to the hilt. The tip reached Terant, and for the first time, Terant bled.

The wizard paused as if in shock. With a word, he activated a burst spell.

Everyone in the hut was blasted backward against the crumbling walls. Some of the aspects crashed into the slate walls of the hut hard enough to crack the stones. Neither hawk nor bear rose.

Kitable was knocked back, but he braced himself against the wall and withstood the blast, one thought in his mind.

Path's open.

He completed the spell.

Terant's Molded Shield shattered.

"Carsh! Throw!"

Crouched by the wall where he had been slammed, Carsh snatched one of his remaining knives with a shaking hand and sent it flying across the hut.

As the knife left the Rydan's hand, Master Terant activated a remain hovering spell. A small Deflector appeared in front of his head and chest, protecting him from the knife.

Kitable's hope fell, but he had underestimated Carsh. The knife hit the wizard's hip below the deflector, sending Terant spinning into the broken ground. Whether Carsh had predicted the defensive magic or sensed it as he had released his blade, Kitable did not know. From the Rydan's self-satisfied snarl, Kitable assumed the Rydan had hit exactly where he had aimed.

Terant did not immediately rise, grumbling and cursing from the ground. When Kitable felt a sudden lifting of magic around him, he realized he had been mistaken.

The Seal had been dismissed.

Kitable threw two spells: the first was to stun the Terant and the second was a Tracker. Magic answered from a bead on Terant's necklace; a defense against thought magic stopped the attack. Terant vanished,

somehow casting a Relocation spell faster than Kitable had thought possible. In place of the caster, a small stone wore his Tracker spell.

"*Daem'd flya!*" Carsh cursed as he slowly rose from his crouch. His right arm—the arm he had made the final throw with—hung at a strange angle, and he cradled it against his chest with his blade-bearing left hand. Blood seeped out of a hundred small scratches from flying debris, and Carsh's left wrist had lost its grass bracelets. Unhampered by his pain, Rydan was, like Kitable, already assessing the rest of the hut.

The bear and hawk were gone, but the rest of the orange-lit creatures stood panting beside their elders scattered around the room by the broken ground. Elder Tril's shoulder was bleeding under his singed white pelt as he patted his wolf and let her leave to nurse her injury. The rest of the aspect blinked out of existence one by one, leaving behind the injured Circle members. None had escaped unscathed.

Tril retrieved his fallen staff and slowly made his way over the rubble and stilted ground to Kitable.

"You never mentioned you could do that," Kitable said.

Tril merely looked pained. "We did not know we could, but it has not saved us."

Of the seven that had started, only five elders were conscious.

"I have called for cutters," Shimmer whispered from beside Kitable, before dropping her bag beside one of the unconscious elders. Shimmer was breathing hard from her exertions, and her face was red from more than just blush, but her shields were all still in place. He assumed she was experiencing mild spell burn from the extended casting. Checking, Kitable found he too had a faint burn remaining in his muscles, but it was easy to ignore. He was not enervated, not this time.

The first Northlander Shimmer checked wore the fur of the north bear over his shoulders. Blood stained the pelt red from his shoulder to belt. It took only a few moments for Shimmer to shake her head and move on to the second unconscious Northlander. Kitable was relieved when the apothecary started rummaging in her bag, for that seemed to imply there was hope for the hawk-feathered man.

"Two aspects have been slain," Tril reported, "and Vat will not rise for us. Master Terant's duty is done. The Circle is broken."

The weight of the world became heavier. Kitable slumped against the nearby wall. Despite everything, they had failed to change the event. He hated divination more than ever.

"What does that mean?" Kitable asked. "Can you not find another to replace the elder? Can you find the aspects? You did, Tril. You found..."

Kitable trailed off as the elder's eyes went distant. The Northlander's body sagged as if his knees would give out.

At some point, the multi-way shield blocking the *visaln* had been lost. Visions were pouring into Tril's mind again, and the elder swayed under the impact. Kitable reached out to hold the Northlander's arm, steadying him.

After a dozen heartbeats of silence, the elder opened his eyes and a tear fell. Despite his obvious sorrow, Tril was smiling weakly.

People had finally braved the Earth Lodge and were now helping the wounded elders move out over the cracked earth and rubble and into the arms of cutters and Northlander healers. Kitable spared them a glance, but none dared approach him or Tril.

"Aspects can be recovered," Tril said, "but when and how is their choice, not ours. A seventh member, however, might not even be born yet. It is rare that seven live during the same lifetime. It took over a hundred years for us to form this Circle. It may be another hundred before it is complete again."

"What happens if there is no Circle?" Kitable asked.

Elder Tril lost the slight smile he had been holding. "Without a Circle, no one can name the DoomDragon. Without DoomDragon, there is no unity. Tradition no longer holds the Northlanders to Darknim." He let out a long sigh. "His own tribe will still follow him, but the others will go home. This war is no longer their concern. We become divided."

Kitable winced and leaned heavily against the wall in disappointment. Tohmas was not going to be happy if half his army marched in the wrong direction in the morning.

When the wall gave a groan, Kitable quickly stood tall.

"We should probably get out of here," he said, shooing people out quickly with the elders in tow. Once everyone was out, Kitable let his Backdoor spell drop. He was not surprised when the entire hut went down with it.

Once he was certain the injured Northlanders were in good hands, Kitable made his way back to give Tohmas the bad news. Carsh, still cradling his arm, walked on his left. Shimmer, flushed and exhausted, left their company for Fixer City once out of the Northlander camp. She invited Kitable to call on her but recommended he let her sleep for a while.

They had re-entered the Esparan side of camp when a rumble shook the air.

Demons, Kitable cursed. Tril hadn't mentioned this...

A red dragon was perched on a peak overlooking the camp.

Come on, Dust, Kitable thought. If he had to, Kitable could do the illusion. It would be difficult, having not prepared for it, but...

Sure enough, soaring in from Fixer City, a silver dragon landed on another peak across from the red dragon. It was small for a silver dragon, but half-again as big as the red dragon it faced. It would be enough to scare off the Red, Kitable was certain. The Silver was bigger and...

To Kitable's dismay, a second red dragon joined the first, casting down stones as it landed. Together, the pair snarled at Dust's illusionary Silver.

Two Reds might be an issue. Could the pair contend with such a small Silver? Dust clearly hadn't been strong enough to make the illusion truly intimidating. They could be bold.

But before Kitable could add another illusion, a second low-flying dragon came up from the far side of the valley. This Silver was massive, far bigger than Kitable had thought possible for a caster of Dust's prowess. The new Silver landed at the base of the mountain under Dust's first illusion, yet could reach the top of it by just standing straight.

"Well done, Dust," Kitable muttered as he broke into a run, heading for Fixer City. "And you were complaining about holding *one* illusion."

He rushed for Fixer City, seeking Match and Mixer to help the apothecary. He waved at Celebrant Sedgan when he passed the man, but the celebrant hardly had a moment to wave back, so engrossed was he in a sermon of some kind.

The enormous bull dragon at the base of the mountains reached up the side of the peak and sniffed loudly at the illusion perched above. Then, shaking Kitable's confidence, it let loose a roar far beyond anything Kitable had heard before. In that moment, Kitable knew the truth.

CHAPTER 10

Dust couldn't cast two illusions of that magnitude. The apothecary could not even cast something as big as the bull dragon. That dragon wasn't an illusion.

They'd attracted the attention of a real silver dragon, as well as the two Reds.

There were no plans for this contingency.

"Demon shit," was all Kitable could say.

When first the red dragon appeared, Dust stared at it, feeling like a rabbit watching an eagle swoop in. He did not know where Shimmer was. That was his greatest fear. She had been with Prince Tohmas. She could be right in the heart of the army. The dragons would no doubt target the command tent first.

Even now, the roosting red dragon clutched at a nearby peak overlooking the army. Its thick neck arched out, the spines along it bristling. Dust figured it was probably licking its lips by now, picking targets from the masses fleeing below it.

Shimmer was in danger.

That was enough to spur Dust to action. Dust clambered onto the roof of his vardo, from which he had a clear view over the waggons of Fixer City. He smelled smoke but convinced himself it was his overactive imagination worrying about the dragons.

He took three long, deep breaths, just as he had taught Shimmer to do before performances, blocked out everything else, and brought his mind to the magic he had been rehearsing.

Rabbits have a nasty kick, he reminded himself. He would have to as well.

He pulled on the magic, piece by piece. It grew increasingly difficult as the power rose within. His hands shook, but he was unsure if it was the fear or the exertion. As he pushed through his limit, his muscles protested the magic he had collected, begging him to release it.

Probably not even half of what Kitable could do.

Speaking clear, calm words was a performer's skill. Dust carefully articulated every word of the spell from memory. He fed the magic into each layer of the illusion, starting with the color, moving onto the

roughened surface, then to blocking the light so it would cast a shadow. Details were placed, from the dragon's partially transparent ear flaps to the glowing amber of its enormous cat-like eyes. Horns and scales were built in shinning white.

Releasing the spell was like jumping into a pit; Dust felt like he was falling. He feared hitting the ground, for it felt like a long drop, but he held the powers under his control, guiding it through the spell he had created.

Shimmer needs me. He had to stop the red dragons.

The silver dragon he created soared into the sky above the camp, starting at the vardo and flying out to the nearest mountain peak. Following Dust's manipulations, the manor-sized beast landed on a peak over the army and extended its serpentine neck toward the red dragons.

The Reds mirrored the action, as if surprised. Unified, they roared.

Dust did not have the energy to hold the illusion and add sound. His Silver simply remained on the peak, peering at its adversaries.

Red dragons were violent and vicious, known best for killing herds of horses for fun, not just food. They were smaller than the black dragon someone had slain to end the Northlander war, and their scales were supposedly weaker, but still no mundane weapon would cut a Red's scale. The silver dragon was a metallic dragon, larger and stronger than any other dragon in the world. The scales were meant to be invincible even to other dragons, and their fire burned the hottest of any. If anything could make two Reds hesitate, it was a Silver.

The Reds seemed to be considering the illusion cautiously, like a beast spotting prey but unable to scent it. So focused was Dust on reading the intentions of the enemy's Reds, he did not at first realize his dragon was no longer alone on its perch.

The ground shook. A grumble rolled over the camp. A second silver dragon, twice the size of the mountain, landed beside Dust's illusion.

Dust's throat went dry. *A real dragon?*

The silver bull-dragon landed in the valley between peaks, then pulled itself up to reach the top and sniff at Dust's illusion. Dust felt his stomach drop past his knees, and he thought he would be sick. The beast was, by far, the greatest dragon he had ever seen, and it, unlike the illusionary dragon, was *real*. A real Silver. There were supposedly only a handful such dragons in the world. Dust could not breathe.

Boulders crashed down from the peak under the Silver's claws, thankfully too distant to fall in the camp. Dust remained frozen, unable to adjust his illusion in his shock.

The bull-dragon, his silver scales glistening like moonlight, stretched his neck around the illusion to examine all sides, then snorted. A tendril of fire flickered out in what Dust assumed was disbelief.

The Reds were clearly hesitant now, and their growls of challenge died off into echoes down the valley. Side by side, the two enemy dragons stared at the pair of Silvers.

The bull dragon turned to examine the distant Reds. It roared and, with a flap of its wings, created a small landslide from the peak. Fire followed, flowing like star-lit water into the sky. The blue-hot flames left no smoke behind.

Dust held on to his illusion but could not find the power to move his fake dragon.

He did not need to. When the red dragons did not back down, the Silver snapped at the sky and took flight. It cast a long, wicked shadow over the camp as it went, and Dust thought he could hear the collective gasp of the people below. Ignoring the humans, the Silver flew at the invading dragons.

Both Reds backed up, then took flight. Faster than Dust had expected for a creature of that size, they were behind over the horizon.

The Silver did not give chase but, roaring a new challenge—Dust thought he would have to mimic the sounds should he ever need to impersonate a dragon—it turned its charge sharply and dove into a nearby cliff face. Blowing fire, it tore at the mountain like a crazed animal, sheering off chunks of rock and tossing them like meteors through the sky. The soldiers below scattered although Dust had no doubt many failed to get clear in time.

"Papa?" Dust's illusion flickered as he lost focus. Giving up, he let it drop. All eyes were on the enormous bull-dragon attacking the mountainside now. The Reds had fled.

He paused to swallow a rejuv pill, feeling his head foggy from fatigue. Having used an unprecedented amount of magic, he had the woolly feeling of enervation as well as the dull ache of spell burn.

Dust made his way down the ladder and, with trembling hands, tied up the mules, just in case. It gave him something to do and made him ready for any retreat call.

"Papa..." Shimmer tried again as she helped him with the mules.

He shook his head. "I don't know, Shim. Not sure where that dragon came..."

He trailed off as Wisavi Kitable arrived, the master wizard strolling briskly yet somehow not looking harried. His eyes were raised toward the mountain peaks, where the Silver gave a final roaring curse and blasted another gout of fire into the mountain. It cut a deep cavern of molten stone into the peak.

Dust's chest released. *Of course it's not real.* Kitable must have been able to augment his illusion, making it vast superior to Dust's. *Didn't need me at all,* Dust mused.

Running a hand over his goatee, Dust let out a sigh. "Well done, Master Kitable. I... I thought it was real. Amazing." He wanted to sound enthusiastic but his panic had sapped him of all energy.

Kitable cocked his head, frowning. "I have nothing to do with that dragon, Weaver. That is no illusion."

The three casters stood for a moment by the immobile vardo. The mules flattened their ears, their normally passive stance anxious.

The dragon took up a place atop the mountain it had smashed and watched for the return of the Reds, the silver scales glistening.

"It seems friendly enough," Shimmer said brightly. "I mean, unless you are that particular mountain. Aren't Silvers usually indifferent to humans?" She glanced at Dust for confirmation. "From what I recall, they don't usually eat us."

"Even so, I think we should get moving," Dust replied, his distress creeping up. He put his back to the dragon, trying to think about something else.

"I agree," Kitable replied. The master wizard glanced back up at the beast. "I will keep an eye on it, in case it develops a sudden interest in us."

There was no confidence in Kitable's voice.

Finding a place overlooking the forces of Galanth had been simple; the army had surrounded itself with mountains. Rakhund had made the trip on the back of one of his dragons, although he had climbed the mountain himself to keep the beasts out of sight until Master Terant was ready. From a peak on the east of the valley, he had a view over the enemy's forces.

The funeral pyre would make a good target once Terant drew off Kitable. They did not know what Kitable could do against the dragons, but they did not want to give him the chance. Further, Terant had taken his previous defeat by Kitable personally and seemed enthusiastic about killing the wizard. Rakhund was content to let the wizards deal with each other. The farther he was from them, the better.

Once he saw the spells, Rakhund called in the dragons and sat back to watch the destruction.

The arrival of a Silver interrupted.

This mountain range was the perfect home for a Silver, Rakhund admitted, but he had never thought to seek one here. Silvers were even rarer than Blacks, and their scales even more powerful. If he could capture and control that little female now, while she was still young, then Rakhund would never have to replace another dragon. It would be harder to enchant a Silver than the Reds, but it would be worth every...

The arrival of the bull-dragon changed everything. There was a true prize. He was mature—surely a difficult mind to break—but he was spectacular.

When the Silver took flight, Rakhund sent his Reds dragons away. He would have to plan this. He could not expect to defeat such a magnificent beast without—

The Silver screeched, and Rakhund heard the word translated by the spells he used for monitoring his Reds.

"Demon!" the Silver shouted, turning sharply from its path in pursuit of the Reds. It flew straight for Rakhund's ledge.

He had been scented.

Rakhund bolted into the tunnel at his back, casting as he ran. Old spells, long neglected, burst around him. With every ounce of energy he had, he coated himself with defenses against dragon fire and the crush of teeth. He ran faster than any human could, aided in the dark cavern by his unusual eyes. Still, as fast as he ran, he was still in the tunnel

when the impact of the Silver rumbled against the ledge at his back. The collapse of stone, shaken loose by the sheer weight, crashed noisily around him. Louder still, both within the tunnel and down the side of the mountain, was the rush of dragon fire.

The silver dragon's fire cut a swath into the rock on Rakhund's heel. He snarled out another spell, insulating himself from the sweltering heat that ripped into his flesh. The unprotected stone of the cavern melted away, dropping Rakhund a dozen feet as the blaze widened the tunnel.

The dragon paused to inhaled.

Rakhund skidded against molten rock, protected by his spells but still stumbling on the uneven footing. Falling to his knees, the molten rock solidified against the cloth of his cloak, weighing him down. The heat scalded his scales, but he could not take the time to brush the searing pebbles off.

A fresh column of fire cascaded toward him.

Wrapping himself in magic, Rakhund crouched low and closed his eyes. He sought his core, where the energy ran deep and strong. He pulled on it consciously, driving his living force into a sphere around him.

The fire crashed into the sphere like a kick. He slid down the tunnel of melted rock as more stones flowed away. The hole in his stomach, his connection to his Reds, tightened, and he felt it shift, strained by maintaining by defending against the Silver's fire.

Steeling himself, Rakhund clutched at his chest, commanding control and refusing to give up the Reds. The shield around him flickered. The heat of the immolating fires burned into him, quickly reducing his cloak to ash.

Just as the scales on his arms and feet began to blister, the Silver paused for a breath again. Into the break, Rakhund dropped all spells and found the dragons' key. Taking the gold-encrusted object in his hand, he commanded the dragons home.

With a final blast of magic, Rakhund smashed the wall of the mountain in front of him, escaping to the outside.

He half fell and half jumped down the side of the mountain, skidding down snow. At length, his descent paused next to a mountain lake. He went straight for the water, as cold as it was, and used it to hide his scent. He lay in the water, floating on his back as his blisters screamed.

He waited.

Nothing followed. A dozen heartbeats passed, then another dozen. The Silver did not pursue. Rakhund slowly eased himself to the edge of the lake.

Not merely mature; that Silver had been old enough to have survived the Demon Wars. The wind had betrayed Rakhund and carried his scent to the bull-dragon. What had followed made sense.

Rakhund pulled himself out of the water, picking cooled, molten stones off his scales and the remnants of his robes. He was tempted to seek out the Silver, but if the dragon was indeed a veteran of the Demon Wars, no binding would hold it now. Even Rakhund's bindings had been broken by the will of dragons before.

He would have to wait until the army was clear of the mountains. A pair of Reds had no hope against a mature Silver, let alone two Silvers, and Rakhund had no intention of giving the bull-dragon a second chance at cooking him.

But the Silver had been wild and unenchanted. They were territorial. Once the enemy left the territory of the dragon, Rakhund would have another opportunity. That would have to be enough.

Escaping the assault of the Circle and its allies, Terant fell against the wall in his courtyard.

He was not surprised by the visitors this time. As he took a moment to catch his breath, the youngest intruder gestured subtly. A spell tightened in his mind and, defenseless, he could do nothing to hinder it.

The man with the gem in his forehead shrugged, a small smile on his cynical face. "Even easier than last time," he said, the words translated by the magic now bound in Terant's mind.

Terant pushed himself to stand, knowing he was vulnerable but not wishing it to be obvious. Gritting his teeth, he checked the knife in his leg. *I'm bleeding but not badly, not yet.* He would have to use a pain destruction spell and have a Cautery spell ready before he touched the deeply imbedded blade.

He wiped his bloodied hands on his robes as he looked up. "I was busy. Have you a reason for your visit?"

The group of three had changed. While the younger man and woman were the same, they had brought a different lead woman. She was the eldest he had seen, but her wrinkles were all around her mouth, making her face into a permanent glower. Her hair was white and short, and the golden symbol on her chest seemed to pulse with a heartbeat.

"You have succeeded," the new woman informed him.

Terant glared at her. "He got through your Seal," he grumbled.

"We only promised to delay him, not defeat him for you," the man holding the thought spell answered. When Terant looked at the stranger, he noticed the gem in the forehead was now red instead of blue. *A different man, a different stone, or a different mood?* It was hard to tell.

"You should have had enough time," came the original woman's response.

Terant scoffed. "A dozen destructions landed, and yet the only damage was to those pelts they wear! I could have done more, if I had had the time, but Master Kitable got there fast enough to distract me."

As he gingerly checked his chest wound, which was not deep and could be bandaged easily, Terant assessed the three strangers. Each moved independently and spoke without shared sentences.

No Linking this time, he concluded.

"Still," the white-haired woman said, shrugging dismissively, "you have broken their Circle."

The man among them made a long face. "These pelts they share with the beasts can dispel. They stole his magic."

"They can defend their masters, Gannon," corrected the younger woman with the streaked hair. The gems along her knuckles and eyes flickered in their own light, matching the hue of her ribbon robes. "They are the bridge, remember."

"Bridge of what?" Terant asked them. "You said they were abominations. Why?"

The older woman snorted disdainfully and turned away. "We are done."

The other two nodded in agreement.

"Then why come here at all?" Terant demanded, pushing off from the wall and regretting it. His leg was not strong enough to hold him. He had to catch himself from falling with his staff.

CHAPTER 10

The smile of the youngest man was malicious. "We were waiting for your failure. You disappoint."

"Today, he disappoints," corrected the woman with the streaked hair. "When next we call, perhaps he will not be as successful."

"One can hope," the young stranger said as the older woman completed a spell that opened a glowing portal. As Terant had multiple defenses in his courtyard against such spells, he was again deflated. He said nothing further while they left.

Once they were gone, he focused on his wounds, hoping he would never see any of them again.

Chapter II

With his dog Stitches on his heel, Darak started cursing before he arrived at the prince's tent, and he did not stop once he found himself in the presence of the princes.

Can't be simple, can they?

While they awaited the arrival of others, Prince Barnon and Prince Tohmas sat down around the main table, Prime Protector Carsh hovering nearby. Darak only had time to note that the Prince of Rabarch did not have his own prime protector before Prince Tohmas called him over.

Darak searched the room as he made his way over to his patron. Prince Barnon was injured: a bad arm. Carsh was trying to hide it, but he had a similar injury.

"Prince Barnon has lost his cutter, Darak. I offered him your services," Prince Tohmas said. Although the words were mild, they sounded like a command.

Feeling under scrutiny with the second prince's presence, Darak did not immediately object. He hated having the weight of one prince's health on his shoulders, but two...

He tried to find a way to politely refuse, but there were no words. Knowing he was trapped with accepting, Darak then tried to find a way to limit his own involvement, but all he came up with was "I'll give it a shot until someone better can be found."

But who goes first? The prince because he's higher rank, or a prime protector because they need their arm for fighting sooner?

Perhaps sensing his hesitation, Tohmas obliged him by nodding toward the other prince in the room.

"Right," Darak muttered, facing the less imposing prince. "Arm," he said, holding out a hand.

The Prince of Rabarch looked impressed as he extended the wounded limb, an expression Darak had never seen on Tohmas' face. "How did you know it was my arm?"

"Dropped shoulder, rotated in to shield the forearm," he said. He paused. "And you're drinking with your left when you look right handed. Eat this," he said, handing the man a pain pill, "then hold this." He placed a gag in the man's hand. "Squeeze it if you feel the need to hit something." He glared up at the prince. "Don't hit me. Knocking out your cutter guarantees poor service."

Prince Barnon gave him a nervous smile.

As he set the bone, which was thankfully not displaced much, Prince Dragal and Prince Sol arrive, followed by a bald, thin man. Prince Dragal glared around the room, and Darak winced and decided to finish tying Prince Barnon's splint from the other side, putting him farther from the Prince of Clandac. Barnon had been kind enough to squeeze the wooden gag, but Dragal looked ready to hit Darak for the pain he was causing his brother. Although the older man seemed unlikely to do a lot of damage, Darak decided not to push his luck.

Barnon accepted the rest of the administrations, his eyes on his brother. Stubbornly, he placed the splinted arm on the table when it was done. Darak could not tell if the man was trying to prove something or seeking to borrow strength from the other.

Taking a deep breath, Darak called for Stitches. "Didn't know I'd have two arms to work on," he told Prince Tohmas, who seemed to be deliberately ignoring the exchange between the other two princes. "I'll grab another arm splint and be right back," he said. Watching Carsh avoid him had allowed Darak to determine where the break was in the Rydan's arm. He left just as Wisavi Kitable arrived. They all seemed to be waiting for someone.

When he arrived back, Darak was pleasantly surprised that Carsh sat down and extended his arm for treatment without protest. The discussion in the tent was becoming heated. From what Darak could tell, BookKeeper Olmer, seated beside Prince Dragal, was a wizard, and the

conversation was magic related. Much of the frustration and ire was directed at Darknim DoomDragon, who had taken a seat across from the Esparan princes but had a vacant chair on either side of him.

"An impressive feat," the bookkeeper was saying to Prince Dragal.

Master Kitable, standing rigidly by the entrance as if not wanting to enter in further, completed the thought; "A caster who pre-set spells among us without our recognizing and then triggered them from a distance while maintaining a duel with me, Carsh, and the Circle? A dangerously impressive feat. One I do not think any single person capable of."

The bookkeeper's eyes, made large by spectacles, narrowed. "You are suggesting what?"

"Seria was there," Master Kitable replied, but Darak did not know the person the wizard was referring to. He finished wrapping Carsh's arm, trying to reduce the swelling around the break prior to placing the splint.

"She defended DoomDragon," Prince Tohmas replied from his seat on an angle to both DoomDragon and the other princes. The prince's thought was tentative, as if up for discussion.

Darak expected DoomDragon himself to reply, but Master Kitable proved faster.

"How many words did she use for each spell?" Kitable asked.

After a thoughtful silence, BookKeeper Olmer gave the answer; "Usually two."

By the dark expressions of the princes and protectors, this was terribly significant. Darak was lost. He focused on threading the ties on the splint.

"She is an ally," DoomDragon grumbled.

Prince Dragal snarled. "One word of activation per spell. What was the second for? An attack? Now my brothers bleed because of the mislaid trust that I warned you all against!" He pointed at DoomDragon. "That man—" The rest of the sentence was cut off when the Prince of Clandac broke into coughing.

It was a distinctive cough, but Darak pretended not to be paying attention. The prince's cutters would have told him. There was no reason to bring it up.

"I offered you an alliance, Princes of Espar." DoomDragon growled like his namesake and leaned in like a hound lifting his hackles. "You

continue to insult my honor every time we speak. Your bookkeeper used many more words for his casting, but none accuse him."

"I seldom have hovering spells of that nature at hand," BookKeeper Olmer objected. "That was two full casts, I will have you know. Not easily done, especially not that quickly."

"Pity it was not three," Barnon said from his place, lifting his splinted arm. He received a sympathetic look from both of his brothers in reply. The bookkeeper frowned deeply.

When the Northlander's expression darkened, Darak took an involuntary step back. Even Stitches whined and cowered behind Prime Protector Carsh, who watched the exchange with a blade spinning around his left hand. Darak could not tell who the Rydan was watching, but Carsh looked like he wanted to put the knife into whoever it was.

To distract himself from the thought of having to treat a knife wound in addition to the fracture, Darak returned to tightening the splint.

"Who else could have known Rairn well enough to reproduce his voice, his face?" Prince Dragal accused. A cough briefly interrupted. "Who else knew we would all be there? You were sitting on the ground! You were waiting for that gust! Did you think her defenses would not be enough?"

"My Circle is broken because of that attack!" DoomDragon snapped, and Darak started mentally checking his bandage supply. The Northlander had an ax, and all of the prime protectors were putting their hands on their swords. DoomDragon was outnumbered, but by the flush of the man's face, Darak did not think that would stop him.

He tried to focus on Carsh. The Rydan was holding still for the moment.

"And we are crippled for it," Prince Dragal retorted. "Apparently your Circle cannot hide us now, cannot block Master Terant, cannot even keep your rabble in line! How convenient for Marfaie!"

Carsh stepped away from Darak, going to Tohmas' side. Darak was about to chase after the prime protector when a roar made him retreat instead. DoomDragon had leaped to his feet. The Northlander slammed a jeweled carbiron dagger, point first, into the table. "Enough! You Esparan! You impossible Esparan!"

Darak peeked out. Darknim DoomDragon was seething.

"Darknim…" Prince Tohmas said softly.

"Enough, Tohmas! For years, I watched the Esparan kill my people. I finally made peace with them, only to watch my people die *for* them. Now I free myself from that alliance to find myself again betrayed and accused. I will not have it!"

Everyone was standing, and every prime protector had drawn their blades.

Darak swallowed hard. *I don't have enough bandages.*

"Darknim…" came the second attempt from the Prince of Galanth.

DoomDragon cut the prince off with a dismissive gesture that left the dagger standing in the wood. "My Circle is broken. There is no DoomDragon without a Circle, and so I am nothing. Perhaps I could convince them to hold for you, but you are Esparan, you all are Esparan, and I do not think you worth the effort. This alliance is over. I will have nothing more to do with any of you. My people are going home."

Without fear, which Darak thought a feat worthy of a god, Darknim DoomDragon walked past two prime protectors bearing swords and left the tent. In acknowledgement of the prowess of man with the dragon-shaped ax, no one stopped him.

For a long moment, there was silence at the table. The princes took turns staring at the dagger in the table. Despite its obvious value, none dared touch it.

"Dragal, you idiot!" Tohmas exploded, slamming a fist onto the table and making all the occupants at the table jump. "Could you not hold your tongue for even one night? We are days from Marfaie, and you have just halved us!"

Darak, regardless of the circumstances, had never heard Tohmas raise his voice. It set Darak on his heel, but the effect was lost on Prince Dragal; the incensed Prince of Clandac met Tohmas' accusation with a snarl of his own "Terant did that! Losing the Circle means they were divided by—"

"Darknim could have made it work! He could have had some of them stay, but now—"

"You are the one who insisted numbers were not everything, boy," Prince Dragal chided, leaning in to lock stares with Tohmas.

Tohmas growled like Darknim had, his hands spread on the table before him. "But they matter. We needed him!"

While the two princes argued across the table, Prime Protector Carsh plodded back to Darak and extended his splinted arm, allowing Darak to finish tying the knots. Although Darak was surprised Carsh was calm during the argument, Darak did not dare miss the opportunity to work on the Rydan. He consciously closed his gaping jaw and grabbed the leather thongs. He kept one ear on the conversation.

"We are enough," the elder prince said fiercely. "Marfaie is weak and we will—"

"Are you incapable of listening? Did you not hear the account of Master Terant's destruction of the Circle, while the pyre was lit with magic? We have *multiple* wizards against us! We cannot underestimate that! We needed the Northlanders!"

"Wizards do not do well in close quarters, and your Rydans have proven capable enough. Are they not strong enough to rid the world of a single wizard?"

Carsh straightened, and Darak hastened to finish the bandage over the splint. He did not want the man running off now.

But the Rydan only bared his teeth and gave Prince Dragal a wicked grin.

To Darak's shock, Prince Tohmas paused. Clenching his jaw, the Prince of Galanth broke the gaze with Prince Dragal and slowly lowered himself back into his chair.

Prince Tohmas Galanth yielded.

The pause lingered. No one seemed to know what to say until Prince Tohmas finally spoke, his voice defeated.

"I'll have the Rydans bring up in the Pack Runner. He'll be useful against the casters. Since there is nothing I can do to change either of your minds, I am going to have to deal with it. We will be counting on our casters to keep us safe until we reach Arcott, since we have lost the cover of the Circle." Prince Tohmas looked up, checking on the casters. Of the two, only Kitable appeared to be listening. BookKeeper Olmer was looking away, lost in thought or pretending to be. "At least I have SoulBurner. I suggest you guard yourself well, Dragal," Tohmas finished.

With Prince Tohmas sitting at the table with his chin in his hand, no one seemed willing to speak. Then, in a still-strained voice, the prince added, "We will have to reconvene after I have had a chance to consider the situation. Give me few candles, if you would."

The three princes stood cautiously, as unsettled as Darak was by Tohmas' depressed mood.

"We will return at sunset," Prince Dragal agreed, his voice surprisingly mild.

After many glances over half-turned shoulders, the three princes and their prime protectors filed out, taking the bookkeeper with them. Prince Sol waited the longest and paused in the exit as if having something to say. He left without a word into the bright sunlight.

Darak finished off the bandage over the splint and then swapped to the other arm to check a pulse.

"Checking your pulse since you aren't exactly forthcoming about the amount of pain you're in," Darak lied. The pulse was a useful way to measure the impact of the poison from last winter.

Meanwhile, Tohmas rose and went to a chest in search of something.

Master Kitable raised a curious eyebrow at the prince once they were alone. "Tohmas, are you—"

"Demons!" the prince cried, interrupting Kitable by tossing a stone out of the chest and onto the table. Darak lost count of Carsh's pulse as a red-glowing stone hit the table. "Son of a demon-kissing..." Tohmas made a rude gesture at the tent.

Master Kitable's eyes found the shining stone, and his face fell. If there was a curse, he muttered it among a host of other words Darak did not understand.

Carsh's pulse, Darak noted, was higher than it had been the last time he had counted it. *A product of the dark root poisoning, the recent activities, or pain?* At least the Rydan's breathing sounded normal, and he'd taken one pain relief this time.

The voice of the Galanth wizard rose in volume, and Kitable had pulled the drawstring of his tunic off as a tool. While Darak watched with his hand still half aware of the beats under his finger, the string hovered over the wizard's hand. It shook, and even Darak felt something pass over him.

Stitches chose that moment to bark at the wizard. Darak let his attention on the prime protector drop to shush the dog.

The stone on the table went black, but Darak dared not move until he was certain the wizard was not planning on sending out any

more waves of tingles. He absently scratched at Stitches' ruffled ears, feeling uneasy.

"He gone?" asked Tohmas,

The glowering Galanth caster nodded. "Scared away. I guess he didn't want to visit us personally. Considering he would be drawn into a tent with a knife dancer, a wizard, and SoulBurner, I'm not surprised."

Darak now understood the prince's initial gesture; he had been rudely gesturing at a magical observer. Since Kitable had apparently tried to bring the intruder into the open, Darak could not blame whoever it was for leaving. Darak did not fully understand what a "wisavi" was, but he knew that people said it with even more reverence than they had said the word "master."

Darak's opportunity to check Carsh ended; the prime protector left and perched on a chair. Tohmas joined him by retaking his seat and picking up the stone. He fiddled with it, considering its plain surface. He was… smirking?

The wizard chuckled, shaking his head. "You knew someone was scrying. I knew something was up. You never get angry like that."

"Dragal doesn't know that," Tohmas replied, and Darak's jaw dropped. Tohmas had been fooling not just the spying wizard, but also his uncles. *Why was he lying to the other princes?*

Although Darak strongly suspected that the same question was burning in the wizard's mind, Kitable did not voice the query. He let out a long breath and said, "If you need me, I will be in my vardo, keeping my head down and my mouth shut."

"Thank you, Kit," Tohmas said. He leaned back and retrieved something from his pouch. His voice was light again, all pretended ire gone. "If you want something to do, look into this. Several of these were found in the fires in Fixer City. This one was on Sedgan's temple waggon."

Kitable accepted the hairpin Tohmas presented and turned it over, closely examining it. He snapped it in half when he was done his assessment. "No magic in it, but it's unique. Could act as an anchor. I'll investigate." The wizard sighed. "I had not heard that the temple waggons were attacked again. How bad is it?"

Tohmas smiled. "The arsonist wasn't a follower of Inac; didn't know Inac's waggons are fireproof. The rest of the fires were in Fixer City. Thankfully, the damage was contained. We'll be marching out tomorrow

first thing, sticking to the mountains. The Weavers say they think they can get the silver dragon to follow, which will protect us from the reds, for a bit." Darak felt the prince's stare land on him. "But we still need a morale boost."

Darak tried to pack his bandages faster, but the prince's attention to him was obvious.

Kitable clenched the broken pin in his fist and nodded. "Then I'll get to it. I need to keep Terant off our backs for the next three days. The dragons will probably wait until we leave the mountains if the Silver is around. But we'll have to come up with something for attacking Arcott. It's a good run from the mountains. The Silver won't follow that far."

Tohmas nodded thoughtfully, dismissing Kitable.

Darak was about to excuse himself—he had decided on the words to use—when the prince pointed to a chair and commanded, "Sit," in the impossible-to-refuse voice Darak dreaded. Before he knew it, he was sitting in the chair with his hands on the table. Kitable headed out into the day.

"Darak, I need you to help me with a problem."

Darak winced. "Prince Dragal's cutters, I'm sure, have things in hand. They're probably better at this than I am. I don't see that many consumptions in the far south."

The Prince of Galanth cocked his head. "Not what I was going to ask you about but interesting that you noticed. What do you know about his condition?"

Darak blew out his cheeks. "No one survives it," he said, thinking the statement obvious. "He's probably on a concoction to control it. Might keep it from spreading a bit. Eventually his cutters will give him Bella's Mix; a combination of frozen freedom, green powder, and orela seed. Then he'll feel great."

The prince narrowed his eyes. "Why don't they use that more?"

"It'll kill him within two days once he starts on it. But he'll go high and happy!" Darak smiled at the prince. "Not my problem. Not yours either."

The prince shared the smile, put at ease. "I supposed not. What is, however, my problem is the lack of balance. The funeral today made me realize that we have been without a Celebrant of Pari all winter. I need proper spiritual guidance for the Healing waggons during this."

"I agree," Darak cautiously said. "How does this become my problem?"

Stitches knew, Darak was certain, for she slunk forward to lay her head on his lap with a deep groan that echoed perfectly what Darak was feeling.

"I want you to become the Celebrant of Pari for Galanth."

"No!" Darak snapped, surprising Stitches so badly she banged her head on the underside of the table. "I am a fragment of the Healing Hands. I am not even a facet of the Pari! I have no training beyond patching broken limbs! Besides—" he ranted, struggling to stop his voice from rising. Desperation edged in. "Besides, according to my own facet, I am little more than a stagnating acolyte on some days, a disappointment to them on the others. How can *I* become a celebrant? Choose a facet at the least! One of the healing mothers or fathers! You cannot—"

"I can, actually," the prince interrupted. "Turns out I have bookkeepers too, and they know a great deal about the laws of Galanth. Apparently, I can appoint anyone I want as a celebrant. I am appointing you."

Darak's hands went cold. "Why me? Choose a facet, my prince, please. They at least know more about—"

"Taking one of the facets from a Healing waggon means raising one over the others, creating possible resentment. Besides, they are true specialists in only the Healing Hands. You are more worldly," the prince finalized in a firm voice Darak cringed to hear.

"I am a cutter! I am a fragment! An underling! I know even less than they do, and I certainly know nothing about—"

"When do you plant cray seed for harvest in the third mooncycle?"

Darak paused. "Right after New Year's."

"Your father was a farmer," Tohmas reminded him. Darak's head dropped. "You told me yourself that you originally trained to treat animals. That gives you a good understanding of the Beast Master as well. With the Healing Hands already covered, that leaves only mining, which, being from Galanth, you will not need. I doubt you predecessor knew anything about dirt anyway."

"Demons..." Darak groaned as his hand found Stitches' sympathetic head on his lap once more.

"I expect you," the prince said, which Darak interpreted as *I am ordering you*, "to converse with the facets often: use their wisdom. You will be their voice among their celebrants. I will put aside a waggon for you immediately so that you can start running services and collecting a

gathering. I will also inform the other two celebrants so they can include you at their next meeting."

"First of the quartercycle," Darak groused into his lap. "They always meet on the first of the quartercycle."

Even though his head was bowed, Darak knew the prince was grinning when he said, "Then you will have a few days to ready yourself."

"I think this is a bad idea," Darak protested, but he found himself unable to meet the eyes of his patron. Instead, Darak looked at Stitches' dual-colored eyes. She was nudging his hand, and he complacently pet her.

"I think you will be brilliant in the position. Tell me if you need anything."

That was it—a dismissal. Darak was done with Carsh, and now the prince was done with him. He rose slowly from the seat and dragged his feet to the door.

This is not merely a bad idea; this is insanity. Darak made a point of avoiding services, not running them. He hated all the ceremony that came with his cutter's vest and the crushed flower of Pari he wore. He had dedicated himself to preserving life, but he knew nothing about what any of Pari's other aspects wanted of him. *Does Pari see what is happening? Does he care?*

When he reached the door, Darak glared back into the tent. "I should never have told you my name the day you were shot in the shoulder."

The Prince of Galanth laughed. "Probably not! But I am sincerely glad you did, Darak. I do not think anyone else could do this."

That assumes that somehow I can.

Grigson was disappointed.

There were no harried retreats. Even the panic was short-lived. Scrying from his hiding place revealed that the threat had passed. Tohmas' forces had survived, although not unscathed.

As he came out of hiding to join the march, Grigson heard the stories. Hundreds of Esparans were dead, mostly from falling stones knocked by dragons, although a few were credited to the enemy wizards. The dragons had been driven off by the support of Inac. Dragons

were her favorite, and a pair of mighty Silvers had come to defend her champion.

Knowing Inac's graces were fleeting and never manifested, Grigson had to seek further to find the truth. He certainly did not believe Inac had anything to do with it.

When Grigson slipped into Fixer City, it was abuzz with religious fervor, driven by Celebrant Sedgan. Everywhere he turned, there were red ribbons flapping in the mountain wind. The people had taken to drawing the double flame symbol of the goddess on their faces with coal or makeup. Although Grigson did not dare get close to the celebrant himself, he saw Sedgan moving through the crowd, his robes deliberately parted to show off the symbol burned into his flesh over his breastbone.

The dragons took up much of the crowd's attention, yet it was not the only story they told. The fires Grigson had started in Fixer City had been extinguished by Celebrant Sedgan, purportedly to draw Inac's attention to the funeral pyre alone. But that very pyre had been under attack. Some people claimed the ghost of Prince Rairn himself had risen to curse the march, but those few were corrected by the masses, no doubt parroting Celebrant Sedgan's words; the ghost at the pyre had been a spell, and it had been broken.

Only one Esparan Grigson spoke to mentioned an accident in the Northlander camp; a building had collapsed.

Northlanders only had one building, the Earth Lodge. He could not determine if anyone had died in the incident, but he doubted strongly it had been an accident.

His inquiries left him with more questions. Dragons, a fake ghost, and an attack on the Northlander Circle... he needed more information.

Grigson sought out Dust Weaver. The Weavers had been keeping an eye on Master Kitable, Shimmer going as far to associate herself with the ex-companion who sparred with Prime Protector Carsh. If anyone had direct information about the specter at the fire, it would be Dust. He might even know about the Northlander Circle, seeing as they were casters as well.

Grigson found the performer in his shop, Match and Mixer, as the overloaded waggon jostled along the mountain path. Theirs remained one of the few with four good wheels, but he suspected that was because

they used magic for repairs. Around them, the waggons of Fixer City were patched and rigged from the long march through the hills. Even those with metal rims were dented nearly beyond use.

Grigson paced himself with the waggon, then hopped up. Dust started. He had nearly been nodding off in the driver's seat, but a kick of fear—or was it respect—made him suddenly alert.

Smiling banally, Grigson settled into a seat beside Dust. "Busy day. You look tired," he said lightly.

Dust straightened his crinkled, colorful coat. "Exciting times," he replied. "What do you want, Grigson?"

Grigson shrugged. His timing was poor; the waggon stuck a stone and jostled him. He had to put his hand onto his seat to avoid falling out. "Heard there were some impression illusions flying around. Figured you'd know about it."

Dust flinched. After the moment was done, he was again sitting straight and strong. He could not disguise the bags under his eyes, but he betrayed nothing of his exhaustion otherwise. Grigson recognized the tell for what it was; Dust going into character.

"The silver dragon was an impressive illusion, I'll give you that, but well beyond me or Shimmer, Grigson. Kitable probably was—"

Grigson cracked a smile so wide, it distracted Dust from finishing his sentence. "The Silver was an illusion? Not the illusion I meant, old friend, but I appreciate the information!"

Dust regained his train of thought as the waggon hit another small stone, which shot out from under the wheel and clattered into a nearby rock. "It was obvious, Grigson. I figured you had spotted it. It hardly moved! It didn't speak, didn't blow fire... didn't really respond to anything around it. It was big, but that was all it was good for."

Grigson tried to read the man but failed. He *knew* Dust was lying about something, but he couldn't figure out how much was lies. *Could there be pride in those words? Or fear?* Someone powerful enough to create such a huge illusion was someone to watch.

"Perhaps the first illusion was just a decoy," Dust added, leaning over to Grigson as if revealing a great secret. Even the fact that Dust was volunteering information worried Grigson. "The second dragon was more impressive. If that's an illusion, I can't crack it. It's been following us

since." Leaning away, Dust steered the waggon around a boulder, then started the mules down a low, wide slope.

I can play this too, Dust, Grigson thought.

Unwilling to rise to the bait, Grigson did not search for the supposed dragon. Instead, he asked, "Shimmer didn't get tangled in the pyre ghost, did she? She's been hanging out with the wrong type of people."

Dust snorted. "We don't like getting involved. Not my problem."

"Ah yes. First rule if it's not your problem, don't worry about it." He laughed. "But if a ghost was trying to get you or your daughter killed, I'm sure it would become your problem. I could help. I've got contacts. I have ways. We could break from the main group once free of the mountains, head back to StonePeak..."

He trailed off, seeking recognition at the mention of the place and the implicit threat it represented, but Dust was unflappable.

"You know, I've been thinking," Dust said conversationally.

"Dangerous, Dust. Don't do something you will regret," Grigson warned.

He did not quite know what to do with Dust's tiny smile. Even Grigson could not tell if Dust's confidence was well-founded or a bluff, and he had lived with Dust for years. He felt certain he would have recognized a bluff, but he could not believe the words that followed were anything else.

"Grigson, has it occurred to you that I know more about you than you do about me?" Dust asked. "You have a secret held over me, I admit. But the secret is passing in usefulness. And how many secrets do you think I remember? How many have I collected over the years, just in case someone came by, trying to pull me back?"

For the first time, Dust ostensibly sized Grigson up. His words were articulated perfectly. "I walked away. Think about that. I *left* StoneTop. No one stopped me, Grigson. No one came after me. Haven't you wondered why not?"

They reached the end of the slope, and the waggon leveled out. Grigson became aware that his hands gripping the seat were warm. In fact, the seat was getting uncomfortably hot.

"Let's just part on amicable terms. Better for all involved," Dust finished.

Grigson fingered one of his rings, wondering if a spell would be useful. He could try, but Dust might have defenses. And since Grigson had not detected Dust cast, the Heat Shield attacking from below had to be Shimmer's doing. She was nearby.

The mask dropped. Dust's cold, green eyes were set like the stones they passed between. "Do not ever threaten me or my family again, Grigson," the performer said slowly.

Grigson stood, towering over Dust while subtly moving away from the Heat Shield spell. As much as he hated to admit it, fear caught in Grigson's gut. He needed more information. Dust had been powerful enough in his own way. "Better for all involved, today," Grigson agreed. "We'll talk again when we leave the mountains. Think about my offer. Might be safer to be out of Fixer City for the long term."

He was lowering himself from the waggon when it struck another stone, one of a size Dust should have avoided. Losing his grip, Grigson stumbled off less gracefully than he had intended. He spent another few moments brushing the dirt off his knees and hands, watching Fixer City go on without him.

For now, he would let Dust think over the options. Whether they agreed or not, it was obvious Fixer City was becoming a dangerous place. At the least, he would need to confront Dust when Shimmer was out of the way. He did not know yet the extent of her powers.

Need to find another way to get the information, Grigson decided. *Someone closer to Prince Tohmas' command tent and away from the fanatical Fixer City.*

Gathering his stashes and making quick preparations, Grigson then sought the Rydan woman Sori among the Fyrd of Arrow. She was perfect. Her companion was a friend of Prince Tohmas. And although she was Rydan and could be used to alienate the Rydans from the Esparans, she was in fact an outcast, so there was no hierarchy to concern him.

He rotated the Blind Love ring on his finger. Sori had been married before, and although she believed her husband was dead, she'd not been there when Prince Tohmas had killed him. No other person had seen him die.

She would want him back.

Initially, Grigson observed from cover. Sori was a tiny woman. Like a prepubescent girl, she had a thin waist, short legs, and diminutive

breasts. Her hair had probably never seen a comb and lay in tangled trusses she had roughly tied up out of her face with a cloth band. Despite the warming spring, she wore hide and furs. The only Esparan items she used were her shoes, which must have been made for a child to fit her.

She worked at a fire among Esparan tents, patching a legging's knee with her weathered hands. A blue tabard lay beside her on a rock, waiting its turn.

He targeted her and activated the ring. Once he was certain it had landed—he saw her blink in brief confusion—Grigson stepped out from the cover of the army tents.

Her blue eyes narrowed. As the magic reached her mind and twisted her vision, the suspicion faded from her face. The woman stood up slowly, as if afraid of startling him, and she moved her hands widely away from the bone knives she had tucked into her heavy skirt.

"Sori," Grigson called. "Come here."

The magic translated his words into whatever language she needed him to speak, and she answered at a trot. Standing in front of him, the woman's eyes were as wide as a startled deer's.

He had expected as much. She had thought her husband dead, after all. *Thought, but never known for sure.*

What he had not expected was her strike; she lashed out at him with a stinging slap across his face. Taken completely by surprise, Grigson failed to block it.

When she reared back for a second hit, Grigson trapped her wrist in his grip and forced her hand down.

"I will allow one," he said softly. "I have been gone too long to not expect such a reaction. A second, and I will retaliate."

Her eyes went down, to the grass bracelets Grigson wore. He had made sure to weave bones into the grass, and his clothing matched her hide. Even if she did not see his true face through the magic, others could. From his stash, he wore the usual hides of a Rydan, his hair slicked back and his belt stacked with flint knives.

Her eyes on the bracelets, the woman let her arm be lowered.

"Sori?" a voice called from behind them, and the woman shifted, unalarmed, to look behind her. Lance Carraway, High Guardsman of Gaidol and one of Prince Tohmas' trusted commanders, stood by the fire. His hand was on his sword, his expression one of suspicion. Behind

the high guardsman, Gaidolon guardsmen stuck their heads out of tents to investigate.

The Rydan woman wrapped her arm around Grigson's and gazed up at him with a warm, happy smile.

"This is Zeken," she said, although Grigson was certain she had spoken in Rydan. He had prepared by wearing a translation ring on his toe. Not understanding what his "wife" said would give away his ploy too soon.

The high guardsman did not relax, but his hand moved away from his weapon, clearly understanding her. "Your first husband?" he asked, eyeing Grigson. He considered what he saw for a long moment, and Grigson returned the stare with Rydan criticism. Rydans did not explain themselves to Esparans. Grigson would only react if the high guardsman challenged him directly. Otherwise, Zeken would have thought the Esparan too far beneath his notice to bother with, and so did Grigson.

"I guess..." the high guardsman muttered, slowly straightening from his aggressive stance. With a sigh, High Guardsman Carraway checked, "You alright, Sori?"

The Rydan woman tugged on Grigson's arm then nuzzled him. Her hand slipped around his waist.

"My husband," she said, as adoring as Grigson had ever seen a Rydan be.

"Fine," the high guardsman said, his voice reluctant. "I'll give you some privacy." He seemed to debate saying something further to Grigson but did not manage to get up the courage. Grigson had seen that before; Esparans did not dare challenge a Rydan. Rydans solved all their problems by fighting.

Once the high guardsman left, the other observing eyes turned away. Grigson was left with the little Rydan woman. She tugged on his arm in a soft plea, and when he looked down at her he found her chest pushed up and her chin lifted.

Of course. What else would a husband want to do with his wife after being apart for most of a year?

She led him back to the fire and spread a bedroll onto the ground. Setting her blades to one side, she lay before him, quickly undoing the lacing of her coat to show she wore nothing but a woven necklace

beneath. Her tiny pink breasts went tight in the chill, her nipples as erect as Grigson felt himself become.

Oh the things I do for my patron, he thought, burying his smirk.

Lowering himself onto her, Grigson lifted the heavy skirt and ran his hand up her muscled leg, surprised by the softness of her skin. She whimpered as his cold fingers brushed higher, but it was excitement, not refusal, and only made him reach higher.

He placed his lips to hers and, there, something went very, very wrong.

It wasn't pain; the sensation was pressure against his back below his ribcage. His body gave away, collapsing heavily against her. Numbness shot down his legs. He could not move, not even to breathe. He could not even feel the warmth of her skin.

The Rydan woman's expression changed, going strangely blank as she wiggled out from under him. Although he could not move, Grigson saw the bloody knife she held. Blood coated her arm to her elbow and dripped from the knife.

"Zekan's dead," she said coolly, her words still translated. "Like you are now, Flyer."

The pain finally bloomed—his back. Agony cut through him. A chill climbed through him, icy fingers so sharp they burned digging through his upper back. The sensation spread until it became a weight, like bags of sand wrapped around him.

The truth landed as heavy as a dragon on his chest.

I'm bleeding out.

"Lance?" Sori asked the surrounding tents. She was not surprised when Lance trotted out from behind a tent, looking mildly sheepish. She had known he would not leave her, not if there was any chance someone would hurt her. He did not trust Rydans any more than she did.

He looked down at the fake Rydan, his expression growing more concerned as the bloody pool from the man's kidney enlarged.

"I'm going to need you to explain this," he said.

Her Esparan was not perfect, but she tried hard for Lance's sake. "Zeken be dead." She held up her necklace. After Tohmas and Carsh

had killed the Rydans, Zeken included, Sori had returned to the site of the killing unobserved and taken her husband's knucklebone to remember him by. No one else would have known his death had been confirmed. "Da bone," she explained, pointing to the bead at the center of the necklace.

She met his stare and realized Lance was blushing deeply. She had not done up her coat.

"So you knew, because you saw Zeken dead, that this was not him," Lance deduced, averting his eyes. "Please lace yourself up, Sori."

Because he asked nicely, Sori did up her coat as she said, "Id be Flya."

"Flyer?" Lance repeated, glancing back at her before he could stop himself. With her coat folded shut and mostly tied up, he did not have to look away. "Magic?"

She was pleased he knew the Rydan word for "wizard." She understood the translation was not quite accurate, but it was the closest she could get. Wizards were supposedly good allies, but all casters of the Rydans were the dreaded flyers and to be feared. Flyer magic was manipulative and dark. Few Rydans had the skills to kill a flyer.

Sori puffed her chest in pride to see the seeping blood flow slow from the man at her feet. She had, with a single blow, just killed a great evil. This was exactly why she kept her knives so sharp.

Lance looked a little less certain. "Come with me please, Sori. I think Prince Tohmas will want to know about this." Lance slung the flyer over a shoulder and began walking. He seemed to ignore the way the blood-stained through his best tabard and darkened its blue to black.

Sori wondered if Tohmas—son of the First Clan's chief even if the Esparans were not aware—would kill her for being a second clan member, but she decided to do as Lance asked regardless. She paused to collect her spare knives as well as the bracelets from Clodn, the chief of the Third Clan who she had killed. If she was to stand before the Hand of the Outlands, she had to be ready.

Lance felt particularly conspicuous as he walked through the camp. Carrying what appeared to be a dead Rydan through the ranks would

not be helping keep the peace with the Rydans. *Will there be dissent from the Rydans now too?* The Northlanders had separated themselves from the main forces, leaving the Esparans with the Rydans. They all knew Darknim DoomDragon had broken from the alliance and was abandoning them. The Northlanders were no longer allies.

After his hasty travel through the camp, Lance was stopped by Protector Ursa outside the command tent, the man distinctive with his long, braided moustache. When he frowned, it reached to his collar bone.

Lance dropped the body onto the ground in front of Ursa. "Since he's dead, I don't think he's a threat. But Tohmas needs to know. He's a caster, or rather he was." Sori hovered a ways back, not confronting the protectors.

Nodding, Protector Ursa ducked into the command tent. Although Lance was expecting to be called in, Tohmas and Carsh surprised him by following Ursa back out. The protectors would probably have not liked letting the Rydan woman into the prince's tent, Lance recognized, but he hadn't pointed her out yet. *Did they realize she's with me? Or does Tohmas just not want blood stinking up his tent?*

Carsh came out first, his stance aggressive as he inched forward like a mountain cat stalking. He snarled, and Prince Tohmas responded by putting a hand onto SoulBurner's hilt, igniting the magic-nullifying aura around Lance and the body.

Nothing changed.

Once Carsh had searched the body, he sat back with his splinted arm on his lap. This seemed to cue Tohmas to come forward. "I think it's too late to question him," Tohmas said.

"I apologize," Lance said with a shrug. "She made the kill. I didn't get a chance to ask questions."

Tohmas glanced up, mild suspicion visible on his usually calm face. "She?"

Realizing that he had forgotten to introduce them, Lance gestured for Sori. He realized his hands, matching Sori's, were caked in blood, but at Tohmas' nod, the protectors permitted the tiny Rydan woman to cross between them and present herself to the prince.

To Lance's surprise, Sori did not stand tall in front of the prince as she usually did when meeting new people. Instead, averting her eyes in

a submissive manner Lance had never seen, she dropped to her knees and pushed two red-strained grass bracelets out in front of her like an offering. They were the type of bracelets Lance usually saw Rydan men wear, although he'd only seen them red once.

Tohmas' face darkened. In a blink, he had a dagger in hand and had stabbing the dagger through the grass bracelet on the ground. Before Lance could even open his mouth to ask, Carsh was crouched beside Tohmas, and both of their gazes were aggressively fixed on the cowering woman.

Lance had known that Tohmas spoke Rydan somewhat, but he was shocked when the Prince of Galanth flawlessly rambled off "*Who ya be, da kihl chief?*" The words sounded like an accusation.

"Sori," Sori answered, her head low. "Naw clan."

Knowing Carsh was First Clan and that Sori had once been Second Clan, Lance eyed the prime protector closely. According to Sori, the First Clan of the Outlander had decimated the others, driving both Second and Third Clans to extinction. Did she deny her original clan because it was dangerous to be seen as Second Clan? He recognized she hadn't mentioned her original clan; did she consider herself clanless?

Tohmas leaned slightly back, although his knife did not leave the bracelet where he had stabbed it in obvious, open threat. "*S'plain.*"

"Clodn," was Sori's muffled answer. She hesitantly peered up to gauge their reaction to the name of the Third Clan's chief.

Carsh cracked a wide smile. "I be lykin'!" he declared. He checked with Tohmas but then stood up from his crouch.

Tohmas reached out and took the bracelet he had stabbed. He left the second as he rose and wordlessly stepped back. His eyes did not leave Sori. He wasn't fearful, Lance recognized, but he seemed to be taking her seriously.

Sori gathered up the second bracelet and backed away slowly from the prince. Once she was a dozen paces away, she turned and left at a run. Tohmas watched her until she entirely out of sight.

"You going to explain that?" Lance asked.

The prince let out a long breath. "You told me a while back that a pair of Rydan women had come to you for help. Was she was one of them?"

Lance nodded. "You know her?" he asked.

"Never met her before now. But I know someone who did." Tohmas lifted the red grass bracelet. "Watch yourself, Lance. This belonged to a Chief of the Outlands. She carries them because she killed him." His eyes went to the dead body lying on the ground at their feet. "Seems she's good at killing people."

"I be lykin'!" Carsh repeated enthusiastically.

"You only like her because she shamed the Third Clan," Tohmas answered, smiling a bit with effort, then bending down to investigate the body more closely. He pulled a trinket off the coat then emptied the pockets. To Lance, he added, "Clodn was briefly Chief of the Third Clan. If a woman killed their chief, then the entire clan is embarrassed. Or they would be if they were not all dead."

Lance was left without anything to say. Sori had spoken very little about her life in the Outlands. He had known she was an outcast—that she had no home to return to—but he had not known why. For killing a chief? The meek little girl who had slept beside him all season was a seasoned murderer.

"Here's something familiar," the prince said, interrupting Lance's contemplations. Looking back at the Prince of Galanth, Lance found the man holding a hairpin.

Squinting, Lance made out an engraved pattern on the item, but it was a rather benign looking object otherwise.

"We found these at some of the fires in Fixer City," Tohmas explained. "This may be our arsonist. I'll have Kitable check..." He trailed off, turning the hairpin in his hand. "And we'll ask the Weavers. Those two watch everyone magic. This fellow had a fair bit of magic on him. They'll know him. You made our lives easier, Lance. He was a threat. I'm glad he's been dealt with."

The prince turned for his tent, calling over his shoulder, "Just don't turn your back on that woman."

Lance stood for a moment longer, his hands prickling as the blood on them dried. He had absolutely ruined his tabard. Even Sori's cleaning and stitching would not save it.

He swung through Fixer City to get a new one on his way back, giving himself time to think. He passed on the summons to the

Weavers as he went. Tohmas was right; they seemed to recognize the dead man by the description and left at a run to confirm the identity.

Chapter 12

Without the Circle, there was no DoomDragon. And without any reason to support the Esparan's attack against Prince Marfaie, Darknim led the Northlanders to the east, splitting from the Galanth forces as they left the mountain trails. He had met with Prince Tohmas the night before, who had given him back the dagger he had left behind. The other princes came out in the dawn, silently watching him lead his people out from the hills. He thought the princes looked relieved and that amused Darknim.

After the first few candles of the march, Darknim let the elders take the lead. At first, he held back to be among the Northlander Hunters, but at midday, Darknim stopped on a boulder, sat down, and let the forces go on without him.

Elder Tril met him.

The elder hunched more now, using a staff to keep from pitching forward. He looked weak, as if a decade had passed in a day for him. He kept his eyes lowered and mostly shut as he presented himself to the man who had once been known as DoomDragon.

"We go on," the elder said. "You will walk your own path."

Although he had not discussed anything with the Circle, Darknim was unsurprised Tril knew of his intentions.

"I will seek an old acquaintance and have words with him but this is not the fight of our people. This, I do alone," Darknim confirmed.

The elder nodded like a sage grandfather, making Darknim suddenly feel young. It was hard to believe; Darknim was older than Tril by nearly twenty years. *How could one winter wear a man so deeply?*

"The fight of our people awaits yet," Tril replied. The elder turned and shuffled his feet away, still nodding and muttering to himself as if forgetting Darknim was still within hearing range. "And not alone. Never alone that man."

Knowing he had little hope of figuring out what Tril had been rambling about, Darknim picked up his bag. He made sure the glass orbs—Wisavi Kitable's creations—were well protected by the thick hide wrapping before slinging the bag over his shoulder and picking up his ax. The enormous black ax, with the dragon on the handle rearing in pain and the tiny human hacking into the body like the dragon was a tree to be felled, still glistened. Darknim felt the power of it now more than ever.

The ax is a problem, Darknim thought as he looked it over. It had gained power since the slaying of the black dragon over the winter, and Darknim felt it as an emotional weight more than a physical one. Kitable had said the ax was likely from the time of the Demon Wars, when demons had ridden dragons through the skies, laying waste to the land beneath them. Entire civilizations had been wiped out in the crossfire, the damage so profound; the twisting, colored lights that could still be seen in the skies after night in the north were thought to be the scarred skies still echoing the magic. Kitable had refused to study the weapon, claiming he was concerned he would damage the relic. Darknim suspected the ax bothered Kitable as much as it bothered Darknim. *Does the wizard fear it as I do?*

But the ax had a purpose, and Darknim would see that through. Afterward, he wasn't sure what would happen. He had little interest in the title of DoomDragon or the ax once the war was over. He did not know what he would do, but the hunting fields of the north were calling him.

The last of the Northlanders passed him, heading east and out of the mountains. They would go south, away from Arcott, once free of the rocks and boulders of the Crescent mountains. Tril was confident they would not be harassed by the enemy, giving Darknim the certainty he needed to head in a different direction.

CHAPTER 12

Darknim hefted his bag and struck out, heading deeper into the mountains to the northwest.

After only two steps, he realized someone was waiting for him.

Calanor Blow, a white sack at his feet nodded to Darknim in greeting.

Darknim halted before the celebrant. "You've not spoken to me yet, so I'm guessing Kitable told you about the little presents I have in the bag."

Calanor smiled and nodded again. As an untouchable, if Calanor used his powers to make his voice heard, he could unwittingly dispel any nearby wizard magic, including the orbs Darknim carried.

"Didn't realize you were coming," Darknim added, eyeing the celebrant's bag. He looked to be carrying enough supplies for a short trip, which Darknim thought appropriate.

The celebrant had donned a long white coat over his robes, everything from his scarves to his booted feet white and grey. Somehow, the Esparan had avoided getting mud on him during the travels, a remarkable feat considering the wet spring weather. He shrugged with a smile visible only because Calanor wore his scarf off his face this morning.

Darknim resumed his walk, the celebrant falling into step beside him with his sack slung over a shoulder. His long strides easily matched Darknim's as together they made their way briskly west along the trail Tril had taught Darknim. Once they left the trampled road the army had followed, the footing became slippery with slush and snow. Darknim hugged his fur cloak tighter over his shoulders, but Calanor did not appear to notice the cold.

"You planning to give me a third form of magic to hit those dragons with?"

Calanor nodded.

Darknim sighed. "I wish I'd never cut your tongue, my friend. It's going to be a rather quiet journey."

Calanor's only answer was a shrug.

It was a relief to be done with Master Terant's attack. No longer did she need to hover around Sabian pretending to flirt. Now, except for a visit

to the command tent to confirm the death of Grigson, she was home in Fixer City. She did not deny that the death of the conman put her heart at ease. She'd never fully understood what Grigson had been doing, but she knew in her core it had been trouble that was better done with.

As a general rule, Shimmer kept an ear on the rumors running through Fixer City. She heard when DoomDragon forsook his agreement with Prince Tohmas and gathered his Northlanders for imminent departure. She also knew that the caster Seria was not to be joining him. The rumors said Seria had found the Northlanders too rough for her liking. However, when the rumors also mentioned how much the woman liked Match and Mixer, Shimmer could only roll her eyes.

While the Esparans and Rydans went north, the Northlanders veered to the east and left the mountains, pulling away from the target of Arcott in the north. A day later, the camp set in the last valley along the mountain road was half as big as it had once been.

With Dust's permission, Seria set her tent near Match and Mixer. Without the Northlanders, the woman seemed to have nowhere else to go. But the proximity of the other caster set Shimmer's teeth on edge. She could not even bring herself to full cast near the woman, fearing something would be overheard and stolen.

She wondered if this was how Master Kitable felt.

Beyond this camp, the road led out of the mountains to the east, then looped north to Arcott. Red dragons awaited them along that trail; Shimmer had seen them while scrying. She was certain Kitable knew as well. They had not been attacked again by the Reds solely because of the ongoing presence of the silver bull-dragon, but they expected that to end when they left his territory. Going out to Arcott down the east road was death, but the paths to the north were not wide or flat enough for waggons. They had to go east.

The command was given to settle in along the branching road within the mountains, but Shimmer heard the Esparan soldiers talking about marching in the morning. Wherever they were going, Fixer City would not be joining them. The waggons could go no further until the dragons were removed from the east road.

The evening was a raucous one in the Rydan camp, the drums and shouting loud enough to be heard clear to the farthest waggon. In Fixer City, the visiting soldiers were solemn. While the crowd waiting

to see her dancing was larger than usual, she noted no one was drinking tonight. Dust was finishing his juggling, but the contributions to their copper tin were scanty at best, matching the dour mood. Still, some Rydan had come out again to watch, sitting in their own crowd near the front. Above these, acting as a silent chaperone, came the boy Shimmer had been pretending to fancy for the last mooncycle.

Sitting on a waggon's overhang with one leg dangling off the edge, Sabian was certainly turning into a handsome man. Shimmer had to laugh at the thought of ever having a real relationship with him. Firstly, she found him too focused—he had a way of giving something his complete attention that seemed almost unnatural—and secondly, she found him dull. He was fast becoming an amazing knife fighter, but carrying a conversation with him required doing both sides of the talking.

Besides, she mused, *my heart is for another.*

As she watched Sabian, another group of Rydans arrived at the campfire from the back of the crowd. Knowing her turn would come shortly, Shimmer ducked behind the neighbor's vardo to adjust her skirts, ready to surprise the audience with a showy entrance.

Commotion stopped her preening. She peeked out for a second time.

Sabian sat straight, both feet over the edge of the canopy. With one hand, he worked a knife in circles over his knuckles. His entire focus was on the new group of Rydans, but she had only had time to give the new arrivals a cursory glance before the gathering of Rydans started picking a fight with an Esparan in the audience. The disturbance was enough for Dust to pause his juggling.

Sabian dropped to the ground and made long strides toward the newcomers.

"*Eesna!*" the boy called as he put himself between the Rydans and the Esparans they were harassing. In his walk over, he had drawn a second knife and held both blades at the ready.

While the Esparans gave the conflict greater distance, the Rydans fanned out around Sabian, sizing him up. The first of the intruders moved to push the boy back, but Sabian shoved the Rydan's hand aside with the flat of the knife. He was still being gentle; he could have used the edge.

Shimmer rattled off a Translation spell, just in time to hear Sabian repeat, "*Eesna!*" and have it repeat as, "Back off!"

She checked on the audience, seeing the other Rydans—regulars at her performances—rising from their seats to investigate. They seemed more confused than concerned.

"Who's that?" one asked, understandable because of her spell.

"Not familiar," the second replied. While they held weapons ready, they did not advance but peered at the group confronting Sabian with growing suspicion.

Rydans survived by knowing every member of their clan. They had to know which warrior was connected to which to avoid offending a more powerful Rydan or miss an opportunity to improve their rank. *If they can't recognize the new arrivals, where did they come from?*

The Rydan confronting Sabian, a broad man with a tattooed chest depicting a clawed hand, snarled. Shimmer watched on, wondering what spell she could use to help without giving away the use of magic. That would only get Sabian ostracized.

"Esparan," the Rydan spat. "Bah!"

This time, Sabian stepped into the Rydan's path when he tried to move past. His calm words were gibberish at first, translated courtesy of the magic.

"Arm forbids this," Sabian insisted as he pressed his right hand, still holding a knife, into his left forearm. "Hand forbids it as well," he added, repeating the gesture into his left palm. "Who are you to argue?"

In other confrontations between Rydans and Esparans, when Sabian made the gesture to the fist or the forearm, the Rydans typically backed down. Shimmer did not recognize the rank of "Hand" or "Arm" exactly, but she had seen the salutes before.

These Rydans did not back off. Instead, they copied the salute with a fist into the arm as if to appease him.

Whatever the meaning of the gesture, Shimmer assumed they had gotten it wrong. Sabian snarled and dropped into a fighting position. He was ready when the first of the Rydans lunged at him, blade out and aimed to kill.

Shimmer's heart lurched. This was no casual brawl. Rydans had the reputation of being vicious, but she had never seen one attack an Esparan. *This is bad.*

Having seen Sabian spar with Carsh, Shimmer was not surprised that Sabian easily slid out of the way of the attacker's knife. He

retaliated in Rydan fashion; he put his left blade between the Rydan's ribs and into his heart. The Rydan collapsed in shock, his wound rapidly bleeding him out.

Translated Rydan from her regulars reached her ears: "Don't know who they are, but Sabian's a Follower of the Arm. I'm not getting involved."

When she glanced over, the other Rydans had calmly retaken their seats, their eyes on the confrontation but without any indication they would interfere.

The additional intruders were not dissuaded by the ease with which their friend had been killed. Together, the five Rydans leaped at Sabian.

If the other Rydans were not going to help, it fell to Shimmer. The majority of the crowd were Esparans and moving away. Enough lingered around the fire watching the fight to be a hindrance to Shimmer's magic. Sabian was tightly tangled with the intruders, making many of her spells...

Dust's voice cut into her mind. *Illusions, Shim.*

She glanced at Dust and spotted the shifting colors of Spell Sight on his eyes. Following his example, she brought the spell to her vision as well.

Oh demons, she cursed silently.

The five remaining "Rydans" shimmered in the yellow light of a powerful light illusion. Underneath each illusionary Rydan was a real person; an Esparan. It was confusing to sort through; where the Rydan illusions had exposed, tattooed chests, the Esparans wore thick leather armor. The Rydans carried short bone knives, but the Esparans beneath were armed with swords. They had helms, but the illusions showed slicked hair and bone beads.

There were intruders in Fixer City, and they were using magic.

This was no mere brawl. This was an attack.

Get Kitable, Shimmer thought back to her father, who nodded and rushed from the scene. She then took a deep breath and left the cover of the vardo where she had been hiding.

Sabian had managed to get a waggon to his back and had only three people to deal with at one time. Two were already bleeding from knife wounds despite the brevity of Shimmer's conversation with her father.

As she approached, Sabian ducked low, kicked out one of the Rydan's feet, then spun out of the half circle where they had pinned him.

The last attacker Sabian passed slashed with a hooked knife that Shimmer's enchanted vision revealed as a straight sword. Sabian dodged the hooked blade and was hit by the sword. A long slash tore his tunic through the sleeve and left a bloody cut across the boy's shoulder.

After enough practice with Carsh, Sabian had developed Rydan stubbornness; he did not acknowledge the injury. He retaliated, planting his knife into the attacker's upper arm. Replacing it from his baldric, he was armed in the next flicker.

Shimmer tried to get a clear target as she made her cautious way through the crowd toward the fight. *I can't afford to hit Sabian. My aim has to be—*

A hand grabbed Shimmer and yanked her back. The press of someone against her back and an arm around her waist unearthed anger and fear from their hiding place in her memories. The words over her shoulder were comfort and concern—someone worried about her safety—but Shimmer hardly heard them.

No one touched her. No one was allowed to.

Alone on an empty country road and too far from the village to call for help, Shimmer's bag was taken from her. She remembered being pinned to the cold earth, her hands held down, a weight on her hips. Her panicked mind searched for the words of a spell to save her, but magic was too new to her and the powers escaped her grasp. She was made helpless by their physical strength.

She rebelled this time, the words of magic no longer foreign or complicated. With an activation word, a heat shield sprang up. She added a clause to it, hastening the increasing heat. The person holding her back cried out, their hands and arms red with blisters as they released her.

Pushing back against whomever it had been, she turned and found an Esparan she had seen at many of her performances. He was harmless, just concerned. And he was backing away from her, fear on his face now.

Ignoring him, Shimmer spun back to Sabian. He dodged his attackers wider still, seeming to know the blades he saw did not match what was striking him. But he did not move far enough to stop a small knife, completely concealed by the illusion, from digging into his thigh up to the hilt.

His leg folded under him. As he fell, he delivered a parting blow by flicking a small knife into the enemy's belly. It was hard to tell if the short blade would kill.

She'd been the prey before. She'd had to hide to save her life, concealed by grungy blankets in a dark corner, or riding between the axels of waggon to sneak through a gate. Magic had changed that. *I don't have to hide. But I can hide him.*

Her target still for a blessed moment, Shimmer dropped a Full Concealment spell on Sabian.

Thanks to her Spell Sight, Shimmer could still see Sabian when the Concealment spell hid him from the view of the attackers. For a moment, neither side knew what to do. Sabian may have known he had been hit by magic, but he did not know what spell. The attackers, on the other hand, could no longer see their prey. Their killing blows hesitated.

Concealment did not handle movement well; when Sabian launched to his feet, the spell faltered, and he was visible. It bought him a moment of surprise, and he used it to deliver a blow across the nearest attacker's throat. As soon as the other "Rydans" saw the strange combination of grasses and dirt illusion move, they retaliated, and Sabian was once more forced to deflect, then dodge. His leg seemed to keep him upright but was otherwise useless.

Wounded and surrounded; she'd been there. She'd been beaten, robbed, left for dead. But she was no longer the victim, and she would not allow Sabian to be either.

Shimmer let out a steady breath and, now clear of the crowd, took aim. The words came quickly and easily, falling from her memory as if the pages were before her. She targeted the center of the Rydan group, shielded Sabian from the effect, and let the spell fly.

Green light flashed out, striking each of the six in turn with a burst of force. The attackers staggered, knocked off balance by powers they could not see. Whether or not he sensed the magic or simply reacted to their lapses, Shimmer could not tell, but Sabian seemed to follow the green light around the circle. His well-aimed knives ended two more lives.

The remaining two attackers managed to fend off the blows from Sabian. While they retaliated, Shimmer spotted a spell approaching a streak of orange. Shimmer had no Eavesdrop spell handy, but she

recognized the auras well enough to know something had been said to the imposters.

A shiver ran down Shimmer's back. *The caster is still around. Where? Who?* Fear cut in. *I'm not ready to duel someone!*

It was as if her assailants were again over her, suffocating her. *This is out of my league.*

But the two intruders responded to the communication by turning and fleeing. Although she aimed to cast a Tracker, Shimmer fumbled a word and the spell failed. By the time she tried again, the fake Rydans were gone.

A five-way summoning spell streaked into the area, landing on Match and Mixer. A blink later, Wisavi Kitable burst through the door of Shimmer's waggon. Shimmer let out her breath, and the final remnants of her haunted memory left. Now safe, she ran to Sabian, who sagged against the nearby waggon. Gathering her skirts, she pressed the cloth around the knife in his leg. It was a Rydan knife, which surprised her.

She glanced at the other fallen, analyzing the wounds but finding their wounds too grievous. All four were dead.

Rydans aim to kill. Sabian was trained by a Rydan. Only makes sense.

Sabian grumbled when she applied pressure to the bleeding but did not object as she tore loose the cloth, wrapping the strips around the imbedded knife.

The remaining onlookers scampered out of Kitable's way. Even the Rydans who had stayed seated by the fire averted their eyes. She heard them dryly comment, "Hand and Arm tonight. Heavy blood."

As soon as Kitable arrived to loom over her, Shimmer stood to face him, her beads and bangles chiming with her movement. Sabian was stable, for now. She would need her bag to do more.

She expected the master wizard to demand explanations immediately, but he instead stood with his mouth briefly agape. Shimmer was wearing her dancing clothes, her legs visible from hip to toe through the sheer garments. Tearing the skirts had left them barely reaching her thigh. The sight of the skin seemed to numb his brain.

It occurred to her the best way to defeat the caster in a duel would be to simply undress and the thought made her smile despite everything.

He cleared his throat. "What by the hells is going on? Your father—"

Shimmer let fall her smile. "Six men attacked an Esparan. They had light illusions that made them look like Rydans. Sabian stopped them, only they attacked him before running off and—"

"A Tracker? Did you get a Tracker on them?" Miserably, Shimmer shook her head. "Useless girl," he muttered.

She felt her face flush. "At least I managed to stop them from gutting him!" she protested, tossing her beaded hair. "He could have been killed!"

The wizard paused, but it was not for long. "I have to tell Prince Tohmas, then find those who caused this disturbance. Master Terant has succeeded in breaking off the Northlanders, and now he is trying to cause a rift between the Esparans and the Rydans." He glared down at her. "Surrender any wounded to the local guardian."

"All dead, except the two who got away. Sabian doesn't leave wounded."

"Pity," Kitable said.

Shimmer swallowed hard, starting to recognize that there were bodies strewn around her. Trying to focus on the important things, she added, "Sabian will need a cutter."

Kitable sighed, staring down at Carsh's Follower. He seemed to consider offering Sabian support, but dismissed the notion. "Come on, Sabian. I'll need you at the command tent." With a flare of the green robes, Kitable marched back off toward the Esparan side of camp.

Sabian limped after him.

She was still staring at the place where Kitable had stood when her father arrived back to Match and Mixer. The crowds milled around, none seeming to know if they should move on. She spotted the haze of an alteration spell around Dust, likely for speed.

"I trust Mast—Wisavi Kitable chased them off?" he asked between pants.

"They knew he was coming," she corrected, remembering the thought magic she had seen give warning to the false Rydans. "They fled, but he's going to track them." Her eyes remained on where she had last seen the irritated green robes when she added, "He hates me."

"Nonsense," her father said.

Shimmer let her eyes drop and shook her head. "It's the way he looks at me, Papa. Every time I see him, he is so full of disapproval. Everything I do—"

"Who is he to disapprove of you, Shim? He's just another person who thinks he knows what is best in the world and is certainly wrong. He has no right to judge you or any other."

As sweet as her father's words were, Shimmer could only shrug and shake her head again. She could still hear Kitable's voice repeating "Useless girl" and it made her stomach knot. The other memories were threatening to return as well. She fought to keep them, and the tears, out.

"Shim?" Dust asked, and she looked up. He pointed with a nod of his head toward their home. Between her and the vardo, the Rydans—the real ones—were standing, squinting at Shimmer as if trying to recognize her.

She had been casting in front of them. Even now, she still had Spell Sight active.

Dismissing the spell, she reviewed what they had seen. None of the spells had been visible to the naked eye, except the Spell Sight. They may have been able to tell magic had been involved, but they could not be certain it had been her. Her back had been mostly to them, and they probably would have been watching the fight. They did not understand magic. Only Carsh had ever demonstrated the ability to detect magic passively.

She could not show weakness in front of Rydans.

Steadying herself, Shimmer gave her father a nod, showing she understood his concern. Facing the Rydans and staring them down, she walked back to the vardo, passing in front of them. She shot them a wide grin and swung her hips as she moved back to the front where Match and Mixer would make a stage, ready to give them something else to think about.

"Oh so jumpy," she said to them. "You came to watch a performance! Did something surprise you? Are my tricks fooling you?" she demanded. Seeing no Rydan was moving to attack, she hopped onto the stage.

"Ladies and gentlemen! Shall we try this again?" she called.

Kitable reported the attack to Tohmas, dragging Sabian in with him. Celebrant Darak joined them, patching Sabian up then returning to his new Temple waggon. There was something prophetic about the way

the newest Celebrant of Galanth left with his hands covered in blood. After all, the man was, first and foremost, a cutter.

After hearing what Carsh's Follower had to say, the prince came to the same conclusion as Kitable had: Terant was trying to drive apart the Rydans and their Esparan allies.

"Explains the thefts," Tohmas added with a gesture to the papers strewn over the table. "I took a closer look once Grigson was identified as the arsonist. Horses, food, and weapons, all stolen across camp, usually with a sighting of a Rydan or the recovery of a grass bracelet. I suspect it was Grigson before he got knifed. I keep telling people that Rydans do not leave their bracelets behind, but no one believes me."

Carsh was already proof of that fact. The Rydan, after getting his arm fixed and curtly telling Tohmas about the defense of the Circle in six words or less, had returned to the collapsed Earth Lodge and dug until he had recovered his missing grass bracelet, which he had pointedly tied around his splinted limb. The grass was brown from dirt and had to be repaired with horsehair, but he had it back.

"Loni is missing as well," Tohmas added. He glanced up at Kitable. "I have no idea if that matters, but maybe he didn't like an untouchable being around."

"It was not Terant," Kitable said.

Tohmas frowned. "I am glad to hear that," he said, pointing to the chair across from him. "If he was responsible for all this, he is becoming dangerously impressive."

Reluctantly, Kitable sat down. He first checked on the enchanted stone that now lived on the table among the wood tokens. It was still a neutral grey color. There was no eavesdroppers tonight.

Carsh moved out from behind the prince to offer Kitable a cup.

"We beat Terant back a day ago, and Carsh put a knife through his hip," Kitable said, nodding thanks to Carsh for the drink. As it had in wine it, not wildwater, Kitable could still speak after taking a drink. "He ought to be still enervated. Even if he's not, he could not have gotten through the defenses around Fixer City, not without leaving a trail. Whoever was casting those illusions had to be already inside the defenses. Besides, the final communication spell set off one of my alarms. Terant's proven he can dodge those alarms."

The prince sat forward and rubbed his temples. "This recent incident, it couldn't be something left over from Grigson?"

Kitable shook his head. "That would be one crazy contingency, and one dependent on too many unpredictable factors. It could not have been left as an enchantment. It has to be someone alive and able to adapt."

Kitable heard the Prince of Galanth's disappointment in the sigh he gave.

"Olmer, the Weavers, or Seria?" Tohmas asked.

Kitable hated that it had come to that.

"Olmer is unlikely," he said. "He's been working for Dragal for three decades and is only a marginal caster." *Although, Clarin professed relative ineptitude before I dueled him*, Kitable admitted. But Kitable felt confident BookKeeper Olmer's limited ability with magic was genuine. The man knew the same set of spells now he had three decades ago. First and foremost, the bookkeeper was a bookkeeper. He had little time for the kind of research Kitable had undertaken.

"The Weavers..." Kitable's sentence fell off. He did not have confidence in Dust and Shimmer Weaver. He had seen their performances, and he had benefited from their assistance more than once. He had already confronted Dust on this kind of betrayal and come up empty. It was still possible that they had somehow evaded him. The girl had to be watched.

"If you trust them," Tohmas said when Kitable failed to finish the sentence, "then just say so."

Do I? Tril had said that Kitable and Shimmer worked well together. He had to admit the elder had been right so far. Dust's illusionary dragon had been helpful, and Shimmer's defense of the Circle had been a large part responsible for their partial success. Tril had also been confident enough in the Weavers to recommend her in the defense of the Circle. That was not something the Northlander elder would have done lightly.

"I believe them innocent," Kitable confessed. "For reasons I do not fathom, that girl and her father appear to be acting in the aid of Galanth."

"Which leaves Seria," Tohmas prompted.

Kitable nodded. "I never did like her," he admitted.

The prince smiled. "Me neither, to be honest. What do we do?"

"I can track back the events of today. If she was involved, I will see it." Kitable looked up at Carsh, then quickly back at his wine. He could not bring the Rydan into this, not with his broken arm. *Besides, I don't need anyone else if I don't have to protect others.*

"Can you defeat her by yourself, Kit?"

"Don't insult me!" he snapped. "Of course I can handle Seria. Without having to also defend a bunch of innocent people, I could have handled Terant too. When you march on the walls of Arcott, I will destroy Terant, that I swear." He paused, eyeing Tohmas carefully. "So long as you are confident, I will not need to divide my attention."

"You've already given Darknim everything he needs. Focus on the casters. We'll take care of the dragons."

Kitable detected no uncertainty in the prince. In that, he had the decision. "Then I will do it now. Someone just put a lot of effort into trying to distract me with the illusionary Rydans. He is feeling vulnerable."

The prince looked down at the mess in front of him; tokens, reports, pages. He let out a long breath. "Earlier than I expected."

"We levelled the Earth Lodge in our last confrontation. Do you really want me taking him out while your forces are at Arcott with me? We could flatten part of the city at this rate."

"Good point," Tohmas allowed. He gathered the tokens slowly. "I have to let you make that decision, Kit. You know magic best. If you believe now is your best chance, take it. I can adjust. Not having to worry about Master Terant would be a good thing."

Kitable let the thought settle for a few heartbeats. After the night of rest after the fight with Terant, he did not feel even the slightest hint of enervation. Terant had not been so lucky. At the least, he was nursing a chest injury and a leg just about as bad as Sabian's. Giving Terant two more days to recover as the forces marched to Arcott would not help their position.

Kitable nodded. "If I can use tonight's events to track his location, I will go after him."

"Then get to it," Tohmas said in dismissal.

Kitable returned to his vardo.

It took only one Reflection to answer his question. With Sabian's injuries as a guide, Kitable had a perfect account of the fight with the

disguised Esparans shortly. Adding the effect of Spell Sight to the Reflection was tricky, and something he did not think any other wizard in all of Espar could do, but it showed him what he needed to see.

The Esparan thugs who had attacked Sabian wore no identifying tabards or ropes of rank. They were armed and wore leather armor, but other than that had few distinguishing features. They would be very difficult to define or anchor, being very similar to so many other Esparans in the area.

But when Kitable saw the orange thought spell warning the imposters, he decided they were not the largest problem. Tracking back the spell, he found Seria watching the fight from under a waggon. She called off the attackers when she spotted Kitable's anchor reaching for Match and Mixer.

It was confirmed; Seria was loyal to Prince Marfaie.

Knowing he had a small window in which to act, Kitable sat down and started casting. He layered additional spells over his usual array, having to reach for his books for particularly complicated incantations. He would need his most powerful and adaptable spells. For the sake of saving energy, he gave them a short duration. When he felt he was just about ready, he added a few extra offences and defenses, an extra Relocation spell, and finally, a Rejuvenation spell.

He cringed as the Rejuvenation ran over his sweating body, calming him and bringing back full energy, but accepted it as a necessary risk. Such an extensive set of casting threatened to exhaust him. He needed to have his wits about him when he met Seria or her master.

He had half a day from this moment to act before the Rejuvenation spell dropped him into sleep, whether he was ready for it or not.

The moon was high by the time he rose from his casting position but Kitable felt as if it was midday. He even cast his final Scry while pacing to burn off some of the energy.

Seria was sleeping, he discovered, in a small tent beside Match and Mixer in Fixer City. Rather than waste a Relocation spell in getting there, Kitable walked. Thanks to the Rejuvenation spell, he could have sprinted it.

He had Spell Sight up before he arrived at Seria's tiny tent, able to analyze the defenses around her shelter. As his mind sought a

route through the defenses, a five-way summoning spell took form above the tent.

Anchored to a binding spell to the north, she was casting a Relocation spell as he watched.

Break the spell or follow it? He had not touched the tent yet. Unless she had detected his earlier Scry, it seemed unlikely she knew he was there. If she could relocate, it stood to reason that Kitable would be able to as well, and that meant getting a clear anchor for further castings. It also could mean finding Terant while the wizard was still recovering from his injuries.

When Seria finished her spell, Kitable attached a Tracker. Soon he was anchored to a location far to the north. A single word brought his Relocation to bear.

And then he was gone too.

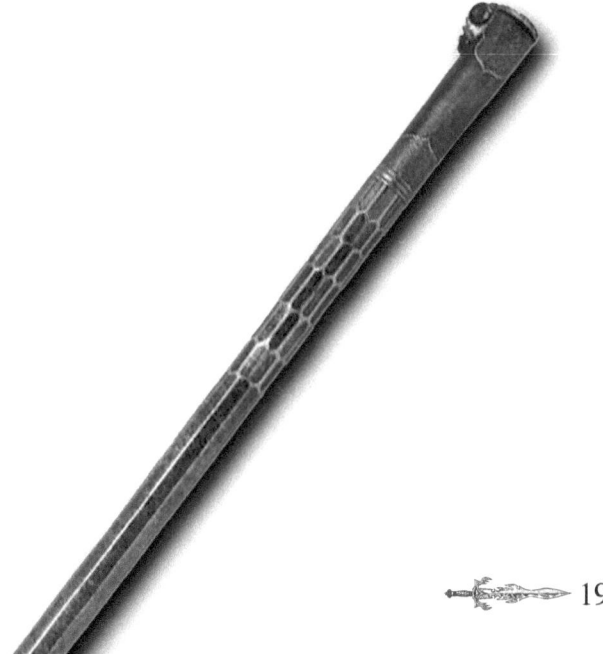

Chapter 13

Shimmer chewed nervously on a lock of her hair as she gazed out the hidden window of Match and Mixer, an uneasy feeling in her gut. The events of the day still had her heart racing despite more than one cup of calming tea. Her Tarot cards lay askew on the table, the ten of swords central: betrayal.

She had not seen Seria since Sabian's fight, even though her tent was only a few paces from Match and Mixer. The single communication that had passed to the illusionary Rydans had been locally targeted, so the caster must have been able to see the area nearest the fight. That meant either an effective Scry or a physical presence, and neither option made Shimmer happy enough to sleep. Instead, she stood in Match and Mixer, watching the tent for the owner's return.

There were hundreds of places that were safer than Fixer City these days. *Why did we not pack up when the army marched north?* There was hardly any money to be made here, and the expense of living was rising. They should have struck out before setting a single wheel in the Princedom of Tanble.

In answer to her silent questions, she remembered the gentle touch of a hand on her neck and sighed. Terrible memories rose when any other touched her. Why did Kitable's touch chase those same nightmares away?

Movement outside the window interrupted her memory. At first Shimmer thought her tired mind was playing tricks on her; the wisavi

himself had stepped into the space beside Match and Mixer and was staring at Seria's tent as if answering Shimmer's thoughts of him.

Concealed by the many spells of the waggon, Shimmer did not hesitate to cast Spell Sight. Soon she was watching a Relocation spell form over Seria's tent, presumably the same spell that had attracted Kitable's attention.

Had Seria been within the tent the whole time? And where is she going now?

When Kitable cast a Tracker, followed by an anchor and his own Relocation spell, Shimmer was so startled she accidentally bit her own finger instead of the curl of hair she had been fiddling with.

He was chasing Seria.

Shimmer leaned forward, her mind spinning. *Is Kitable on the offensive after the confrontation with Terant? Does he suspect Seria is involved too?*

Scrambling, Shimmer placed a ribbon on her pillow, showing her father she would be back soon, and grabbed her bag. There, she paused.

Kitable did not want her help, or so he had repeatedly told her. *And how much help will I be?* Still, she wanted to know if Seria had indeed betrayed them. Shimmer glanced back at her sleeping father. Dust had been friendly with Seria, so if Seria had been behind Sabian's attack, then Dust had to know. Shimmer had to find out.

It's just surveillance, like following Clarin or Kitable, like we always do. It was worth a slight risk if it meant finding out the truth.

Taking a deep breath, she began casting, attaching to Kitable's anchor to follow his spell north. It was a lengthy spell, but the moment it finished, she was whisked away. She reappeared on a stone surface at the center of a beam of moonlight despite nearby walls.

She ducked into a shadow to get her bearings.

She had appeared in an open courtyard. The moonlight reflected off silver threads in the ground underfoot, a pattern in the stone that had likely been targeted by the original caster of the Relocation. With only one entrance to the courtyard and nothing else in the small area, she assumed the space was solely designed to act as an anchor for Relocations.

Her Spell Sight showed clearly that the door was enchanted. She hesitated, staring at the auras and trying to make sense of them. Once beyond them, escaping would be difficult. *Last chance to go back.*

Pulling her traveling cloak over her colorful clothes, Shimmer set her mind to identifying the various spells on the door. *I have to know.*

The enchantments, she slowly recognized, were all aimed at keeping people out of the courtyard, not blocking people from leaving it. One was an alarm, and she carefully slid around that one once she had gathered her courage.

Enchanted blue lights lit an ornate, swept hallway beyond the door, but there was no sign of Kitable or Seria.

The sound of voices drew Shimmer down the corridor with cautious steps. Some part of her was beginning to shout at her for her insanity, but her curiosity drove her on as to a second door.

The spells on the second door had been bent. *Trust Kitable to use alteration where others would use destruction,* she thought with a smile. Some of the spells probably would act as alarms if they were broken, but that risk was eliminated with his tactic. It also left her an easy way in.

The room beyond was an enormous hall. A dozen pillars held the domed, carved ceiling aloft. Furniture and fixtures were sparse; few chairs and tables were scattered about. Firelight poured from the west wall, casting the long shadows of pacing people across the tiled floors.

"Caught!" a man's voice shouted. "Simple illusions, and you were caught at it!" Shimmer recognized the voice from the Earth Lodge battle, Master Terant.

Seria's high voice replied, "How was I to know Sabian would get involved? Or that he would survive?"

"Too late now. Your work there is finished."

Shimmer flattened herself against a pillar, then slowly peeked out. Master Terant had removed his outer robe and tunic, leaving bare his chest wound, which had been cauterized. The man carried a staff to help him walk, a limp obvious. Seria stood, head bowed, near the edge of the ornate fireplace. Although Shimmer tried to focus on Terant's hovering spells to identify them, the movement of the caster in front of carven hunt scenes on the lit fireplace mixed the spells like the churning of leaves.

"Tohmas' forces are two days away, maybe less," Seria confessed, her voice a hesitant whisper. "They will be visible from the high towers by tomorrow if they leave the mountain cover."

"No," Terant replied. "No, Tohmas has ordered them to remain where they are. His soldiers will not brave the fields, not with Rakhund's beasts patrolling it."

Seria stood silent for a moment, her lips pressed into a line. "They must have a plan," she tentatively said.

"Tohmas has been sending groups into the mountains" Terant replied, slowly turning around and pacing back toward the woman. "The Northlanders have gone east and are no longer a concern. It is just Tohmas and his Rydans now." The master wizard cracked a sinister smile. "They will be stopped easily enough, if we can get magical interference out of the way." He glared at the smaller woman. "You waited as I told you to?"

Seria nodded eagerly. Shimmer saw two of Terant's spells flicker like the flexing of muscles. She thought she saw them change colors. "And you left your anchor visible?" he continued.

The woman nodded more enthusiastically. She was beginning to grin, the firelight casting shadows over her face and making Shimmer's gut tense. She had the distinct impression something was going very wrong.

"Then let us begin," Terant finished.

With her next word, Seria activated one of the bright spells hovering around her. The magic passed over Shimmer, and a Seal spell, much like the one that had kept them from the Circle, went up. Shimmer ducked in reflex. *Time to leave,* she decided, still not knowing where Kitable was. *Too close.*

But the door she had just slipped through blocked by a conjured wall of stone. Physically and magically, she was trapped.

"So," Terant said with a tap of his staff as he faced the seemingly empty room. "I would guess we once again have the honor of meeting the great Master Kitable, this time alone. Right, Master Kitable?"

Shimmer's heart dropped into her gut, where it stopped beating. *Where had Kitable gone? Had Terant and Seria noticed me? If they think I am Kitable—*

Panicked, she dared not move from her hiding place. In all her spying on other wizards, she had never before been caught.

The thought was left unfinished when she spotted movement. Stepping out from the gloom, she was relieved to see the familiar green and silver robes of the wisavi. Kitable was bathed in auras, and his blue eyes were already sparkling with Spell Sight. There was nothing that could not be described as awe-inspiring or magnificent about him now.

There was no banter; just as Master Terant opened his mouth, Kitable activated a spell and light crashed into the Tanble wizard's defenses. Instead of being a single Eight-layered Dispel, it alternated between each element in turn, burying through several layers of shields. Terant shot a spell at Kitable in answer, but it only took out the first of his shield.

From there, Shimmer had a hard time keeping track. There were dispels and conjures, careful alterations and a series of dominations that made her shiver with their potency. Seria added a few spells of her own when she thought Kitable distracted, but the wisavi proved himself again by easily deflecting those minor disruptions. He even shoved Seria aside with an additional spell in passing.

Behind her numbed awe, terror snuck into Shimmer. She had helped Kitable before, but with Carsh as her proxy. She could not even recognize the majority of the spells thrown about the room now. Both Kitable and Terant cast with ease that belied the complexity of each casting, leaving Shimmer far behind. If either enemy caster attacked Shimmer, she doubted her ability to counter.

Seeing Seria stumble to avoid one of Kitable's force spells, Shimmer swallowed her apprehension. Seria had deceived them. She would not allow that to happen again.

Activating a hovering Force Bar, Shimmer pinned Seria where she had fallen. The woman struggled at first, sorting through the auras. Soon enough, she cast a destruction to free herself. Shimmer ducked behind the pillar, waiting to see if she had been spotted.

As moments dragged by without retaliation, Shimmer chanced another look. The duel had not progressed. Despite his leg, Terant moved as lightly as Kitable, proof he was using at least some pills and probably some thought destruction magic to control his pain. The

flagstones were scorched black throughout the room, yet their auras of hovering spells and shields looked undiminished.

I can't get through that!

The thought of being helpless made Shimmer rebel by reflex. There has to be something. No one was invulnerable.

He's too well protected, Shimmer decided. *But the ground isn't.*

Shimmer began a cautious spell, tracking the duel as she performed a full cast. Seeing Kitable stagger under the weight of a fire spell prompted her to cast faster, but she tripped on the words, and the entire spell was lost in her eagerness. Kitable rolled, extinguishing the brief flames, and retaliated with a piercing jab of light from a trinket. Terant dodged, but the spell left a seared hole in the mantle under the carved bear's foot.

Seria, having worked herself free, attacked again, but a hovering spell from Kitable countered as he came to his feet and threw the girl into a whirlwind. She stumbled, dizzy.

Shimmer restarted her spell and recognized vaguely that something magic had reached out to her. Certain she had not yet been spotted by either party, she assumed the magic had been the side effect of another spell and finished her own casting.

As she came to the end of her spell, she held the final word, waiting for an opportune moment.

Terant launched a multi-way destruction spell that cut through several of Kitable's shields before being stopped; Kitable's defenses were almost gone. In exchange, Kitable managed to get a force spell through Terant's Molded Shield. It slashed a thin line from Terant's freshly-cauterized chest injury to his left hip, the first blood either had drawn.

Without pausing for his injury, Terant launched orange thought magic, and Shimmer almost lost her spell when she recognized that none of Kitable's remaining shields would to defend against it.

Kitable fell to his knees, the orange tendril of magic fixed to the center of his forehead. With gritted teeth, he fought the spell, but Shimmer feared it would not be enough.

This will have to be good enough, she decided. She finished her spell, feeling a burn flare but quickly fade.

The stone beneath Terant's feet vanished. He fell, his concentration lost.

Kitable took advantage of Terant's lapse and activated a pin on his collar. A burst of multi-way magic surrounded him, pushing the spell from his mind. A shield remained, windy auras now defending him from further thought spells.

Terant heaved himself up using his staff, throwing a spell at Kitable as he moved. He had, somehow, put up a shield of green force.

Kitable dropped and rolled under the new attack. Taking refuge behind a pillar, Kitable came slowly to his feet. With a word, Terant activated a black alteration spell, bending it to touch down on the pillar. To Shimmer's surprise, the pillar sprouted arms. Reaching behind, a stone hand clamped down onto Kitable's shoulder. Shimmer heard a loud crunch.

For the first time, Kitable activated a plain, uncomplicated spell; a one-way destruction of earth magic. The wispy pattern of black eliminated a chunk of the stony fingers and freed him.

Seria moved in, raising her hand to target Kitable, and Shimmer reacted instinctually. Knowing she could not attack the woman directly, she used a familiar spell to drop a kettle's-worth of water onto the woman's head. Suddenly blinded by the water poured atop her, Seria lost her spell.

Kitable favored his shoulder as he cast his next spell, but he brought it to life before Seria could get her sopping hair out of her face. The enormous, multicolored, glittering wall appeared between Kitable and Terant.

Shimmer winced; it was bafflingly complicated. Despite having briefly seen it once before, she did not even know where to begin in deciphering it. At the bare minimum, she could tell the spell destroyed a person, which seemed helpful as it was advancing toward Terant and was angled to keep Seria away from Kitable.

Shimmer did not see the panic she had expected. Terant glared at the intricate spell bearing down on him, his hovering spells flickering around him like angry fireflies. When the spell was close enough to destroy the hair from his knuckles, Terant spoke.

Kitable's spell vanished, revealing Kitable preparing another spell. He seemed so surprised by the dismissal of the spell, his casting paused for a flicker.

Terant's staff was gone. Whether it had been consumed by the wall or used up by the counter, Shimmer did not know.

"How many do you have, I wonder?" Terant shouted.

With a final word, a new version of the complex wall appeared. The colors angled themselves, pinning Kitable against the corner he had retreated toward. The magic dissolved the pillars as it passed, making the stone disappear without a pebble remaining.

Shimmer took stock of her remaining hovering spells but came up empty. None of her spells were offensive, a Concealment spell would not be enough, and she did not have time for a full cast. She could not even see Kitable through the enormous spell.

Before she could come up with something, Terant gave a shout of frustration. He released the wall, causing it to snap out of existence and revealing nothing behind it.

Shimmer's heart soared. Kitable was gone!

Hefting his leg now that he was without his staff, Terant cursed and limped toward the last place Kitable had been. Sheepishly, Seria tossed her hair, trying to keep the wet strands from her face, and joined her master.

"We will track him! Find the anchor to..." Terant let the sentence fall off as he examined the place Kitable had so recently left. Shimmer, with Spell Sight, also saw the hundreds of cloudy purple anchors. Shimmer smirked. Not even Master Terant could track them all. They had no way to know where Kitable had Relocated to, or how he had slipped through the Seal.

Shimmer smothered a whoop of victory. It was not as good as defeating them, but Kitable had escaped!

A spell slammed into her side, striping her spells from her in one wave. The next spell slammed her to the wall a stride off the ground, her hands pinned to her sides and her feet a stride from solid ground.

Impossible! The attacks had bypassed her shields entirely. *When did he get a binding onto me?*

Despite her confusion, Shimmer felt no dread. She was satisfied by the approach of Terant and his apprentice for Kitable was safe. Terant and Seria were easily her betters, but she had accomplished her goal. Nothing could take that victory from her.

"Well," Terant said, "what have we here? Kitable may have escaped, but now we have his apprentice to keep—"

"Apprentice?" The word burst from her before Shimmer could stop herself. Laughter, liberating her from the last of her apprehension, escaped alongside. "Me? You must be joking!"

The scorn on their faces lost potency, confusion sneaking in. *Well, I'm an actress*, Shimmer decided. The pair of casters would kill her if they believed she was helping Kitable, but she could convince them otherwise. Seria did not know Shimmer well enough.

Terant's eyes narrowed. He cast a circle of white light between them, easily recognized as a Lie Light even without her Spell Sight.

"Then what are you doing here?" he demanded.

Shimmer shrugged, the motion limited by the magic holding her and the weight of her bag, still slung over her shoulder. "I was following Kitable."

"Following him? Why?"

"My father and I keep an eye on wizards we have to live near. I used to follow Clarin around," she truthfully informed them, "but now that he is gone, I have time for Kitable. He did not know I was tracking him." Every statement, taken independently as the Lie Light did, was true.

The suspicion in Terant's eyes was lessening, and Shimmer was not the only one who could tell.

Seria stepped forward. "I saw you assist Sabian during the scrap yesterday! You are loyal to Galanth!"

"I am not loyal to Galanth!" Shimmer snapped back, which in itself was also true. "As for Sabian, I am fond of the boy, or had you not noticed?" It had been part of their ruse for protecting the Circle, but how would they know that? As for being "fond" of Sabian, Shimmer liked the Vait boy enough to make the statement true. If they read deeper into the word, then it was their fault. "Besides, it does well to make powerful friends. Carsh would have nothing to do with me, and Kitable treats me like an idiot. Who else can I approach?"

Master Terant was now smiling. "You are a native of Fixer City," he began thoughtfully.

"For the moment."

CHAPTER 13

"Are you loyal to Prince Tohmas?" he asked, and Shimmer shook her head. When it became evident the motion—completely undetectable by the Lie Light—would be insufficient, she rolled her eyes and added, "No."

She was not loyal to Tohmas, no more than her father was.

"Are you helping Galanth?" he pressed.

"No." *I'm helping Kitable. I don't care what became of Galanth, so long as Kitable is safe.*

Through a pause, the older man examined her. Shimmer made her calm and sincere. *I don't need to fear him. I am not his enemy.* The character she took on believed these things. Her appearance would show it.

"I think you may be of use to me," Terant finally concluded, and Shimmer smiled to see the expression on Seria's face. She made sure the smile seemed vindictive, not joyous, and contained no hint of relief. "Drop her," he directed.

The spell holding her released. Shimmer landed on her feet and, thanks to a dancer's grace, did not stumble even as her bag swung heavily.

Falling into a new performance, Shimmer looked at Seria with a boasting stare, her mind spinning. Letting him believe there was rivalry between them would make her willingness to help them more realistic. Being suddenly too helpful would be suspicious.

"You are going to help me break apart Tohmas' army," Terant informed her.

Shimmer sat into one hip with her hand resting at the top of her skirt. "I work for a price," she told him. *Not that I'd work for you for any price, but Lie Lights don't care about context. I'm not lying.*

The man sneered and delivered a dark grin. "First," he said in an eerily quiet voice, "I will give you your life. If you work well, then I may consider offering you compensation. We can negotiate the price then."

Shimmer nodded, holding onto her false calm. Any word spoken now would have to be a lie.

Seria was indignant. "You cannot trust her! She has been traveling with Tohmas!"

"I have been traveling with Fixer City," Shimmer corrected. "Armies are pretty good customers, so long as you stay away from the front lines. You sound like a child throwing a tantrum. How is it someone as simple as you are the apprentice to such a powerful—"

"Enough," Terant interrupted. "Seria, stop worrying. I am not going to turn her loose. Of course I am going to Geas her."

Shimmer's stomach knotted, but she forbade any sign of her unease from surfacing. He was watching her closely, anticipating her reaction. She gave him nothing.

"Are you going to object?" Terant said after she failed to reply.

Shimmer laughed falsely. "No," she replied honestly. "There is no point, I assume."

"Good girl," he said. "Then let us get on with it. Once that is done, we will lay the plans that will rip apart Tohmas' precious alliances."

While Seria glared, Shimmer followed Terant to the side of the room, where she had to carefully control her breathing as he took her bag from her and applied the most terrifying spell she knew over her mind.

During the war with DoomDragon, Kitable had discovered that his enemies knew about his crystal pendant. He had almost thrown the enchanted trinket away but, after some consideration, he had instead decided to instead change the Relocation spell on it. He had completely redone the anchoring component.

If he did not know where he was going, neither would his opponent.

Building the many random anchors in, then defining what would be "safe" had been difficult. He realized that he had defined a vertical distance that was a little higher than was prudent when he relocated two strides in the air and fell right into a bag of flour.

It was a softer landing than the stone floor or any of the boxes in the storeroom would have been. Kitable mentally thanked the flour for being so conveniently located as he stood to brush the dust off himself.

He had to move quickly. It was possible that Terant would try a few of the many anchors and get lucky. Or if Terant figured out the spell Kitable had used, he may realize the anchors would pass through the Seal spell but the Relocation spell itself would have been blocked. There was only one direction Kitable could have gone in light of the domed Seal spell: down into the rest of the manor.

And down he had gone. Due to a lack of windows, he could not tell how far down his spell had taken him, but it felt like he was underground

by the cool temperature. Where exactly he had landed compared to the hall he had just left was a mystery.

A mystery that is going to have to wait, Kitable realized. Voices were approaching the room where his spell had randomly dropped him.

Barrels, bags, and dried meats allowed him to recognize the room as storage, but it was too small to let him hide. The door was wide open, light pouring in from the hallway beyond. None of his remaining spells were appropriate for concealment, and he had no time for a full cast. Instead, he pulled off his robes and shoved them behind a barrel, leaving him in a pair of grey trousers and a simple undershirt. He grabbed the nearest bag, his hand pinching. He would have to remove the crystal shards from it in a moment.

When a pair of men walked through the open door, Kitable was transferring potatoes out of a sack into the make-shift pouch of his shirt in the darkest corner of the store room.

"Got enough?" one of them asked at Kitable's back.

He had been in Galanth for long enough to have picked up a prominent south accent, but Kitable's origins had been Lour. It was not quite as good as being from Tanble, but it was certainly better than being Galanth.

When he replied, his words sounded, to him, as if he was a child again. "Should be. Running low, though," he mumbled.

The two men pulled down a cured ham from the rafters and held it between them. "We should be getting more soon, or just grab a few more from upstairs."

Kitable perked up. "Where?" he asked, reaching into the bag to keep his face, and his enchanted eyes, from being seen. He may need Spell Sight and dared not dismiss the spell yet.

"Go up a floor or two. Your best shot's on the main floor. Just don't let the cook see you there or it'll be your head."

Kitable knew the tone; he had heard a similar tone when Master Sylas had spotted in the corridors, sending the apprentices running for cover.

He gave an agreeing grunt. The two servants left without another word.

Kitable paused, propping himself against a crate and dumping the potatoes from his shirt into a corner. So far, Terant had not followed.

That is promising. Now I just had to get out of the Manor of Arcott, assuming that is where I am.

It has to be a manor; too many floors. Those two didn't seem bothered that they didn't know who I was. A very large manor then.

He checked his hand in the door's light. The crystal activation had to draw blood, but these small cuts were few. He pulled the pendant's tether off from around his neck, removing the last shards. He shoved it into a half-empty jar of honey.

Satisfied he had removed the slivers of crystal, Kitable reassessed the room and decided there was nothing of value here. *Need to look outside. There will be defenses.*

Wrapping his green and silver robes in the emptied potato sack and promising to clean them later, Kitable slung the sack over his good shoulder. He reviewed the trinkets, but there were only three still available for activation: his shield pin, an Anchor Block rope, and a ring that thickened the air around him to discourage enemies from approaching. It was mostly to keep fighters at bay since a more savvy opponent could force their way through it.

It took him almost half a candle to find a set of stairs so carefully was he avoiding people, and it took another half candle to find the second set. Once he was on the main floor, he easily found a window to look out.

A disappointingly impressive layering of auras looked back at him. He put down the bag to lean against the wall and consider them, grateful for the Spell Sight he still wore.

The Seal was still up for one thing, but that was not a barrier to physical travel and did not overly worry him. What did concern him, however, were the other spells wrapped around the building.

Breaking down the spells by their auras took time. They were not offensive shields—they couldn't be if Terant wanted people to come and go from the manor. Instead, it seemed to target magic itself. A thread of purple connected all the components of the spell like a ribbon woven through braided hair.

So what does the binding do? It's got a reversal on it, like it goes backward up a spell...

When realization hit, the implications landing like a physical weight on him, and Kitable leaned back against the window frame. *Genius, yet unheard of. How did he come up with that?*

Terant's spell didn't counter a given element or domain of magic. It connected to *magic* itself as it passed through, then tracked the target and turned the magic into a binding spell. That meant any spell, regardless of its composition, would trigger the binding and give Terant a direct binding to the offending caster.

Casting would bind Kitable instantly.

Can't be right, Kitable corrected. *I should have been attacked during the duel when I cast.* He reviewed the recent conflict with Terant. *There were bindings. My Anchor Block stopped them...* He had thought either Seria or Terant responsible at the time, but this made more sense.

The consequences of the shield around the manor continued to evolve as Kitable stood thinking. Even if he tried to cast a new hovering spell, the magic he drew in would set off the alarm and activate the binding. And his Anchor Block was gone now.

If I cast anything, Terant will not only know where I am, but he'll also have a binding on me.

He searched the auras, but there was no way through. Physical passage was blocked. Magic would be tracked. He was trapped.

He crept back down the stairs. The Rejuvenation spell was a meticulous timekeeper and would exact its toll soon enough. If he failed to figure out how to escape the manor in the next eight candles, he had to find a place where he could sleep without drawing attention to himself.

And in all that time, the Galanth forces were vulnerable. If Terant discovered Kitable's absence, there would not be an army to go back to.

Chapter 14

The full forces of the Esparan, for once unburdened by Fixer City and the Temple waggons, set camp beyond the mountains. From a high viewpoint, Tohmas could see a red dragon patrolling the horizon. He watched, but it did not come closer. Looking behind him, he caught a glimpse of the silver of the bull dragon that had followed them through the mountains. Whether it was real or an illusion, he did not know anymore. It continued to watch, daring the Reds to enter the mountains again.

He had no idea if the Silver was a blessing from Inac or just a coincidence, but he did not dare count on it following them outside the mountains. Dragons were territorial. The army was on its own once free of the mountains.

Knowing he had to be patient, Tohmas decided it was time to again converse with the princes. Arcott was one long day's march ahead. Once there, they had to take the city and bring down the treacherous prince who had been waging war against them in secret for a decade. The faster that happened, the better the spoils to be had.

Darknim's departure was no concern, but the injuries to Carsh's arm in the defense of the Circle was another matter. The prime protector was practicing throwing with the splint on, but he was much slower. Tohmas needed Carsh when they attacked, broken arm or not. Tohmas had no one else he could trust.

Kitable had been missing since the night before. Tohmas had recruited the Pack Runner and Sabian. He hated to think it, but Kitable's absence was worrisome. Not only was Tohmas concerned about his wizard and Follower, if Kitable wasn't available to deal with the casters, he risked losing everything to the enemy's casters. He'd prepared the Pack Runner and Sabian, knowing Carsh was now unavailable. *This is going to be a lot closer than I'd like.*

But there was no going back. If the Reds attacked early, or if the wizards got around Kitable's efforts, or if Marfaie's forces repelled them at Arcott...

Tohmas clambered down the rocky hillside toward camp, Carsh falling into step at his back. Neither used a light, accepting the shadows.

The plan had become a litany in his mind.

But all of it depended on the dragons not getting involved. That was in Darknim's hands, a fact Tohmas would not reveal to the other princes. Tohmas himself would not know the results until he was on the field already, at the mercy of the beasts should they survive. That was an unpleasant thought.

He banished his uncertainty. He owned Inac's blessing. The Goddess would ensure victory was his. He trusted Darknim and the Northlander's abilities. Some degree of risk was inevitable.

In the dusk, the encamped forces had erected no banners and lit no fires. The soldiers had been ordered to leave all non-essentials behind. The only light now came from the moon and shielded lamps.

The soldiers believed their location was hidden still by magic, but Tohmas knew that was a lie. The concealment of darkness was the best he could offer against the threat of enemy casters. He had prayed that Kitable had been successful already.

Standing in the circle of lamp light outside of Dragal's tent, Tohmas found all three of his "uncles." When he heard the conversation, he stopped to listen instead of declaring himself, pausing in the shadow of a nearby tent.

"I will not do it!" Barnon was insisting. "You are my brother, Dragal. I cannot!"

Dragal's words were broken by pauses for short breaths. "And as your brother... I am asking this...of you. Both of you. I will not return... from Arcott. If they do not get a sword into me, you do it."

Carsh grunted beside Tohmas. Tohmas agreed. Dragal should have done it himself, not burdened his family with the responsibility. The other sons of Zayban were equally weak for refusing to help.

Sol leaned on a barrel by the entrance and shook his head, his arms crossed over the crest of a shield on his chest. "Dragal, you still—"

"I am a dead man." The Prince of Clandac coughed, then spat blood to one side. His breath was rapid for a man just standing still but that was no surprise. "My daughters know what to do when I do not return." He paused again, wheezing. "Tell me... you will do it. I would rather... die in battle than—"

"No!" Sol sharply replied. "You have had bad bouts before. Why do you think this is any different? Return south if you must—get out of the cold air—but do not tell me that this is your end, Dragal. We only just lost Habal. I do not want to lose you too!"

Knowing each moment spent eavesdropping perpetuated the danger of being caught at it, Tohmas decided it was time to interrupt.

With brisk steps, he entered the light, interrupting them as if oblivious to their conversation. "Ah, how wonderful I have found you all here! I think I have figured out how best to use the Rydans. Have you a few moments, good princes, that we may converse?"

Yadder, yadder, he scolded himself.

The three princes all stood straight upon his arrival, cutting off their conversation. Dragal mumbled something about advising the young as he followed Sol and Barnon into the tent. Tohmas cautiously shadowed them, wishing they could talk outside, away from the *rehbrehd* disease. Carsh was muttering wards against sickness.

Won't be much longer, Tohmas reminded himself. Tohmas expected Dragal to jump at the opportunity to be at the heart of the fighting when Tohmas suggested he and Dragal seek out Prince Marfaie in his manor directly. Although Dragal would never ask for Tohmas' help in saving face, he did not have to. Unlike the optimistic brothers, Tohmas considered Dragal's death unavoidable.

But if he went down during the battle, the gap in command would be a problem. Someone had to be available to take command when he fell. Tohmas intended to be that person. He just had to ensure the timing was correct.

CHAPTER 14

Like every wizard Shimmer knew, Terant cast his hovering spells long before dawn. Still in the large hall, Seria and the master wizard sat by the fireplace. Shimmer was sealed away under a one-way wind barrier that prevented her from eavesdropping but allowed Terant to hear if she started casting.

It would not have mattered. Thanks to Seria's boasting, Shimmer knew there was a shield over the manor that tracked magic being drawn in. The moment she cast, she would be caught and bound. With Master Terant's continual presence in the back of her mind through the Geas, that would mean instant death.

So instead of casting in the morning as she usually did, Shimmer sat on the floor and watched the sunlight change in the high windows of the empty, cold hall. She let her mind wander, keeping it away from plans of escape. She couldn't risk the Geas spotting something.

More than once, she felt tension in the back of her head like a brewing headache. It intensified twice, which made the hairs on the back of her heck stand up. She felt vulnerable.

When she felt the encroaching powers, she filled her mind with menial things: what dress she would wear today; how much did it bothered her to have her hair so unbound; how cold was the stone in the early morning, not like the warmed wood of her home vardo. Dust had done that enchantment so many years ago, he claimed to have forgotten the code...

Each time, the feeling slowly released, and she was left with a distant memory, a hazy thoughts of the man holding the binding. She could feel his smugness.

When Terant and Seria were done casting, they informed her it was time for breakfast. Terant seemed to have a chore—perhaps adjusting spells to better protect the manor from the imminent attack—so he told her to remain in the kitchen and not cast any spells. The magic in her mind flared, pressure but not pain, and she knew she had to obey. She wondered if someone not adept at sensing magic would have noticed the influence or just accepted the thoughts as their own.

Terant and Seria left the kitchen.

To allay the suspicions of the kitchen workers, Shimmer preened at the center table, finally putting up her hair. It was the best she could do to look presentable in her underclothes. She still saw some of the younger staff snickering, blushing, and pointing at her when they thought she wouldn't notice.

Might as well make myself useful, she decided. She dried dishes, scraped the bread tray, then chopped asparagus. Over time, the kitchen staff stopped paying her as much mind. After a halfcandle, she minced their last garlic clove and was sent to fetch more.

Technically, she told herself, *this entire area could be considered the kitchen.* After all, if someone said to go pick up food from the kitchen, it could be the room or any of its storerooms. The kitchen did not have any windows, but it was possible one of the hallways would.

She wanted a look outside.

Shimmer had only managed a dozen steps down the hall before the Geas flared and stopped her. She was certain the storage rooms were all within those paces and anywhere further would no longer be "kitchen." He had ordered her to remain in the kitchen.

Tension rose in her mind, and her stomach lurched.

"Damn garlic," she said, bringing her thoughts into order by pulling them into a spoken sentence. "My hands will reek for a quartercycle! Where do they keep the soap?"

"Where are you going?" A voice said in her mind.

Shimmer flinched, working to keep her thoughts steady. "Didn't know you could do that," she said, choosing her words cautiously. "You scared me."

"Sending requires an anchor. I have one," he said, his voice filled with self-satisfaction. The threat was obvious. Plenty of things required an anchor. Many of them were unpleasant. Some of them were deadly. And he *had* an anchor in the Geas.

"Answer the question," he commanded.

The magic tightened unpleasantly in her mind. "Looking for a window," she said aloud, not trusting her thoughts unless she focused them on speech. "Your kitchen is stifling. And they needed more garlic."

The pause lingered. She felt something shifting at the far end of the anchor, like a ship pulling on a mooring line. *Straining? Was he casting two spells? Trying to do something while maintaining the Sending?*

"You will be leaving soon," Terant said. *"Behave until then."*

The voice retreated, the pressure gone from her skull.

Shimmer took a shaking breath, staring down the corridor in frustration. With Terant's attention on her, continuing down the corridor was dangerous.

Before she could turn back, a hand appeared from around the nearest corner, dragged her forward, and slammed her against a wall. Her breath rushed out of her lungs, leaving her unable to cry out.

But when she identified her assailant, all thought of protest faded away.

"Kitable!" she whispered in relieved awe. "You are—"

It was only then that she noticed the knife he held to her throat.

"You deceptive, demonic—"

Shimmer's tears of relief turned to fear. "Please, no, Kitable. I swear, I'm not against you!"

Her blood went cold. He had murder in his eyes under the scintillating shifting colors of Spell Sight. She knew he could kill—she had heard all of the stories about his duels and knew them to be incomplete—and she could feel his rage through the arm that pressed against her chest.

"Then why are you here, girl?" he snapped, emphasizing his suspicion by pushing her harder against the wall at her back.

"Because Terant asks yes or no questions under a Lie Light!"

It was a cryptic thing to say, but it was true, and the answer made Kitable pause.

His glower lessened, bemusement sneaking onto his face.

"Yes" and "No" were too easily manipulated mentally by variables. He knew that.

"Only fools let the target of a Lie Light set the terms of their questions," he muttered. He peered at her anew, the suspicion in his stare fading. "The man alters spells to literally undo them, interconnects others together tight as weaving, and has cast spells that blur the definition of the elements, yet he asks yes or no questions under a Lie Light?" A hint of a smile played over his face.

Despite the proximity of the blade, Shimmer nodded.

The grip on her loosened, and the knife lowered. He seemed confused. "That is probably the most ridiculous thing I have ever heard. I

believe you." He stepped back and released her. "I shouldn't," he added with visible frustration. "Somehow, I find I do. Besides, if I did not, I would have to cut your throat and that just..." His sentence trailed off as he tucked the knife under his belt.

She realized she was staring and made herself look away. She could see him thinking, but it was a harried process instead of his usual calm contemplation. He seemed to be speaking himself; "I've killed so many, yet now I hesitate. Figures." He threw his hands up in the air. "Fine. You followed me, didn't you? Then fooled him into not suspecting you. Seems plausible."

"You look awful," Shimmer said gently. Kitable's shirt was torn, and there were small bloodstains, like flea-bites, around his left side. Visible through the loose collar of his undershirt, a bruise stretched from the middle of his chest down his arm.

Following her gaze, he smiled coyly and pulled the collar slightly wider. "Yeah, a nice bruise from an enchanted pillar. Nothing is broken, at least I don't think so." He rotated his shoulder to prove his statement, then shrugged. "Not the worst I've had. What about you?"

"I..." Shimmer fought the urge to check the shoulder for him. "I followed you, but kept out of sight so they did not..." She stopped herself deliberately. The first time she had met Kitable, she had been just about as incoherent. Now, she blamed her renewed fluster on the fact that she was so surprised to see him in the manor.

That, she told herself with an exasperated sigh, *and he is showing off his battle scars.*

She had to clear her throat to gather her thoughts.

"I'm under a Geas," she blurted.

He frowned like a farmer finding gophers in his field. "Great," he grumbled. He leaned toward her, and her breath caught. It took her an extra moment to realize he was activating a spell.

Her words caught, but she got them out; "Don't cast any—"

"I know about the shield," Kitable interrupted. "I'm assessing the Geas. I might be able to use one of my hovering spell. It shouldn't attract his attention or trigger the defenses." He let out a slow breath and finished examining her. "It should work. I can confound it for now."

"Confound it?" she said, realizing abruptly he had moved closer to her.

His voice was matter-of-fact, his enchanted stare tracking invisible magic threads around her without quite landing on her. "It will show him what he expects to see, for a bit. A thought creation. I had one ready since he's not great with thought magic. So far, he hasn't bothered shielding against it as much as other elements. But I didn't get around to using this one." He paused and his eyes focused on her at last. "What were you were supposed to be doing?"

"Getting garlic," she said, her voice involuntarily a whisper.

His eyes unfocused as powers rose from his hovering spells and reached out to her. Lacking defenses, the magic easily took hold.

Part of Shimmer's mind felt strangely stretched as he released the spell. She blinked and had the distinct feeling she was pulling apart a braid of garlic. Again and again, she tested the heads of garlic for a good one.

With the next blink, she was standing across from Kitable. It was as if a dream spun on the fringes of her mind.

"Is this how you feel when you Scry with eyes open?" she asked, trying to see through the double vision: in one moment, Kitable and, in the next, her own hands sorting garlic.

Kitable shrugged, his wince less this time. "Sort of. It won't buy us much time. I'd warn you how dangerous a Geas is, but I recall you are familiar with them. But even if he doesn't happen to check on your thoughts and detect the ruse, what are you going to tell him when he wants to know where you were? With a Geas, you can't lie to him."

"I'll just tell him I got cornered in a storage closet by an attractive man in kitchen clothes, who never did tell me his name."

There was a slight pause—she didn't know if it was surprise or consideration—then, to her shock, he laughed.

"You *did* trick him despite a Lie Light, didn't you?" For the briefest instant, he looked impressed. In a blink, his amusement vanished. His voice formalized. "Now that you have a few moments of reprieve, what is your plan?"

Shimmer lost her smile as well. "He wants to use me for something. I'll probably be back in Fixer City later today." The more she focused on him, the easier it was to ignore the garlic braid in her fake thoughts. "He's not very good at giving commands though. You're right about thought magic being hard for him. I'll slip out from under his control."

His expression grew pensive. "Tohmas can help if you can get to him. SoulBurner can dispel the Geas without repercussion."

Tohmas? When had it become "Tohmas" and not "Prince Tohmas"?

"My father can handle it. I will be..." *He's concerned about me!* The realization made Shimmer's words trail off. *Concern for his duty or for me?*

Instead of finishing the sentence, she corrected herself and asked, "What about you? Why are you here?"

With resignation, he shook his head. "Because I cannot leave. The defenses on the manor prevent me from sneaking out until my spells expire, and I cannot call down any new spells without setting off..."

"...a binding," Shimmer finished for him. "But that only triggers if you draw magic through the shield."

He narrowed his eyes on her. For a second time, he seemed confused, and she realized he was not following. "Steal from him. If *he* draws the magic through, the binding's on him."

He considered the suggestion carefully, his musing comforting Shimmer into forgetting where they stood, risking discovery. "That ... that requires I am physically close enough to detect the magic as it passes, but I'd have to be within the shield. No, his location was high up. I can't reach that without being detected. A Scry is better, but I have no hovering spell for that. Impossible. And the difficulty of targeting magic as it passes in the raw form... a challenge by itself. Plus I'd have to know when he will be casting." He shook his head, as if suddenly remembering her presence and opened his mouth, but Shimmer interrupted.

"He casts at the third candle of the morning."

"Still nearly impossible," he pointed out.

She smiled. "Nearly?"

"The idea has merit. I will think on it." This time, when he smiled, he was meeting her gaze, finally *seeing* her in a manner she didn't think he had before.

The pressure in her mind changed, and Shimmer lost all track of Kitable. Her thoughts were filled with sorting through the garlic, checking the cloves for desiccation before picking one.

The moment lasted a lifetime. Shimmer's heart sped further as she felt Terant's presence. If he saw through Kitable's creation, her life was forfeit. She was suddenly aware of her father's warnings against getting

involved and the foolishness of having followed Kitable as he chased Seria. She and Dust should have turned away from Prince Tohmas' army long ago. Her infatuation was going to get her killed.

The thought of checking the garlic braid held, and the pressure slowly released. When she again brought sight to her eyes, she found Kitable looking at her warily.

"I should go," she said. "He checked in."

Kitable nodded. "It won't fool him twice." With a wave of a hand, he tossed aside his own spell, dismissing it and any trace he had been there. Her mind snapped back together, whole but tired. With his other hand, Kitable handed her a head of garlic.

"Be safe," was the last thing he said to her as she left.

She wanted to say something in return, but the threat of the Geas loomed over her.

Shimmer was back in the kitchen, mincing garlic, when Terant returned with Seria. He asked what she had been doing, but since she had been keeping her hands busy, she managed to fill the answer with dishes and chores.

"Time to get to work," Seria informed her jauntily as they joined her.

Terant halted on her opposite side, not looking the least worn by the morning's casting. In his hands, he held a small chest. Shimmer felt the magic on it potently, rising gooseflesh on her arms. Never before had she felt so dense a concentration of power.

"I have a job for you," he said, extending the chest. It looked like rich jewelry box built of smooth wood and decorated with filigree.

Shimmer recoiled from it, unable to recognize the auras but certain of the potency.

Master Terant gave her a wry smile. "You will carry this into Fixer City. Place it beneath Kitable's vardo then open it."

With each command, the Geas in her mind flared, and Shimmer was compelled to obey.

Steeling herself, Shimmer took the chest. It was surprisingly light, making her dread even more the power it represented. She tried to make her voice sound even. "What is it?"

Terant scoffed; "Just some alteration magic you wouldn't understand."

Trying to keep her thoughts in line when she wanted to slap the man for his arrogance, Shimmer asked, "Do you happen to know where the vardo is?" She knew that answer. Kitable concealed his vardo thoroughly from Scrys. Had Terant known where it was, he wouldn't have needed Shimmer at all.

"I'm sure you can find it," Terant replied, his smile unwavering.

Shimmer shrugged. "Probably, but if I have to carry this thing around, I'll need a bag. And I need to get dressed. Nothing subtle about me running around Fixer City in my undergarments."

Terant waved her off. "Get the chest under Kitable's vardo today, girl. You may stop for clothing. You may not cast any spells or tell anyone about the Geas."

She distracted herself with examining the box to avoid thinking about the commands. She would find holes in them later, when Terant was not hovering so close on hand.

After Shimmer left, Kitable moved for a fourth time. He settled in a small corner in another storage room behind empty baskets expecting next year's harvest. Had he been religious, he might have prayed no one would discover him, but since the gods had as little interest in him as he had in them, he instead simply made a hole for himself among the boxes and blankets and sat down.

Shimmer's suggestion continued to nag him. He knew it was impossible, yet he had no good options, and the idea would not be dismissed. If he could indeed steal magic from Terant as he summoned it, it would be possible to create a spell to escape the shield around the manor. Once free, he could renew his spells and attack once more.

He was almost at the end of the time the Rejuvenation had bought him. If he fell asleep now, the three remaining spells bound to him would expire during his slumber. He would be completely helpless except for his limited trinkets.

I need a Scry. For some inexplicable reason, he trusted Shimmer, and that meant Terant would likely be casting again at the third candle of the morning. He needed to be nearby. Since he could not see doing

so physically, doing so as disembodied senses would suffice. But he had no Scrys left in his hovering spells and casting would let Terant find him.

Unless I use the magic I already have, he considered. Terant had once broken down Kitable's hovering spells, essentially un-casting them, in order to kill him with the overload of magic. In theory, if Kitable could do the same thing, he could re-use the magic from his remaining hovering spells.

The three remaining spells were not powerful. Even if he could un-cast them all, he doubted he could create a potent enough attack to harm Terant or find a counter for the shields around the manor. He couldn't be sure if the three spells—assuming he could un-cast all three—would be enough for a Scry. He'd never quantified magic comparatively before.

It was an unfortunate day to be atheist.

He settled into place. With no better ideas, he decided to try.

The first he tried was the weakest spell; a one-way earth creation spell. It was meant to generate a heavy weight, whether as a tool or as an attack.

Kitable kept it simple. He took the spell and cast it backward, breaking it down piece by piece. The tendrils of magic felt slippery in his mind as he teased them out of the creation spell, surprising himself at how easy the spell could be untangled into its component elements. But the threads felt as though they were pulling to get somewhere else instead of eager to come to him. During one manipulation, the entire spell fell apart, and the released power washed through him as it dissipated. The heat flashed then was gone.

He let out a slow breath by habit, easing aside the ache of the spell burn. The ache lingered, but wasn't enough to distract him.

Kitable's vision refocused on the store room and his cover of baskets and blankets. His skin prickled with sweat. His head was beginning to ache from both the mental effort and the new spell burn. For a moment, he almost gave up entirely on his plan. If he had not witnessed Terant's spell, he would never have thought about recycling magic in this manner. How could he expect to figure the technique out so quickly?

Just a Scry, he told himself. He couldn't do much with the magic he had left, but all he needed was a basic Scry. *What else can I do anyway?*

The Rejuvenation would run out shortly. The spells would expire, becoming useless, before he woke.

He closed his eyes and focused on the next spell, a Spell Sight. Repeating the process, he uncast it, teasing it out line by line. As the magic came loose, Kitable kept his attention close, aware of every fiber of power. After three lines had been reversed, the spell fell apart as the first had, but this time Kitable wrapped his mind around it. It strained against him, like a leashed hound pulling, but he yanked against it, tightening his hold.

The pressure released. The magic settled in his mind like an in-progress spell awaiting the next word.

While holding the first ball of power, Kitable repeated the process with the last spell, and soon he had a much larger ball of magic held in his mind. Although he was able to split his attention, the magic refused to remain divided: as soon as the second spell was untied, it fused with the waiting magic of the first.

For a blink only, he allowed his excitement. It was possible! For the first time, he had un-cast a spell, changing a spell into its basic elements. It was exhilarating to glimpse the new possibilities unfolding to this ability.

But in the next moment, he reminded himself that the Rejuvenation was due to fall, and he still had to do something with the magic. If he fell asleep too early, it would be lost.

Meticulously, Kitable crafted a basic Scry, which he added a Contingency to and so bound to himself as a hovering spell. Fortunately, there was enough magic for the spell. Unfortunately, there were leftovers. Once the spell was finished, all the magic in his mind was loose.

The burn washed over him, digging through his muscle to burrow into his bones. He slouched, gritting his teeth against a cry as the powers seared through him.

Before he could reorient himself, Kitable's mind drifted, as if the supports had been knocked out from under him. The Rejuvenation had come to take its toll.

His last thought was a quiet curse to the spell burn. *Waking is going to be hell.*

He was asleep before he could even lie back.

Chapter 15

Dust did not worry when Shimmer disappeared overnight and failed to reappear in the morning since he had the ribbon on her pillow. He wished her success in whatever she was doing and went about setting up Match and Mixer normally.

Early that afternoon, Shimmer returned.

While she found a change of shirt and slipped her skirts over her slip once more, she said, "Father, dear, will you be alright to manage the shop alone? I have something to do." A handkerchief and some looped earrings completed her ensemble as she waited for his reply.

Her voice was perfectly normal. One word, however, instantly made his heart beat speed.

She had called him "father." Just as "the" Match and Mixer hailed danger, Dust only called Shimmer "daughter" when there was trouble, and Shimmer only called him "father" when she needed help.

That isn't her bag, he recognized. They both had supplies that never left their sides, ready for easy escape. She had taken hers last night, but no longer had it.

Thanks to many years of practice, he kept his voice despite his misgivings. "Well, I'm all caught up on sleep." With a complacent fatherly smile, he finished, "Oh, go have fun!"

"Thanks," she said, giving him a peck on his cheek.

Once Shimmer was out of sight, Dust slapped Spell Sight up and crept after his daughter. The orange magic anchored in Shimmer's mind,

evidence of thought magic, was obvious. He analyzed it as Shimmer walked through Fixer City. When he finally figured it out, bile rose in his throat.

A Geas.

Shimmer had paused at a shop, waving over one of her local contacts; Caddic. The boy reached only her waist but had gone through a growth spurt lately. The extra food he could buy with Shimmer's payments would be helping that.

A little too loudly, Shimmer asked, "Where is Master Kitable's vardo parked?"

The boy proved worth his money; he detailed a route straight to the vardo. Shimmer paid him and continued on her way.

Knowing his destination—Shimmer was expecting him to overhear her—Dust activated a four-way alteration spell usually used to enhance his juggling. It served well to give him the needed speed to reach the vardo first. Like Fixer City, the vardo had been left behind in the mountains to await the return of the soldiers.

When he skidded to a stop alongside the waggon, Dust found himself at the end of the surprised stare of Kitable's waggon driver, Colt. At first, he did not know what to say to the deaf man, but this wasn't his first visit to the vardo; Colt extended his stone for Dust's use. Touching it, Dust rattled off his problem, but the waggon driver shook his head.

"Kitable is not here."

"Not worried about that," Dust said. "I'm just going to cast a spell on the waggon, if you don't mind."

Colt looked suspicious, but Dust pleaded with him, and the waggon driver finally consented. Dust chose the first step of the vardo, where none of Kitable's defenses reached.

Dust finished with a moment to spare. He ducked behind the vardo, using the auras of the defenses to conceal his enchanted self, as Shimmer arrived.

As if nothing was out of place, Shimmer addressed Colt as a friend and asked if Kitable was around. Even though Dust had given the waggon driver no directions, Colt replied, "Yes. Go ahead and knock."

He knows more than he lets on about magic! Dust thought.

Shimmer gave him a sad smile. "No need," she said. "I've got a present for him."

Dust's heart sank. If Shimmer did not go up to the door, she would not trigger the dispel.

Instead of going for the door, Shimmer untangled a chest from her bag. Even from a distance, Dust sensed the potency of the magic. Colt wrinkled his nose as if feeling something amiss then shied away. His certainty shaken, Colt glanced directly at where Dust was peeking out from behind the vardo. Thankfully, Shimmer's attention was on the chest, and she did not seem to notice Colt's apprehension.

Fine, I'll do it the long way, Dust decided.

As he cast a full dispel, Shimmer approached the vardo and placed her strange chest under the edge of it. She moved without grace, a manufactured action.

Dust cast as quick as he could but the words could not come fast enough.

As he finished the dispel, Shimmer flipped open the chest.

Magic erupted out like a volcano.

As she walked through Fixer City, Shimmer kept her thoughts one step ahead. First, getting into the vardo. Then, finding her clothes. Then, dressing. She had been commanded to tell no one about the Geas. She could not say anything to her father.

But in the back of her mind, she knew Dust recognized something was amiss the moment she arrived.

The Geas prevented her from using a hand signal, and Shimmer knew she could not force words out that would directly contradict the command to not tell anyone about the spell. But words had many meanings, and her father knew her well.

Saying "father" was not revealing the Geas. It was just a word.

As soon as the word was out, Shimmer deliberately avoided thinking about it, feeling Terant's presence too close. Once dressed, she headed into Fixer City. The pressure of the Geas followed her.

"Find Kitable's vardo," Terant commanded into her ear. *"Once you have determined he is in, set the chest down below the vardo and open it."*

Her heart skipped, recognizing that Terant's unaltered plan meant he had not spotted her hint to Dust. She forced the thought from her mind and focused on Terant's words.

"I know someone who can help," Shimmer muttered. Ignoring the fact that Dust probably knew where Kitable's vardo was, she filled her mind with memories of Caddic, one of her agents in Fixer City. She paid for information regarding other wizards frequently. Caddic kept himself appraised of their movements in case Shimmer came by to ask. Kitable had been good at hiding for a while but recently had been relying on the Circle's protection. It had become easier to find him.

Caddic was the only option she gave Terant.

"Good enough," Terant replied.

To Shimmer's chagrin, she found the boy swiftly. And, sure enough, he knew where Kitable's vardo was. With the Geas pulling her on like the tug on a leash, she followed his directions.

Thoughts of her father continued to creep in. She needed Dust's help soon, but she'd seen no sign of him. The chest in the bag made her anxious. Something felt entirely wrong.

She paused when she found the vardo, the auras around it indomitable before her. Her ribs seemed to tighten around her heart, the enemy's trinket awkward in its bag over her shoulder.

Fear snuck in around her every thought, for herself, for Dust, and for Kitable's vulnerable position back in the Manor of Arcott, thus far undetected. If Terant found out the wisavi was not here, would he go seeking him?

She needed a distraction, and her scattered thoughts did not give one.

The flash of a colored cloak leaving the clearing caught her eye. Colt, manning the campfire by the vardo, turned away from it and faced her expectantly.

She knew that cloak. But as she felt hope, Shimmer suddenly realized why she felt so wrong about the chest. He'd said it was alteration, one she wouldn't understand. Hadn't Kitable said Terant altered spells to undo them?

The implications grew. If he reversed the spells on the vardo, he could use their energy as an attack. He could both destroy all the defenses and obliterate Kitable in one swoop.

But Kitable was Arcott.

Terant had commanded she confirm Kitable was in. She didn't think she could keep Kitable's whereabouts secret if directly asked, and it was about to become apparent the Master Wizard of Galanth wasn't home.

Nausea rose.

The presence in her mind grew, and Shimmer slammed down on the thoughts, bringing her whole focus onto the chest. She knew what the spell would do, and she set her thoughts onto marveling at them.

"Something wrong?" he asked.

She had been a performer since childhood when performances had dictated whether she ate or not. Different circumstances required different skills, even different personalities. "Shimmer" was only one name she could use, only one person she could be.

For the sake of her secrets, Shimmer became a character. She had called this one "Bliss." Bliss had no love for anyone besides herself, making her stronger and more willing to do whatever she needed to in order to survive.

"I will get this done," she replied in her thoughts alone, stubbornly forcing confidence and selfishness to the fore of her mind. *"And once I do, I'll be free to go, right?"*

Amusement drifted into her mind, an intrusion of its own as the emotion was clearly not hers.

"Of course," he said.

Without a doubt, it was a lie.

Refusing to let go of Bliss' arrogance, she trusted in her own usefulness. He might not release her, but he would use her again. That much was certain.

She entered the campfire circle at the base of the vardo's steps. Colt recognized her and offered the orb that allowed him to hear her.

"Is Master Kitable in?" she asked. Somehow, even Bliss' voice sounded different.

"Yes. Go ahead and knock," he replied.

Her heart skipped.

"Why do you doubt him?" Terant demanded, his voice pounding like a headache.

She winced, her head throbbing as she fought back. Any reply would be a lie.

"Don't knock," she thought. She let her fear through, fear of discovery and of the many dangerous spells that defended the vardo. Then she brought Bliss' absolute confidence back. *"Knocking will trigger wards."*

"The driver knows it," Terant surmised. *"He's defending his master. Fine. Let's be done with this."*

Shimmer's head ached again, her vision clouding. She felt her mouth move and heard her voice speak despite the words not being hers.

"No need," she said to Colt. "I've got a present for him."

"Let go!" she cried reflexively, helpless as she spoke and her body moved. *"I will do it."*

She still had no control when her own hands placed the chest under the stairs of the vardo. The pain in her head screamed, scattering her thoughts.

"That, dear girl," Terant said, a boom that echoed in her skull, *"was a lie."*

Panic swept into Shimmer, although her body did not show it. Had she been in control, she would have trembled and cried out, knowing that her life was forfeit the moment the chest was activated, for surely he would be done with her now that she had revealed her disobedience. She fought against her own muscles, but there was no response. Her vision blanked in pain, her head feeling cracked wide by the pull of two forces within.

She was aware of only one thing; her hands opening the chest.

Sharp as an icicle, magic struck her from behind.

The tether in her mind snapped.

Her head cleared.

Suddenly in control of her body, Shimmer ducked and ran from the vardo as the spells around Kitable's home were undone, folded into themselves, and burst. She cast as she ran and had a Molded Shield up by the time she threw herself behind a neighbor's vardo. She crashed into Colt and, unsurprisingly, Dust. Colt stared at them both, bewildered, while they covered their ears against the thunderous explosion of magic she had left behind.

Colt was already looking around the corner, judging the damage, by the time Shimmer got up. She rattled off a quick Anchor Block, then joined the waggon driver in investigating the explosion.

Kitable's vardo was in ruins. Splintered wood littered the ground out to twenty paces, some flying with enough force to be sticking out of the nearer waggons. The force of it had extinguished the campfire entirely and scattered the cinders.

Shimmer puffed her cheeks. "Kitable is going to be furious when he finds out."

Glancing back over her shoulder, she saw her father finally letting go of his ears and standing up. He dusted himself off but gravel and dirt remained stuck to his trousers and shoes.

"Thanks for the dispel!" she added.

He nodded, but his face was grim. The sight of it bothered her; it was an expression she saw seldom. It never boded well.

"I'm fine, papa," she told him, reaching out gingerly. "I knew you could—"

Colt grabbed Shimmer first, his hands wrapping around the Molded Shield but not touching her skin. He pointed frantically back toward the exploded vardo.

Checking, Shimmer saw Seria appear in the rubble.

Confirming the death? Shimmer wondered. *Or following up on me?* Terant would know his spell had been broken. With her basic defenses up now, he could not target her directly any more.

"Demon shit," she cursed. "Seria."

Dust's voice was heavy as granite. "I'll get this one."

He activated a spell, covering himself with a powerful illusion. The green and silver robes followed his arms and body when he strode purposefully around the corner of the vardo they had hidden behind. His voice was not part of the spell, but he mimicked voices well. He had even added dozens of little tiny balls of lights around him bound with purple threads to mimic hovering spells as seen with Spell Sight.

As the perfect duplicate of Kitable, Dust squared himself before Seria.

"Pathetic excuse for a spell," he declared in a southern Galanth accent. "You missed!"

Shimmer followed her father around the corner, playing a new role.

Shimmer pointed a damning finger at Seria. "Wisavi Kitable! There she is! Seria works for Terant still!" Shimmer declared.

Seria paled to match the gravel.

"Foolish girl to come alone," Dust declared. "Let her feel the wrath of my magic!"

Dust adjusted his illusion and brought together some of the little balls of "spells," winding and twirling them around.

Seria panicked and cast reflexively. Neither Shimmer nor Dust tried to stop her. In a blink, she had vanished.

Dust dropped the illusion. Grinning now in a more typical manner, he spun to face the speechless waggon driver and tipped his hat. Shimmer, meanwhile, burst into laughter.

"Wrath of my magic?" she asked as Colt kicked at some of the explosion's shrapnel.

Dust shrugged. "Got carried away," he confessed. He searched the new clearing, grimacing. "Sorry I didn't get the dispel in fast enough though to stop you before the chest went off. What *was* that?"

"Terant has a way of breaking down spells. I think that was what he did. Destroyed the defenses with its own magic. Good thing Kitable wasn't home," Shimmer answered. Dust paused mid-bow to cock an eyebrow at her. "We need to tell Prince Tohmas where his wizard is."

"Telling Tohmas may be an issue," Dust said. "He's headed north. They're about to storm Arcott."

Shimmer let out a long breath. "Then we'd better catch up."

Colt cleared his throat loudly, drawing their attention. Fixing them both with a stern stare better suited to a scolding parent, he said, "You get to explain this to Master Kitable."

Evidently deciding there was nothing worth salvaging in the wreckage, he sat back down and started to rebuild his fire. Since he did not offer his orb, Shimmer presumed he did not want to hear her reply. She eyed the damage and grimaced.

"I guess that's only fair," she admitted. "But I've got to save him first!"

With a spell for speed, they took off through the foothills.

Kitable awoke in darkness with something abrasive over his face. Thrashing, he pushed aside the blankets that had fallen on him. It took a moment, but he soon explained the storage room to himself, and his thoughts immediately went to his spell.

The comforting buzz of the hovering spell answered his thought by spinning around his head. He let out a sigh of relief and promptly regretted it. His ribs, lungs, and shoulders sharply ached.

When he tried to sit up, pain shot through him. His muscles, deep against his bones, burned fiercely and temporarily made him lean back. Too much power had been left with the casting.

Not as bad as some spell burn I've had, he told himself, gritting his teeth and sitting up. He had more important things to worry about now that he was awake.

Figuring the time was easy; Rejuvenations was strict a timekeeper. He had cast the spell at midnight the night before, with a duration of twelve candles. The spell sustained for the allotted time, then forced recovering sleep for the same time. That meant a full day, to the candle, had gone. It was officially midnight.

The position he had slept in had left him chinked from skull to pelvis, but before seeing to his discomfort, Kitable pulled a sandglass from his pouch and set it carefully aside. In between turns of the glass, he stretched out his shoulders and arms, then sought food. When the sandglass ran out on the fifth turn, Kitable settled back into the seat and activated the Scry he had prepared.

He could not add Spell Sight, but with his senses trained to the Scry, Kitable was able to detect, and avoid, Terant's defensive spells. Through the Scry, his senses circumvented the manor in search of something magic, all the while staying well within the massive shield that would instantly reveal him and bind him.

It took him another half-candle to find the open courtyard where he had Relocated to in pursuit of Terant. Once he had sighted the patterned silver stones, he remembered the corridors he had taken and followed them back, staying outside the manor still but trying to approximate the location of the hall where he had confronted Terant.

Starlight and moonlight were all he could navigate by when he found the huge domed ceiling of the hall. To enter in? There were wards, and he could not manipulate or dispel them now. And if he drew too close, would Terant or Seria not detect the Scry? Discovery was death until he gathered more magic and more spells. He dared not move in.

He was still considering the problem when magic passed near his disembodied senses.

He jerked to the side, searching the area for an explanation. A sharp pain shot through his temple; he'd hit his head in his distraction. Hoping he'd not made enough noise in his hiding place to attract attention, Kitable scanned the region around his Scry. Nothing confronted him. Whatever the spell, it had clearly failed to bind him, but had he been targeted? Stumbled on a defense? Was Terant aware of him?

Silence answered for several breaths. The next time the magic approached, he sensed it more clearly. It was raw powers, not targeted, not a spell. Understanding followed. *No reason to get closer*, he realized. Terant was calling magic—casting earlier than Shimmer had reported, else Kitable had lost track of time—and that meant the magic was passing through the complex to reach the wizard. Some of the magic threads were passing close enough for him to detect them.

Upon the next flare of power, Kitable reached out a conscious thought and grabbed a snippet, leaving the majority of the magic to carry on as summoned. He paused, the gentle warmth of magic swirling in his mind. Was there enough of a difference to draw attention? Kitable had never thought of magic as quantifiable, and he hoped Terant had not either. How much could he take without it being obvious?

More magic passed by. As far as he could tell, Terant was carrying on.

Dividing his mind further, Kitable maintained his Scry with one part of his thoughts, then reached out for another bit of Terant's magic when it passed by. He repeated the action until the ball at the front of his mind was even larger than it had been the day before, pushing at the edges of his divided attention.

Although he felt confident in his ability to divide his thoughts, he could not cast two spells at the same time; as far as he know, that was an impossibility. Any spell he cast would dissipate all of the magic, using what it needed and leaving the rest to burn him. Casting close to Terant might alert the enemy. Even remaining where he was ran a risk. He was still vulnerable. If Terant or Seria spotted him, he would be dead upon the first binding.

I'm only going to get one spell from this, he admitted to himself.

As much as he wanted to do more, Kitable released the Scry and was instantly back in the storage room. The comforting buzz of magic remained with him, the bulging powers in his mind straining to escape.

He held the magic carefully, considering every word of the spell he planned to build. Terant was a master of layering elements and domains. To escape the manor without being bound, Kitable needed something well beyond a simply Anchor Block. Every angle, every element, every approach had to be considered. It had the benefit of using a lot of power, so hopefully, it would leave little spell burn. He connected it to a Contingency, setting it as a hovering spell, and released.

He'd taken too much magic, fearful of being short and wasting the entire endeavor. Now, the remaining magic poured through him, adding a new layer of heat and pain to the muscles already aching from the last spell burn.

Kitable slowly got up. His muscles tightened in protest, as if he had ran to Wayburn and back. He leaned against the wall. Already tired, he could hardly stand through the pain.

It will fade, he told himself, forcing his feet to move. He had to get moving. He had a chance to escape.

And then what? Once through the shield, it would be a race to get additional spells up before Terant discovered him. Normally, his morning array took candles to cast, but he might only have moments. He needed something decisive and powerful, something that could end a duel in one shot. But Terant was so well defended. No single spell could get through such varied magical defenses.

With one exception, Kitable realized.

He knew how to break down spells now. He could do what Terant had done in HillTop. He could reverse Terant's spell. It seemed only fair.

Cautiously, Kitable sought a way out. Dawn had spread through the manor, slowing his progress further. He managed only short distances before his body protested and needed a rest.

At length, he found a door leading outside and pushed it open. The shield hung before him, invisible yet nearly tangible in its potency. Stepping outside would trigger it.

The sunrise cut low across the houses, leaving long shadows like criss-crossing rivers along empty streets. The noise of the city felt dampened, like the cold air was a blanket muffling the distant clang against an anvil or the stomp of a horse being bridled. The chill condensed his breath and gave him gooseflesh through his thin shirt. His robes—Galanth's green and silver—were still in the bag over his bruised, sore shoulder.

A bell tolled and the pre-dawn hush broke. Footsteps clattered across stone thresholds, and weapons clanked. Shouts went up, followed by drums and horns.

This was the second day. Tohmas was already here.

"Good distraction," Kitable muttered to himself as he pushed off the wall and took a deep breath. He licked his lips, focused on the hovering spell, and activated.

Without waiting to see if it had worked, Kitable bolted out the door and took to the streets, casting as he ran. He needed one spell, and one spell only. Then, he needed to find Terant before the master wizard found him or destroyed all Tohmas had worked to build.

In the pre-dawn, Tohmas was back on the vantage point in the foothills, looking for the dragon. He was still standing there under the weak dawn when the beast passed over them.

The enormous shadow rose out of the gloom, the red of its scale lit by the fiery sunrise. Horses and dogs went mad in the camp, struggling against their tethers, and the alarm horns sounded. Most soldiers cowered as if wishing the beast would fail to spot them. No doubt they knew basic cloth or even the lee of a stone would not save them if the dragon brought fire upon them.

Tohmas waited in the open, his hand on SoulBurner. He knew the blade could cut dragon scale if it had to. From a higher vantage point, he may even reach a vital part.

But it passed over them without pausing. With a gust of wind, it carried onto the northwest, away from Arcott.

Tohmas laughed. "The way is clear!" he called. "To Arcott!"

Unburdened, the forces traversed the fields at a brisk march. The Rydans rode on the wings, keeping their excited warhorses under tight control but taking any opportunity to goad on the Esparans nearest them. They would break from the main forces when the city came into sight—that much Tohmas expected—but until then he needed his forces together.

Watching the many fighters and riders make their way across the fields unaccosted by dragons, Tohmas' confidence wavered. The dragons'

departure might only be temporary; Darknim was one person facing the beasts and their master. And what about the casters? Kitable was missing still. No one had reported him captured or killed, yet Tohmas dreaded what would happen if Master Terant or his apprentice attacked and Kitable was not there to confront him.

Inac grant us victory, Tohmas prayed, holding the grip of SoulBurner, and hoping the light of the sword was enough to draw the Goddess' attention. It wasn't enough to merely take Arcott. Tohmas needed survivors. He had more plans for Espar that required sufficient force. Losing too many against the walls of Prince Marfaie's capital doomed it all.

Interrupting him, the illusion of a silver dragon flew down from the clouds, glittering in the early light and guided by a colorful caster jogging with flickering lights under his feet. The Weavers were joining, Tohmas was pleased to see. That would give him something to challenge the casters with.

But where's Kitable?

As the dragon passed over, a roar rolled over them. At this distance from Arcott, Tohmas suspected it didn't matter that the mouth did not open.

Just as the Rydans spotted the city and broke their horses into a run, the first spell appeared. The Fire Blast, similar enough to other attacks for Tohmas to recognize, attacked the dragon over the Rydans. The illusion flew through the flames as if they were nothing. *Perhaps*, Tohmas mused, *had the dragon been real, such a spell would indeed have been nothing to a Silver.*

A second blast struck to no effect. The third spell crash among the Rydans. There, the herd was thrown off their feet, those who did not fall balking at the fires that were smothered by slush and snow. Under the rapidly-dispersing steam, the Rydans brought their horses under control and fanned out.

And then they jumped, clearing an obstacle that Tohmas could not see.

Among the Esparan, the horns called a warning, then a halt. The many fyrds ahead of him stopped their advance awkwardly.

In the pause, a runner reached him.

"A trench appeared!" the breathless runner reported, handing over Prince Barnon's token to confirm the source of the information. "Wasn't

there two breaths ago, but now it's there, six strides across. The Rydans went *over* it. Straight over! I mean, some fell in, but the horses just *jumped* the damn thing!"

Tohmas grinned at the shock in the boy's voice. Rydan horses didn't like to have their charges interrupted. But a warhorse with an armored rider could not make that leap. The Esparans would have to go around.

"Far Criers! Direct Rabarch and Gaidol to the west gate. The rest south. Solta holding back to relieve us at the gate."

Another blast of fire crashed into the front lines as they obeyed. The cries of the soldiers reached Tohmas, sending a shiver down his spine. Carsh merely growled, Bashuran edging forward to hunt down the caster. For once, Tohmas suspected he hated the casters as much as his brother did.

The only thing he could do was advance. If he or his allies could reach the caster, there would be retribution, but he could do nothing from this distance.

The division of the forces seemed to confuse Arcott's magic defenders, their larger assaults slowing as if they knew not where to aim. Spreading out the forces worked well to protect them from the spells.

Still no Kitable. Better make use of who we have, Tohmas decided.

He nodded to Carsh. With an ox horn, he signaled the Pack Runner to move in. Sabian would be on his tail somewhere in the masses ahead of him. They would take the wizard to task soon enough.

Despite the fall of arrows and the barrage of magic, the Rydans had reached the wall beyond the trench. There was no gate, but Rydans didn't need gates. Raised on the edge of the DragonTail Mountains, they knew cliffs and peaks well. The wall had long spikes jutting out along upper reaches of its ten-stride height to repel ladders, but the Rydans merely stood on their horses to reach the first of the spikes. Soon, rows of Rydans were making leaps between the spikes like firedrakes up a rock face.

As Tohmas cleared the edge of the trench that had magically appeared to block their charge, Prince Dragal and his sparse protectors joined him. The Prince of Clandac looked small atop his warhorse, as if the long march had eaten him up. Tohmas knew the cutters had given the prince some new drug to try, and it seemed to be doing a fine job of keeping the cough under control for the moment. Tohmas remembered keenly what Cutter Darak had told him about those dying of consumption and their final "high and happy" days.

"Gates are still closed," Dragal reminded him, as if he had expected otherwise. "You planning to climb the walls too?"

"Rydans will open the gates," Tohmas replied, coming to a halt, and waiting for the rest of his company to join him.

A horn of alarm sounded; magic was present at the west approach.

Despite wishing for Kitable, Tohmas shouted, "Weavers!" He waited for the caster to look over. His daughter had joined him, Shimmer Weaver a step behind her father, her fiery hair tied back and the air around her shaking with powers. "Head west with Prince Barnon. We need you on the caster."

"What about the wall?" Shimmer shouted back. Sure enough, magical fire exploded along the top of the north wall. Tohmas heard cries from the Rydans despite the distance. Someone sounded an alarm; it was Rydan and translated as "flyer."

The sight of a flyer was a terror many of them had never known. To them, flyers meant death. Although he doubted they would flee, the warning would shake many of the warriors.

Carsh snarled, but Tohmas shook his head. He needed Carsh with him.

"Sabian and the Pack Runner are on this one. You two get the west." Tohmas told the young Weaver.

"Which one is Terant?" she asked, frustration in her words. He did not know when or why, but this had become more personal for her.

Good. Passionate people fight harder.

"Most likely the west gate," Tohmas said. "Most of the fighting is over there. If he wants to hit hard, he'll have to be there. This looks more like Seria."

She and her father rushed off impossibly fast. It was as if their feet did not even touch the earth as they ran, their footprints singeing the ground.

He took a moment to let his surprise fade. He had been skeptical that they would obey him, but Inac did seem to be looking over him today.

Reminded, he checked the skies; he saw no dragons, real or illusionary. Dust's had dropped.

"Best call up for the waggons," Dragal interrupted. "We could be stuck here for a long time in siege."

Tohmas shook his head. "Trust me, Prince Dragal, this one will be ours before the day is out."

"Just so long as Marfaie does not escape," the Prince of Clandac warned.

"We will get him," Tohmas promised, but he was careful not to specifically promise who would get that honor.

To the south, a horn told Tohmas that Barnon's fyrds had reached the gates and were bringing up the ram, a plan in case the Rydans did not make it. They repeated the warning of magic interfering with their purpose.

"Foolish to spread ourselves so thin," Dragal muttered.

"The defenders are thinner than us," Tohmas replied. "And this way, no magic can get us all." *I hope.*

Finally, proving him right, a horn of success sounded. Tohmas turned Honest Justice to the south, Dragal with him. Bashuran, Carsh perched on his back, was soon following, but both rider and steed kept one eye on the fighting.

Tohmas had to leave them to it. These fyrds would have to deal with Seria on their own, just as the west fyrds would have to deal with Terant. Tohmas touched the hilt of his sword and prayed again that Inac would grant them victory.

It was time to move into the fray himself.

Chapter 16

T erant burst from his chambers and ran through the halls, not caring who saw or what they would say. The marker in the northwest had been tripped, not by a few people but by thousands. Climbing the nearest stairs, he sought a vantage point atop the Manor of Arcott and looked out. Seeing only the cleared fields and crags of the north, he cast a Scry and reached out disembodied senses.

Cautiously bringing his enhanced vision to the north, ready for wards and distracting spells, he found the advancing army. Nothing blocked his investigation, a fact that bothered him.

Where's Kitable? He knew the Northlander Circle had parted from the main forces and were no longer in play, but the Master Wizard of Galanth would not have been so cavalier in allowing such a Scry.

Unless I'm being deceived...

The Rydans rode at the flanks in a divided mob, their huge horses at a trot that could outpace most cantering beasts. Between the horses came the main Esparan forces. Terant spotted the four banners of the sons of Zayban. Above them flew the illusion of a small silver dragon.

Demons, he cursed inwardly. When last he had checked, Master Kitable had still been in the mountains, the forces undecided on an approach. Seria had reported seeing Master Kitable there, and Terant had detected no Relocation spell since. He would have known if Kitable had left! How was the army *here*?

Prince Marfaie did not tolerate incompetence.

As Terant watched, a Fire Blast slammed into the illusion of the dragon. While it looked impressive, it did nothing.

Clearly Prince Marfaie knew about the invaders already.

Targeting his patron, Terant activated a Sending. By the time he was done, the second Fire Blast had landed, erupted, and been equally useless against the fake dragon approaching them.

The dragon is only an illusion, my prince, he said. *Please save your energy. It will be needed.*

One final Fire Blast went off, like a parting kicking from a bully, but at least it targeted the live people below the dragon. Even though the explosion was five strides in diameter, it was too small to hurt more than a few of the galloping riders.

Now he could see them without the Scry as tiny spots on the horizon. He had designed his hovering spells around dueling Kitable, not repelling an army. But he had time. A full cast would suffice.

Terant dropped an earth destruction spell in the path of the charging army, expanding it with six extensions until it reached the entire length of the walls. He aimed it ahead of the charging forces, unable to gauge their speed to ensure effectiveness. More than anything, he wanted those horses stopped.

The ground vanished without obvious flash of power. In the flat turf, he suspected they would not even see it until they fell. He was disappointed when only a few Rydan steeds stumbled. The others, somehow spotting the obstruction, leaped over the trench.

The spell had created a hole six strides wide. No warhorse, especially not an encumbered one, should have been able to make the leap.

He had hoped for chaos and confusion, but the jumping horses gave sufficient warning to those behind. They called a halt.

At least the main forces would have to go around. It was a far cry from the consequences he had hoped for.

An alarm bell belatedly sounded over the city. While Terant heard the horns calling out new directions to the invaders below, he headed down from the tower. Marfaie's warriors scrambled in the hallways now, rushing to posts in readiness.

Targeting Seria, Terant ordered, *"Get to the north wall and cut them down. I will go where I am most needed. Tell me the moment Kitable appears."*

"As you command," answered his apprentice.

Breaking into a run, Terant followed the anchor he held on the prince, recognizing the man had taken a place in his hall. Prince Marfaie would be angry enough that the army had reached this far, but Terant was not the only one to blame. A dragon should have already confronted the intruders. So where were Rakhund and his dragons?

If the dragons took care of the army, Terant could save his energy for Kitable. But if the enemy wizard did not appear soon, perhaps the death of a prince or two might convince the vengeful Esparans to back off.

He found Prince Marfaie sitting in the manor's grand hall. The man had an open Scry in front of him, viewing the battle. As Terant entered, he saw Seria pitch a dozen Rydans off the north wall. It struck Terant as odd that the prince was without defenders, but they had lost many during the earlier stages of the war and needed all swords on the walls now. With his training, the prince could defend himself well enough. His short staff was still within reach.

The scene in the Scry changed. One of the prince's commanding Bears led soldiers through the streets.

"North wall is secure. Take your men to the west gate," Marfaie commanded.

The soldier visible in the Scry straightened, nodded briskly, and redirected his men.

They are taking the appearance of new magic in stride, Terant mused. *Perhaps they think I am the source still.* But it would be hard to hide Marfaie's powers now that he was showing it in the grand hall. They would have to be grateful for the additional advantage their prince's power represented.

Looking up from the projections, Prince Marfaie locked eyes with Terant. Terant felt the rebuke like a strike to his gut. It had been his duty to watch the approaching enemy and keep them from Arcott. He had failed.

"We will be discussing this later, Master Terant," the prince said, adjusting his Scry once more. "I want you at the west gate. Prince Barnon makes his approach."

Terant censored himself. He wanted to object that the attack had not come from the direction they had expected, or complain that Seria's report about the army's location had been wrong, or even point out

that Kitable was still missing, but none of those things would matter to the prince now. Now, they had to repel the invasion. He was still useful, for now.

Waving his hand, Marfaie adjusted the visible Scry and showed the west gate, named the Tusk Gate for the narwhal tusks mounted atop it. Ranks of soldiers had attacked, battering the gates with a ram. The wood was holding but seemed unlikely to last long. The keep and its surrounding city did not have much endurance left after decades of dry, cold winds.

"Yes, my prince," Terant said, bowing his head.

"And Master Terant, kill the princes. Use Barnon if you can, but kill him. I want them ruined, but I want them dead more." The prince twisted his hand, adjusting the Scry to face him once more. "I will hunt down his brothers. It is high-time this ends."

It did not phase Terant to hear the change in orders. The death of the sons of Zayban had been inevitable, princes or not. Their deaths had always been planned. The invasion had jumped the timeline. Now, they would all die by whatever means required.

"We will not be able to target Prince Tohmas directly because of SoulBurner," Terant warned.

Marfaie shrugged, lifting his glare from the Scrys. At once, Terant became aware of the black tattoos across the prince's face that marked prowess in battle. He had almost forgotten the prince had skills well beyond that of magic. "You prefer grand shows of force, I know," Marfaie said. "I am accustomed to the indirect approach. I will deal with Tohmas. He has answers I seek." The Scry showed the banner of Galanth briefly, but Tohmas was not visible within the view, hidden by SoulBurner. "The Rydans would never follow this far for an Esparan's slighted pride. This is not vengeance, I am certain. Something is at work here. I will get answers." He turned back to Terant, the Scry adjusting to the south gate. "If they breach the manor, you will find me in the temple," he finished absently.

Terant studied the Scry of the gate, making his plan. Then, using the Scry, he tossed in an anchor to guide his Relocation spell. Instantly, he stood above the contested gate.

First, he broke their ram and threw the soldiers back. Then, spying the man bearing the black rank rope of princehood, he decided on a

thought spell. They were not his strongest, but this man did not know how to resist it.

Once he had outlived his usefulness, Barnon would die.

Darknim and Calanor traveled with little sleep, making their way over the rocky ground to the far northwest of the mountains. Deep banks of snow remained hidden in shadows. Come evening, the mountains gave way to a single long crag of raised cliffs, and the melted edges of snow turned to ice.

The rough weather of the north stripped earth from the surface, leaving stones bare and good shelter hard to find. The cliffs were steep and crumbling. Darkening clouds high above the peaks rushed on distant winds, but the air around them was coolly still. They would have to scale the crags to reach the caldera where Rakhund and his dragons resided, an arduous climb.

They camped for the night, hidden among the rubble at the cliff's base. Darknim expected to need a fire in the cold that frosted his equipment, but the campsite never chilled enough to require it. Calanor had no winter blanket, Darknim noted. In the celebrant's presence, Darknim did not require one either.

Knowing the timeline was tight, they awoke before dawn to begin their climb. They sorted their belongings, slinging the essentials onto their shoulders and making their way up through the pre-dawn grey. Darknim transferred two of Kitable's dozen small orbs, stored in individual small hide pouches, onto his belt. He left the others in the bag over his shoulder for the climb. He shed his heavy fur coat, expecting it would fail him both in the climb and in the confrontation he expected at the top. He fixed his ax to his back in readiness and his sling and stones on his belt.

At first, Darknim worried about Calanor, but despite a lack of hands, the celebrant easily scaled the cliffs at Darknim's side. Although he could see no magic, Darknim suspected untouchable powers held onto the stones. *He's probably better off than I am!* Darknim mused. *My fingers will numb on these pockets of snow!*

Together, they climbed carefully, Darknim cautious not to jar the glass orbs. He needed the orbs to break near Rakhund or his beasts if he was to free the dragons from the spells binding them. Once freed, the dragons should pose little enough danger to Tohmas' forces. That was the point, although Darknim still had not sorted out how to handle two freed Reds. Unlike their more passive cousins, red dragons were indiscriminate in their carnage when angered.

In the lee of the mountain, the wind was calm for their climb. As the sun rose, a fog settled in, likely more of Calanor's doing. Darknim thought to warn the celebrant about the timing of this endeavor—they were cutting things very close with Tohmas' planned departure from the mountains—but found it unnecessary. Calanor, unarmed and un-armored, did not sweat nearly as much as Darknim did, despite keeping pace.

At the dawn, they reached the caldera. Keeping low to the stones, Darknim slunk toward the crater's edge. As large as it was, the fog masked much of the edge and helped conceal him against the black stone. Far below, the shimmering heat from its scales burning away the fog, a lazing dragon was curled against a far wall. The first of the spring's grasses tried to find opportunities in the crater's cracks, the snows melted by the dragons' innate heat.

The dragon's enormous maws rested next to its barbed tails, its wings furled against its spiny back. The bright red scales looked muted in the low natural light of the cloud-covered sun, but its yellow eyes seemed to verily glow when they snapped opened.

Darknim ducked and held his breath.

As Calanor joined him on the crest, a gentle wind rose, passing behind the dragon and toward Darknim. Darknim looked at Calanor, who shrugged. He wondered how the celebrant had known to hide their scent— it wasn't something he had expected from the city-born man— but did not dare ask. The hearing of dragons was equally renowned.

After a hundred heartbeats, he looked again. The dragon had returned to slumber.

Rakhund lived somewhere here, Darknim knew, but he could see no cave openings along the crater walls and no hint of a dwelling. The crater remained stark. *No sign of Rakhund. And where's the other beast?*

He wondered what would happen if they dispelled only one dragon. *Will Rakhund notice? Rush to intervene? Would it be enough to spare the Esparans?*

The sun slowly cleared the horizon, the weight of time falling over Darknim as the sky brightened. Tohmas was leaving the mountains on the approach to Arcott by now. Delaying further would have the Esparan forces subjected to the patrolling dragons.

Only one way to find out, Darknim decided. After checking Calanor was aware of what he was doing, he took one dispelling orb from its hide bag and carefully tested the weight. Satisfied, Darknim fitted the green-swirled glass into his sling. Stunning a rabbit at fifty paces had been necessary for successful hunts in his youth. The throw at a huge non-moving target was comparatively easy.

He flung the orb, aiming to crack it against a stone near the dragon's nose. The hard ground would suffice no matter where it landed.

His aim was perfect, but when the glass orb landed, it did not shatter. Although he could not see details, the black rock became soft, as if spongy. As he watched, squinting from a distance, the orb landed, bounced lightly, then rolled to a stop, safely unbroken and so inactive.

Magic, Darknim recognized. It could not be the wizard magic, for that appeared as colored lights to him. No, this was different.

Rakhund.

Before he could make a new plan, a flash of red appeared before him, hanging like an octopus in the air. The tentacle of power reached out, hooked his bag strap, and pulled before he could move. He lurched back, but it was too late: his foot slipped, sending him careening down the steep inside cliff of the caldera.

Pain shot through him as he glanced off a boulder, then he fell once more. The crumbling slope scraped against his fingers as he sought purchase. The ax on his back lagged behind, crashing into him repeatedly and forcing him to duck his head into a brace position. Through the din of stone on metal, he made out the shattering of glass.

His dragon scale shirt protected him, but his exposed legs and arms were abraded and battered. It was all he could do to tuck them in, trying to avoid breaking a bone.

A torrent blasted up against him. His tumble slowed then entirely stopped. Held against the slope by the force of the gale like an errant leaf, he came to a halt.

My thanks, my friend, he thought, wishing Calanor could hear him.

Gathering his senses, Darknim assessed his position. He was on a ledge above the floor of the caldera by a dozen paces. Over the edge, a stride away, the drop was sheer. Had he tumbled over, it would have been fatal.

He let out a long breath, trying to steady himself. The fall had left him bruised all over. His ribcage ached in protest with his deep sigh. But he hadn't struck his head, and nothing seemed broken.

The wind died down slightly, releasing him to stand on the ledge. Now in control, he climbed down. He landed on the floor of the crater as the wind completely settled.

Looking up, the fog prevented him from seeing Calanor atop the caldera. He thought that for the best as he faced the enormous red dragon that lifted its head at the intrusion.

It lay a dozen paces away and did not seem concerned by his presence at first. Its yellow eyes seemed to drift to orange as it watched, the air around it shimmering with heat. It seemed, for a long moment, to be waiting.

A flicker of movement caught Darknim's eye to his left.

Rakhund emerged from the shadows as if he had been a part of the cliffs themselves. His heavy cloak hid his features; Darknim had never seen his face or the skin of his hands. He had only heard his voice as a whispered grouse of broken Esparan.

Swiftly wrapping the sling he had clutched during his fall around his wrist, Darknim reached for his belt pouch in search of an orb. He found a flattened pouch containing the crunch of broken glass. He had no idea where his bag had gone either, but he remembered the sound of breaking glass. No doubt it had been smashed as well.

His heart sank. Even as DoomDragon, he had no powers with which to match Rakhund.

Pushing aside his despair, Darknim unslung his ax. He did not know how he would be rid of the dragons now, but killing Rakhund seemed likely to work. It was also his only option.

Rakhund growled, the sound similar to what Darknim expected from the dragons themselves. The man's cloak flickered in unfelt wind, subtle red energies gathering around Rakhund's core then extending down his arms. To Darknim's right, the dragon slowly stood.

"That ax is not yours to use. I have long wanted to take that which should be mine," the rumbling voice from within the black hood said.

Darknim hefted the ax. "Come and claim it."

Not wanting to find out what the red energy could do, Darknim charged. He expected the dragon would move in to defend its handler but was pleasantly surprised that it remained distant. He soon understood why: with a sound like he was clearing his throat, Rakhund brought his red magic into distinct threads that tangled the ax blade, dragging the blow to a halt. Darknim strained against the press of the magic, fighting to bring the ax down upon his enemy. His strength was for naught. The blade could not cut through the red light.

The magic wrapped his hands and a sensation crept up his arms. He couldn't initially decide what to call the energy that came with the red light, but he settled on it being made of emotions. The red magic felt smug, like an arrogant parent against a child. Darknim felt confidence in his own failure reaching out to scold him. He was no match, not in any way. He would fail.

His Northlander spirit responded instinctually; he would not be defeated.

Darknim kicked, taking Rakhund by surprise and landing the blow against the man's shin. Rakhund's attention diverted, the twisting red magic briefly released the ax. The dragon blade caught on the black cloth as it bounced harmlessly against Rakhund's shoulder. The sleeve tore open.

To Darknim's shock, the arm was plated in crimson scales akin to those of a firedrake, a smaller cousin of the dragons.

Not dragon, Darknim realized. *Demon.*

The red dragon's claw slammed into Darknim during his distraction, throwing him back a dozen paces into the cliffs. His armor bent to absorb the blow, but he still cried out as it dug through the padding. Being made of the hide of dragons, the armor did not break, saving his ribs from completely shattering. He collapsed onto his knees beside the cliff, gasping.

The ax landed on the stones near Rakhund's feet.

Scatterings of lore and history connected in Darknim's rattled brain. It was no wonder Rakhund controlled dragons when Kitable claimed controlling a dragon was next to impossible. No wonder he claimed the ax; the ax was not from a time before the demon wars; it was demonic.

By the time his vision cleared, Darknim was surrounded by fog. Back the way he had come, he heard Rakhund growling curses.

Taking advantage of the concealment, Darknim drew a stout dagger as he moved wide to flank the creature. Demon or no, killing him was the only means he had to stop the dragons.

Sudden heat rolled over him, and fire engulfed the place he had fallen only a moment before. In the blast of dragon fire, the fog was swept away. Instantly, Darknim stood exposed, only two paces from Rakhund. Across from him, Calanor was also revealed. The celebrant was reaching for the ax lying at Rakhund's feet.

The dragon looming above drew its head back, smoke curling from its nostrils, readying another blast.

But Calanor was too close to Rakhund. The dragon paused.

Rakhund's hood had fallen in the wind of fire, revealing his visage. The face lacked hair; no beard, no eyebrows. Two curved horns extended smoothly along the contours of Rakhund's skull from above the temples. The nose was no more than thin slits between plated bone-like scales. Below, the eye teeth extended in snake-like fangs. Even without obvious lips, it seemed to Darknim that Rakhund sneered.

The eyes unsettled Darknim the most. Even at a distance, they glowed red.

In defense of Calanor, Darknim lunged. Rakhund shrugged instead of defending, but Darknim soon understood why; the demon's scales effortlessly deflected the strike of the carbiron blade. Tohmas' well-crafted dagger, once gifted to Darknim, shattered.

Ignoring Darknim's attacks, Rakhund kicked the celebrant. By the sound, the blow broke ribs as Calanor rolled onto his back, arms clutching on his ribs. Like a man bothered by an insect, the dragon stomped down to crush the celebrant. The air around Calanor shimmered as the food slammed down, blocking Darknim's view.

Fury swelled in Darknim, rage replacing reason. He lashed out but more snaking, red tendrils reached out before the strike could land. Wrapped in tightening coils of magic, Darknim was forced to a complete halt.

Rakhund stooped and retrieved the ax, the dragon snarling over his shoulder, its eyes on Darknim.

"Stupid dreamer," the demon hissed, lifting the ax as he faced Darknim. His wide mouth opened in a partial grin, a forked tongue flicking as it struggled in Esparan. "No finesse. No skill. No match, not for me."

Beside them, the dragon stepped in, revealing the bloody robes of the Celebrant of Totho. The fog had vanished entirely.

The demon looked up at the dragon, the cruel snarl still on its face. "DoomDragon, how fitting is it that you will be slain by the one beast you claimed to be able to best!"

Held by Rakhund's red magic, Darknim could not move.

The dragon lowered its head, the white teeth bared.

The sick feeling in Shimmer's stomach vanished when the battle started. The memories of the Geas still upset her, but now she had a direction for her anger.

They had cast as they joined the army. Overnight, sleep had evaded her, but she was here, now, and she was ready. She had been controlled, and she had to prove to herself that such a thing had consequences.

And she knew Kitable was still trapped in the manor. She might be able to help him.

They were to do Inac's justice today. They were going to bring down a Prince of Espar and right a wrong. Prince Tohmas was leading them to victory in the Goddess' name.

Dust rode beside her as they advanced, his dragon illusion still gliding above them on invisible winds.

"Be careful," he said to her. "Inac may drive men into battle, but she doesn't always bring them out the other side!"

Shimmer nodded, trying to steady her nerves. She had dozens of shields surrounding her, yet she felt as though armor would have

brought her more comfort. Her greatest fear was facing a wizard, but she knew she had to. Terant had bound her. She could not walk away now.

Just as the city came into view, her enchanted sight revealed the swell of red fire elements. It flew high, crashing into the illusion of the dragon.

She forced a laugh. "Surprised they fell for it!" she shouted to her father.

Dust only had the energy to shrug, the long maintenance of the illusion starting to take its toll.

After three Fire Blasts, a new spell appeared between the forces and the walls. At first she contemplated trying to counter it, but the power that rose baffled her. It was not until it was released that she recognized what the caster had done.

It was a windy spell of black that crashed down like a rockslide. It lay low enough that those at the front would not be able to see it, yet it destroyed all earth stretching for a width of six strides.

"Call a halt!" Shimmer shouted. She jumped up and down in search of a far crier. She spotted Prince Sol nearby and targeted him. "Call a halt! There's a pit ahead!"

She was shocked he listened to her, but the horns called out. The forces stopped. From her vantage point, she suspected some of the fighters were only a hands breadth from the drop, saved by the command to stop.

The trench reached the length of the walls. Where it crossed the path of the Rydans, it had little effect. The warhorses leaped it.

"Weavers, head west with Prince Barnon," Shimmer heard. She turned to see Prince Tohmas keeping a respectful distance from her, SoulBurner not drawn but within easy reach. He pointed the way.

"What about the wall?" Shimmer asked, glancing back. She thought she had spotted magic auras atop the wall. A caster was not far.

"Sabian and the Pack Runner are on this one. You two get the west."

Swallowing hard, Shimmer nodded. Her father, she was surprised to see, checked with her, not with the prince. He was not obeying Prince Tohmas; he was working with Shimmer.

"Which one is Terant?" she asked the prince.

"Most likely the west gate," Prince Tohmas said. "Most of the fighting is over there. If he wants to hit hard, he'll have to be there. This looks more like Seria."

Having decided, she turned her attention south.

They were among Prince Barnon's soldiers for the ride south. The Rabarchian soldiers brought up a ram and hammered the brittle wood of the gate. Above, a paired set of narwhale tusks shook with each strike, creating a strange buzzing noise.

Several spells happened in succession, so fast as to be nearly simultaneous.

An Anchor, then a Relocation Spell, appeared on the wall over the gate. Suddenly Master Terant stood above them all, his auras blinding her with their complexity. A Force Spear crashed into the ram, snapping it into three pieces, then bursting out to slash at the soldiers. They fell back, their leather armor easily pierced. Then a thread of orange magic—thought magic—reached out into the soldiers.

She assessed his auras as fast as she could but could only conclude Master Terant was defended against everything. Shimmer pushed that thought aside. No one was invulnerable.

Seeming to sense her apprehension, Dust touched her shoulder. "You sure?" he asked one last time.

Putting her acting skills to work, Shimmer squared her shoulders and buried her apprehension. "Let's take him out."

He gave a nod then activated a binding. In the chaos of battle, speech would be impossible, but their connection could be heard over any din.

Together, they headed to the gate. Letting the arrows bounce off her Missile Deflector, Shimmer ran until she was beside the broken ram and surrounded by Rabarch fighters. Her boots stuck in the mud that was forming, blood loosening the soil, the aftermath of Terant's spell jutting from the ground as mangled armor and broken weapons. Behind her, Prince Barnon had commanded the retrieval of some of the wounded, while those who had not been struck moved in to collect the largest ram fragment and renew their efforts. The soldiers gave her a wide berth, seeming uncertain about how to treat the strange woman in their midst.

"Hey, Terant!"

Master Terant leaned forward, his scowling visage visible over the lip of the wall. "Ah, the deceptive little shrew!" he called down. "Well done, girl. I had expected my spells to consume you."

"Your Geas was shit," she replied, trying to keep her heartbeat from running away with her. *Faking confidence is almost as good as the real thing,* she reminded herself.

He lifted one eyebrow. "You came all this way to insult me?" A spell was forming above his hands, and her Spell Sight revealed it as destructive. *And nasty,* she added mentally as it continued to enlarge and grow more complicated.

"Good enough, Shim," Dust said through their connection.

She held her ground. "I'm not here to insult you. I'm just distracting you, you idiot!" Shimmer performed a theatrical curtsy. As she stood, she cast a small force spell at his feet.

Dust's wind spell blasted against Terant's back. When he took a step to keep his balance against the gusts, the force spell caught his foot. He fell, head first, off the wall.

Activating an item, his descent was stopped by green powers that righted him and allowed him to hover in the air perched atop a disc.

"Stupid girl," he said. His next word activated a hovering spell.

Shimmer did not have time to analyze the incoming magic and instead resorted to dodging it. Despite the speed gained from her Sprint spell, the dispel caught the edge of her shields, tearing through several. Terant shot a similar spell at Dust, but her papa conjured a decoy and the attack was wasted.

She threw out a dispel, only to see it spun around to strike her shields instead. "Pathetic," Terant added, tossing another attack at her. Her heart lurched when she recognized her Anchor Block had been dispelled by his earlier destructions. Even though she ducked under the spell, it looped around and pierced another set of shields by coming at her back. Her Sprint spell died.

Another few of her dispels made their way into his shields, but she felt like she was chipping at fortifications. It felt useless.

Dust bypassed the magical defenses by throwing a stone at Terant's head. He wrapped it in an illusion which made the fist-sized stone look like a boulder.

Terant had Spell Sight active, but this was one of Dust's finest illusions. In addition to the size, he had surrounded the boulder with a smooth black aura like that of an earth creation spell. With insufficient time to interpret the combination of real and fake auras, Terant dropped off his Force Disc to duck under the boulder, which pinged into the wall behind him without even marking it.

Shimmer made the earth under Terant vanish, but the man activated his trinket and was soon standing on a Force Disc once more. When Terant tossed a dispel at Dust, her father attempted the Decoy but this time, the attack ripped through the first spell, a second, then a third. The disguised Eight-layered Dispel hit Dust in the chest. Instantly, he was without hovering spells.

Terant grinned and activated two identical spells, one in each direction. Shimmer, despite her remaining shields, was immediately sealed in a circle of force that glowed green around her. When Terant lifted his arms, the two orbs floated into the air, taking the two Weavers with them. Chuckling, he rose into the air and retook his place on the wall above the gate Prince Barnon's men had finally broken through.

Shimmer suddenly had a magnificent birds-eye view of Arcott.

Most of Prince Tohmas' forces were still trapped at the east gate, a growing crowd with a thin line of people forcing their way through the gate. Fighting was spattered through the narrow city streets, Rydans darting between houses from the walls to the large central manor. Prince Barnon was through the west gate, thanks to Shimmer and Dust's distraction, but it seemed unlikely the prince would hold now that there was nothing to stop Terant's magic.

Thanks to her Spell Sight, she clearly saw the thread of thought magic she'd spotted earlier, although now she saw how it connected Terant to Prince Barnon.

The two orbs containing Dust and Shimmer crashed together. Dust cursed loudly enough to catch Shimmer's attention, magic flaring around him as his casting was disrupted. She mentally scolded herself and tried to focus. The force magic would keep their spells contained mostly, but there were exceptions. Gawking at the battle would help no one. They needed to get out of the orbs.

With their advance through the gate, one of Barnon's soldiers had climbed the wall and was now striking at Master Terant himself. Not

surprisingly, the sword could not penetrate his shields, but it did draw Terant's attention off Shimmer and Dust for a moment.

Terant cast a sweeping glare over the scene, scowling. The Tanble soldiers pressed them from all sides, but the Barnon's people had a foothold.

Tossing his hands dismissively, Terant threw the spheres containing Shimmer and Dust away, rocketing them into the sky. He then tossed spells into the mix. Shimmer could not see what he cast or whom it targeted.

There was not time enough to think of more than one solution. Every morning since she had been six, she had cast the summoning spell that filled the teapot with water. Today, it was going to take more than the eighteen words it took to fill the teapot, but she had to hope it would still be completed in time.

They were heading for the trench on the far side of Arcott, Shimmer recognized, as she raced through the summoning spell and many, many extensions.

With the wizard kept busy by the Weavers, the ram pounded through the main gates on the west side of Arcott. The wide planks split at the hinges.

"Advance!" Barnon eagerly called.

Shoving the gate out of the way, the forces of Rabarch pushed into the city. The high towers on either side allowed the defenders to drop stones over them; every soldier entered with their shields high.

Proudly, Barnon joined his soldiers in overrunning the black and grey-clad defenders with the dark streaks across their faces. Wading in, Barnon helped clear the space nearest the gate, buying time for his soldiers to get up the towers and claim them.

A surprisingly firm shove from the Tanble men broke through his soldiers, cutting in behind him and blocking the gate. He was suddenly split from the majority of his fighters, including most of his protectors.

He paused, uncertainty flooding in. Would it be better to wait it out? He was not confident enough in his skills with sword and shield to cut a path back.

"Shall we take care of that?" someone called, and Barnon was startled to find himself joined by a tall man wearing blue and white. Thankfully, the face was familiar, Lance Carraway. High Guardsman Carraway, like all his Gaidolon guardsmen, rode his warhorse proudly, towering over Barnon and his footmen. He had no idea where the man had come from.

For a moment, Barnon's head hurt, and he had a hard time seeing. His heart skipped as an inexplicable fear rushed through him, feeling like a rabbit set upon by hounds. He wanted to tell them to do it, to clear the gate, but he could not decide on the words.

The sensation cleared as Barnon heard the high guardsman declare: "Gaidolons to me! We're going bear hunting!"

The enthusiasm was echoed over the many blue tabards as they filed together in a double row, riders at the front and warriors on foot behind. The horses lead, those on foot following with a second bellow.

Barnon's eyes followed Lance's impressive black horse as it pounded over two enemy soldiers to let his rider out the other side of the blockade, then spun to kick two more of the tattooed fighters. The sword in the Gaidolon's hand added a few more bodies to the pile. Tohmas had a tendency of surrounding himself with people who responded well to stress, so it did not seem unusual to hear the Gaidolon laughing in face of the threat.

Shouldn't I feel happy about this? He's succeeding.

No emotion rose. Blithely, Barnon tried to direct his soldiers to aid the Gaidolons, but his words sounded wrong. Between him, his protectors, and a selection from one of Rabarch's fyrds, they held the line but did nothing to push them back.

His sword arm was tired. The headache reemerged.

By the time Barnon glanced at the gate, Lance was on foot, his horse kicking the last of the defenders into the reach of another Gaidolon who skillfully skewered the enemy. The surviving few recklessly fled into Arcott's streets, and Barnon's protectors cut them down, although Barnon himself could not bring his sword to bare.

Something is wrong, he thought. But no matter how he tried, he could not figure out what or even why he thought that.

High Guardsman Carraway limped back over to Barnon, still wearing a silly grin. His horse followed patiently. New soldiers wearing

red and white tabards could now squeeze through the entrance. Smirking soldiers in blue and white now waved from the tower tops.

"Door's open! Where to next?" Lance asked, and Barnon thought to smile although he did not seem to succeed. Next, they were to flush out the rest of the Tanble fighters that would resist but....

He lost his train of thought when something cold closed over his mind. A shiver coursed through him as a silent voice spoke in his ear.

"Call a surrender, dear prince. Give the order now."

While he internally screamed objections, he felt his mouth open to obey.

Before a word left his mouth, Lance's fist collided with his jaw, knocking Barnon off his feet.

He wanted to kiss the man for the gesture. Knocked prone and his jaw aching, he could not give the order. He still felt the cold clamp on his mind, but it seemed to have paused.

But Barnon's protectors moved in against Lance, and Barnon could not call them off. Lance only had time to start an explanation, delivered with his hands up complacently to the protectors, when *he* stopped mid-sentence.

Lance's face became pained. No doubt, it mirrored Barnon's. However, to Barnon's surprise, the man shouted: "No!"

It all made immediate sense. He was being enchanted, as Barnon had been. There was magic in their minds seeking to divert the attack on Arcott.

Lance froze, his muscles rigid. Was he forced to be motionless for the angry Rabarchian protectors, or was his lack of animation because he was fighting the spell?

Loyal to their high guardsman, the Gaidolon guardsmen surrounded Lance in a defensive circle. While they defended against Barnon's protectors, they were also facing the caster in grey and black that hovered above the entrance.

Master Terant had reentered the fray. The pain returned in Barnon's skull.

"Call a surrender," the voice said again, and this time no high guardsman was available to punch him.

Lance resisted, Barnon told himself.

Defiant, Barnon brought every thought to keeping his mouth shut. Lance had spotted the magic but others would not. His word could damn the west gate's approach. Others were counting on him.

"Call a surrender!"

Although he could not speak, Barnon thought the word as loudly as he could.

"No."

The voice grunted. *"Fine. If you would rather die, I can do that too."*

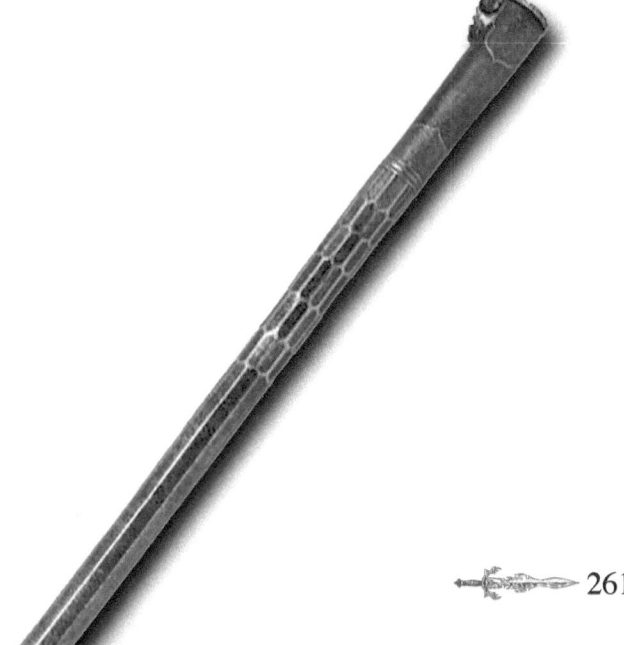

Chapter 17

Shadowed by the Pack Runner, Sabian stopped at the base of the wall. Two strides above him, spikes as long as swords jutted from the otherwise smoothed stone. He could not see what was happening at the top, but there were flashes of light and cries of outrage or pain from the Rydans who reached the top.

The Pack Runner leaned against the smooth wall, glaring in disapproval at the delay. "Up!"

Up? Sabian didn't have a horse to jump off as the others had done. He couldn't reach the spikes.

But as the Rydan wove his hands together into a stirrup, Sabian understood. Climbing onto the Rydan's shoulders, Sabian reached the first spikes. A dagger clenched in his teeth, Sabian scaled the wall.

The occasional falling body impeded his climb. Reaching the top, Sabian found Seria selectively picking off any who reached the top, too pressed to attack those making the climb. Seeing her effortless toss a spell at a Rydan and send the hapless man plummeting, Sabian wished the Pack Runner was with him. Instead, the Pack Runner had remained on the ground below with his dogs and was stalking along the base of the wall like a hound who had treed a squirrel.

Sabian understood at last: he had been sent up to chase the squirrel down.

Once he crested the ramparts, Sabian crouched in readiness. Seria turned her attention to him, her pale eyes shimmering in colors. Her fair face bore a snarl.

"Sabian," she began in a low voice filled with mockery. "How's the leg?"

He answered by throwing a knife at her heart, but her defenses deflected it wide.

Missile Deflector. Shimmer had used it too. Closer strikes were required.

As he started forward, she raised her hand and spoke a word. He tried to dodge, but the spell slammed into his chest like a ball of ice digging into his ribcage. His leg folded under him, dropping him to one knee. But he managed to drop low before falling from the wall.

He concentrated as Carsh had taught him, pushing aside pain or fear. Whether he had been injured or not, he was going to kill the caster. Magic could not hold in a strong mind. He would resist.

After a flicker, the pain and cold were gone. He breathed again. As harsh as the sensation had been, it had not caused any damage.

She did not seem overly concerned when he raised himself back into a crouch, but she was a little more harried with her next spell.

This time, he could feel something approach, and he knew he had to move. Without pausing his charge, he leaped to the left and sprung off one of the wall spikes before launching himself back onto the wall.

The spell missed.

"Not bad," she said, her voice calm as he slammed his dagger overhead at the base of her neck. He did not even manage to get her to shift with his strike. His knife glanced off an invisible barrier that he tangibly sensed as a tingle in its proximity.

The feeling suddenly intensified. New magic pushed him back.

After a season of training with Carsh, Sabian felt the presence of magic like the prickle of a cactus over his skin.

The edge if the ramparts disappeared under his foot, but he managed to catch the spikes once more as he dropped past them, leaving only his knife to fall. Sabian had a new one in his hand by the time he swung himself up and, deliberately, into her legs.

This time she stumbled and fell to her knees. Seeing her prone, he, in experiment, threw a short knife into the sole of her foot.

She had not seemed to be hovering. It stood to reason that the shield she wore was not under her feet.

The knife sunk into the flesh, and she screamed in pain. Before he could throw another blade, Seria ducked her feet under her. Another spell was forming, he knew, but he could not tell where or how it would hit him. There was nothing to do but take a few steps back and hope he would sense it in time to dodge it.

The tears in Seria's colorful eyes and her grotesque grimace made her look like a folklore witch as she casted. Even before the larger part of the spell was complete, Sabian felt something brush against his wrist.

Shaking his hand did not dismiss the sensation. *A binding,* he decided. Wisavi Kitable had explained the spell to the princes repeatedly. Once bound, the spells would not miss their target.

Sure enough, she released her magic.

Sabian ducked low and extended his arm above his head. He waited until he felt the swell of magic intensify to near-contact, then dropped his wrist out of the spell's path. Knowing it would follow the binding, Sabian bolted forward.

The spell was fast but, for two strides, he was faster. While the spell pivoted to follow the anchor on his wrist, Sabian dodged over Seria's shoulder, caught her by the throat with his right hand, and ducked behind the wizard.

When the magic fire exploded against Seria's shields, Sabian's hand erupted in agony. He instinctually yanked his hand into the cover of his other arm, but the skin was already blackened and burned by fire. He could not remember dropping his second knife, but his charred fingers were certainly empty.

The fire had gone wide around her shields, providing cover for the rest of Sabian. The shield equally protected Seria from the flames, but the heat still made her flush red.

It had not harmed her, but he was within all except her closest shield.

He grabbed her with his good hand before she could cast. Throwing himself to the right, Sabian pitched them both off the wall.

Bashuran could have outpaced Honest Justice, but they stayed side by side as they rushed to the east gate. Tohmas was aware that arrows occasionally tried to stop him, but the archers lacked accuracy and strength at this distance. By the time he was approaching the gates, the arrows had stopped.

He found a group of Rydans leaning against the open gate. Esparan soldiers had claimed defensive positions to keep the Tanble warriors from reclaiming the exit.

Every last one of the Rydans stood straight and grinned at him before giving the salute to the Hand and Arm. They had done well to escape Seria and make it to the gate to fulfill their duty.

His nod gave them leave. They had earned the right to sack the city. With tooth-baring whoops, they ran into Arcott ahead of the Esparans with Tohmas.

"You going to be able to call them off later?" Dragal asked, riding up beside Tohmas on a brute of a bay.

Why do you think I will? I don't think Arcott will still be standing at sunset.

Instead, he replied, "They will obey." Then, playing another role for a breath, he added, "Are you certain you wish to..." His gesture to the entrance completed the sentence, and as predicted, he got an incensed look from Dragal.

"Get going, boy. I want Marfaie's head for the grief he has caused my brothers."

Tohmas resisted the urge to point out that Sol had the greater claim to delivering justice. The closer Dragal got to the fighting, the better Tohmas thought it would be for them both.

"Let us ride," Tohmas agreed in a well-feigned defeated voice. He even let Dragal lead as they passed through the rabble of soldiers at the gate. He drew SoulBurner to follow.

A central manor towered over the city, beckoning them in. Despite its status as a capital, Arcott seemed small compared to Wayburn. There was enough space to maneuver, but not enough space for anyone to escape.

With an entourage of protectors, they made their way through the narrow streets to the manor. Understandably, the manor had sealed itself. Its walls a meager six feet. Any soldier on horseback would be

able to reach the top and climb over. But to get the horses through, he would have to open the gate. Although he suspected even iron and wood could not stop SoulBurner, any approach would put him at the mercy of the defenders' arrows. His shoulder throbbed, warning against that approach.

Speaking of arrows, he thought as the walls around the manor's gate suddenly bristled. The soldiers along the wall loosed their arrows. Unlike the Rydans, who bore double blades, Tohmas held SoulBurner in his right hand and, true to Esparan form, a shield in his left. He lifted the shield to protect himself, forced to rely on Justice's leather armor to protect the horse.

To his right, Carsh sat atop Bashuran just outside of Inac's light, and Tohmas saw the Rydan sit tall in readiness. With his good arm, Carsh easily caught one arrow. A second plunged in from the right and his only defense was to lift his bandaged arm. The arrow stuck into the splint's wood, and Carsh left it there in amusement. They would have to congratulate Darak on his sturdy splinting later.

Confused when no arrows challenged him, Tohmas lowered his shield. To his shock, the arrows were destroyed the moment they passed into SoulBurner's red aura. Fires consumed the shafts, leaving the flint arrowheads to drop into the mud and slush around Tohmas.

Inac's light, carried by the enchanted sword, was defending him.

Grinning, he hefted the sword and, with Carsh the only one to figure out his train of thought fast enough to follow, rode up to the gate. Carsh wisely ducked into SoulBurner's light.

His protectors followed a heartbeat later, which was a shame. Still, their timing meant only one other volley descended on them, and their shields kept most safe.

At the fortifications, Tohmas turned Honest Justice and cut SoulBurner into the gate.

A stone glanced off his helm, dazing him. The sharp edges of the helm, despite being padded, dug into his neck and briefly stunned him.

I guess stones can't be burned up by SoulBurner's fire, he thought, shaking his head to clear the disorientation.

Carsh gave a call, and the blur of hides and blades passed through the edge of Tohmas visible. Leaping off Bashuran, Carsh went up the

wall and into the defenders atop the wall. He vanished, but cries of battle fell from above.

Feeling harried now, Tohmas lifted his shield over his head and took the brunt of the stone rain that continued. Finding the gap between the great gates, he slipped SoulBurner through. SoulBurner cut through the wood, the metal of the reinforcements, and then the bar that held the gate shut.

The stones had stopped by the time Tohmas pushed the gate open from the back of the horse.

Bashuran followed Tohmas into the manor grounds immediately, pushing through Tanbles to reunite with his rider and trampling any who got in his way. Protectors were next into the fray, spreading swiftly out to claim the walls. Within a few flickers, Dragal was riding up in Tohmas' wake.

"Reckless boy!" came the chastisement. "Do you want to end up on a pyre? You may have been lucky thus far, but you cannot count on luck to keep you safe!"

Tohmas bit back a laugh. *Do you not see how the arrows are no threat as long as SoulBurner lights my way?*

Censoring every other reply, Tohmas looked down, nodded gravely, and said, "You are right, uncle. I got carried away. I am sorry."

"Follow, boy," Dragal insisted, "lest you get yourself killed next time!"

Tohmas checked his reply sharply and said nothing. His patience for being treated like a child was fast reaching an end.

Immobilized by magic he could not break, Darknim saw the gaping maw of the dragon approaching and could do nothing. His arms at his side and his fists clenched, Rakhund's powers held Darknim fast.

A burst of wind, as strong as the one that had saved Darknim from the fall, rushed through the area. Tearing through the dirt and stones, the air became hazy with debris that stung Darknim's face. Even the dragon had to brace itself to avoid being pushed back.

Rakhund was knocked aside, but he surrounded himself with a blazing shield of red light and resisted. The magic holding Darknim released.

At the mercy of the powerful blast, Darknim flew across the floor of the crater. He lost sight of the demon and the celebrant in the spitting dust and snow stirred up by the wind. The last thing he saw was Calanor weakly coming to his feet to face Rakhund.

The wind petered out gently and let him come to a stop. Darknim was left staring back the way he had come, fifty paces away.

He knew there was little hope of killing the demon. He was all but unarmed. Sling stones could not cut through scales. Darknim's short knife, crafted from flint when he had first become a hunter, could not be expected to succeed when a well-forged carbiron blade had failed. Nothing short of an enchanted weapons would cut either the demon or dragon scale, and the ax was in the hands of the enemy.

Above the settling dust cloud, the dragon looked over its shoulder at him. He expected it to rear back for releasing fire or dive at him in bite; its long neck could easily cover the distance. But instead, it stood placidly watching. Lacking a command to attack, was it happy to wait and see who would survive?

Below the beast, the dirt and dust settled revealing Rakhund and Calanor facing each other. Rakhund brought the ax up to strike and wind pushed him back, but Calanor was barely holding his feet, his proud stance slouched and weak.

Darknim stepped forward, watching the dragon for a reaction but seeing none. Gaining confidence with each step, he headed back into the fight. Although he doubted he could be victorious, he would not leave his friend to fight alone.

As he moved, the low sunlight flashed on something at his feet. Hidden in a cradle of soft stone unlike any Darknim had seen before, Kitable's glass orb flashed in the light.

Calanor pushed me deliberately back, he realized. He had sent him to get Kitable's trinket.

Darknim scooped up the magic item and broke into a run. He brought his sling out, thinking it ironic that the weapon that had once stunned rabbits for a supper might be the one to fell a demon. He slotted the orb into the leather pocket as he closed the distance. A shadow passed over, then a second dragon crashed down into the crater back the way he had come, a roaring growl shaking the ground

along with its rumbling landing. Heat rolled over him, the red already close on hand.

The first dragon lifted the hackle-like scales along its neck. Its eyes flared crimson as Darknim neared Rakhund, ready to defend its master. A black band of stones on its wrist went golden with symbols, a command being given. The dragon reared back and blew fire.

Darknim rushed under the plume of inferno, ducking under the dragon itself. The heat of both the fire and nearby dragon prickled his face, but he dared not retreat. Hidden behind the feet of the confused beast—too large to move quickly—Darknim spotted his real target, the demon.

Calanor was sprawled on the crater's floor before Rakhund's towering form. Blood seeped through the celebrant's robes and onto the stones around him. The demon's cloak now hung open and wind-torn, revealing more rust-colored scales. The ax's black metal was outlined in pulsing red tendrils that ran between the weapon and the wielder as if tying the two together. The great blade was about to swing down onto the celebrant, and Calanor, on his back, seemed to lack the strength to move.

Darknim swung his sling sharply twice and let the orb fly. He aimed to hit Rakhund's side, hoping to crack the orb and release the spells within. To his dismay, the orb didn't fly as sure as a stone—it was too light. Instead of hitting Rakhund, the orb dropped toward Calanor's prone form, toward the one person whose touch would destroy the wizard magic within.

Although he had thought the celebrant entirely spent, Calanor lifted a weary hand up as if to defend himself. The orb struck his hand.

And broke.

The orb had not struck the celebrant. It had struck the stone the Celebrant held in his hand.

Wizard magic exploded out.

The red light emanating from Rakhund's core was swept away instantly, put out like a candle's flame in a hurricane. The ax, as if being thrown, flew out of Rakhund's hand and smashed into the rock face behind him. To Darknim's shock, the perfect blade, which had withstood centuries of use without sharpening, shattered against the stone.

Rakhund roared in outrage, his paw-like hands covering his face as he wheeled away.

Above and around him, Darknim heard both dragons roar, but he did not know if it was rage or elation. If they were going to kill him, they would succeed, Darknim knew. But he was determined to see that the demon died first.

Taking his chances, Darknim sprinted out from the cover of the dragon, his little bone knife in hand. It had never been used as anything beyond an eating tool. The edge was dull, but the point was sharp.

Just as Rakhund brought his hands away from his face, Darknim thrust the little knife into the eye socket of the monster. The blade dug deep and broke at the handle.

The cursing, thrashing demon went down, taking the chipped hunting knife with it and leaving Darknim holding only the leather-wrapped handle.

Darknim froze, feeling useless. He had nothing left.

The demon did not stir but lay twisted backward on the bare stone of the valley at Darknim's feet, the smallest bit of flint visible in its left eye. A small trickle of dull black blood tracked down the cheek.

The dragons, as one, screamed, and the sound deafened Darknim.

Darknim rushed to Calanor's side. The shadow of a looming dragon sent them into darkness. Not knowing what else to do, Darknim placed himself over Calanor, the celebrant too weak to even groan now, and tried to ready himself for killing dragons.

Without ax. Without help. Without hope.

A serpentine neck reached out tentatively, the wide nostrils snorting smoke. Like the demon, the dragon's teeth protruded like boastful swords. The great golden eyes squinted partially shut, Darknim guessed in confusion, as the muzzle tentatively sniffed the dead demon.

The dragon's growl made the stones tremble. The huge head withdrew, but Darknim recognized the rearing posture; there would be fire. Grabbing Calanor as gently as he could, Darknim dragged the celebrant closer to the valley wall just as the Red let loose its incinerating fire.

The fire left a trough of melted stone in its wake, leaving not so much as a fleck of ash. In the flash of white flame, the demon was immolated.

The heat flooded around them, stifling the air. Darknim felt his exposed skin, along his open arms and face, burn. Determined to protect the weakened celebrant behind him, he did not move. As brief as the blast was, the stink of melted skin and singed hair choked him. His leathers smoked. Only where he wore dragon scale was he spared the searing heat.

The flames winked out, and the dragon snorted in satisfaction. Turning, it took flight. The second great form followed. Together, the two flew away.

Freed, Darknim thought with a smile that made his freshly-burned face sting. He brought a hand to his face and found his beard partially missing. He gingerly pulled himself up, trying to assess the damage by feeling.

The backs of his hands were blistered, as were his arms from wrist to shoulder. His legs, from ankle to knee, were black. Now that the threat was gone, the pain rose.

He searched the crater for something to soothe the burn, but all the snow in the area had been melted away. When he turned his searching toward the celebrant, he found Calanor sitting up. Shielded by Darknim, only the edges of Calanor's scarves were singed. The blood seeping from his chest and legs had soaked through the white robes, and the bruises along his face made him look like a brawler, but he was conscious when Darknim thought he had no right to be.

"Come," the celebrant's thought-speech said.

Darknim knelt before Calanor, baffled but in too much agony to consider disobedience. Unsteadily, Calanor gently touched Darknim's face like a mother brushing aside a curl of hair on their child. Where the frost-bitten stump of the celebrant's arms touched, cold flooded over Darknim.

As Calanor touched his arm to each of Darknim's blistered, burned hands, Darknim felt the pain of the burn lessen. By the time the celebrant released his touch, the agony had faded to a mild ache.

Calanor collapsed backward against the rock, unconscious.

Shivers shaking him, Darknim leaned over his friend, tearing away the robes to view the man's crushed ribs and the bleeding gash along his hip. To his shock, the celebrant was still breathing and even moaned when Darknim took the scarf from Calanor's neck and wrapped the

bleeding limb. The breathing remained steady, somehow the chest was not flooded by blood despite the extensive injuries.

"God of breath," Darknim muttered as he wrapped the chest roughly with the torn robe. The shivering was passing, new pale skin appearing where blisters and exposed burnt flesh had been only a moment before. He felt his strength returning, the pain fading to a dull strain of worn muscles.

Darknim sat briefly in the silent crater once he had finished his work, testing his own resolve.

He had done what he had set out to do. He was finished.

But without help, Calanor would still die.

Deciding that there was nothing left to gain in the crater, for any evidence of the demon or his ax was immolated, Darknim lifted over his wide shoulders and began the trek to the nearest civilization: Arcott.

He found a sloping path along the sharp crater walls. By the time he reached the top, he could see smoke rising from the city on the horizon.

Putting his head down, he marched onward.

There was silence in Barnon's mind as the cold feeling intensified. He held to his convictions: he would not speak. He could not take the chance that the warriors would see the magic as Lance had. He would not betray the plans they had made. His brothers were counting on him.

The caster's presence lingered in his mind, reviewing all the plans Barnon recited in his determination to hold to them. Although he worried he would be revealing the plan to the enemy, he used the images to fuel his disobedience.

Sol to the east. Barnon in the west. Dragal to the manor with Tohmas and Carsh at the first opportunity. Rydans to open the gates, then cause chaos. They had the numbers.

His head ached. As he reviewed the plans, the pain sharpened.

Just as the tearing agony of his head shattered Barnon's focus and, with it, his resistance, Barnon heard a cry come from within his own mind, but it was not in his voice.

CHAPTER 17

The magic holding him disappeared. Barnon woke on his knees, surrounded by concerned protectors. His hands were over his ears to block out the shout, and he let them fall as he felt the last traces of pain vanish.

Shaken, he was slow in standing. When he finally found his feet, things started to make sense.

Lance had quickly recovered from the absence of the spell and was on his horse once more. Following the high guardsman's gaze, Barnon looked to the top of the wall, where a man in plain shirt and trousers stood. His beard needed trimming, and his hair had a wild look to it, but it was the same stern-faced wizard Barnon had often seen at Tohmas' side. Master Kitable had joined the fray.

Although Barnon could not see the enemy wizard anymore, Kitable's fixed gaze implied a location just above the gate.

"What took you?" Lance shouted up at the Galanth caster.

"Get moving, you idiots!" Wisavi Kitable replied without so much as a glance at Lance.

Heeding the warning, Lance assembled his men. Barnon did the same and met up with the high guardsman to coordinate their attack. The region near the gate was light on enemies, the protectors having done their duty.

Lance looked apologetic and, surprisingly, amused. "Sorry about the ah…" He gestured with his fist, and Barnon had to smile. Doing so made his bruised jaw throbbed, so he took a moment to stretch it out.

"I appreciate it, actually. I would have returned the favor, had I been able."

Lance laughed. "I bet you would've! Where to, Prince Barnon?"

"As per the plan. Rabarch will hold here, Kitable will deal with Terant, and we will flush the rest of the city into the open."

The high guardsman lifted his sword in salute to the prince, then, with a grin, mimicked the shoulder-slapping salute of the Rydans. "Lead on!"

Soon Barnon was moving through the streets once more.

Once the sounds of alarm reached his ears, Kitable pushed off the manor wall and stood straight. Hefting his sack, he waited, ready, until he finally heard a Galanth horn signaling a magic attack.

Activating his spell, Kitable seared a hole in the defense, cauterizing the edges with all eight elements to blind the spell. Taking two long strides, he passed through.

He was already casting by the time he cleared the shield, counting on Terant now being occupied by the invasion.

He had no Spell Sight, but fixed that by casting it as he broke into a run. Once he was done, he activated all his remaining defensive trinkets, giving himself, among other things, an Anchor Block. Then he launched into the new, longer spell. Knowing how to uncast spells had made the rest of the spell easy to create, especially after having experienced it himself.

Two horns had sounded, but his exit from the manor put him closer to the western horn, and so he ran that direction. He had no way of knowing if it would be Seria or Terant he faced, but assuming he could make his one attack count, he could destroy either one of them.

Rounding a corner, Kitable found himself at the back of the Tanble defenders. Rabarch and Gaidolon squads were holding back the Tanble Bears to keep the gate open. With the Spell Sight, two tendrils of orange were visible, which proved that their battle was more complicated than just swords and shields. The more he considered it, the smarter it became. If Terant targeted the right people with his thought magic, it would be more effective than merely blasting a handful of soldiers. It may end up saving a lot of energy, and in a prolonged confrontation such as this, that was vital.

Terant was easy to find thanks to his multitude of auras. He had placed himself above the gate able to survey both sides of the wall. The enchantments around him kept him safe from the mundane weapons of the soldiers.

I'm less mundane, Kitable thought. Ready, he activated his spell.

A cascade of colors, visible only to enchanted eyes, cascaded onto the enemy wizard.

Every spell was undone, devolved into its raw elements and sent back along its bindings to the body it was tethered to. Instantly, Terant was filled with all the magic he had summoned that morning, no longer

spaced by time but all brought down upon him in a blink. With the magic came spell burn.

The master wizard collapsed with a cry.

Although the excessive influx of magic may kill the man, Kitable was not positive it would be enough for a wizard as strong as Terant. Dropping his sack by the wall, Kitable climbed the nearest ladder. As he stepped out on the ramparts, he was finally recognized.

"What took you?" High Guardsman Carraway demanded.

Kitable scowled but dared not take his eyes from where Terant had fallen. "Get moving, you idiots!" he answered sharply, and as he did, magic hit him from the side.

He had only minimal shields. The spell bound itself to him and dropped him to his knees.

Terant, his face red from either fury or spell burn, climbed to his feet. Kitable's Spell Sight revealed Terant's glowing ring as the source of the attack—without a hovering spell associated with it, it had been spared by the attack.

When Kitable opened his mouth to cast, he recognized the spell.

Pain lanced through every muscle in his body, and the spasm threw him onto hands and knees. Involuntarily, his mouth slammed shut. His spell was lost.

"Perfect circles," Terant said from his place over the wall as he dragged himself up. Despite the strong voice, Terant moved like a man walking on cinders, confirming the success of Kitable's spell. "You hit me with a spell I used on you, and I hit you with a spell you used on Seria. Honestly, though, I think I was more effective, Kitable. You forgot to add the Augmentation to the Full Reversal spell."

Augmentation, Kitable thought with a mental groan. Terant had augmented Kitable's spells then undone them. He had doubled the blow with that simple twist. Kitable had never thought of making the enemy's spells stronger before.

But even if Kitable's attack had been only half as potent, it had been effective. Spell Sight revealed a lack of hovering spells and shields. As effective as an Eight-layered Dispel, Terant was without defenses. If Kitable could just strike him now...

Taking deep breaths between each word, Kitable forced the spell through the pain. Although his body shook, his mind held each part of the spell in careful reserve as it was built, word by excruciating word.

Halfway through the cast, Terant seemed to realize what he was doing.

"Do not be stupid," the caster said with a snort as he advanced, his magic ring still lifted and pointed at Kitable. "No one casts through a Black Agony. All you can do is suffer."

Wasted words, Kitable thought. He ignored them and forced out the next part of his spell.

"Foolishness," the Tanble caster said, but he activated the ring once more to curtail Kitable's efforts. A new wave of pain flooded over the Galanth wizard.

To his surprise, the second wave did not seem as bad as the first. His senses, he had to admit, were overwhelmed and going numb. Pain had taken over every part of his body, but his mind still held onto his spell. The only difficulty was in getting his mouth to form the words between waves of throbbing.

Terant advanced, drawing a knife from his belt. He was better able to manage a blade than another spell through his spell burn, Kitable assumed.

Although Kitable could form the occasional word, there was no hope of convincing his body to move through the Black Agony. He did not try. He focused entirely on the spell he was forming. It was small, but he did not need force, he needed precision

Master Terant was only a pace from Kitable when he was stopped by Kitable's only useful remaining defense, his ring. Now that he had come close enough to slit Kitable's throat, Terant found himself slowing in the thick air.

Before he could solve the mystery of the barrier, Kitable finished his spell.

Unable to be certain a trinket of Terant's would not interfere, Kitable manually aimed the spell. His aim, as Terant had once described it, was impeccable. The Force Bar caught across Terant's neck, threw the man onto his back, and pinned him to the top of the wall by his throat.

While lying on his back, trapped by the force over his throat, Terant activated another item. An anchor reached out, giving Kitable a

precious moment to act. Casting through the Black Agony for a second time, Kitable chose a short, simple spell.

The spells were completed simultaneously.

The wind alteration from Terant's trinket hit Kitable in the shoulder. Kitable's spell required no aiming: he could target his own spell blindfolded. The Reduction he cast on the Force Bar locked into place.

Terant cursed, but his next words were choked off as the bracket of force, lying across Terant's neck, shrank. Still holding firm to the wall as it reduced in size, it severed the vulnerable throat with a wet crunching sound. His kicking protests stopped abruptly, the body falling limp.

The Reduction spell continued. Angled down toward the gate, the severed head slid down the trail of blood and dropped into the gateway below.

Kitable finally released a breath of relief.

Pain lanced through him, the Black Agony no less potent without its master. When Kitable tried to cast once more, he discovered what Terant's last spell had been. Like Seria, Kitable had been enchanted with a Vox. He had even recognized the Permanency from the auras. Unable to cast without speaking and unable to speak without casting a spell to free him from the Vox, he was trapped.

Holding still minimized the Black Agony, but he could not remain on his hands and knees atop a wall all day. Eventually, he had to hope that one of the Galanth would find him or, better still, Tohmas and his sword. Until then, Kitable was completely at the mercy of whoever stumbled across him. The ring had many charges and would keep the air around him uncomfortable to pass through, but if enough people pushed against it, it could be broken.

Just as he prepared himself to wait, Kitable heard someone approaching along the upper wall.

The first thing he saw was colorful cloth. He lifted his head through the Black Agony to glimpse her face, but a wave of pain overwhelmed him, forcing his head back down involuntarily. His limbs gave up on holding him. He was soon crouched over as if praying at an altar.

She was soaking wet and leaving puddles behind her, but she was the most beautiful thing he had ever seen.

"Black Agony," Kitable heard Shimmer's voice say softly. Each word seemed hesitant as she added, "A four-way alteration."

Five, he tried to correct, but no words escaped him. His voice had been blocked.

She stopped when she hit his shield, but a spoken word and a subsequent flare of a hovering spell saw his defense dispelled. Shimmer was soon kneeling before him. She laid a hand upon his aching back, but he could not feel it through the throbbing.

"I do not have a four-way dispel," she confessed, "but this should work."

While her word of activation was a whisper, the spell flashed out strong. The chilling touch of dispelling magic washed over him like a strong north wind.

The pain stopped.

Kitable let out a slow, unsteady breath and lifted his head.

"Eight-layered Dispel," he identified, grateful to hear his voice function.

A grin exploded on her face. Shimmer was already pulling away from him. Soon Kitable was again eye-level with her skirts, convincing him to rise to his feet.

"My first one," Shimmer boasted. "Got it from BookKeeper Olmer. He let me borrow one of his books. Apparently, he can't cast it though. It uh... has a Linger so any of your items may..."

She paused as she leaned back and looked him over. He was still only wearing his shirt and trousers, his measly trinkets few and mostly spent.

"You look awful," she told him, and Kitable fought not to grin. He felt, despite the remnants of pain, excellent. Victory had that effect.

Composing a strict stare, he replied, "You are wet."

She brushed aside a few dripping locks of hair, then gave up on the individual strands and shook her head. Water flew in all directions. "Arcott now has a moat!" she replied with a laugh. "A few people are going to be really annoyed when they check their water-skins—summoning is so much easier than creation—but you should have seen it! We were trapped in force cages, only they were spheres. Couldn't target through it, couldn't dispel it fast enough, but Papa summoned wind to guide us, and I summoned water. I filled the damn trench! The whole thing! Nothing like a million pots of water to cushion a fall! It was brilliant! I'm not even feeling—"

To stop himself from laughing, Kitable snapped, "Oh stop grinning!"

Harried, he turned and lowered himself down the ladder.

"Not a chance!" Shimmer called after him. "I dueled Master Terant and lived, summoned the better part of a lake, and managed to cast my first Eight-layered Dispel effectively! It's a marvelous day!"

He had his back to her, so he knew she could not see him smile at the enthusiasm in her voice. "Where's your father?" he asked.

"Got wrapped up in transporting people. Force discs can take a lot more weight than people can," she brightly replied.

She fell silent when Kitable did not reply and remained on the wall as he retrieved his sack and donned his proper green and silver robes. He would need to be identified as he traveled through the city now. He had enough enemies to worry about without being attacked by allies in error.

Once the robe was dusted off, still smelling keenly of potatoes, he removed the grin from his face and looked back to see Shimmer still watching him from a place on the wall, smiling softly to herself.

"You coming, Weaver?" Kitable asked.

Her face lit joyfully. Sliding quickly down, her feet not touching a single rung of the ladder, she was off the wall and at his side instantly.

"Shimmer," she corrected with a toss of her red hair.

He winced as he got sprayed. "If you want to make yourself useful, Miss Weaver," he amended once he had wiped his face dry, "then help me find Seria before she rips apart my prince's army. The other horns claiming magical interference sounded from the north, I believe."

She nodded eagerly and skipped along beside him over the rubble as they made their way to the north wall, casting new defenses and attacks with every step.

"And stop being so cheerful," he added, but Shimmer just laughed and carried on despite him.

Chapter 18

T he spikes broke Sabian's fall; he bounced off one after another. The final drop was a dozen feet straight down, but he landed on top of Seria and other bodies. Stiff limbs and half-buried weapons bruised him, although none broke the skin.

The moment they landed, Seria grunted out an activation word.

Cold magic washed over Sabian. His muscles seized, locking him in place with his blade in hand. It lingered painfully, only loose enough to allow his chest to rise and fall in panting breaths.

Despite the ache extending from shoulder to ankle, he strained against the powers holding him. He could not allow the caster to escape! But like a wrap of pure stone, he could not move.

Untangling herself from the other bodies, Seria rose to her feet. Within the confines of her magic, she had been protected from impact. A red mark on her elbow and shoulder were the only signs of her fall, but she still favored her bleeding foot. Muttering curses, she pulled herself from the rubble and delicately swept her hair from her face, her sneer proud as she looked down on Sabian.

"Pathetic."

Through the chill of the magic, the impact of her kick was blunted, but he still felt sharp pain in his ribs.

The sound of baying hounds reached his ears.

CHAPTER 18

Sabian smiled, and Seria paused, her expression confused. But before she could speak, a knife pierced into her wounded sole, held up to rest it. She fell, exposing her feet unwittingly.

Brought the squirrel down to the hound, Sabian mused.

The Pack Runner delivered a second knife into her foot in the next blink, taking advantage of the weakness Sabian had discovered. Brought to her knees, she threw out her powers in a circle, cutting over Sabian and leaving his skin numb. Yelping in pain even as it determinedly charged, a huge black hound crashed into her next, its jaw snapped at her throat. The teeth were blocked by her impenetrable shield, but she still screeched and fell back under the weight of the attack.

A new spell burst out, fire erupting like a volcano and throwing the dog off. More hounds cried out on their approach. When the magic cleared, Seria had come to her feet, holding her wounded foot down against the ground to defend it. Two dogs lay dead in the scorched debris surrounding her.

Singed and bleeding, the Pack Runner rushed in. Like the hound, he went for her throat and his bare hand got purchase on the shield there. He could not crush her through the shield, so he stabbed his bone knife at her face. It shattered against the shield, but her head snapped back under the force of the blow.

Two more dogs, one with fur still smoking, snarled at her heels. They bashed their teeth and claws into her Molded Shield, seeking the flesh below the invisible armor.

Harried on both sides, Seria lost her balance.

Despite his immobility, Sabian smiled vindictively.

Not bothering with another blade from his baldric, the Pack Runner used his hold on her throat to slam Seria into the wall. Her head bounced off the shield, jarring her activation words into dehiscence. The dogs snapped at her dangling feet, drawing blood.

The Pack Runner drew her back and slammed her once more into the wall, smashing her head into its own defense with the force of impact. Again and again, Crawthran pounded the caster into the stone.

Her body was limp by the time Seria's skull cracked. The blood, trapped by the Molded Shield, filled like a pot for blood pudding. Sabian felt suddenly sick. The sight of brain matter now mixed with blood was something he had never seen.

Even after she had stopped moving, the Pack Runner continued to pound her head against the wall a few more times before tossing her body aside. The hounds followed the throw, taking turns pulling on shielded limbs as if seeking to tear one off.

Ignoring the corpse, the Rydan dropped low and circled Sabian, sniffing like a bloodhound.

He would sense the magic, Sabian knew, but what could he do? And why would he help? He knew the Rydans had no tolerance for uselessness.

To his shock, Sabian found his mouth moved when he tried words. "I brought her down," he said.

The Rydan cracked a smile. "Goh," he replied. He nodded sagely as if justifying an acceptance. Sabian had succeeded. The Pack Runner was satisfied.

Crawthran moved out of Sabian's line of sight. Even Knife Dancers did not know how to break spells.

A howl called, and Sabian heard the hounds scramble westward. Lying on the ground still frozen, Sabian was left behind.

Either the spell would wear off or it would not. If it wore off, he would be able to rejoin the fight. If not, he had to hope someone came by who could free him.

The flyer was dead. He had done his part. His Leader should be proud of him. That was all he needed.

Tohmas had to marvel at the size of the building. He was familiar with small huts and tall grasses, not multi-story, towered, complicated buildings, especially not when his enemy apparently did not want to be found. For once, Tohmas let Dragal lead.

They broke into the main building, cutting their way through defenders. Unlike Tohmas, the tight quarters were familiar to the protectors, and they fell into familiar defensive and offensive combinations Tohmas had never seen. He took in all he could as they pressed through the manor toward their invisible goal.

As they went, their gathering shrank as, one by one, he left teams behind to secure his exit.

Corridors were difficult, and the enemy had the advantage of knowing the space. It did not come as a surprise to him when a rank of Bears, Prince Marfaie's elite, emerged from a side passage into the midst of his men and cut their force in half.

With Dragal, Tohmas took a side room and set up defensive positions as he waited for the rest of his forces to push through. Soon the protectors were trading blows with Bears in the narrow doorways. Proving they were the best of the south, the protectors gave no ground. In bursts, the clatter of spears, shields, and swords deafened him, interspersed with unsettling calm. Smaller groups advanced out, pressing the enemy to regain their road out. Wounded trickled back, but these were few.

Secure for now, Tohmas examined the room. Like many sitting rooms he had visited when conferencing with princes, it had two entrances on opposite sides of the semi-circular room. The far wall looked out through stained glass windows, quite a rarity so far north.

While the protectors held the enemy at bay, Tohmas checked the windows curiously. Carsh, chuckling to himself, finally pulled the arrow out of his splint. It had not pierced deep enough to reach him, the tip now chipped in the wood.

The windows looked out over a small courtyard. Tohmas could see the slit windows on the far side, prompting him to pull away. *If I can see that distance, so can an archer.*

Looking back through the room, that realization gave him an idea.

He needed Dragal gone; the Prince of Clandac continually disrupted Tohmas' alliance with the Northlanders, and he could influence Sol and Barnon when Tohmas wanted his voice to be paramount to the brothers. *Besides, Dragal asked for death,* Tohmas justified to himself. Since the enemy had not yet provided that, it had to be arranged. But Tohmas could not allow himself to be incriminated in Prince Dragal's demise.

The enemy's arrow Carsh had provided was an opportunity.

The protectors were all blocking the doors or standing ready to relieve those who were fighting. This left Tohmas, Carsh, and Dragal alone at the center of the room. Dragal himself seemed distracted by shouts warning that Bears had made their way over to the other entrance as well.

Tohmas took the arrow from Carsh and, with a nod of his head, pointed at Dragal. The Rydan immediately stepped back and switched his long knife for a short throwing blade. He faced the window behind Dragal, leaving Tohmas to come up behind the Prince of Clandac. The exchange of blows at both entrances made it easy not to be heard.

Once he was positioned behind the prince, the arrow's shaft in his left hand, Tohmas spoke softly. "Dragal," he said, and the man turned his head. "I heard what you said to Sol and Barnon. It's for your good."

Tohmas dug the arrow into the man's lower back, aiming it at the inside of the kidney to sever the arteries there.

Matched to him, Carsh threw his knife through the window.

Dragal cried out, half cry and half cough. The sound was further confused by the simultaneous sound smashing glass. The protectors nearest the princes spun to see Tohmas catching Dragal in his fall.

"Dragal!" Tohmas exclaimed in feigned dismay.

"*Daem'd archer*!" Carsh shouted helpfully, lunging to the window to peer out in search of the supposed attacker.

"Away from the windows!" Tohmas added.

Aided by the protectors, Tohmas laid Dragal away from the dangerous windows. The bleeding soaked through bandages in a heartbeat. Dragal's coughing fits made it worse, but Tohmas thought the man was still smiling slightly through the pain.

Dragal's hand found Tohmas' collar, and Tohmas let himself be pulled down to hear the prince's final words.

"Good boy."

Dragal collapsed, blood spurting from his wound with every cough.

Tohmas stepped back to let the Clandac protectors tend to their prince. Despite being confident he had hit the deadly target, he asked about the nearest cutter, then directed his men to force the enemy back so that they could get a path out.

But by the time the ranks had been cut down, his green-coated forces replacing them at both exits, the Prince of Clandac was dead.

Smiles left the troops. Dark faces peered back at him as the declaration was made, and Tohmas, dutiful of appearances, cursed loudly. Because he had been the man to catch the prince in his fall, none of them questioned the blood on his hands.

CHAPTER 18

Half of the protectors of Clandac went with the body when Tohmas sent them back. The other half, willing to carry on the mission their prince had died attempting, carried on under Tohmas' command.

They were fighters. They knew what happened when fighters died. Mourning came later. For now, they had to press on.

Tohmas was only disappointed Darknim had not been around to see it.

Now he had to find Marfaie.

Tohmas slew Dragal, but Carsh did not give the event a second thought. His brother had done exactly as Tamv had asked: rid Espar of its princes. Tohmas was good at spotting opportunities. That was why he was a good Leader.

Carsh was pleasantly surprised by the speed with which the Esparans accepted their prince's death. They must have known about the illness in the man's chest. Dragal had come north looking for death. Now he had found it.

As they left the sitting room, parting from the Clandac protectors assigned to take the murdered prince out, Carsh sensed a tingle of magic passing. It marked the third such flare of powers during their exploration of the manor, but it was too brief for Carsh to target. For a moment, Carsh missed Kitable. The wizard would have been able to tell him what spell had been present.

He ensured he had his second knife in hand, despite the splint. He had to give Darak credit for doing the job well; the splint had survived the impact of an arrow without breaking! He may have lacked his usual finesse with his splinted arm, but he made up for it by using his other arm.

They pressed on, the Clandac protectors taking orders from Tohmas. *Tohmas' army is growing again.*

Outside the room, the first two corridors were quiet. In the third corridor, a group of warriors attacked, more of Marfaie's Bears. Their faces marked with four claw tattoos, they gave battle cries like a roar and charged the protectors.

Carsh stayed between the charge and Tohmas, joining the protectors in keeping the enemy at bay. It may have irked his brother, but the spaces were too cramped for the sweeping slashes of a long sword. Carsh and his knives were better suited to the close quarters.

He threw only one knife, having depleted much of his supply. When a Bear reached him with a small ax, Carsh dodged aside and struck back with his long knife. He had to count on the sharpness to slice into the throat, his splinted arm lacking strength to force it through cartilage. The fine tip pierced the targeted jugular and dragged through. He was pleased to see the pulse of blood that followed. He had struck the carotid. This one would die quickly.

While the man fell, Carsh snatched the short knife off the enemy's belt. He flipped it to test its balance, then threw it with his good hand. It perforated the lung of the next Bear, knocking the attacker off his feet. The vulnerable throat was within easy reach of Carsh's long knife. He moved in to kill.

He skittered to a halt when magic swept over him, distracting him and leaving the Bear alive for a moment more. An oblivious protector stepped in to end the life of Carsh's enemy.

The magic was building. "Flya touch!" he shouted.

The protectors glanced at him, unsure.

Tohmas gave a short whistle, probably by instinct, telling Carsh he was on his way, bringing the protective light of Inac. Only Carsh would recognize the whistle.

A wave of magic flooded down the hallway like a river. It brought pure, distilled pain with it, crippling the protectors around him and bringing them to their knees. Carsh grit his teeth stood determinedly in place, his skin prickling as if infused with snake venom. He searched ahead seeking the flyer but saw no one.

SoulBurner's light reached him. The pain vanished.

The Bears at the far end of the corridor charged into the lapse, and it was Tohmas, unaffected by the spell, who met them. SoulBurner stabbed through the first's armor and to his heart. Unlike a normal blade, the sword slid easily free to slice through the next opponent, unhindered by bone and flesh.

Carsh joined him in the next blink, the stunned protectors following. Defended by SoulBurner, there were no more waves of pain. Soon, no enemies remained.

"It was a caster," a protector reported as Carsh took a moment to retrieve what knives he could, whether from where he had left them in the dead or fresh blades from the fallen. "I heard him casting! Didn't see much of him, but he had a staff."

Tohmas paused, his jaw tight. If this was Master Terant, something had gone wrong with Kitable. Facing the master wizard had never been the plan.

"Protectors, stay here," Tohmas commanded.

Carsh grinned. The opportunity to slay the flyer was finally upon him! He quickly arranged the new blades in the baldric. He had only two Rydan knives left, the rest Esparan and not designed for throwing.

"We are not leaving you to—" the protector objected.

"I have SoulBurner," Tohmas pointed out. "None of you have a hope of stopping Master Terant. Having more targets for him will just make things more difficult."

"What about Kitable?"

"Whether or not he's around to help, we still have to deal with this caster."

The protector nodded with a frown.

"At least take Carsh," someone else suggested, and Carsh laughed. Tohmas could not stop him from going in! Tohmas had SoulBurner, but Carsh had a lifetime of knife dancing to keep him safe. Besides, he had *tunnabot* planned. It was his duty to seek the caster, and it was his right as a Rydan to kill the man who had broken his arm.

"I couldn't keep him out if I wanted to. *Tunnabot*." Suddenly recognizing he had slipped into Rydan, Tohmas translated: "The caster broke his arm. He gets a shot at revenge." He cleared his throat. "You all can make sure we have a road out." Turning a corner in the hallway, he left them behind. Carsh lead him forward, the red light of SoulBurner reaching beyond him to light the way.

The brothers said nothing as they advanced, but Carsh felt Tohmas' eyes on him, seeking hints of impending attack. He would be ready at the first sign of magic, but there was no attack, or at least none were detectable through SoulBurner's light.

All defenders defeated or fled. At the end of the hall, they found a pair of ornate doors. The two doors were divided, and each half intricately decorated with the various symbols of a given god.

A temple.

Carsh put his hand gingerly on the smooth metal. A tingle reached up his arm, magic clearly present beyond the doors. He growled and flipped his knife in his grip. They were close.

"Flank or close?" Tohmas asked, recognizing that Carsh had found a target.

Carsh was the knife dancer; this was his fight. Tohmas would defer to him.

Flank: they could separate and try to surround the caster swiftly by surprise. Close: Carsh could remain with Tohmas to utilize SoulBurner's protection.

If he had to keep close to SoulBurner, Carsh would be limited. Sneaking up would be better.

"Flank," Carsh answered.

"I be bait," Tohmas agreed, sheathing SoulBurner for a moment to stop the revealing light. Unclasping his shield and tossing it aside, he adjusted his sword sheath for a left-handed draw and selected a knife for his right hand. The shield was of no use against a caster. And this would be a battle in Rydan style. Both hands should carry blades.

Rolling his shoulders in readiness, Tohmas faced the doors.

Carsh nodded, having done nothing more than flip his grip on his knife once more. He had a familiar Rydan blade in each hand, his baldric filled with pillaged knives not as suitable.

Ready, Tohmas kicked the doors wide, stepped through, and taking advantage of the flare of light that followed SoulBurner's draw, pulled the sword from its sheath.

Carsh darted through the glaring light, counting on his brother's display to distract the flyer within. He threw himself under a bench and paused there, searching the room.

Four rows of pillars lined each side of the enormous X-shaped hall. A central dais loomed under a domed ceiling, surrounded by rows of benches and stools. There were four alcoves, one at the end of each of the arms of the X. The corridors were so long and dark, Carsh could not see far enough down them to know if anyone was hiding within.

Pools in the south, gardens in the west, beds of embers in the east; Carsh recognized the four gods. Esparans always built temples in an X shape.

He could not see anyone yet, but there was magic in the air. For one, the room was lit with pale flameless light that SoulBurner overwhelmed closest to them. There was something else somewhere across the room, but it was too far away for him to locate with accuracy.

"You enter alone, Prince of Galanth? I am surprised," a voice said, echoing from everywhere and nowhere at once. Carsh felt goosebumps as the words reached him; they were masked by magic, probably being thrown to avoid giving the concealed flyer away.

The voice is wrong. Carsh had heard Master Terant when they had fought. This voice was deeper.

Tohmas took long strides forward, his sword and knife raised now that a threat had been identified. With SoulBurner's aura, he could not be targeted by spells. The red light would keep him safe from projectiles as well. Makes good bait, Carsh mused.

"Only I carry SoulBurner, Terant. My goddess seeks vengeance!" Tohmas told the flyer. The name was wrong, but Tohmas could not have known as much. In truth, it did not matter; Carsh would kill any caster. And so long as Tohmas could get the flyer talking, they would find him.

Staying under the benches, Carsh crawled to the east arm of the X. The nearby embers made the shadows under the seat particularly deep to hide him.

"Terant?" The voice laughed. "Terant is dead, Prince of Galanth. You should congratulate your wizard; he finally proved himself. I always knew Kitable was the better."

From his position between the north and east arms, Carsh heard the voice coming from somewhere to his left. *Either the dais or the corner of Pari...*

He slunk toward the central podium, being careful to not scrape his splint on the floor.

Originating from somewhere near the dais, Carsh sensed magic lunging at Tohmas. There was no reason to be concerned: Tohmas had SoulBurner. The magic could not touch him. Carsh went back to slinking under the bench and around to the northwest corner of the temple.

When Tohmas jumped back, Carsh realized that he had been wrong; the floor holding Tohmas vanished. Quick on his feet, Carsh's brother scrambled across the cracking stone and managed to get to solid ground. SoulBurner's light could not penetrate stone. The magic had destroyed the space below the surface, leaving a crumbling, thin layer.

Now facing a trench at least three strides across, Tohmas would have to go around to reach the caster or Carsh.

"*Daem'd flya!*" Tohmas snapped, lifting SoulBurner in useless threat to the room. "You coward!" he clarified in Esparan.

Only a bit farther. Carsh sensed the tension of magic beyond him as he approached the dais from behind. The powers consolidated; the caster was a stride off the ground, flying near the center of the room. He was also entirely invisible. *Have to narrow it down.* As he slunk on, Carsh delicately swapped his Rydan blades for three Esparan ones, holding the last one in his teeth. Tohmas was making a cautious way around the trench, having found one side had left solid ground between the trench and the wall.

Carsh moved in closer, feeling the first magic shield pass over him as he slid under the benches into closer proximity. A second then a third shield ran their foul magic over him as he passed through. A larger locus of energy was ahead of him. He would find his target there.

"I am practical," the flyer replied, the voice again bouncing in the hall and denying Tohmas any chance at locating his enemy.

The flyer activated a spell, tossing it into Tohmas' path, a wall of stone blocking the only path around the trench. "And your goddess, you say? Oh, let me tell you about your goddess. About the woman who pretends to speak for Inac but is nothing but a—"

The next shield passed over Carsh, but the flyer's words suddenly stopped.

Certain he had been detected, Carsh sprung from hiding. Although the push of magic slowed him, it could not stop him. Next came pain, but he only felt it in his mind, and so he ignored it. He flicked out a fan of three Esparan knives. The two middle ones hit something solid.

He pulled free a Rydan blade for a targeted strike.

A spell answered before he could attack. He recognized it from Terant's duel; Carsh was thrown backward. Without a wall behind him

to smash against, he fell among the overturned benches and cushions, bruising his pride more than anything.

He charged back in and leaped after the moving target of hidden magic. The caster had fled vertically, heading for the far domed ceiling where the images of the gods peered down at the scene.

He had to drop the knife from his good hand, but Carsh caught the invisible man's foot. Dangling in the air as the flyer retreated up, Carsh fumbled to pull a fresh Esparan knife from his baldric. The splint made it far more difficult.

"You wretched Rydan!"

Despite being kicked about, Carsh swung his bad arm up, the knife in hand, and cut into something that felt like flesh. Blood seeped out.

The caster squawked.

Carsh was surprised. Flyers were usually harder to hit.

A spell gained force above him as he tried to get a second knife to join the one embedded in the target. When the spell reached a disturbing energy level, he changed his mind and released.

The spell followed him down like an avalanche, the cold nipping at his calves as he folded and rolled aside to avoid most of the impact. The skin on his un-bandaged arm and his back prickled with frost as he cleared the area. He had no doubt the full power of the spell would have turned him to ice.

Before he could rise, magic blasted into him. In a blink, he was dragged through the broken benches and slammed against the far wall between statues of Pari. There, held by wrists and ankles, he was pinned off the ground.

When he strained, the magic wrapped around his throat and tightened. He froze like a hound held by the scruff. He dared not even whistle.

He did not need to.

Tohmas re-entered the room at a run, having taken a longer start down the corridor behind them. Reaching the edge of the trench, he jumped.

It was not a feat Carsh had expected of his brother, and it appeared to take the caster by surprise as well. Although he landed roughly, Tohmas cleared the pit. SoulBurner's light was suddenly within twenty paces of Carsh.

At the edge of SoulBurner's light, between Tohmas and Carsh, a man appeared and dropped onto the ground, instantly dispelled. Carsh was disappointed that the flyer had lowered himself; he only fell a stride onto the hard stone floor of the temple.

The broad man scrambled away, trailing a short staff as he cleared the light of the enchanted sword. Carsh saw fine leather armor and a fighting cloak, something he had never seen a caster utilize before. The stranger appeared to be a few years younger than Dragal but moved with speed Carsh would have thought magical, if not for the fact the caster had just been dispelled.

He had five lines of tattoos over his face and dozens more down his exposed arms.

Realization dawned on Carsh. Five marks meant this person outranked the Bears they had confronted earlier. Only one person outranked them; Prince Marfaie.

The Prince of Tanble is a flyer.

He mentally shrugged.

He needs to die.

Tohmas headed for Carsh, allowing the caster to leave the red light. But before the light washed away the magic restraints on Carsh, the caster yanked free a stone from his belt and shouted an activation word, pointing a damning finger at Tohmas.

The magic materialized as a dozen stones, each the size of a fist. All twelve shot out toward Tohmas at once, aiming to keep the brothers apart.

It was a surprise to see the stones pass through the light, for Carsh had witnessed the powers of the goddess keep arrows at bay, but these plowed through uninterrupted. Tohmas took the first on the right shoulder, and it knocked him sideways. He braced himself, sheltering his head.

A stone struck his left hand.

The red light was suddenly gone, SoulBurner knocked from his grip. The enchanted sword skidded across the floor and into the magically-created hole Tohmas had jumped.

Helpless, Carsh hung from the wall. A strange feeling snuck into his gut.

For a moment, he felt a flicker of fear.

Tohmas was vulnerable. A single spell could kill either of them.

Surprise and speed were the assets of a knife dancer. One word could mean death against a caster. Constant engagement was key—it kept them from casting. But Carsh could not prevent the flyer from freely casting if he was pinned.

I failed.

He tried to curse but only a growl could escape the choke on his throat.

He saw understanding dawn over Tohmas' features. If he left to retrieve the sword, he left Carsh at the mercy of the caster. But if he did not get SoulBurner, he could be targeted by magic and killed.

Snatching up a fresh knife from his belt to replace his sword, Tohmas charged Prince Marfaie instead, following the style of a knife dancer. Now armed with a knife in each hand, he launched himself at the enemy. A flyer forced to save his own skin had no time for casting.

Carsh brought his rage against his fear, filling himself instead with determination. He was a knife dancer. He would slay this flyer. It did not matter that he was trapped for now, or that his arm was broken, or that his brother had been disarmed.

The thought of the arm and its splint gave Carsh an idea.

He turned his knife in his right hand, sawing the edge against the ties of his splint. The bindings holding his arm was over his wrist, over the splint. If he could free the splint...

The caster's stance changed when Tohmas charged, his feet sliding into a strong fighter's stance. Marfaie brought up the short staff into two hands like Rydan warriors with a *stafnye*. And the short staff appeared to be ringed with metal now that Carsh checked it. It was not a magical trinket. SoulBurner's touch had been irrelevant to it. This was a weapon, a weapon Prince Marfaie appeared to know well.

Before Tohmas could reach him, Marfaie stabbed with one enforced end of the staff, a direct blow for Tohmas' face. His brother had to abandon his charge and, with a knife, used his right hand to knock the staff aside. Tohmas slashed with his left blade, but the opposite end of the staff cracked across Tohmas' body and slammed into his knuckles before he could get the blade close enough to damage the enemy.

The knife fell from Tohmas' hands. Carsh suspected he may have broken a finger.

Tohmas hesitated, falling back a step to move beyond the reach of the weapon for a breath. He, like Carsh, did not seem to have expected a fight. Flyers knew magic, not battle.

But the pause lasted only a blink. Marfaie was speaking nonsensical words, casting. If the spell went off, they were dead.

Carrying one knife, Tohmas ducked into the battle once more, coming under the swing of the staff. With his open hand, he caught the back of the weapon. His muscles strained to hold it in place, stopping the far end from swinging up into his gut while he slashed at Marfaie.

Marfaie turned, using Tohmas' own strength against him and allowing the staff to go with Tohmas' bracing. The staff rotated, the opposite end slamming into Tohmas' shoulder. Surprised, Tohmas fell with the blow.

The tie on Carsh's splint snapped under his blade. Twisting his broken arm, which screamed in protest, he wiggled the splint, trying to loosen it.

Carsh could feel magic building once more, Marfaie using any pause in the fray to layer more magic into his attack. And with the hold of the magic across his throat, Carsh could not warn Tohmas. Tohmas may not even know the caster was managing to cast, bit by bit.

Landing briefly on one knee, Tohmas blocked the blow of the staff butt with a forearm to protect his throat, the armored leather bracers there blunting the blow enough to prevent a broken bone. Dropping his knife, he went in open-handed, grabbing at the staff with both hands. He managed to hold it for long enough to pull himself to his feet before it slipped out of his grip. The hardwood was lined with metal. Blood clung to the length of the staff as it came free, Tohmas' hands cut by the metal edge.

Finally loose, the splint cracked open. Carsh slipped his arm down through the splint, freed from the restraint and leaving the splint still held to the wall.

Pushing back against the agony of his broken arm, he snatched the best of the Esparan knives from his baldric and threw it.

His arm bones adjusted as he released the blade, making his vision blank in anguish. Although his throw landed, it lacked strength. When it dug point first into Marfaie's back, it did not cut into the spine as Carsh had intended.

Marfaie cried out more in alarm than pain, but the magic he had been preparing dissipated. He glanced back at Carsh, gauging the threat in a blink, then faced Tohmas in time to dodge Tohmas' punch and swing low at Tohmas' ankles. It was a common *stafnye* attack; Tohmas skipped over it and landed a fresh punch. Marfaie had leaned far enough around to keep his head out of harm's way, gaining only a bruise to his thick shoulder through his own leather armor.

Carsh reached for a second knife, unsure how much he could do with the broken arm but willing to try. Perhaps a less-defended area. The back of the knee or...

Prince Marfaie snatched up a new trinket from his belt as Tohmas lunged. With a single word, he vanished.

Tohmas stumbled to a halt in shock.

But Carsh could tell that the caster had simply stepped aside, allowing Tohmas to fall past. Although Carsh could no longer see him, the tingling presence of magic was still potent.

Tohmas froze for a long moment, waiting. When nothing happened, he slowly stood straight and snorted.

"Coward," he said, giving a sigh as he checked his hands briefly. By his brief frown, the bleeding was not enough to worry him.

Carsh strained against the remaining restraint, trying to force words through the choke on his throat. The flyer was not gone; he was right there! Tohmas could not sense or see him.

While Carsh saw concern on Tohmas' face, he did not seem to understand what Carsh was trying to say. Instead, his brother turned his back and jogged to the pit where SoulBurner had fallen.

But the threat was still standing silently behind them, poised.

For a beat, Carsh's chest hurt sharply. He screamed against the hold on his throat, but the sound was strangled and useless. Even his broken arm hung limp and uncooperative.

"Pit's not too deep," Tohmas told Carsh. "Be right back!"

He dropped into the trench after SoulBurner.

Magic exploded in multiple directions. One conjuration spell filled the hole where Tohmas had vanished with water. Next, the cold spell Carsh dodged earlier touched down on the surface of the water. The pit froze over instantly, trapping Carsh's brother.

Prince Marfaie appeared in front of Carsh, the black tattoos crossing from forehead to chin making his face dark. When he smiled, his teeth were stained, the brown shade unique to chewing tarol root.

"Well, well," Marfaie said, flicking his hand as he rested his staff against his hip. The force magic summoned scooped up Carsh's free hand and pinned it against the wall above the still-suspended splint. His healing bone shifted again. Carsh saw lights behind his eyes, the pain shooting through him from wrist to gut. For some reason, that bracket of energy was tightest, holding his bones compressed against themselves and keeping the pain from dissipating.

Marfaie grinned widely, his breath like fish. "Since you have decided to visit, I think I am owed some answers. We have time, don't we? Let's start with why you are here."

Vile powers reached out, digging into Carsh's forehead. He fought back, straining against his immobility until his arm's pain covered him with sweat and tossed his stomach. His heart again clenched in his chest, skipping. Despite it all, he could feel powers coursing through him, penetrating every fiber of his body.

It felt like an ice worm in his skull, but he could not even bring his hands up to try and dig it out.

"Wretched Rydan," the caster cursed as he leaned in, peering at Carsh in surprise. "Who is that?"

Chief Tamv flashed behind Carsh's eyes. Carsh tried to pull away, but the thought was there, on display for the flyer to see.

"Father and Leader," Marfaie translated. "Conqueror. A would-be conqueror of Espar."

Rage filled Carsh, his heart pounding and aching. He could not allow the flyer to take his memories, take his thoughts, but all the rage in the world could not stop him.

Through the haze of his watering eyes, Carsh saw the ice turn red behind Marfaie.

That thought was stolen in the next moment. Marfaie's expression fell. He spun to face the threat.

A loud crack filled the temple. The tip of a sword jutted from the smooth surface of the ice.

"Demon-cursed, impossible man!" Marfaie cursed.

Bathed in red light, Tohmas pulled himself out of the cold water and rose onto bare feet, the glorious light of the goddess defending him. He was in a half crouch in readiness and his leather armor was gone, as were his shoes. He seethed, his body shaking with fury and determination.

He charged.

But before Tohmas could reach the flyer, Marfaie threw his hands skyward, snapped out a word, and vanished. This time, Carsh sensed no lingering powers. The man was truly gone, taking the stolen thoughts with him.

The caster had escaped. Worse, he'd revealed Tamv's plan to the enemy. Carsh had failed.

Having been fooled once by Marfaie, Tohmas remained ready for battle. He freed Carsh from the magic with SoulBurner and felt he could take on any wizard with his brother at his side. But Carsh dejectedly put away one of his knives, leaving only a pillaged Esparan blade in hand, worth keeping only because others were in short supply.

Carsh sensed no magic, Tohmas interpreted. The threat had escaped.

"*D'aems.* I'd hoped to kill that bastard," Tohmas' cursed, sheathing SoulBurner. He shook himself, spraying water. A chilling wind from Totho's corner still cut through the wet. Carsh stood for a moment, pensive. Tohmas waited, hoping his brother would detect another location of magic for them to hunt down or reveal that the wizard had perished, not vanished. Instead, Carsh spoke in plain Rydan.

"He knows. He was in my head." Each word was reluctant.

A shiver ran over Tohmas, and it had nothing to do with the ice water. If the flyer had been in Carsh's head, their secrets were revealed. Tamv would be furious. Even as Tamv's sons, Tohmas expected no leniency. Carsh could be disowned or, if the insult was deemed profound enough, killed. In confessing that a flyer had taken information from him, Carsh was admitting failure, something that contravened their Rydan upbringing fundamentally. Carsh was trusting Tohmas with everything.

They were brothers. They defended each other against all foes, including Tamv.

Tohmas swapped to Rydan. "What did the flyer see?" His tone was gentle.

"Tamv," Carsh said, meeting Tohmas' stare with renewed confidence as his request for aid was met with acceptance. "Conquest."

So Marfaie knows of Chief Tamv's intentions for Espar. That could undermine the groundwork Tohmas had built for Tamv's conquest. Tohmas was still manipulating the princedoms and their princes to reduce opposition to the Rydan's control. If the princes learned the true intention behind his actions, none would be willing to join him, leaving him to take every last princedom by force. That would fail. He needed at least *some* believing his rhetoric of a better world under a single rule, even if he did not believe it himself.

"Marfaie will not get far, not if Elder Tril has done his duty," Tohmas comforted. Carsh was fingering his firebug charm, invoking the blessing of Inac it carried. They had to pray Tril had been successful. Tamv did not tolerate failure. "Back to the main forces. He'll be ours by nightfall," he promised.

Carsh let out a sigh and headed for the door. It was telling that he was so distracted by the breach of his mind that he did not bother to look for plunder. Even if the Rydan would never damage the sacred device of a god or goddess, there were other valuables scattered through the temple.

Tohmas had no need for pillage, but glancing back at the pit that was still frozen, he contemplated trying to retrieve his armor or his boots. They'd been so heavy in the water, he'd abandoned them.

"Meh," he decided. He walked out barefooted.

They retraced their steps through the manor, collecting protectors as they went and meeting few remaining enemies. After so long in the dark, stagnant corridors, the fresh wind of the late afternoon lifted Tohmas' spirit. The sun hung over the distant mountains in crimson. The evening was deepening.

A long day, but a good one, he mused.

Honest Justice was not outside when Tohmas left the manor. The protectors had, as instructed, ensured the exits remained open, but it had come at a cost. In one of the clashes, the royal horse had run off.

Bashuran had gone as well, but Carsh had only to whistle to bring the black horse to him. Tohmas was relieved to see the familiar gelding lagging behind Bashuran by a hundred paces.

A gash across Justice's right hind fetlock opened the skin to the ligaments. Despite his severe limp, the horse presented himself to Tohmas in readiness.

At the least, Tohmas planned to have Darak look at the injury, but there was no saving the horse's purpose. He was un-rideable for now and would never fight again.

While Tohmas treated what he could of the damage, another group of protectors returned, having completed a search of the manor, and flushed survivors into the streets. They were joined by Celebrant Loni, who had been released from a cell beneath the manor. How she had ended up there, she did not explain. Tohmas thought that for the best.

Once Justice wore a bandage, Tohmas led the horse into the streets, surrounded by mounted protectors on every side.

Walking, with Tohmas' permission, at his side, Loni preached in bursts as it suited her. She trailed behind on an occasion to play a crowd, catching back up after the distraction lost her interest. Ultimately finding a large enough group cowering in a temple's entrance, Loni allowed Tohmas and his mounted guard to go on ahead. He was content to move on without her until he heard:

"Behold! The mark of the goddess who has claimed her champion!"

The Celebrant's voice rose above the clatter of horses, cutting with confidence. When he looked back, Loni had climbed onto the side of the temple and was perched on a window sill, pointing a long finger at him. In the evening light, the little color visible beneath the filth covering her once-glamourous gown sparkled golden.

"*D'aems*," Tohmas muttered again.

He was still barefooted. While the scar on the bottom of his foot was over a decade old, this marked the first time the Esparan had seen it. The flame-shaped scar on the sole of his foot had been meaningless in the Outlands, but the Esparan would view as a miracle likely to match Sedgan's branded chest; the mark of Inac.

Should have thought of that sooner, Tohmas thought. As much as the title had initially irked him, he had come to accept it was, if nothing else,

a tool to be used in the conquest. Inac would surely support anything that brought him victory.

Tohmas walked on, leaving the celebrant still perched on the temple window behind him, but the crowd came in clumps behind him, whispering on his heel. The protectors adjusted their formation, bringing their horses together into a cautious rear guard.

He offered no explanation. Telling him he had stepped into a fire by accident in his youth and burned his foot would ruin the miracle. The crowd did not really want to know the truth anyway.

As he left the city, the horns told the entire story. Success had been found at each gate, but there were still skirmishes being fought. Responses came without needing him. Barnon and Sol reported setting up camp. The last of the Galanth soldiers were called from the city in victory, then sent against holdouts in the west. A fyrd moved into the manor as well, using it as a local fortification from which to launch further attacks. Whatever Tanble forces remained, Tohmas was confident they could be sorted through later. No hold in the city was great enough to be a threat to him or his army, not now.

There were no sightings of dragons. Tohmas assumed Darknim had done his duty.

Once in the open land outside the conquered city, the protectors offered Tohmas their horses to save him the long walk to the camp. Declining their offers, Tohmas whistled, certain the sound would carry into the Rydan's ranks.

The protectors tensed, no doubt believing any whistle meant trouble. Carsh alone knew the sound and smiled, which offered the protectors no comfort.

Schlavarai answered her rider's call.

At a full gallop, the mare appeared in the trampled fields of Arcott and presented herself to Tohmas eagerly. He almost expected Honest Justice to be offended when he had the dappled Rydan mare kneel and let him mount, but the older warhorse merely snickered then followed quietly. She dwarfed the other warhorse handily; he could not object.

Without halter and saddle, it was impossible to completely stop Schlavarai's excitement at having been called to ride again. Her long legs pranced into a dance of joy that forced the protectors to kick their horses into trots to keep up.

Arcott was done. It was time to plan the next stage.

Chapter 19

Climbing the south wall provided Kitable with an impressive view of where Seria had been killed. A group from the Fyrd of Traiton milled about at the base of the wall, removing bodies to the pyre and, ever practical, removing equipment. When they saw him, they nervously looked away.

Can't blame them, Kitable thought. *It's not like I bring calm and relaxation where I go.*

Keeping his eyes on an aura of magic, Kitable came down the wall. Shimmer followed him down the parting corridor of soldiers.

The guardian of the fyrd, a scar-faced man with a white eye, joined Kitable as he reached Seria's body, but Kitable held up a hand to stop the man from speaking.

"Need to be sure she's dead first," he told the man.

Seria had been struck against the wall hard enough to chip stones from the fortification. The transfer of force, even though her Molded Shield, had cracked her skull. The blood was contained by the Shield until dispelled the magic, whereupon it leeched into the nearby mud.

Entirely dispelled now, lacking any auras of magic, illusionary or otherwise, Seria remained dead.

"Who could have done this?" Shimmer whispered at his back.

She sounded nervous. The Molded Shield was one of the finest defenses a wizard had. Seeing how it could be bypassed was sobering.

Now certain Seria was not a threat, Kitable turned his attention to the guardian.

"Yes?"

"Another body over here," the guardian said, jabbing his thumb over his shoulder like a dagger. "Looks like it's breathing though."

The body of interest had been placed apart from the piles of bodies of the Rydans who had failed to climb the wall. Sabian lay awkwardly, unable to flatten to the ground or adjust his bent limbs through the freeze of magic. By the slowing of her steps as she approached behind Kitable, he suspected Shimmer had finally sensed the magic.

The guardian, grumbling something like "not my problem," rejoined his men.

The magic persisted, wrapping around the boy from the top of his head to his pinky toe. The auras were mainly alteration.

"I could do a four-way—" Shimmer suggested.

"You would kill him," Kitable corrected.

The girl blanched, her mouth hanging open.

"Gauging by Seria's appearance, he has been frozen like this for more than a candle," Kitable said. "Average duration for Nahon's Lock is three candles, but she could've made it shorter. He may not have a lot of time." He knelt beside the boy as he explained, ignoring the seep of cold mud through his robes.

Shimmer knelt on the other side of Sabian. "But if it wears off, he'll be able to move."

"Nahon's Lock was written as a restraint, but it becomes an attack when left for too long," Kitable said, sorting through his remaining spells and findings them inadequate. He would have to full cast the counter. "Seized muscles build up toxins."

"So, if you release him, you release all the toxins," she said tentatively. She frowned deeply. "That kills him? But if you don't do something soon, the spells runs out, and he's dead too."

Kitable did not think the statement merited a reply. She was right; if he did not counter it, Sabian would be dead, and Carsh would be annoyed. Kitable did not want an annoyed Rydan.

He focused on the Nahon's Lock spell and cast. Halfway through, he could tell by her lit eyes that Shimmer had figured out what he was

doing. She said nothing as the line of the dispel he had created touched down on the top of Sabian's head.

"Have you anything in that bag of yours for pain?" he inquired as he moved the spell down the frozen body. It was slow, for the spell had to cautiously maintain the rest of the Lock spell as it advanced, but it was worth it. The toxin could be dealt with in small amounts.

"Always," she replied. "Why?"

"Give it to him the moment his mouth is clear of the spell," he directed.

"He will choke! If his muscles are frozen, how can he swallow?"

"The spell does not affect all muscles," he corrected. "It allows for breathings and, ironically, for speech. As I said, it was made as a restraint. Locking all muscles would kill someone instantly; your heart would stop." He cocked an eyebrow at her. "In other words; he will swallow fine." He could have also spoken at any time but had remained silent, Kitable admitted.

He moved the dispel down as Shimmer rummaged through her bag. She waited until his dispel reached below Sabian's chin then coached him into swallowing the pills. He initially refused, but she overruled him by pointing out that she would simply force-feed him if he did not take the pills voluntarily. She seemed to have a good idea of how much pain he was going to be in shortly.

It would feel like spell burn, with every tensed muscle releasing their burning ache.

"This one's for the muscles," she added, providing a second mottled pill. "Forced relaxation!"

Demons, Kitable thought, *she's bright. She thought about where the pain is coming from, not just that pain is present.*

Every time their paths crossed, she surprised him with how quickly she was able to creatively adapt. When they had been confronted with poisons they could not neutralize, she had instead removed the toxin itself. To avoid getting in the way when defending the Circle, she had tailored her spells to assist Carsh. She and her father had confronted Terant and lived... *I'll have to find out how.*

As much as it shocked him, he wanted to know how she had survived her duel with a master wizard, and why she had turned up wet, and

why she continued to travel with Fixer City when business would be so much better elsewhere, and where she had come from, and…

When Kitable looked up, he met Shimmer's colorful eyes, for she was staring at him. A smile surfaced. She began to fiddle with a curl of her long red hair.

Kitable had to consciously move the dispel again for he had forgotten about it.

Tril had been right: they worked well together. Further, he felt indebted to her. Beyond the dispel that had freed him on the walls of Arcott, she had also helped him escape the manor. He had forgotten about her presence there, and now he wanted to know how she had escaped the Geas. For some reason, it did not surprise him that she had succeeded.

I'm a master wizard; I can offer apprenticeship.

There was not enough room in his vardo, but since she was traveling with them anyway, it would still be possible to teach her. He could show her proper magic. She could help him with new spells. He was amazed that he was even considering losing his solitude, but if the company was her, it was not as unwelcome.

He had never asked anyone to be his apprentice before. He had never known anyone good enough. Shimmer was still inexperienced and certainly would need plenty of guidance, but she had such potential.

Would she refuse? Maybe she liked her life by the fires of Fixer City. Maybe life working with him would be too boring.

By the time the dispel reached Sabian's ankles, Kitable had made up his mind. Shimmer was talking to Sabian, to make conversation he presumed, but she looked back at Kitable once the spell slid off the man's feet, and Kitable let it drop. Sabian had yet to reply.

I will ask her, Kitable decided.

The moment he opened his mouth to speak, a voice interrupted: "Kit!"

Shimmer cracked another broad grin. "Prince Tohmas calls you 'Kit'?" she teased, and Kitable had to roll his eyes.

"He is the only one who gets away with it," he replied. He shouted back, "What now?"

The green and silver-clad Prince of Galanth arrived atop a huge dappled horse Kitable did not recognize. He lacked armor and boots but wore a grin large enough for two men as he dismounted.

As Sabian scrambled to his feet—an impressive feat considering the likely state of his limbs—Kitable rose and tried to brush the mud off his knees. When he glanced at Shimmer, she was standing with her bag slung over her shoulder once more.

Tohmas paused, one hand on the horse that stayed by him despite lacking bridal or lead. "Am I interrupting?"

"No," Kitable replied immediately. "We were just rescuing our unfortunate friend from some lingering spells, lest he end up taking a permanent nap."

"Demons!" Shimmer cried. Her eyes searched the sky. "Nap! What time is it?"

"Fifth candle," the prince replied, his voice curious.

"Oh! " she said with a grimace. "I need to get back to Match and Mixer before—"

Kitable could see her auras; he knew which of her spells was counting down, even if she did not know the count. To be ready for battle, Shimmer must have cast the spell early. That meant she was painfully close to the forced slumber her Rejuvenation spell required.

"Sit down," Kitable interrupted. "You are too close to the expiration to chance running through Fixer City right now. If you pass out too early, you could land unconscious among unsavory types."

The girl thumped herself down onto the cold ground, then folded herself forward so she would not topple when she slept. "Damned Rejuvenation!" she cursed as she settled. "I should have used Papa's pills, but they don't last long enough, and we needed a full recovery from all those spells to get through Terant... that... bother."

She fell asleep there, relaxing into her propped position.

"I can take her home," Sabian weakly offered.

Kitable glared at him. "You will amaze me if you find yourself capable of holding one of your knives right now, boy. Sit down before..."

He had never expected Sabian to listen to him and so was shocked when Sabian immediately dropped to one knee. It took a moment more for Kitable to recognize why.

Carsh had arrived at Tohmas' side. Sabian's position—bent with one knee not quite touching the earth—was something Kitable had seen the Rydans do, but he did not know the meaning of it.

It was a minor miracle that the boy was capable of standing, let alone taking the half-knelt position. His muscles must have been burning through the pain pills. He was probably as sore as Kitable's worst spell burn, but the boy just did not seem to notice. He held the position diligently while Carsh towered over him. The Rydan's eyes flicked over to where Seria had fallen, then returned to the boy bent before him.

With his head lowered, Sabian could not see Carsh's small smile. The evidence of his Leader's approval was long gone by the time the Rydan spoke and Sabian looked up.

"Ged," Carsh stated.

Sabian rose and left at a walk that did not quite conceal his pain, but Kitable had to give him credit for his efforts.

Carsh stepped back and raised an eyebrow at Kitable. Shimmer lay serenely on the ground between them, her colorful dress now marred with additional mud. The Rydan's smile was suggestive.

Reckless, Kitable thought. Rejuvenations had to be carefully managed. A caster should not cast one if they were not monitoring the passage of time. It was an extremely dangerous spell if unmonitored.

Hypocrite, a part of Kitable replied. But his circumstances had been different, he convinced himself.

Tohmas pressed his lips and seemed to deliberate on addressing the situation with Shimmer.

"Thank you," Kitable interrupted. "I think you prevented me from doing something very stupid."

Tohmas chuckled. "Kit, your stupid is another man's moment of genius, I assure you."

The prince was wrong. Kitable felt he had indeed almost done something very unwise. His life was arranged the way he wanted. He did not need help, nor did he want it. Shimmer was a distraction.

"What did you want?" Kitable pressed instead of dealing with the compliment.

"I need you to send eight messages, one to each of the princes. Is that possible?"

Kitable mentally counted, then frowned. "Yes, but with Barnon, Sol, and Dragal here, there are only seven princes who are not present."

"Dragal is dead," Tohmas replied, his voice factual. It made Kitable start: the death of a prince should have been more notable. He hadn't heard anything. And Tohmas did not seem to think the topic merited conversation, as he quickly continued, "I need you to send a message to each of his..." Tohmas paused and cracked a smile. "To the men who married his daughters."

"His sons-in-law?" Kitable clarified.

"I could not decide if it was sons-in-law, sons-in-laws, or son-in-laws. Esparan is so strange!" Even Kitable had to smile. Some part of him was disappointed that he was light-hearted after learning that a Prince of Espar was dead, but the rest of him shrugged it off. Dragal had been sick and old. His time had come. It was no surprise.

"The message?" he asked instead.

"Funeral announcement. We will be heading down to Solta for the event, but I want them to have time to attend. Possible?" Tohmas asked, holding out a piece of vellum.

Kitable scoffed. "Straight forward," he confirmed as he accepted the vellum and perused it. "Best give me eight copies though. Easier to send one to each location. I will take Miss Weaver home, then get right to it." He was rewarded with another smile from his patron.

"As soon as you are able," Tohmas said.

Kitable handed back the funeral invitation and scooped up the sleeping girl. Shimmer nuzzled against him, gently moaning in her sleep. It was a bizarre sensation.

Prince Tohmas cocked his head at Kitable, a question almost voiced between them.

Kitable shook his head. *A distraction,* he reminded himself. *A distraction I do not need.*

"I'll get her back to her father," he said. He did not look back as he headed out to find Dust Weaver.

It now made sense.

Marfaie had been frustrated enough when Prince Tohmas had disturbed his carefully laid plans for the sons of Zayban, but he had settled it by simply replacing Habal with Tohmas in the plan. Turning DoomDragon against Marfaie had aggravated Marfaie further. Now Arcott had fallen, Tanble was lost, and Marfaie was furious.

But he had his answers. He now knew why.

With the Prince of Galanth charging him, enchanted sword again in hand, Marfaie left. This was a battle he could fight another time when the circumstances favored him more.

Using a wooden ring around his neck, he activated the Relocation spell and fled. The view changed instantly. From the ornate temple, Marfaie moved into a valley far outside of Arcott.

They could not follow. Now, he had time.

"All for nothing!" he shouted, pounding his staff into the soft turf.

He had seen the Rydan Chief in Prime Protector's mind. The entire war, all of the defense of Solta, all of it had nothing to do with Marfaie or Zayban or Solta! All of it was an excuse! Marfaie himself was nothing but a front!

He released a long breath, settling himself. *I escaped. I will have vengeance yet.* He would tell others what he had yanked out of the Rydan's surprisingly disturbing mind. They would stop Tohmas Galanth of Galanth. Marfaie had a new war to fight.

Ready to move on, Marfaie looked around. He had supplies in a shack by the nearby river. He needed to bandage his back and leg before going any farther, and then he would...

In the gloomy light of his valley, Marfaie was shocked to discover he was not alone. His heart skipped several beats when he recognized a Northlander, then several more.

He uttered an activation word but a burst of cold air blocked it. Seven Northlander elders in furs and feathers formed the circle around him, staring with wild eyes. Beyond them, a crowd of Northlander warriors filled the spaces between the scraggly trees.

Frantically, Marfaie searched his memory for another enchanted trinket or something that would help him escape. Lifting his staff in readiness, Marfaie braced himself for battle.

But the bearded man wearing a wolf-skin gestured and a cold wind swept over him, carrying his magic with it. The wind then sealed around him like the embrace of a ghost, holding him stationary.

The silent grins around him intensified. The wolf-skin Northlander barred his teeth like the beast on his shoulders.

Two hunters came up between the Elders of the Circle of the Raven and took Marfaie's arms. A third removed his staff.

"Vile, traitorous Rydans..." he cursed quietly as they led him away.

The day drifted to an end, the spoils of Arcott claimed by the conquerors and the rest burned. The sons of Zayban lit the pyre for their dead brother and remained there in vigil. It was no surprise to find tears blurring the eyes of the youngest of the brothers. Tohmas found Sol startlingly stoic.

They had no accusations or denials for him when he joined them at the pyre, although Barnon asked what had happened. The abbreviated version of the death appeased them, and they all fell into a resigned silence for the remainder of the evening. Tohmas suspected the answer did not matter to Sol.

After dusk, the Northlander forces arrived back among them, following Darknim DoomDragon, who they had met on the road to Arcott. They carried Calanor Blow, wounded but alive. Under the care of the elders, the beaten celebrant was improving quickly.

Darknim DoomDragon joined the vigil by the pyre briefly, his once-tanned skin thickened with burn scars that seemed old despite having occurred only in the last few days. Sol and Barnon accepted the presence of the Northlander with a nod of respect.

"Welcome back," Tohmas said, glancing over at the Northlander. "What happened to your ax?"

Darknim's smile stretched his burned, eerily smooth skin. Even his beard looked unevenly singed. "Broke it. I'll have to make a new one."

Tohmas did not know what consolations to offer. He knew of no one who could replace the black-winged ax. The craftsmanship of the ax originated from the ancient past and still surpassed anything a smith could forge today.

Into the ensuing silence, Darknim leaned over and whispered, "He's in the tent, by the way. The elders did their part."

Satisfied he had seen all he needed to at the pyre, Tohmas was pleased to have an excuse to leave. "Prince Sol, Prince Barnon, join me," he called.

When Barnon lifted his head, he seemed to want to refuse, but Sol quickly stood, and the younger prince followed his brother's lead. The two remaining sons of Zayban followed Tohmas to his tent.

Tohmas held a hand up to Carsh, and the Rydan stopped. For this, Tohmas did not want any reminder of the Rydan's presence, not if Tamv's name came up. The Rydan pranced anxiously but sidled away in acceptance, counting on Tohmas to control the damage the Prince of Tanble could cause with his stolen knowledge.

It was hard for Carsh, and Tohmas saw the conflict in his brother's face. Rydans did not use torture or courts. To them, all was death or legacy. If he killed Marfaie, Carsh would prove that he was the flyer's better, but in giving Marfaie over to others, he was letting go of that prestige.

As much Tohmas wanted to let Carsh finish the confrontation, discretion was required.

Passing into the tent, Tohmas found Prince Marfaie, his bearded and tattooed face marred by long bruises and his leg wrapped in a rough bandage he had bled through. He was held firmly by two Hunters, a pair of the Circle Elders standing a pace behind him in readiness.

With one long stride, Tohmas brought the Prince of Tanble into reach and punched him before he could speak. As he had intended, the cry the man gave out was muffled by his now-broken jaw. Marfaie struggled to right himself, the grips of the Hunters on his arms unrelenting.

Shaking his hand to clear the effects of the impact, Tohmas looked at the Hunters who held the prince.

"I can handle him from here." Tohmas drew SoulBurner. Elder Tril, his feral eyes reflecting the light of the sword like a wolf caught in torchlight, grinned widely. He gestured to the rest of elders, and the Circle followed him out. The Hunters let Marfaie crumple to the ground and left.

Only Darknim remained.

Keeping Marfaie, who was slumped over spitting blood into the dirt, in the light of SoulBurner, Tohmas turned to Darknim. "When you said you thought Marfaie would get away, you failed to mention that it was because he was a caster."

"You did not know?" Darknim answered, going to stand over the slumped Prince of Tanble. He placed a boot on the man's back. "You spoke all the time of the magic being faced at Arcott! You said you feared he would match Wisavi Kitable even. You could not—"

"Terant!" Tohmas chuckled in understanding. "Maybe Seria or Clarin too! *D'aems*, he had so many wizards working for him, it's hard to keep them apart. But I didn't realize he was a caster until he hit us with the first spell."

"Marfaie..." came the whispered realization from behind him.

Tohmas stepped aside to clear the way for the sons of Zayban who had obligingly followed him. Darknim shoved his foot out, throwing the defeated prince down for easier viewing.

"You clearly fared well enough," DoomDragon quipped at Tohmas.

Tohmas shrugged. There was no reason to dwell on the misunderstanding. Even if the magic had been unexpected, it had been dealt. Arcott was theirs. Marfaie was captured.

"I thought he had escaped," Sol said softly as he glared down at the man who had assaulted his princedom for a decade.

"The Northlander Circle knew where he was going," Tohmas explained, gesturing to DoomDragon to pass on the credit. "We set a trap for him."

"When the Northlanders left, it was on purpose," Barnon realized aloud, his voice filled with awe.

"Had to be. Terant watched us often. I dared not let anyone know, else Marfaie would have changed his Relocation spell." If Marfaie had known Tohmas was aware of his possible escape, he would have devised a new plan. It had been vital that Marfaie believed his path to freedom was safe. Tohmas had not known it was the Relocation spell that he had been trying to maintain, but the effect was the same.

"And I needed DoomDragon aimed at the dragons," Tohmas added.

"Which I have freed," Darknim gravely said. "The reds are no longer under Marfaie's control. Thus, to honor our alliance, I offer this prisoner

to you, Princes of Espar. Marfaie has slighted your family. I offer him up to your justice."

The eyes of the sons of Zayban finally went to DoomDragon, and Tohmas was pleased to see a small nod of appreciation. Marfaie, crumpled below them, did not seem to notice when the gazes returned to him.

"I have a request," Tohmas intervened, thinking of Carsh. Esparan justice required Marfaie to be starved as a traitor. Unless he could make amends, he expected to find Marfaie pinned to his starvation post by a Rydan knife, intercepting the justice of Espar. That would drive the factions apart.

"He and his casters should be forgotten. Their names will never be spoken aloud. They must fade from history."

Death would shame Marfaie, proving Carsh was superior, but the far greater punishment was to be denied legacy. He could give this much to Carsh.

The two princes nodded. They bent, then carried the defeated Prince of Tanble out of the tent. By the cast of their expressions, Tohmas knew that he would never see Marfaie again.

"I will have the Circle follow to keep his powers under control," Darknim offered.

Tohmas considered the matter done, even though Darknim did not leave the room or call out to the Circle that had already left the tent. They would know.

And with his jaw smashed, Marfaie would not be revealing anything to Sol or Barnon. It was as good as Tohmas could do.

He let out a sigh, feeling the pressure of the unknown lift from him. Finally done, he sheathed SoulBurner and sought a wineskin. Darknim deserved a drink.

As Tohmas put his hand on a wineskin, Darknim asked, "Are you going to ask me if he said anything?"

Tohmas winced. The very fact that Darknim asked the question revealed that some of what Marfaie knew had been shared.

Not done then, he admitted.

"To what end? I cannot change it," Tohmas said, waiting for more. His left hand was itching to use SoulBurner, but he refused to surrender to the Rydan in him that demanded silence. Moving to his immense table, he placed a pair of cups on the surface. The Esparan way was better here.

"Who is Tamv?"

"The Chief of the Outlands," Tohmas replied honestly, but DoomDragon was too clever to let that be the only answer.

"Who is he to you?"

There were many possible answers, but Tohmas could only justify one. As much as Tamv would not approve, he had to answer truthfully.

"My father," he admitted, passing a cup of wildwater to Darknim.

The Northlander took a long drink as if needing to gather his thoughts. He frowned under his patchy beard. The fresh scars creased deeply.

"I did not expect you to admit it," DoomDragon confessed. "Why tell me?"

Tohmas finished his own cup in a single swallow, then smiled the weakest smile he had all day. "Because if I did not, I would have to lie to you. In less than a mooncycle, Darknim, you would have reason to doubt me. And when it was finally revealed, you would hate me for having lied to you. So, there you have it."

Rydans would have threatened Darknim, but Tohmas wanted to treat the Northlander like a Rydan Follower. That meant the bear of a man was owed the truth and, frighteningly, trust.

The moment he mentally identified Darknim as a Follower, his path was set.

He rose from his seat and opened, with a key, the one chest in the room he kept locked and, thanks to Kitable, enchanted. A stack of vellum, each identical, looked up at him. He selected the top one.

"Is everything Marfaie said true, then?" DoomDragon asked.

In reply, Tohmas handed DoomDragon the writing. "You read Esparan?" he asked, and the bearded man nodded. "Then there's your answer. Tell me what you think."

There was a long silence as the Northlander read and an even longer silence as he pondered the implications. At length, the Northlander sat down and finished his drink.

"Ambitious," he first said, and Tohmas sat across from him, refilling both their cups. "You would claim all of Espar as yours. Why?"

"Because Espar is divided. Her princes bicker and her people suffer. I can stop all that. I can unite her."

"And Tamv?"

"He wants control," Tohmas confessed.

A skeptical gaze answered from under Darknim's grey mat of hair. The stare went from Tohmas to the vellum, then back, several times.

"Will you join me?" Tohmas finally asked.

The Northlander put down the paper and sat back in his seat. He contemplated Tohmas carefully, as if reviewing every word they had ever exchanged. At length, the Northlander sat forward.

"Tohmas Galanth, worlds are turned by men like you. Regardless of what I say, you are going to do this."

"I am."

"Tanble is mine?"

"As promised," Tohmas confirmed regardless of the man's ultimate decision. He had made a promise to a Follower, and he would never welch on such a vow.

"Then we are with you," Darknim agreed. He placed a hand on the vellum and slid it back to Tohmas. "I would be a fool to turn away now. We will wear your green and take Espar from the princes who try to stop you. They will fight, Tohmas. You know that."

"We can handle it," Tohmas assured him as he took the paper and put it away. The trunk clicked as it locked once more. "Nothing will stop us."

THE END

SNEAK PEEK OF KING

King

The damp of the ground was cutting through his breeches as he knelt before the flickering flame of the altar, having insisted the servants keep the damn meeting table on the waggons and leave him be. He had no plans for formal conversations tonight. His soldiers knew the camp routine well enough to no longer required directions. Carsh, his brother by deed but not by blood, had gone down into the Rydan side of camp in search of company. Like most Rydans, Carsh was still celebrating the sacking of Arcott and the death of the Prince of Barlaby. The Rydans were looking forward to their next battle and would have grown restless should the rumors reach them that the war ended.

Carsh's presence among his fellow Rydans had another purpose; he would beat down any suspicions of peace, just as Darknim DoomDragon was doing for the Northlanders. Keeping to themselves, the Esparans were the only ones who had yet to be told the truth. Tonight, they relaxed and looked forward to the prospect of real beds the next night.

Tohmas let them keep their illusion. Spies could not hide among the Rydans or the Northlanders, but a well-placed traitor among the main forces could learn too much from the Esparans. He had to wait before informing his Esparan forces of the grander plans in the works.

Finishing the prayer, Tohmas leaned back and turned his attention to the three piles of painted stones arranged at his knees. The largest pile to his left was clumped together, not requiring organization; markers

of the princedoms he knew and controlled. The other two piles were laid out so each colored symbol faced him, ready for his consideration.

"Always so hard at work," an alto voice said from the other side of the tent.

Instinctually defensive, Tohmas tensed before fully recognizing the voice. He stayed his hand, leaving the sword on the altar, turned to face her, still on his knees respectfully.

The Goddess of Fire lay sprawled on his bed, one hand draped comfortably over the edge. Her attire was one part elegant and one part scandalous, ranging from golden chainmail draping her upper arms to a skirt cut for riding but too shear to protect even her modesty. One hand was gold-tinted, but her other glinted like glass. She seemed thinner, and her hair was more blonde than red. Her clothes were partially transparent, but he was grateful for even that slight cover. He had seen her without any coverings; no conversation was possible then.

He had come to expect to the goddess' visits since they had left Arcott and would have been disappointed if she had failed to attend tonight. Before that, she had appeared to him sporadically, although most commonly after battle celebrations. With the frequency of her presence now, he had ceased worrying about being caught with her. Everyone, from Tohmas' brother to the princes who had marched with him in the Northlander War, knew that the candles after sunset were his time. They did not know why, but they knew not to intrude.

There were nights when she came as the Lady of Lust and others when she was the Bitch Goddess. Most visits were from the Warrior Queen aspect of the Goddess of Fire, although some elements of the Lady of Lust shone through all of her manifestations.

He forced his stare away from her, feeling desire rise.

"Is this what you wish of me tonight?" he asked. The time was short to finish his plans for each of the princedoms, but even a prince of espar obeyed his Goddess. She would know best how to utilize the time he had left.

She slid from the bed and onto gold-touched feet that made no sound despite the assortment of bangles decorating her ankles. She wore no sword tonight.

"No, no other plans, Champion," she cooed, her accent slipping from southern to strongly Lourite. The shift reminded Tohmas of his

training with Chief Tamv, when he had been coached to trade his Rydan accent for a Galanth one that better suited his Esparan blood.

Inac approached, and Tohmas lowered his head. When she touched his shoulder, her hand was frigid. It had burned before; perhaps it changed on her whim. He took the cold to mean he had to finish the matter at hand, not be distracted by the increasing need her long, graceful legs stirred in him.

"Your allies number the greatest," she said softly, keeping him on task.

Tohmas' eyes went to the pile on his left, the stack representing the princedoms he had already brought under his control. Among them was a quartz stone he had selected as Darknim DoomDragon's marker. He had thrown aside the stones representing Barlaby, Meloch, and Tanble, as those princedoms had been conquered by Darknim before Tohmas had brought the Northlander to his side.

"Show me," Inac said, the accent now nearly Rydan as she paused behind him.

He felt her gaze on his back, like the heat of a candle behind him, as he gestured at the first pile. "The sons of Zayban are already mine."

"The three that live, yes," Inac replied. "But Sol and Barnon are not the force their brother Dragal was. And the third son is yoked to your blood by a dead marriage. The hold is brittle."

The word "marriage" was bitter. Her realm was lust, not the sweet love of her sister goddess, Ocea.

Tohmas's stare went to the brown and white stone that represented his uncle-by-marriage. "Prince Deiton is a coward with no heart for fighting. He will follow where the sons of Zayban lead," Tohmas said. Beside the stone was Dragal's blue and yellow stone. "Dragal's sons-in-law are taking his place, keeping the family strong. Sol says they will divide Clandac between them, but I have a better offer for them. This much is simple. We have the north and centre of Espar between us six." The quartz stone in the pile was key. Darknim knew the offer Tohmas intended to make. He had already approved the plans for Dragal's heirs.

"You did right to finish off Prince Dragal," Inac said, her voice husky. "Now we can press on without interruption."

She knows. Of course she knows. Dragal had sought death, although he had never specifically requested it from Tohmas. Still, Tohmas had provided it. He had been well within Rydan customs and laws, and he

doubted the Northlanders minded, but the Esparans would be outraged if they knew he had stabbed an arrow into the back of a Prince of Espar. Princes did not kill princes. They did not see illnesses needed purging. In their eyes, Tohmas had committed murder. He had no intention of telling any Esparan about it.

Inac was the Mistress of Justice; her approval freed him of all guilt.

"I am glad you approve. My uncles would damn me, should they discover it," Tohmas said.

"Their hands are no less blood-stained. They were the death of Prince Marfaie. But he was a traitor to his title as prince," Inac said. It was strange to hear the name spoken aloud; Rydan tradition insisted the names of the damned should never be spoken aloud. Tohmas presumed Inac did not care, being a goddess.

"You did right. And they did right. Vengeance can be just."

Vengeance, in the form of slow maiming and starvation, had left the corpse of Prince Marfaie at the border to Solta. Starvation was traditional for traitors in Espar.

He had slain four princes now, one by choosing not to act, one by poisoning, one by respecting the man's request for relief, and one by giving him over to his enemies. Only a mild sense of guilt remained for the first. None of the others upset him.

"Now, your enemies?" Inac asked, her hand siding behind his neck to rest on his left shoulder. The scar there tingled, bringing Prince Dorakon of Gaidol to the forefront of Tohmas' mind. His eyes went to the white stone with the blue centre.

"Prince Dorakon hates me. I won the bet and made him look like a fool. He will fight me." Leaving Dorakon's stone where it lay, he picked up the green and yellow stone beside it. "Prince Neillen is tied closely to his brother, so I expect him to follow Dorakon and set Nothor against me. But Neillen did not come for the funeral. He sent an emissary, Lord Garmont, who is soon to marry Prince Neillan's sister-in-law." He paused for his thoughts to coalesce. The connections between lords and ladies of Espar puzzled him. Instead of assessing a hierarchy of skill, as he had in the Outlands, he memorized bloodlines with little understanding as to their importance.

Maybe he could find leverage somewhere in those connections. "And Damoria," he finished, listing the last stone in the right-hand pile,

"has a feud with my princedom that goes back two generations. Prince Wevan has sent his son. Apparently, the last time the young Warrah and I met, I bloodied his nose, and he gave me a black eye." Tohmas smiled. Although he did not remember the encounter, he appreciated the simplicity of their relationship.

Inac lifted her hand from his shoulder. The chill lingered. "And the others?"

A yellow stone with a grey anvil for Lour, a blue stone with a red bird for Polthian, and the white stone with the brown horse for Trulin lay between the two piles, unassigned.

"We will see," he said.

She came around, standing before him. Like her feet, her legs were gold-tinged. He could see up to her hip through the long slit of her crimson skirt.

The chill left his shoulder, heat rising instead. It started in his chest and moved down suggestively like a lover's caress.

"You will suffer for this quest, but it will be for the best."

Since the first night he had seen her red dress in a Rydan *shella*, Tohmas had felt her will in everything he had done. Chief Tamv had presented the idea to go into Espar, but Tohmas had heard the echo of Inac's will in his voice. The time was ripe now, even it if was earlier than any of them had expected. That was because of her assistance. She was ready to lead him on. With her at his side, he could do anything.

When she beckoned, Tohmas came to his feet. Physically, she was a head shorter than him, but in her presence, he felt small.

"Give me SoulBurner," she commanded, and he immediately retrieved his enchanted blade from the altar and dropped to a kneeling position to present it to her. Although the sword would only glow red when held in his grip, its enchanted aura filled the tent when her hand wrapped around the hilt.

His soul stirred to see her standing with the green and silver blade flickering flames in hand. It marked the first time he had ever seen the blade from a distance, and he now found himself cowed by it. He felt like a brand had been laid on his soul.

"I have a final task for you," she announced, and he adjusted into to a Rydan ready stance with one leg bent and his knee not quite touching

the ground. "Your undertaking must have an heir, Champion. This realm I created must stand. You must have a son."

Inac was goddess of war, fury, justice, and passion. He had not expected her to comment on matters of family.

"Is it not Ocea who would need to give her blessing?" he asked.

Inac tossed her hair in the firelight and sneered with a dismissing wave of her hand. "Fine, fine," she said indignantly. "Ask her permission. Fall in love, if you want, Champion, even marry. You will always belong to me."

He bowed his head in acceptance. Into the silence, he spoke the prayer of Inac.

By the time he had finished, the blade lay on the ground and the Goddess was gone. The heat through his body dwindled then vanished. The tent was once more filled with a damp chill, his knees wet from kneeling and growing cold.

But his soul still felt bound to her and, as he re-sheathed the sword, his heart locked onto the command.

He would have an heir. He had to have a son. If that were so then, by Esparan, Rydan, and Northlander law, he had to marry. Only then would a son be his heir as well.

The thought confused him. He knew war well. Women were easy. *But a wife?*

He had come to no conclusion by the time he changed the light on Inac's altar and slept.

Glossary

Barlaby: Far north princedom of Espar. Overrun by Northlander
    CURRENT PRINCE: Prince Lorian Rairn.
    COLORS: White and White.
    CREST: None

Calendar: Universal calendar pre-dates the Demon Wars. Roughly
    based on the moon's phases:
    YEAR: Eight mooncycles of forty days, and one mooncycle (the
        ninth) of a variable length, thirty-five or thirty-six days.
    MOONCYCLE: forty days.
    HALFCYCLE: twenty days.
    QUARTERCYCLE: ten days.

Celebrant: Esparan priest, traditionally assigned to a single deity of the
    four. Overseeing a group of Acolytes.

Clandac: Central Esparan princedom.
    CURRENT PRINCE: Prince Dragal Galanth. Eldest son of Zayban.
    COLORS: Blue with Gold.
    CREST: Scythe

Companion (Black rank rope): Esparan Companions are not soldiers
    by profession. They become soldiers when they are required, but
    have other occupations.

Currency (Esparan)

> LEG: Wedge-shaped copper coin with a hole in it for threading on a string.
>
> TABLE: Eight legs strung together.
>
> SLIVER: Wedge-shaped silver coin with a hole in it for threading on a string.
>
> SLICE: Eight slivers strung together.
>
> SPOKE: Wedge-shaped gold coin with a hole in it for threading on a string.
>
> WHEEL: Eight spokes strung together.

Damoria: South west princedom of Espar, corner of DragonTail mountains and Outlands. Enemy of Galanth.

> CURRENT PRINCE: Prince Wevan Damoria.
>
> COLORS: Red with Yellow.
>
> CREST: Dragon

Espar: The overall region north of DragonTail mountains.

Esparan (race): People of Espar. Pale skinned and featured peoples. Religion of four elemental gods.

Forsinth: Princedom of Espar, known for pottery and claywork. Close ally to sons of Zayban

> CURRENT PRINCE: Prince Deiton Darvin-Galanth. (Widower of Elinea Galanth)
>
> COLORS: Brown with Silver.
>
> CREST: wine pitcher

Galanth: Southern Esparan princedom on borders with Outlands.

> CURRENT PRINCE: Prince Tohmas Galanth. (Son to Habal Galanth)
>
> COLORS: Green with Silver.
>
> CREST: Tree

Gaidol: Princedom of Espar with prolific trading routes. Borders contentiously with Trulin. Close ally to Nothor.
> CURRENT PRINCE: Prince Dorakon Lodaton
> COLORS: White with blue.
> CREST: Shark

Guardians (Red rank rope): Each Esparan city had a single Guardian named by the Prince. A Guardian may or may not have a Prime status, depending on the size of the city.

Inac: Esparan fire god. Female. Also known as the Bitch Goddess, Dame Justice, Lady of Lust, Warrior Queen.

Knock: An Esparan gesture of agreement. Originally from a time of blood-bonds, where the two people would press their fists together and cut across the two hands to bind their words and spirits. More recently, no cut is used, just the knock of fists.

Lour: Western princedom of Espar along the Crescent and DragonTail mountains. Deep iron mines. Finest metalsmiths in Espar
> CURRENT PRINCE: Prince Loritat Naygan.
> COLORS: Gold with Grey.
> CREST: Anvil

Meloch: Far north princedom of Espar, currently overrun by Northlanders
> CURRENT PRINCE: Prince Garit Carnilan. Deceased.
> COLORS: Black with Red.
> CREST: Raven

Northlander (race): Race of the far north; a hardy people organized into clans but united by a Circle of the Raven, which comprises of magic-users. When the circle is complete (7 members), they name a DoomDragon (all clan leader).

Nothor: Eastern coastal Esparan Princedom. Known for shipping and mechanical innovation. Close ally to Gaidol.

> CURRENT PRINCE: Prince Neillen Lodaton.
> COLORS: Green with Gold
> CREST: Ship

Ocea: Esparan water god. Female. Also known as the Maiden, The Benevolent Mother, the Weeping Goddess.

Polthian: Esparan Princedom on southern border, close to Outlands.

> CURRENT PRINCE: Prince Emacen Polthian.
> COLORS: Blue with red.
> CREST: Eagle

Pari: Esparan earth god. Male. Also known as the Mountain King, The Beast Lord, The Traveler, Healing Presence.

Prime (single strand of silver in a rank rope): A distinguishing rank above the main associated one in Esparan ranking. For example, a Prime Protector would be one step above a protector and command them.

Protectors (Green rank rope): Bodyguards of a Prince of Espar. Commanded by a prime protector.

Rabarch: Esparan Princedom.

> CURRENT PRINCE: Prince Barnon Galanth (youngest son of Zayban Galanth)
> COLORS: white with red
> CREST: Dragon head

Rydan (race): Tribal people of the south Outlands, consisting of three clans (First, Second, Third), each ruled by a Chief. Primarily raiders and nomads, with a strong emphasis on horsemanship. Rydan horses are powerful warhorses, bound to a given master for life.

Solta: Central princedom of Espar, currently under siege by Northlanders.
> CURRENT PRINCE: Prince Sol Galanth (Second youngest son of Zayban)
> COLORS: Red with back
> CREST: Shield

Tanble: Northern Princedom of Espar, currently overrun by Northlanders.
> CURRENT PRINCE: Prince Vornan Marfaie (believed deceased)
> COLORS: Black with grey.
> CREST: Sword

Totho: Esparan wind god. Male. Also known as the Tempest, The Gust, North Star.

Trulin: North East Espar Princedom. Breeders of powerful warhorses.
> CURRENT PRINCE: Prince Kelland Trulin.
> COLORS: White and Brown.
> CREST: Horse

Wardens (Blue rank rope): Under the Guardians, these are permanent Esparan soldiers who guard the city and maintain the peace. The number of Wardens answering to a Guardian depends on the size of the city. If a call comes from the Prince, the Wardens become responsible for a company of ~20 companions.

Wisavi: A wise-man and advisor to a Rydan Chief.

Author Bio

At a young age, Deborah's rampant imagination kept her up, lending great detail to all the terrible things lurking in the night. In desperation, her mother suggested she invent her own stories to distract her brain. She has been doing that since, channeling her ideas into sword and sorcery-style fantasy novels and shorts.

In her other life, Deborah is a veterinarian. She lives in Sooke, BC, Canada with her husband of 13+ years, their two sons, and three demanding felines.

WWW.DLAMBERTAUTHOR.COM

INSTAGRAM: @dlambertauthor
TWITTER/X: @dlambertauthor
FACEBOOK.COM/DLAMBERT42

Book Club Questions

1. What did you think of Rakhund when you first met the character? Were your expectations met by the end of the book or not?

2. There is no magical healing in this world. Does that make the world more or less enjoyable to read about?

3. Kitable claims domination magic is the worst type of torture. Do you agree? What type of magic do you think is the most abhorrent?

4. At this point, what are Tohmas' primary motivations?

5. Who is more powerful: Tohmas, DoomDragon, or Prince Marfaie? How do their powers differ?

6. Shimmer and Dust are close, but Grigson reveals that they keep secrets from each other still. How does that change your view of their relationship? Does everyone keep at least one secret from anyone else in real life?

7. Which cultural or world-building details that jumped out? How do they differ from other fantasy novels you have read or are they similar?

8. Which enemy concerned you the most: Grigson, Terant, Rakhund, or Marfaie himself? Why? Did your opinion change by the end of the book?

9. Tril comments that DoomDragon is "Never alone." Do you agree? Why or why not?

10. After battling Marfaie, Carsh feels he has failed. Do you think he has reason to be ashamed? How did Tohmas' reaction help? How does that interaction affect their relationship?

Discover more at
4HorsemenPublications.com

10% off using HORSEMEN10